Drew Gummerson, 30, is based in the Midlands and has lived in the United States, Australia, the Czech Republic and Japan. This is his first novel and he is working on a second.

The Lodger

DREW GUMMERSON

First published 2002 by GMP (Gay Men's Press),
PO Box 3220, Brighton BN2 5AU

GMP is an imprint of Millivres Prowler Limited,
part of the Millivres Prowler Group,
Worldwide House, 116-134 Bayham Street, London NW1 0BA

www.gaymenspress.co.uk

World Copyright © 2002 Drew Gummerson

Drew Gummerson has asserted his right to be identified as the author of
this work in accordance with the Copyright, Designs and Patents Act 1988

A CIP catalogue record for this book is available from the British Library

ISBN 1-902852-40-0

Printed and bound in Finland by WS Bookwell

Distributed in the UK and Europe by Airlift Book Company,
8 The Arena, Mollison Avenue,
Enfield, Middlesex EN3 7NJ
Telephone: 020 8804 0400
Distributed in North America by Consortium,
1045 Westgate Drive, St Paul, MN 55114-1065
Telephone: 1 800 283 3572
Distributed in Australia by Bulldog Books,
PO Box 300, Beaconsfield, NSW 2014

for Tiong Han

The advert

WANTED: Lodger to share with professional male. Large room newly decorated. All modern conveniences. £40 pw. No bills. Relaxed friendly atmosphere.

One

The phone was ringing.

Shit!

I knew it was early. I always wake up early and I wasn't awake. Ipso facto. I pulled open my eyes and looked across at the luminous hands of my Westclox. Seven forty-five.

Shit!

I slipped out from under the warmth of my duvet and hurried down the stairs naked. I hate missing a call. I work with my mind and a missed call is just the sort of thing that can distract me, can niggle all day. 1471 doesn't always work, especially on foreign and business numbers. I didn't want to waste hours wondering who it was, who it might have been. I was good at wasting hours, very good. I didn't need much of an excuse.

The phone was bouncing on a wooden chair in the hall. It was very loud. It was a replica of a 1929 Siemens' Neophone. It was cerise and had an aluminium dial and was made out of Bakelite. Nice if you like that kind of thing. I did and I didn't. I was ambivalent.

I picked up the receiver.

"Hello," I said.

"Has it gone?" said a voice on the line.

"Excuse me?"

"The room?"

"Um..." I said. "No."

"Great!" said the voice. Very cheery. "Fantastic! Marvellous!"

Too bloody cheery. It was after all very early in the morning. Already I was imagining pre-dawn showers and sunrise hoovering, knocks on my door and cups of tea by my bedside with smiles and pat phrases telling me I was missing the best part of the day, early to bed and early to rise makes a man healthy wealthy and wise. And all that crap.

"You're the first," I said.

"Early bird catches the worm," said the voice.

"Yes," I said. I was beginning to realise how cold it was. I had goosebumps on my arms, legs, and was starting to suffer from cryonics of the balls. I was hopping from foot to foot.

"Where are you?" said the voice.

"City centre," I said. "Curzon Street."

"Nice," said the voice. "Very handy. I can be there in five minutes."

"Five minutes!"

"Yes. Or maybe sooner. What a stroke of luck. Curzon Street."

I looked down at my naked state. And then I looked at myself in the stick-on frameless mirror in the hall. Short hair they tell you is easy to keep. It's a lie. Tufts were sticking up in every direction. I was only a colour wash away from Bart Simpson.

"Look..." I began to say but was interrupted.

"One question," the voice said.

"Yes?"

"How big is the garden?"

"The garden?" I said.

"Yes. How big is it? How many metres? Square?"

"Um..."

"Yes?" said the voice.

"Well it's not a garden as such."

"Not a garden. What is it then? As such."

"Well it doesn't have grass," I said. "It's concrete and gravel. There are Italian conifers and rock plants. There's a barbecue area and a kind of wooden structure with an awning. You can sit there when it's hot."

In fact, I was proud of the garden. I had done it myself with a little help from a Ground Force fact sheet. I had hired machinery, removed turf, compacted soil, erected posts. Me. By myself. I had finished it just as summer had finished the year before.

"No grass you say."

"No," I said.

"I don't think Clarence would like that."

"Clarence?"

"My goat."

"You have a goat?" I said.

"Yes. Clarence. He's my goat."

"Oh."

"You didn't say no pets."

"No."

"Usually they say, No Pets. I checked carefully. The one above yours he most definitely said no animals. And below as well. But you, nothing."

"A goat isn't really a pet, is it?" I said.

"She's very good. You won't know she's there. And she is, she's my pet."

I was now very cold.

I closed my eyes. I imagined a scene. It was summer. Nicholas, my four-year-old nephew, was round. There was the smell of sausages grilling, the sound of cans fizzing open. We were laughing, joking. I had turned the music up. Hannah Jones's trademark scream signalled the start of another Almighty hit. And in the corner, straggly and stinking was a goat.

"Look," I said, "no offence but I don't want any animals. I work from home. I don't want any distractions. I like peace and quiet."

"She doesn't bark you know."

"Right," I said.

"She doesn't roar like a lion, screech like a parrot. She sleeps on my bed and I never even know that she's there."

Sleeps on his bed. A goat in the bedroom.

I'm not fussy, not really. But I did have carpets to think of. I did have floorboards in the lounge. I didn't want hoof marks. Do goats have hooves? It wasn't something I ever wanted to find out.

"I'm sorry," I said. "But..."

"I get the picture," said the voice. "You don't want a goat. You should have put it in your advert. NO RUMINANTS. Thank you."

The line went dead.

It was an inauspicious start to finding a lodger, a lodger I didn't want, a lodger I needed. Financially. Economically. Getting a lodger was something I had thought long and hard about. I was happy as I was, alone, by myself. It suited me down to the ground. But I needed the money.

Over the previous week I had convinced myself that I could find a low-maintenance lodger, someone who was quiet, who would pay their rent on time, who wouldn't get under my feet, in my hair. I had convinced myself that I could find the lodger equivalent of a Madame Tussaud's waxwork, someone who had all the physical attributes of a human being, but none of the mess.

With this in mind I had bitten the bullet and filled in the boxes in the classified ad section of the local paper. I had cut it out and sent it off with a cheque. And this was the result, a wake up call from a man with a goat. Already I had a feeling that things were going to get worse. Things generally did.

I was just about to go upstairs and climb back into the warmth of my bed when there was a sound outside the front door and the post landed on the mat.

"Cooee," said a voice.

I looked towards the door, towards the voice. The flap of the letterbox was open. Through the flap I could see a pair of blue eyes
staring at me and thoughts of goats and lodgers disappeared. I had
been right. Things had just got worse. I should have known then
that it was going to be a busy morning. I should have had the sense
then to run up the stairs, pull the covers over my head and not
come out until the summer.

"Cooee!" said the voice again.

Unlike the voice on the phone, this was a voice I recognised. It
wasn't a voice that was easily mistakable. It was an inharmonious mix
of Leo Sayer practising scales and a seventeenth-century castrato
mid-op. More than anything, it wasn't a voice I wanted to be hearing, not this early, not ever.

I wanted a simple life. Easy. I wanted to be Greta Garbo. I wanted to be alone.

"Cooee!" said the voice a third time, even louder.

"Morning Simon," I said. The voice belonged to Simon. Simon
was the postman.

"Cold, isn't it?" said Simon through the letterbox. "And the cold
isn't the only clue telling me I'm not on Rhodes. You see, I'm not
looking at the Colossus, am I? Not looking at the statue of Apollo.
Not huge. If you catch my drift."

I looked down again. I was still naked. Completely. My balls had
practically disappeared. They were stressing, quite strongly, that
they would never have need of the underpant equivalent of an
uplift bra. They could lift and separate well enough by themselves.

"Piss off, Simon," I said. "Go and push your epistles into boxes
where they're wanted."

It wasn't the first time Simon had seen me like this. Naked. We
had had sex once. He had never forgotten, I was trying to. I liked
the idea of having a door between us. A door without an oblong
hole would have been better. I felt I was an unwilling member of an
impromptu buckshee peepshow.

"Got a special delivery for you," said Simon. "It doesn't fit in your hole. Too wide. Want me to take it back to the office?"

"No," I said. I sighed. Male I could resist, mail I couldn't. "I'm coming."

I rattled the chain from its catch and flung open the door. Even colder air hit my body and I folded my arms. Simon was before me. He had big blue eyes and short blond hair. Some people would go for that. Not me. Not more than once. Blonds weren't my type.

"Well," I said, "where is it?"

"Is that all the thanks I get?" said Simon. He had a pout on his face. "Do I look like the newest employee of Parcelforce? Should have come in a van this should. But for you, I'd do anything. I'll take it, I said and Heidi the postmistress said, what you? and I said, yes me, no problem."

"Simon," I said. "I'm cold. Hurry up."

"Hark at you. Where's your horse Miss goddam Godiva? And how about me? Out in all weathers I am. Snow, sleet, hail..."

I had had enough. I placed a hand on each of Simon's slender shoulders and pulled him to me, battered leather postbag and all. His lips were still moving as I started to kiss him. His eyes widened for a second and then closed and he sank against me. From experience I knew this was the best way to shut his type up. His type being silly young queens. Fifties Hollywood action always stopped them cold. When I felt his hands on the cheeks of my bum, pulling them apart, I decided it was time to stop. I pushed him away. He wiped his lips with the back of his left hand and looked down.

"Still cold."

"Yes," I said. "Never again. I told you."

"Honza, you're a bastard."

"I know," I said. I was. I am. I'm a bastard. Because nowadays I don't want love, I don't want commitment, I don't even want a post-coital cigarette. Fuck and go, that's me.

"I should go," said Simon.

"Right," I said. I nodded. "It's probably for the best."

Simon started to turn away.

"Simon?"

He glanced back.

"Yes?" he said, his eyes expectant.

"My letter."

"Oh yes."

He opened the flap of his bag and pulled out a just-larger-than-A4 envelope, handed it to me and shuffled disconsolately off. But I didn't care about him, I only cared about the package in my hands. I recognised it immediately. I didn't need to look at the handwriting to guess the sender, I didn't need to check the postmark.

Rejection. Another rejection.

"Morning Honza!"

"Morning Honza!"

I looked up and realised I was still standing in the doorway, naked, looking at the envelope. Martin, my next door neighbour's son, and his best mate Steve were walking past. They were wearing their school uniforms. They were smiling at me. I smiled back and waved.

They waved.

Martin glanced down towards my abdomen and grinned.

"Cold morning, isn't it?" said Martin.

"But it has potential," said Steve.

"Piss off Martin," I said. "Piss off Steve." And I closed the door.

I went through into the downstairs room, flung the envelope onto the laminated breakfast bar and crossed from the warm rugs of the living-room floor to the cold tiles of the kitchen. I had just flicked on the kettle, put a spoonful of instant coffee in a cup when the phone started to ring again.

I cursed and made my way back into the hall.

I picked up the receiver.

"I was just calling about the room advertised in the paper..."

The phone went once more before I had finished my toast and once while I was in the shower. I was already beginning to wonder if getting a lodger was such a good idea. I loved my privacy, loved being alone and being able to do what I wanted when I wanted. And then I remembered the bills. I remembered the gas bill and the electricity bill and the Visa bill all held neatly in place by a Tom of Finland fridge magnet on my industrial metallic blue fridge.

I had no choice. I was gripped by my uplifted balls.

I didn't get much work done that day. In fact I didn't write more than ten lines. The first, and I tried to tell myself, major reason was because of the phone. It never stopped ringing. And it was always enquiries about the room. Was it south facing? Would it suit someone over seventy? Would it suit a shift-worker, a drummer, a born-again Christian?

Ninety per cent of the time I knew instantly that I was speaking to someone who I hadn't a cat in hell's chance of getting on with. Even the short conversations I had were painful, full of silences, awkward moments. I can do bullshit. But usually I bullshit for only one thing. Sex. Everyday bullshit I wasn't good at. And the thought that I would have to do it every day with a stranger in my house depressed me, filled me with foreboding.

The second, and I hated to admit, real reason I didn't get any work done was because of the rejection, the rejection of my novel that the envelope I had received that morning contained.

Rejection.

I didn't like rejection. It didn't fill me with joy. Not exactly. And it wasn't conducive to inspiration. When someone has just implied you are crap it makes it difficult to carry on, to think of stunning sentences, apt adjectives.

So I sat in my workroom upstairs in front of my keyboard gazing out of the window at backs of houses doing nothing. I watched as a neighbour hung out white sheets in the wind, disappearing every now and again in an abundance of material. I noticed and then checked by my watch that every fifteen minutes the ancient man who lived two doors down would nip out into his back garden, hold out his hand palm up, look up at the sky and then go back inside.

I was fascinated by any distraction.

And the only real distraction was the constant ringing of the phone.

So, all in all, I didn't work much.

By twelve o'clock the phone had rung twenty times. I was counting. By twelve o'clock I was wishing that I didn't have such a classic phone. I was wishing that I had one of those sleek modern Binatone phones I had seen with a handset which you could carry to any part of the house. But I had always held out from getting one. I didn't like the idea of being always available. The entrance, the hallway was a public space. The rest of the house was mine. Private. A sanctuary. That's how I liked it.

But constantly going downstairs was driving me mad. And every call had been for the room. Every call had been in answer to my advert. So the twenty-first, I was surprised to hear, was my agent. It wasn't a pleasant surprise. Not really.

My agent wasn't my favourite person. It wasn't that she didn't get me work, it was just that she got me work I didn't like. I was pigeonholed. It felt more like I was, as the Americans would say, corn-holed.

Fucked.

"Been trying to get through for ages," said the voice on the line. It was breathy and hurried as usual. She spoke like a correspondent from war-torn Sarajevo phoning in a story while under enemy attack.

"Have you?" I said. "I'm getting a lodger. The line's been busy."

"A lodger?" she said. I could hear her mind working. "Might make a nice article," she said.

I didn't say anything.

15

"Yes," she said. She fired out ideas. "Gay man gets lodger. Sexual favours for rent. The history of gay lodgers. Living with the other side. Sleeping with the enemy."

"It's just a lodger," I said. "Easy. Full stop."

"But..."

"No," I said. "No lodger articles. Not one."

"OK," she said. "Right," she said, taking the rejection in her stride. "I may have another piece for you."

"Oh," I said.

"For *Attitude*."

"Oh," I said.

"On the attraction of gay men to straight and vice versa."

"Oh," I said. "Kind of Real Men are from Mars, Gays are from Uranus?" I was joking.

"Yes," she said. "Exactly. I thought of you straight away."

"Oh," I said.

"You're good at that kind of thing."

"Yes," I said.

"You want it?" she said. "The article?"

"Yes," I said. I didn't. I spent a great deal of my life doing what I didn't want to do.

"You don't sound very keen."

"I am," I lied. "But haven't you got anything else?"

"Like what?"

"I don't know," I said. "How about some travel writing? I've always fancied the Amazon."

"Gay man goes native," she said, missing the point. "I'll think about it. Might be nice. I'll fax you this then, the gay/straight thing. The pink divide."

"Yes," I said. I said it tersely, finally.

There was a pause on the end of the line. There wasn't the expected goodbye.

"Honza?" she said. Her voice was quieter. It was no longer that of a war correspondent but that of a shocked witness to a devastating famine.

"Yes?" I said.

"This lodger thing, perhaps it's for the best. It's time you lived with someone else. It's time you got over Joshua. It wasn't your fault."

"I know," I said. I put the phone down. I started up the stairs and was on the fifth step when the ringing started again.

It was about the room.

Was it big enough for a family of three?

The bloody room.

Bloody agents.

Bloody rejection.

By five o'clock I decided enough was enough. I had a headache and I had arranged three interviews for the next day with the people who sounded the most normal, down to earth, not mad. One was coming at ten, one at ten thirty and one at eleven.

I unplugged the phone.

I filled the bath, shook in some Radox and leaving the door open I slipped in the soundtrack from *Queer as Folk 2*.

Some people relax to classical, Mozart, Verdi. Some people relax to New Age, Enya, Enigma.

I relax best to pop. Pop is the way to live your life. Shit comes shit goes. But the beat goes on.

Two

Interview one

For a start she was late.

This made me happy. I wanted to not like her, to say that she wasn't right for me for the right reasons. You see, I didn't want a female lodger. I don't know why, I hadn't thought about it, didn't want to think about it. Most of my closest friends were women so it wasn't that I didn't like women. In fact, most of the time I preferred the company of women. There was no hidden agenda. Sex didn't get in the way. Well, not usually.

But something inside me was telling me that I shouldn't have a female living here.

And if it wasn't that I didn't not like females then it must be that I actively wanted a man. And that raised other questions. Boyfriend and relationship questions.

I didn't want a boyfriend.

Not again.

All this from an advert for a lodger.

I got up to make a cup of tea and then there was a knock at the door. I went and opened it.

"Hello," I said.

"Hello," said the woman standing there.

My first impression was small and hippy. Tie-dyed and unbrushed.

"I'm Honza."

"Oooo that's a funny name, isn't it?" she said. She giggled, revealing tiny teeth. "Foreign are you?"

"Not really," I said. "My father was Polish but I was born here."

"In this house? That's nice."

I didn't correct her mistake, I didn't enumerate the countries in which I had lived. She was pale and I feared she would pass out at my peripateticness.

"I like roots," she said. "Roots are good. Roots schmoots."

"And you are?" I said.

"I'm English," she said. "One hundred percent English. An English rose but not so prickly."

"No," I said, "your name?" I hadn't written it down. I'd forgotten.

"Oh," she said, "I'm Mary. But not quite so contrary."

She laughed. She put a hand up to cover her mouth.

When she had finished I moved aside and gestured for her to come in. She genuflected on the step, did a strange movement with her left arm in front of her face and walked into the hallway. And then she stopped.

"After you," she said. "Men first." She started laughing again, covering her mouth with her hand again.

It's difficult to finish something before you've started. You have to be dishonest, go through the motions. You know in a second if someone is right, if something is right, if the hat fits, the jumper suits and yet it's polite to lie, to lead someone on. We are trained in the art of deception from our earliest age. That's what our culture expects of us and it's hard to be different.

With Mary before me now, I had the morning-after-the-one-night-stand-the-night-before syndrome. You know it's over but you make a show. You give them a phone number, not your phone number, and you take theirs and you promise to ring. You cook them breakfast and they give you a painful goodbye blowjob with toast crumbs in their mouths which somehow end up under your foreskin and that means you have to have another shower and they take that as an invitation to join you and then when they are finally gone, finally out of the house, you lean back against the door and you could shout for joy to have the place to yourself again, to be in your home on your own.

That's why I like sex in saunas, in toilets, late at night in nearly deserted train carriages, on the windy sand-blown foreshores of decrepit English resorts. It's not that I'm promiscuous, not really. Speak to any straight man. Tell him there's a place he can go where he can have sex when he's horny, when he's a hard-on and a mind to use it. No strings, no ties, nothing. Tell him he can screw as he wants and then can just walk away and he'll be there before you've even given him the address. He'll be off like a shot, tongue hanging, crotch bulging. And then he'll come back, sheepish, and ask where. Where is this place, this nirvana, this Elysium.

I can do the relationship thing, the commitment thing. I can. But I don't want to, not anymore. Not now. I got hurt.

Badly hurt.

But that's another story and Mary was waiting.

She'd stopped laughing.

"In here," I said and she followed me into the living room. "This is it." I spread my arms wide.

No response.

I turned around.

Mary had turned to stone in the centre of my floor. Her eyes had stretched wide and her mouth had dropped open. She looked like a cartoon mouse having seen a badly drawn cat.

"Is everything OK?" I said.

"That..." she said moving her lapis lips.

She was pointing at my Montage two-seater soft-sueded velvet-effect sofa.

"Yes?" I said.

"Is it leather?"

"No," I said. It wasn't.

She smiled, transmogrifying back into a skinny anaemic relic from sixties radical culture.

"Thank God," she said and sat down.

"It not leather," I said deadpan. "It's camel."

She screamed and leapt up.

That could have been my way out. I could have let her believe that the skin that had just touched her skin had once adorned a beautiful humped dromedary roaming the vast plains of the Sahara desert carrying Bedouin tribesman from oasis to oasis.

I didn't. I told her the truth. You see, where boloney was the best option I often found myself lacking.

I showed her round the rest of the house.

I told her that my bedroom and my workroom were out of bounds. She asked what my work was and I said I was a writer and she said that she was considering writing about her life. It was very interesting.

She liked the bathroom. The toilet was not too high she said.

And then I showed her the room that would be hers. But wouldn't.

She said something about Feng Shui and I nodded and she said that it wasn't very ethnic and I agreed. I said the 1991 'vik-ter chair and 1929 Deskey-Vollmer copy occasion table weren't ethnic at all but I said perhaps we could drape sarongs over them. I said that maybe I could buy moulded candles and jasmine joss-sticks. She almost clapped her hands. Almost.

I was very nice.

I said I would let her know about the room.

I was a bastard.

Interview two

Bang on eleven there was a knock at the door. He was on time. That was a good start.

I checked my list, the list that I had failed to put Mary on to.

David.

Actually I didn't need to check. I could remember the name. But making lists and checking them was something I did. I wasn't a control freak, not at all, and I wasn't particularly orderly. It's just that lists wasted time.

I like to waste time. Or, at least, fill my time with things that seem to be useful but are in fact not. I like to create the illusion of busyness because then I don't feel guilty about the little that I actually do, about the few words that manage to seep onto disc at the end of each day. I can sleep more easily if I have made a few lists. I have done something.

So I crossed David's name off the list.

David. Number two of three. The second part of a trilogy. The middle panel of a triptych.

I opened the door.

David was huge. He filled the whole frame and I couldn't see the street. I couldn't see the houses opposite, I couldn't see the cars parked in the road.

I didn't want to see them. I only wanted to see David.

David was gorgeous, beautiful, amazing. He had looks that would make a narcoleptic stay awake, an insomniac sleep. A heroin addict would go cold turkey for him and do it smiling, an alcoholic would drink only water for seven days and seven nights and each sip would still taste like wine. Get the picture?

David was nice.

"Hi," I said. I could feel my face going red. Blood was surging everywhere, rushing to extremities, creating new ones.

"Hi," David said and held out a hand.

I took it. The handshake was firm, the skin like burnished beech. I didn't want to let go. Ever.

"Can I come in?" said David.

I realised I was just standing there. Like the proverbial idiot.

"Sure," I said. I stood aside.

There wasn't enough room for the both of us in the corridor. At least, not enough room with space between us.

That was OK, I didn't want space between us.

We stood facing each other, knees touching.

"Where do you want me?" said David. His eyes were smiling.

I know the clichés, but believe me, his eyes were smiling. They weren't dancing, they weren't doing a jig, but they were definitely smiling and yes, my heart was beating. It was beating fast I mean.

"In there," I said. I nodded into the front room and followed him in. I would have followed David to the ends of the Earth. And back.

"What do you think?" I said. I spread my arms and turned to look at him.

"Nice," he said. He was staring straight at me. He had that look in his eyes. I knew that look, I'd seen it before many times. It was desire. "Very nice," he said. "Can I see the room?"

I didn't run up the stairs, that wouldn't have been elegant, wouldn't have appeared demure. It might even have whiffed of desperation. But I did take the steps two at a time and I could sense David close behind me. I could almost feel his thick thighs in tight jeans, taut chest under T-shirt. And I knew, without looking back, that David was looking at my bum, knew what he was thinking.

At the top I stopped.

"These rooms are mine," I said again, repeating the spiel, thinking pornography. "That's my bedroom and that's my workroom."

"Right," said David. He nodded. "What do you do?"

"I'm a writer."

"Oh yes," said David. "I'm thinking of writing a book about my life. It's very interesting."

"Right," I said.

"And my room," said David. "Where is it?"

"There," I said pointing. "At the end."

"Well come on," he said. He smiled again, "Show me."

David was in the room before me. Once more our bodies were almost touching. The room was big but David seemed to fill any given space or maybe I had just gravitated towards him. David had a body that would always be the object of attention, the centre of affection. I looked at him, he was looking at the bed.

"Is it big enough for two?"

I gulped.

I was going to answer. I was going to say something innocent, honestly. But I didn't get a chance. David's hand was around my waist and his lips were pressed against mine. He had a bit of stubble. I like that. I've kissed men and I've kissed women. It's the same mostly. The tongue's the same, the lips are the same. But stubble makes the difference. You know you've got a man.

I spun us round, our tongues fighting, my hands on David's bum. The bed was behind me now. I sat down, pulling my face free, gasping for breath. David was still standing, expectant and looking down. His groin was at eye-level. We both knew the score.

I put my hands on his belt.

I like sex. I like everything about sex. I can fuck or be fucked, I can suck or be sucked. I can do it on my back, on my front and once I even did it standing on my head. But what I like most is that first sight of cock, that first glimpse of manliness. Big man is not always concomitant with big dick. The two do not always go hand in hand. So as all is about to be revealed there is an anticipatory rush of adrenaline, a fantastic image of gargantuan appendage, and at that moment before show-time my own cock is at its most sensitive. The featheriest of touches and it would become a fecund geyser.

I unbuckled David's buckle. The two leather ends hung loose.

I put my hands on his trousers. I noticed they had a button fly.

Button fly jeans are the sexiest item of clothing ever created. No question. I slipped the top metal disc with its indented logo through its strongly stitched hole.

Not that having a big cock is the be all and end all. Don't get me wrong. At the end of the day it doesn't matter, size doesn't matter. I was bigger than Joshua, my previous boyfriend and we had had amazing sex, brilliant sex. And I had loved him. I had loved him so much. I had loved him until it hurt and I couldn't love anymore. Until I would lie awake at night and watch his face at peace and I would stoke his thick black hair and wish that I could take his pain away, wish that I could banish his demons, make everything right for him in that turmoil of the world in his head.

David put his hands in my cropped hair and tried to pull my head closer.

Not yet.

Once the top button is undone, the others come apart easily. The design is ingenious. I often dreamt of meeting the man who had invented this perfection of flies. I wanted to shake his hand, I wanted to kiss his cheek. All day this desideratum of fastenings holds all in place so securely and then with a gentle tug apart it comes. The acme of easy access.

I gave that tug now and pulled the jeans down to David's knees.

Oh my God!

David was more Goliath than David.

David was huge. He was almost bursting out of his briefs. I say briefs, but anything would have appeared brief next to that huge distended tumescence. I was in shock. It was an explosion of a bulge. I could have done with anti-flash goggles. It was the mother of all cocks, the father of all dicks. And now I let my head be guided in. I nuzzled the material, nudging the prick. I ran my nose and lips along its erect length. I breathed in, revelling in the miasma of washed cotton, dried piss, that unmistakable indefinable aroma of male genitalia.

David, pushing back my head, grabbed each side of the elasticated pants and pulled them down in one swift movement. The cock popped out, slapping against my face and then my mouth was around it.

Size doesn't matter I said, but it's the big ones you remember most, the ones you think about in bed at night, in the morning on waking. You look in the mirror later and open you mouth as wide as possible and marvel that the dick could have been as wide as that Munch-like hole, that Culkin orifice. And you wonder if you'll ever find it again. That's what drives you on on your nights alone, cruising.

I gripped the shaft and started to move my head up and down in time with my hand. Saliva was dribbling down, easing the movement. And then I felt powerful hands under my armpits and I was being lifted up. David was kissing me again, moving his hands down to my own jeans. He wasn't slow like me. He knew what he wanted and he wanted it now. David ripped down my trousers and underpants together and flipping me around, he pushed me face down onto the bed. I heard the tear of a condom packet and then he was on top of me, lying on top of me.

I felt him between my cheeks, the pressure mounting. I reached around and checked the condom was there and then I relaxed, relaxed into the pillow, took his weight on my body, his presence inside me, right in the depths of me. He was licking my ear and his thrusts were starting, then increasing, gathering pace and I could feel the sexy caress of his rucked shirt against the flesh of my back. I could feel the urgency within him.

What can I say?

David fucked me.

Plain and simple, he fucked me.

He fucked me until he grunted and came and I did the same.

And I loved it. Every second of it.

We lay breathless. Me under him. Him on top.

At the door downstairs there was a knock.

"Shit!" I said. "That must be then next one for the room."

David smiled. That twinkle in the eyes was back.

"To look at the room," I said.

David stood and started doing up his jeans, straightening his clothes, righting perfection. I did the same, quickly, as I heard another knock at the door.

"Give me a ring," said David.

I wanted to say that I already had but that would have been corny, so I didn't, I just said that I would. I followed him down the stairs. I was looking at his arse. I loved the way the double stitched seam semi-disappeared into the beauty of his natal cleft.

"It's perfect," said David quietly in the doorway. "I want it. It's just the right size."

He kissed me on the nose and went out.

Interview three

Standing on the step was a lanky youth. He had short blond hair and red spots. He was leaning against the jamb smoking a cigarette. He was wearing a blue boiler suit with the word Ryder stitched in white on the left-hand breast pocket. Behind him, almost blocking the road, was a huge articulated lorry. It too was blue and on the side in mud-splattered white letters was the same word, Ryder.

He was Andy. Number three. The conclusion. The end.

"I'm late," he said. He dropped the half-finished cigarette onto the floor and crushed it beneath a steel toe-capped boot. "I can't stay long. Derek's waiting."

He said Derek like I knew who Derek was. Like me and Derek went back a long way and Derek was someone who I wouldn't want to disappoint.

"Right," I said. "You better come in."

He walked straight past me and into the lounge. I was only two seconds behind him but by the time I arrived he was already sitting on the two seater sofa, legs apart, furiously scratching the inside of his thigh.

"What do you think?" I said. I spread apart my arms. My heart wasn't in it. David was still inside me, inside my mind.

"Nice telly," he said. "Neat."

He was gazing at my Sanyo thirty-two inch widescreen tv with Nicam stereo. He had blue eyes. They had lit up.

"Do you get digital?"

"No," I said.

"Never mind. It's still great. Neat."

I had never heard anyone outside an American movie say neat before. And I'd never heard anyone say it with a Derbyshire accent. Never.

"Shall I show you upstairs?" I said.

"If you like," he said. He smiled.

"This way," I said.

Stupidly I pointed at the staircase. It was stupid because it was obvious. It was obvious that I didn't have either a goods or a passenger lift in the kitchen. It was obvious that the stairs were the way up.

Andy leapt from the sofa and bounded up the stairs three at a time.

I found him in the bathroom. He was leaning over the toilet bowl hawking phlegm from somewhere deep in his throat. He spat and turned to face me.

"Forty quid a week?" he said.

"Yes," I said.

"Not thirty-five?" he said and grinned. The grin split his face.

I grinned too. I don't grin. Not usually. Grin is what prepubescent teenagers do when they find out Britney Spears and the Spice Girls have singles being released in the same week and it just happens to be the week they got extra pocket money for helping mum weed the garden. It's what kids do when they can have both chocolate and vanilla ice-cream and they don't have to eat all their carrots. It's what Cheshire cats do in trees until they disappear completely. I smile, I laugh, but I don't grin. A grin is innocent. A laugh is knowing. A grin isn't about humour, a grin is pleasure.

"Forty," I said. I was still grinning. "No bills. I'll show you the room."

In the hall I told Andy the usual story about my bedroom and the workroom being out of bounds. I told him I worked from home.

"What do you do?" he said.

"I'm a writer."

"I can't write," he said. "Look."

He held out his left hand. There was a thumb. There was a little finger, a ring finger. There was a middle finger. There was dirt under the nails. There was black grime in the raised lines of his joints. There was no index finger. Not at all. Not even half a one, not even a stump. Where the finger should have been there was nothing. There was only the smooth rounded edge of a knuckle.

"I'm left handed," he said. "I can't write. I can't hold a pen. It keeps slipping away. You're lucky."

I wasn't sure if he meant that I was lucky that I could physically write or lucky that I had the talent to do it. So I said, "The room's at the end."

I hadn't made the bed. In my haste I'd forgotten. The bed to me looked like someone had just been fucked on it. Andy didn't seem to notice. At least he didn't say anything. But what would he say?

He was walking around opening drawers, closing drawers, checking cupboard doors. He ran his hand over the surface of the table. He stopped in front of an original John Hassall, Skegness is so Bracing London Transport poster with the fat man bouncing along a deserted beach. He looked back over his shoulder.

"Neat," he said.

He picked up the green plastic Ekco Type U122 1950s radio. I could see his lips beginning to move.

"Neat?" I said.

He grinned. I wished he would stop doing that.

"When can I move in?" he said.

"Oh," I said.

"I can probably start late on Monday. Let's see. Today is Wednesday. Yes. Monday would be the earliest. Monday morning."

I hated doing this.

"I have other people to see," I said. I was thinking of David and his huge cock. "There's been a lot of interest."

Just then there was the loud sound of a horn.

"That's Derek," said Andy. He wasn't grinning now. "I'd better go. Derek's waiting."

"Yes," I said.

I followed him downstairs. I wasn't looking at his arse. He was skinny. He didn't look like he had one.

At the door he stopped, his hand on the knob. Hesitating. I thought he was going to ask about the room. I was thinking how I could let him down gently. I guessed that he was still living with his mum and dad. I was guessing that mine was the first room he'd seen. I was guessing that he had thought it would be easy, easy to find a room and move out.

I felt for him. I'd been there. I was coming all over all fatherly. I thought we were going to have an awkward moment where I would have to say no, be firm and tell him the room was in fact already taken but that he shouldn't worry because there were plenty more fish in the sea, plenty more rooms in Derby, so I was surprised when he just said, "Can I use your toilet? I need a piss."

"Go ahead," I said. It wasn't much but I still felt benevolent.

He was off again, bounding up the stairs, hurtling into the bathroom. He didn't close the door. And he didn't aim for the side, as you do out of politeness to make it more quiet. The stream was strong, the sound of splashing loud. I could even hear how many times he shook. It was three. He didn't wash his hands and then he was flying down the stairs as the horn sounded again.

"Thanks," he said. "Gotta go."

"Yes," I said.

"Bye."

"Bye."

As he climbed into the cab I found I was still watching.

He slammed the door shut and looked at me through the open window.

"Thirty-seven fifty," he shouted as the truck pulled away. "Final offer."

This time I was to blame. I grinned first.

Three

I was in the middle of a telephone conversation with my mother. I hadn't told her of the incipient addition to Curzon Street yet. I knew what her reaction would be. She was telling me of Aunty Irene's new hat. It was as interesting as it sounds.

"So Irene bought a new hat," she said.

"Yes," I said. I was clutching the phone on my lap, biding my time.

"It doesn't suit her," she said. "It has a wide brim. It's blue. It has white spots. It's dappled, she said but I know a spot when I see one. When are you going to wear a hat? I said. You never know who's going to get married, she said. Well, I told her not to wait for you. Honza won't be getting married, I said. Not unless the Church of England allows gay marriage. Can you imagine? Or he goes to one of those Scandinavian countries, I said. I wouldn't put it past him. But I don't know if she'd wear a hat there. It's cold. I told Irene she'd be better off with ear muffs if she was thinking of your wedding. More practical. I asked her if she'd kept the receipt."

You don't believe me, but this is how my mother talks. She doesn't breathe. In my hall I imagined her at home in hers. I imagined her next to an oxygen canister. I imagined a tube in her ear pumping air down to her lungs allowing her to do what she enjoys most without pause.

"Mum," I said, "I'm not getting married. Never." I knew this would shut her up and give me a moment's grace to get in my news. "But I am getting a lodger."

"A lodger?" she said. She raised her voice slightly.

"Yes."

"A lodger or a lodger lodger?"

"What?" I said. I was lost.

"Honza, I can never keep up with you. You'll be the death of me." There was a sigh on the end of the line as if to say I was going to be the death of her right there and then.

"Mum?"

"When I was young words had meaning. They had one meaning. A flatmate was a flatmate…"

I began to see where she was going.

"… a lodger was a lodger. Gay meant happy. Now it means what you are and then you tell me it doesn't. Now you tell me you're not gay, you're queer. You've gone from being gay, happy, to queer, funny. What are you going to be next? Delirious. I can't wait."

"Mum," I said, "I'm just getting a lodger."

"You told me that Joshua was just a flatmate. First you had a flatmate, now you're getting a lodger. Can I expect a call next month to tell me you're getting squatters?"

"Things were different then."

All roads led to Rome. All conversations led to this.

"For two years. For two long years you didn't think to tell your own mother that the woman in your life was a man."

"I never said I had a woman."

"You said partner. Partner this and partner that. You used the word partner more times in an hour than they do in a whole series of *Ally McBeal*. What was I supposed to think? And you were always hanging around with that Fiona."

"Mum, Fiona's a lesbian."

"I didn't know that then."

"She wore dungarees," I said. "She rode a Harley, she listened to kd lang. All at the same time."

"I listen to kd lang. She's got a nice voice. Am I lesbian?"

"No mum," I said. "You're not."

"So this lodger," she said, "have you told him?"

"Told him what?"

"About you."

"I told him I was a writer."

"That wasn't what I meant. You know what I meant. Not everyone is as tolerant as me. God knows my tolerance has been a cross to bear. Just the other day I read an interview with the Chief Rabbi in the *Sunday Times*. He was talking of the promotion of family values, talking of instilling in our children a sense that marriage was our common heritage. He was making some good points."

I was trying hard not to lose my temper. I was trying very hard. I was failing. Talk of Rabbis always did it for me.

"Mum," I said, "when I fuck him I'll tell him then. It'll give us something to talk about post-coitally."

There was a silence.

"And have you thought about Nicholas?" she said. "What about him? He needs stability."

I'll give my mum her due. She certainly knows how to go for the kill, how to twist the knife.

Nicholas was the bastard progeny of my soi-disant reformed junkie prostitute sister. Nicholas was four years old. Nicholas was beautiful, gorgeous, perfect. He was my nephew. I had been present at his birth and I had loved him from the first moment I had seen his bloodstained head. I loved him more than anything. More than anything. On Saturdays he stayed with me. On Sundays he stayed with me. He could have stayed for ever but Julie, my sister, she didn't want.

"You can't be too careful these days," my mother was saying. "These paedophiles are everywhere."

I put the phone down. I unplugged the cord. I kicked the chair. Hard.

Fuck!

You try and live your life. You try and do the best. You try everything you can to kill the beast reality.

I went into the lounge. I poured myself a vodka. I slipped Natalie Browne into the minidisc. I turned her up loud until the beat was banging my eardrums. I danced around my checkerboard russet rug on my beechwood floor. I sang at the top of my voice.

"Things could be fabulous. Things could be marvellous. SOON."

Four

It was Monday morning. I was awake before the alarm. Today the lodger was moving in. He said he would be early. I yawned and stretched and scratched my flat stomach. There was a strange feeling within, under its taut line. I'd had the feeling before. I'd had it stepping off the plane at Narita airport. I'd had it diving into the translucent waters of Sydney's Palm Beach. I'd even had it when I read in *Boyz* that Madonna was planning to tour the UK.

It was excitement.

Was I really excited about a lodger, a new addition to my household?

In the past year I had got used to being on my own. I had come to enjoy my solitary life, was protective of it. I loved being by myself, being able to stretch out on a double bed, to go where I want, eat what I want and yes, sleep with who I want.

I rubbed my eyes. What was I thinking?

There was no reason why a lodger should change any of the above. I wasn't getting a boyfriend, I wasn't getting a mail-order lover by courier delivery. It was just an extra body in the house. A face across the breakfast bar. Someone to help with my spiralling expenses, to help balance my books. That's all.

So what then was this feeling?

Maybe secretly I was excited about the company.

Maybe secretly I had been lonely.

I smiled. No I didn't think so. Lonely. Me? No way José. On your bike Mike.

I pulled aside the duvet, jumped out of bed and walked naked into the bathroom.

I walked naked.

I stopped on the Gerlor sand-tile vinyl flooring and caught sight of myself in the wrought-iron mirror. Naked. I wouldn't be able to walk around naked when Andy was here. There was probably an ancient law forbidding nudity in front of lodgers. Hollywood was probably making a thriller about it. It would probably star Demi Moore. But I didn't care about laws, not really. And I was sure Andy could cope.

But I couldn't do it, could I? It would be like saying look at me, look at my body. Andy could interpret that as a sad older man after a cheap thrill. And that would be wrong because I'm not. I'm not sad, old or lonely. And I don't need cheap thrills. I'm still more than capable of getting my thrills off my own bat thank you. But having Andy as a lodger would mean I would have to modify my behaviour. A little.

Andy.

I thought he would be pleased when I called him. I thought he would sound pleased. I thought he would thank me. I thought he would be effusive, over the moon. He wasn't. Not exactly.

"Can I speak to Andy?" I had said.

"Speaking," he had said.

"I'm calling about the room."

"Yeah?"

"It's Honza."

"Yeah?"

"You can move in. On Monday."

"Right," he had said. "I'll be there early. Monday morning. Thirty-seven fifty. OK?"

And he had put the phone down. He hadn't waited for an answer but I could imagine him grinning on the end of the line.

I had turned down two pound fifty and regular sex for him and that was all the thanks I got. I'm talking about David.

It hadn't taken me too long to reject the idea of having David as a lodger. About as long as it took for the warm pleasurable pain to disappear from my sphincter, about as long as it took for me to change the sheets on the spare room bed. David was nice but I didn't want nice. I wanted an easy life. I wanted space. I wanted to be left alone. I didn't want a boyfriend. And David had boyfriend potential written all over him. How could I write with David in the house? How could I concentrate with him in the proximity?

Mary, the hippy, had been a been a non-starter. So that left me with Andy. Andy in his boiler suit, spots on his face, fag in hand. Andy was the easy option, the safe bet. I didn't fancy Andy. He wasn't my type. This gentleman didn't prefer blonds. Andy could be cartwheeling naked around the living room and I wouldn't bat an eyelid, I could still focus on the screen in front of me. But there was another reason too. A deeper more cogent reason why I believed that me and Andy would get along. It was because of what he didn't say.

Whenever you tell someone that you are a writer you get one of two reactions:

One: To some people, as soon as you say the word writer, you see "wanker" flash across their face. It is as if by being a writer they somehow think that you think you are better than them. They think that you are pretentious and above yourself. They think that you think you are TS Eliot or James Joyce or William Faulkner. I have learnt from experience how to recognise these people. I have learnt to spot them across a crowded bar and now I tell them I am a welder, I am handy with a blowtorch. I don't mention the word writer at all. I do my best to look like I don't even know what a pen is. And usually it works. Usually I get the fuck and everyone is happy.

Two: This reaction is more common. David did it, Mary did it. When I say that I am a writer then this kind of person will say that they have always thought about writing too, they have been thinking of writing about their life. It is very interesting they say and they really think it would be. Yawn. I'm not being a bastard but after a long day at work would you really want to curl up and read, for example, of twenty-six-year-old Janice's life serving chips in the fish and chip shop? Mr Brown he likes peas on his chips. Mrs Brown she likes gravy. Their son Terry. He likes peas and gravy. No chips. Yuck!

I am a bastard.

But Andy didn't give either one of these reactions. He had just shown me his deformed hand and then looked around the room. I felt instantly that I could write with Andy in the house. I admired his genuine lack of interest.

Andy would be OK.

I got in the shower, soaped my body, dried off, got dressed and went downstairs. The usual routine. I had nearly finished my first cup of tea of the day when there was a knock at the door. I looked at my watch. It was eight-thirty.

I went into the hall and opened the door.

Andy was leaning against the jamb smoking a cigarette. He was wearing his blue boiler suit with Ryder stitched in white on the pocket. There was a huge lorry almost blocking the road. It had the same word written on the side in mud-splattered white letters, Ryder. By Andy's feet was a scuffed stuffed holdall. He dropped the cigarette on the floor and crushed it under his steel toe-capped boot. He picked up the holdall.

"Can't stay long," he said and nodded to the lorry.

"Derek's waiting?" I said.

"No," he said. "Derek's day off. Jim's waiting. Jim's a bastard."

Bag in hand, Andy bounded up the stairs three at a time and then moments later he came back down them again, jumping from the sixth, landing with a crash. I was still standing in the hall. The door was still open. At the door Andy hesitated.

"Honza?" he said. "Can I use your toilet?" he said, hopping gently from foot to foot. "I'm dying for a piss."

"It's your toilet now too."

"Yeah. Neat." Andy grinned and then was up the stairs no slower than before. He didn't close the bathroom door and I heard him shake off, three splashes. This time he jumped from the seventh step and the crash was louder.

"I'll be back at about six," he said. "I'll see you later."

"OK," I said. "See you later."

I closed the door. I didn't want to see him grinning at me from the truck window. I don't know why, I just didn't.

I managed to do quite a lot of work that day. As soon as Andy had gone I went upstairs and sat at my desk. I flicked to the appropriate section of my much-thumbed *Writers' and Artists' Yearbook* and found a publisher whose name somehow sounded hopeful and who I hadn't yet tried. I spent two hours writing a new covering letter, agonising over adjectives, trying to sound quietly confident and yet not arrogant.

When I was at last pleased with the letter I printed it out and slipped it in the front of the proposal for my novel. I put the whole thing in a brown envelope and carefully wrote the publisher's name and address in capital letters on the front. I had done this many times and every time it came back to me. This time I hoped it wouldn't. I hoped I would receive a letter saying they liked my style and wished to see the rest of the manuscript. If they did, it was there waiting for them, by my feet under the desk.

"Please," I said out loud. "Please. This time."

I picked up the letter and went out to post it and while I was out I also got keys cut for Andy, front and back doors. Then I went home. Within an hour I was back in my workroom having had a quick sandwich downstairs.

Jane, my agent, had sent the e-mail she'd promised on the phone. She hadn't written much. She thanked me for the article I'd sent, no comment on its quality, and told me I had two weeks to write this piece on the gay/straight attraction for *Attitude*. She didn't give me any more information, just that.

Jane and I used to get along better. We used to e-mail daily and send each other hugs and kisses. We'd spend hours in chat rooms talking about nothing, anything. Then we'd fallen out. It was petty and mostly my fault. She didn't like my novel and I hadn't taken her rejection too well. Now our correspondence was purely business and as an agent I couldn't fault her, couldn't fault her on the fact that she supplied me with a steady stream of work. Except of course that it was always gay related.

But we can't always do what we want and it was a job.

And today's job was the gay/straight attraction.

I started as I always started any article. I made myself a cup of tea. I drank it and then I made myself more tea. I paced around, up and down, down and up. I trawled my mind for memories of straight men. I sat cross-legged on the floor like Buddha. I pulled out my diaries and I made a list of likely contacts, people I'd had but who professed to like their partners cockless; John the plumber, Adam the sales manager, Giovanni the hairdresser (married, two kids), some of the many who existed on the cusp of sexuality. I would call them and pick their brains, do them an injustice and try to stereotype them for my journalistic piece. They would be defined in reductive phrases, phrases I didn't believe in.

I worked steadily until I was disturbed by a knock at the door downstairs. I looked at my watch. It was six fifteen. I knew it would be Andy. My lodger.

He was leaning against the jamb smoking a cigarette. There was no sign of the lorry.

"Hi," he said. "Sorry I'm late."

I shrugged.

"Is it OK?" He held up the cigarette and nodded inside.

"Sure," I said. "Come in."

Andy followed me into the living room and stood in the middle of the floor.

"I got you keys," I said. I passed him the two keys from the breakfast bar where I had left them. He took them in his left hand, the one with only four fingers, and stared at them.

"The gold one is for the front door," I said. "The silver one for the back."

"Thanks," he said. He finished staring and put them in his pocket. He grinned. "Dad never gave me a key. He said I would lose it."

"Oh," I said and then added. "How old are you, Andy?"

"Twenty-one. Twenty-two next birthday." He took a drag on his cigarette.

"Oh," I said again. "And what did you do when your dad went out?"

Andy shrugged. "He doesn't go out. Not anymore."

"Oh," I said and we both stood there.

I went into the kitchen. I could feel Andy behind me, following. I could smell the smoke. I opened a cupboard and turned back to my guest.

"This one's for you," I said. "For your food."

"Right," said Andy. "Neat." He nodded his head. "Nice."

"And the cutlery's in here," I said, pulling out a drawer.

"Knives and forks," said Andy and nodded again. He took out a fork and examined it closely. "Stainless steel," he said and then he looked at me and grinned.

I felt like old Tom Oakley from *Goodnight Mister Tom*. Old Tom takes in young Willie Beech, an evacuee from London, during the Second World War, cares for him, looks after him, teaches him to read, write. I was already wondering if somewhere down the line Andy was going to start calling me dad.

"This is the fridge," I said. I patted the metallic blue appliance, "and this is the cooker. You have to be careful with it, it's a bit temperamental. More than once I've singed an eyebrow. And don't even go near it naked, especially not with a match."

"Naked?" Andy said. He raised one of his own currently unsinged eyebrows.

Andy didn't look like the sort of person who would ever attempt to cook with no clothes on. That was probably something we didn't have in common. One thing of many things.

"Well, semi-naked," I said. "For example, in the summer when your out in the garden in your shorts."

"You have a garden?" said Andy. His eyes widened. "I never had a garden before."

"Oh," I said and then added, "But you have shorts?"

"Of course," said Andy. He took another drag on his cigarette. "One pair. Black. I play football."

"Oh," I said. "There you go then. Don't cook in your shorts. Any questions?"

"Um..." said Andy and nodded to his hand. I noticed he was standing with his right elbow bent at right angles, his hand cupped. Above this impromptu container he was holding the cigarette. The ash was long and drooping.

"You want an ashtray?" I said.

"If you have one."

I did and I fished it out. Andy stubbed out his cigarette and as he did so there was a loud and long gurgle from his inside his boiler suit. He looked down at his stomach, he looked up at me.

"Sorry," he said, "I'm starving. Haven't eaten all day. Is there an shop near here?"

"Out of the door, turn left. You can't miss it."

"And an off licence?"

"Next door," I said. "If John is working there, he's bald and has an eyepatch, tell him that Honza sent you and he'll give you a discount."

"Neat," said Andy. "I'm going then. Want anything?"

I shook my head and said that I didn't and then I followed Andy into the hall. I watched the door close behind him. I hoped he wouldn't get lost.

I went back upstairs and surprised even myself that I got back into my work so easily. Usually for me, that's the hardest thing, starting. Usually I sit there for hours, doing nothing. But this time I was straight into it. Brainstorming. Firing out ideas, making a list. I was already on my second page when there was a knock at the door downstairs. I wondered who it was.

I went down and opened it. Andy was standing there. He was holding two plastic shopping bags.

"Haven't you got your key?" I said.

"Yeah," he said, "didn't like to use it."

"Well use it," I said. "That's what it's for."

"Sure," he said.

I wasn't certain whether he meant was I sure he could use it or sure he would use it.

"Come in," I said.

Andy squeezed past me in the hall and I went after him into the kitchen.

He put his two bulging plastic carriers on the breakfast bar. I sat down on one of the stools, put my elbows on the counter. Andy opened his cupboard. I watched him unpack. I watched him put one can of baked beans in the cupboard, then another and another. In all I counted eight tins of beans and one can of spaghetti alphabet letters. He placed this on the shelf below the beans. I wanted to ask but I didn't. The other bag contained two loaves of thick-cut white bread, two pints of full-fat milk and eight cans of Heineken. He held them up.

"Thanks. Ten per cent off. Want one?"

"Thanks," I said. I took the offered can.

He opened his and I opened mine. Beer spurted out of both and we both slurped bubbles and froth from the tin rim.

45

"A toast," said Andy and held up his can.

I held up mine and we clinked across the breakfast bar.

"To new beginnings," said Andy.

"To new beginnings," I said and we drank and it felt quite pro-found as if we really were starting something new, something spe-cial was happening.

Beer spilled down Andy's chin and he wiped it with the cuff of his boiler suit.

"I'm going to cook," said Andy. "OK?"

I looked at the neat row of tins in the cupboard, the door of which was still open.

"OK," I said. I had to ask, I just had to. "What are you making?"

Andy didn't flinch and there was no pause, not even a milli-second.

"Bouillabaisse," he said.

And we both laughed, shooting beer out of our mouths, slam-ming our hands down on the laminated top between us.

Five

After dinner Andy washed his pots, one knife, one fork, one plate, one pan, and left them on the draining-board to drip-dry. He took another can out of the fridge and offered another one to me. I declined and then he looked at his watch.

"*Coronation Street*," he said. He nodded at the television. "Can I?"

"Sure," I said.

He came and sat next to me on the sofa bringing the beer and the ashtray with him. The sofa wasn't the only seat. There were also two matching chairs, in the same soft-sueded velvet-effect, one under the front window and one adjacent to the breakfast bar, but Andy didn't sit in either of those. He squashed in on my left, legs spread, forcing me to shift over. He placed the can in the V of his crotch and took the remote control as I offered it to him.

We were just in time to catch the opening music, those famous red-bricked houses, the cat walking along the wall. Andy lit a cigarette.

"Do you watch this?" he said.

"Sometimes."

"Me too."

In fact, since Raquel had left Curly and left the show, *Corrie* had lost its kudos for me. It was no longer a street I wanted to walk down. Its campness had gone. But I felt I should sit there and show solidarity on our first night together. I felt it would be rude to lock myself away and spend hours surfing the internet, writing or researching. I felt I should stay with Andy, make him feel at home.

"Martin's going to tell Gail about his affair," Andy said. "Christ!"

"Oh," I said.

"There'll be fireworks. I wouldn't want to be Martin."

"Me neither," I said. "I wouldn't want to be married to Gail."

"Me neither." Andy took a drag of his cigarette. "Gail's horrible." She appeared on the screen. I flinched.

Gail, I had always thought, should be pleased that anyone would want her. If Martin had strayed, played away, then any authenticity the show might claim to portray of real working-class life should dictate that she wouldn't even bat one of her rat-like eyelids, should just be pleased that Martin didn't leave her altogether, should be pleased that she had someone who would want to wake up next to her face every day.

Mind you these were the same scriptwriters who expected us, the viewers, to believe that the gorgeous demigod and neophyte disco diva Adam Rickett had issued from her loins. *Coronation Street* was more fantastic to me than a novel by Salman Rushdie. But Andy was hooked. Alternatively puffing on his fag and sipping from his can his eyes were glued to the set.

The adverts came on. Andy stood up. He put his can carefully on the floor.

"I'm going for a piss," he said.

I felt he expected some answer.

"OK," I said.

His footsteps were loud on the stairs as he raced up them and then on his way down he jumped again and crashed to the floor. I would have to have a word with him about that. Or would I? How would I say it? It wasn't the sort of thing I had ever had to do before. I didn't want to come across patrician to his plebeian. That's not the relationship I wanted to have with my lodger.

Andy sat down. He scratched the inside of his thigh. He picked up his can of lager. The adverts finished and we watched the second half.

In the end Martin didn't tell Gail. She went to the hospital with Sarah Louise instead. She found out Sarah Louise was pregnant. She opened her mouth in an O. What an actress!

At eight o'clock as the credits rolled and the show finished Andy said, "*EastEnders*." He already had the remote in his hand in the air pointing. He was looking at me.

"Fine," I said.

"Do you watch it?" said Andy.

"Sometimes," I said.

If *Coronation Street* had lost its kudos, *EastEnders* for me had never had it. Seeing Barbara Windsor like that, stuck behind a bar in a brown suit, made me almost suicidal. I wanted to see her next to a pool, her pink bra pinging off into the water. I wanted to see her in a hospital ward bending over to pick up a deliberately dropped stethoscope, her green gown riding up to reveal pert cheeks. I wanted to hear her trademark cackle. She had the dirtiest laugh I'd ever heard. It was a laugh that could make a whore blush at fifty metres. Having Barbara Windsor in a show and not using that laugh was like employing Jeff Stryker, star of *Powertool One* and *Two*, to do an insole commercial. It was like getting Tom Jones to head your cabaret and asking him not to sing or to wiggle his hips. Hell, it was like asking Anne Robinson not to wink.

But Andy loved it.

"Go on Peggy," he said as Barbara stood up to Dan the barman and half owner of her pub. "Do you think she'll get him out?" he said.

I shrugged. I didn't know. I didn't care.

"Yes," I said. "I think so."

He smiled. "Me too. I wouldn't like to get out the wrong side of her bed."

"Yes," I said.

Andy seemed to know what was on each channel without ever looking at any tv pages. He knew that after *EastEnders* it was *Police! Camera! Action!* He thrilled in the chase and nudged me in the side with his elbow. He knew at nine thirty that it was *One Foot in the Grave.* He laughed like a drain, rocking next to me and he continued rocking and laughing as *One Foot* gave way to *The Fast Show* on BBC2 at ten o'clock. He even had me laughing although I didn't know what I was laughing at or at least I didn't know what was funny on screen. I only knew that he was funny, that his laughter was infectious and the next time he went to the fridge I accepted his offer of a drink.

"Cheers," he said and we clinked cans.

It appeared that after *The Fast Show* there was nothing Andy wanted to watch. He flicked through each of the channels in order and then back down again. He put the remote on the arm. He took a drag on his fag. He took a long swig from his can.

"Honza?" he said.

"Yes?" I said.

"I forgot."

"Yes?" I said.

"Hang on a second."

Andy leant back on the sofa, lifted up his midriff and was either trying to squeeze his hand in the back pocket of his boiler suit or scratch an itch on his bum. He wasn't having much success. There was a look of extreme deliberation on his face. The boiler suit, by the way, he hadn't taken off yet. He was still blue from collar to toe. Finally, after a lot of fumbling Andy gave up and lowered his midriff. He couldn't get his hand in or he couldn't reach the scratchiness. With a sigh he stood up. The pocket or the itch was now accessible.

"The rent," he said. "Sorry. Earlier. I forgot."

He had pulled out his hand and was looking at the collection of coins and notes there. He was concentrating and I could see his lips moving. They stopped moving and he looked puzzled. He scratched his head and he went over to the breakfast bar. I watched him as he counted out the money, coin by coin, note by note. Eventually his hand was empty. He scratched his head again and then checked his back pocket. He checked all his pockets. Nothing. He looked over at me. I was still watching him.

"The rent," he said.

"Yes," I said.

"Thirty-seven forty-nine. OK?" He grinned.

Goddam it. I grinned too. "OK."

He yawned, opening his mouth wide, stretching his hands in the air. He brought them down scratching his chest on the way.

"I'm tired," he said. "Have to be up early."

There was a pause. He didn't say anything. He yawned again. Louder and longer.

He looked at me.

"Why don't you go to bed?" I said.

"Right," he said. "OK. I will."

"Do you need anything?" I said. "There's a fresh duvet on the bed. There're towels on the bedside table."

"A glass of water?" he said.

"Sure."

"I'll get it," he said.

"OK."

At the third attempt he found the cupboard with the glasses in.

"Goodnight," he said.

"Goodnight," I said.

"Thanks," he said. He was still looking at me.

I almost expected him to come over and kiss me. Not passionately, not like an ardent lover, but as a good son would his mum. He didn't. He went out of the door and I heard him banging up the stairs. Three at a time. At least.

I smiled to myself.

Day one over. Done and dusted. No problem.

In the morning I didn't hear Andy leave. When I woke up the house was empty. It was quiet and it was just like any other day, any other day I had had without a lodger. I walked into the bathroom naked. I emptied my bladder naked. I went downstairs and had a cup of tea naked. Who said that having a lodger was going to change my life?

The first night had been painless and now I had the house to myself. I was glad that I had chosen Andy and not David, followed my head and not my groin. My instincts had been right. Andy was easy, Andy was simple. He wasn't the sort of person who was ever going to cause me pain, make my life complicated, fuck my head.

On pouring my second cup of tea I noticed a note on the breakfast bar. It was written on the torn off corner of some kind of delivery docket. The letters were almost illegible. I picked up the paper and held it up to the light. After much scrutiny I at last managed to make out the words. It said, "Back about six, Andy."

You see, how easy was that?

I had breakfast, had a shower, got dressed and set to work.

I had a productive day.

Until the phone call that is. It was a phone call that would change my life.

Completely.

In the morning I had checked over my notes from the day before. The gay/straight attraction piece would be a doddle. I would be able to finish it off, wrap it up, in a couple of days. I had put the pages aside and then inserted the disc that contained the beginnings of my new novel. I'd only just started, only written the first few chapters but the story was in my head, bursting to come out.

This was the stage I enjoyed the most, the first draft. I didn't have to think at all, the words just appeared, my fingers bounced over the keys. I could write the whole thing, four hundred pages, in a couple of months. It was the revision and the editing that was hard, that caused the headaches. What I had so excitedly typed, felt so proud of, I knew in retrospect would be crap, unreadable. I knew it would take hours and hours of polishing into shape. Anything worth anything takes effort, time.

But today I was really flying. I was full of the feeling that was better than any drug, more mind-blowing than any stimulant ever could be. I was a writer of fiction, creating worlds with my fingertips. I almost didn't hear the phone. Almost. It was three thirty.

"Hello," I said. I was short of breath. I had run down the stairs.

"Honza. It's me."

It was my sister, Julie. My heart started beating fast. My stomach twisted.

"Julie," I said, "how's Nicholas?"

"He's at day-care," she said. "He's fine."

And I breathed more easily. If Nicholas was OK then everything was OK. I only cared what happened to Julie in so far as it affected Nicholas. I didn't like my sister. Not at all. She was an occasional drug user. She was almost an alcoholic. She was mostly a prostitute. In my youth I thought she was cool, outrageous. I'd looked up to her. But since she'd had Nicholas I wanted her to change. I lived in fear that she would phone up and tell me something terrible had happened to my nephew. When he was a baby I was terrified that she would drop him on his head, leave him somewhere. For weeks I couldn't sleep. Despite my worries she had, even I had to admit, proved herself a good mother. But with all her problems, her good motherhood seemed to be balanced on a knife-edge. I felt like I was constantly waiting for her to fall off, to cut herself, damage him.

"So..." I said. Julie only called me when she wanted something.

"Mum says you've got a lodger," said Julie.

"Yes," I said.

"What's he like?"

"He's nice," I said.

"Nice nice or nice?"

What was it with my family?

"He's just a lodger," I said. "To help me pay the bills."

Julie laughed. It was a laugh of disbelief. My family thought I was rich. I'd worked in Japan for two years and I'd earned good money. Business men had paid about eighty pounds to spend an hour in my company and I didn't even have to sleep with them, only teach them English. And a book I had written on camp had made me a few thousand. But I wasn't rich at all, the money had gone.

"Tell me about him," said Julie.

"He's young," I said. "He wears a boiler suit. He eats baked beans. He's not my type. He's not even gay. He's straighter than a fucking arrow."

"OK," said Julie. "No need to go all defensive on me."

"OK," I said and I didn't say anything else. I was waiting for Julie to get to the real reason why she'd phoned.

"Sandra's teaching me to dance," said Julie.

"That's nice," I said. "What kind of dancing?" Somehow I knew it wouldn't be the tango.

"Erotic," she said.

"That's nice," I said.

"She says you can earn good money, dancing."

"In Derby?" I laughed. This new scheme seemed hair-brained even for Julie. Derby was not on the map, not renowned for its erotic dancing clubs. And then it hit me just as Julie said the words.

"In London."

"London?" I said. I picked the phone up and sat down on its chair.

"Sandra knows this girl," said Julie. She was talking more quickly now. "She's got a place. She says I can stay. Mixie, this girl, she says she makes a hundred a night. Two hundred if she's lucky."

"What about Nicholas?" I said. Please, no.

"Mixie says he can come too. Of course, I couldn't leave him. I love him. Mixie says there are lots of girls in the house. She says there'll always be someone to look after him. He's not a baby anymore."

"He's four," I said.

"I know," Julie said. "And then he'll be five and six and seven. I know how it works. This is my big chance. I've got to take it."

Her big chance. If it hadn't been for Nicholas I would have been sad. I would have been sad that my sister should think that her big chance was being ogled in some seedy club. But I wasn't sad, I was angry. I was sick. I didn't want to lose my nephew.

"Julie," I said, "what about day-care? What about school? What about mum, me. You can't go."

"Honza, don't be like this," she said. "I'm going. In three weeks. It's arranged."

"Please," I said. "Don't. You can come and live here. We'll sort it out. You don't have to go to London. We can sort it out."

"Sort what out?" said Julie, her voice hardening.

I wanted to say her life. But I didn't. I didn't say anything. Julie filled the gap.

"Honza," she said. "You don't get it, do you? I want to go. I don't want to be stuck in Derby for the rest of my life."

"You're not stuck," I said. "I'll help you."

"Help me?" said Julie.

"Yeah," I said. "I can help."

"Honza," said Julie. "Fuck you!"

She put the phone down. In truth I didn't blame her. I'd sounded patronising even to myself.

I went back upstairs.

I sat in front of my keyboard. I looked out of the window. For hours. The same thoughts were going round in my head. My sister was going to be an erotic dancer. She was taking my nephew to London. I wouldn't see him anymore. On a Saturday morning he wouldn't run into my arms screaming "uncle, uncle". On Saturday night he wouldn't sneak into my bed. He wouldn't ask if he could bring just one toy with him and he wouldn't fall asleep almost horizontal on the pillow. He wouldn't do any of those things.

Around and around went all the things he wouldn't do. And outside it grew darker and colder.

There was the sound of the key in the door.

I looked at my watch. It was just after six. It was Andy.

I went downstairs.

"Hi," said Andy. He was standing in the kitchen. He was wearing his blue boiler suit. He was smoking a cigarette.

"Hi," I said.

"I'm starving," he said. He opened his cupboard and looked at the tins.

"What are you having?" I said.

He turned to look at me. He almost smiled. "Coq au vin."

"Nice," I said. "Would you like some beers? On me. I'm going to the shop."

"Thanks," said Andy. Now he smiled. "Yes. Neat. Thanks."

I went out. I bought beer. A lot of beer. Enough to sink a ship. Enough to drown my sorrows.

When I got back from the off licence Andy had already eaten and was at the sink washing his dishes. One knife, one fork, one plate, one pan. He stacked them neatly on the draining-board to drip-dry.

"How was dinner?" I asked.

"Awful," said Andy. He turned to look at me. "Too much coq, not enough vin."

I laughed. Despite myself I laughed.

"Want a beer?" I said. I heaved the plastic carrier onto the breakfast bar.

"Thanks."

I passed him one of the green tins and put the remainder in the fridge.

"*Emmerdale*?" said Andy. He nodded at the television.

"OK," I said.

We went and sat down. We sat in the same positions as the day previously, him on the left, me on the right. Side by side. He wore his boiler suit. He didn't talk much. He stood every now and again and told me he was going to the toilet or he nodded thanks when I offered him another beer. He always rested the can in the V of his crotch. He smoked a lot. We watched television. *Emmerdale, EastEnders, The Bill, Peak Practice, Tarrant on TV*. Time for bed.

I could have spent the evening on the phone. I could have talked to my friends and talked through what I was going to do about Nicholas. I could have listened to their sympathetic advice. But I didn't. I was OK just watching television with Andy. I didn't want to think about Julie, Nicholas, London. I didn't want to think about it at all. Mindless tv helped. The beer helped. We drank it all. Five cans each. And then three more for me.

I surprised myself, I slept like a baby.

When I woke up the house was empty.

I walked to the bathroom naked.

By Friday I was already used to the sound of Andy's key in the lock. I'd go downstairs, I'd ask him what he was cooking. Wednesday risotto, Thursday sushi.

"You don't cook sushi," I had said.

"I'm not having sushi," Andy had said. "Not really."

"Right," I had said.

We watched telly. We drank beer. We got along fine.

Having Andy in the house was like having a low-maintenance pet. He was a dog who took himself for walks, whose mess I didn't have to scoop up in a plastic bag and who cracked the occasional joke. He was almost the waxwork I had dreamed of.

My only concern was Nicholas. I thought about him a lot but I never came up with any answers. There weren't any. If Julie was going to London then she was going. I couldn't see how I could stop her. And anyway, she hadn't gone yet. I usually tried not to worry about things that hadn't happened, only the things that had. The things that hadn't happened might not happen.

Julie had a good track record for not doing what she said she would. She had never been to America, she had never become a pop star, she had never learnt to speak Egyptian (a non-starter I had told her, the language is Arabic), she had never slept with either Tom Cruise or George Clooney. She had never even learnt to walk straight in stilettos.

By Friday I had convinced myself that she wouldn't go. It was just another one of those things that would be forgotten about. It would be consigned to the metaphorical dustbin along with the never-bought Egyptian phrase book, with Tom Cruise's never-left underpants, with George Clooney's never-blunted razor.

So on Friday I actually managed to get some work done again. I spent the whole day in my workroom working, not just looking out of the window. I wrote a whole chapter, ten pages. I read it through, changed a few bits and then I saved it to disc. I made a back-up copy.

And then my stomach rumbled.

I looked at my watch. It was six thirty. Strange, Andy wasn't home.

I went downstairs. Nobody. I sat on the sofa, on my space on the right. I switched on the television. I flicked through the channels. I had the choice of three news programmes, *The Simpsons* or *TFI Friday*. I left it on the latter. I could imagine Andy would like this kind of rubbish. Loud music, annoying presenter, semi-clad girls dancing in the advert breaks. It was him all over.

At five to seven I heard the sound of the key in the lock. Andy walked into the room. He didn't sit down.

"What you watching?"

"*TFI*," I said. I turned from the screen to look at him.

"Friday?" he said.

"Yes," I said. "*TFI Friday*."

"You like it?" He was scratching his armpit.

"Yeah," I said.

"Not me. I think it's shit. Can't stand it. The rubbish they put on."

I didn't say anything. Andy stopped scratching. There was a pause. He put his head on one side. "Honza," he said, "is it OK if I have a shower?"

"Sure," I said. "Of course."

"Thanks. I'm going out. With my mates." He turned and bounded up the stairs.

Andy was going out with his mates.

In Andy's mouth the word mates had sounded like some homogenised group, like team or squad or gang, a collection of people never mentioned in the individual. I imagined he always went out with mates and never with a John or a Barry or a Steve. I imagined Andy and his mates rattling around Derby city centre drifting on an unseen current from one bar to another. They would order pints, they would all drink the same. They would get drunker together and laugh louder together. After the pubs shut they would all have chips. If there was any trouble with another group they would take all on not one on. They only thing they would do alone was go home. There would be a momentary frisson as the group identity slipped away and each became himself again until the mates met up the following week.

Andy crashed in the hall. He appeared in the room. He had a towel wrapped around his waist. He wasn't wearing his boiler suit.

"Honza?"

"Yes Andy?" I said.

"Um..." he said. He was gripping the edge of the towel, holding it up, "can you show me how the shower works? I can't turn it on. I turned the knob. There's no water."

"How long have you been here?" I said. I stood up.

"I moved in on Monday, remember? Monday morning. It was definitely Monday because I was with Jim. Jim's a bastard."

"No," I said, "I know. I mean, haven't you had a shower yet?"

"No," said Andy. "I don't know how it works. That's why I'm asking. Can you show me? I'm meeting my mates in half an hour. Please."

"Sure," I said. I smiled. He smiled.

He took the stairs three at a time even wrapped in a towel. In the bathroom I showed him the button to turn on the shower inside the airing cupboard.

"Thanks," he said. "Easy."

I went downstairs. I heard the spurt of the shower as it started.

I don't know why but I expected Andy to come down dressed in a boiler suit, not the blue one he had been wearing all week, not the one that was grimy and stained and smelt of stale sweat but a new blue one, all sharp lines and smelling of Drift, or maybe a white one undone at the neck revealing jutting collar bone. So when Andy walked into the lounge I almost didn't recognise him.

I was hit by the smell first. I was watching wresting on Channel Five. Don't ask. A week earlier, before Andy had moved in, I hadn't even known I could get Channel Five. The smell was kind of somewhere between Issey Miyake, Tendre Poison and Pledge floor polish. The potion was either very strong or Andy had practised his finger exercises on the pump. I turned and Andy was standing there.

He was wearing blue jeans, a blue Ralph Lauren shirt with button-down collar and blue Adidas trainers. He had put gel on his hair and it was spiky at the front. Like mine.

"I'm going out." he said. "With my mates."

"OK," I said.

"I'll be back late."

"OK," I said.

"Don't wait up," he said. He smiled.

"OK," I said. "I won't." I smiled.

"Bye Honza," he said. "Have a nice evening."

"You too," I said. "See you."

And Andy was gone. Only the smell lingered.

If at this point you expect me to tell you that I felt my heart cleave, that I suddenly missed Andy, that I wanted him to take me with him, or worse than that, that you thought I had fallen in love with my live-in then you've got me all wrong. I felt nothing but happiness at the thought of having the house to myself.

Well not myself exactly.

As soon as Andy was out of the door I was in the hall. I picked up the phone. I dialled the number.

John answered. He was surprised to hear from me and I said I was sorry and said that I had been busy, very busy but I had been thinking about him and I knew that it was short notice but would he like to come over. I could hear yes in his heart, no in his head. I could hear desire and pride slugging it out. I said I would cook for him and I had missed him really, I had been busy honestly. Please, I said, I want you. Desperately. There was a short silence and then he said yes he would come. He would be there in ten minutes.

Ten minutes. I was better than I thought.

I never did cook. We were in my bed five minutes after he arrived. John had one of those big cocks I thought about in my moments alone. Big and thick like a folded up umbrella. He fucked me then I fucked him. He wiped sweat off his brow with a Kleenex.

At eleven o'clock I told him he could go.

"What?" he said. He was smoking a cigarette. He was lying on his back in my bed blowing rings up to the ceiling.

"You have to go," I said. "I have to be up early."

"You're joking, right?"

"My nephew's coming," I said.

"And?" he said.

And. And. And would lead to a very long answer. If I explained

"And", then I would have to explain about Nicholas's life. I would have to explain how Nicholas called me uncle but said I was his daddy, how when he was upset he would scream daddy, daddy and cling on to me crying. I would have to explain that I didn't want Nicholas to see me with a succession of men, that when Nicholas was here then this bed was his if he wanted it and I didn't want it crowded with strangers. I would have to explain that I wasn't ashamed of my sexuality but if Nicholas saw me with a man then it would be The Man, my partner and he would have another uncle, an important uncle who would be around for him. I would have to explain that in my nephew's messed-up little life I was his stability, I was always there when his mum was strung out, when she had an unexpected client and had nowhere to leave him. I wanted me to be the constancy in his universe.

I didn't say this. I only got out of bed and picked up John's discarded underpants. I threw them to him.

"Thanks," I said. "It was nice. Very nice. I'll call you."

John didn't say anything but he got the message. He stubbed out his cigarette and started pulling on his clothes. As he finished tying his shoelaces he said, "Honza, you're a bastard."

I knew that already.

"I'll call you," I said.

He just looked at me and walked out of the room. I heard the front door closing.

I went down to the kitchen. I made myself a sandwich and a cup of tea. I had missed dinner. And then I went back upstairs. I changed the sheets and covers on the bed, had a shower and got under the duvet. Julie was bringing Nicholas at nine o'clock. She had called on Thursday and asked if she could bring him an hour earlier that usual. She hadn't mentioned dancing or moving to London.

I soon fell asleep. I dreamt of the big dick part of the evening and not the, "Honza, you're a bastard" bit.

*

I woke up. Or rather something woke me. I opened my eyes. It was dark. I turned my head and looked at the luminous hands of the Westclox. It was three-thirty. There was that sound again. It was a banging. Then I heard my name being called. Loudly.

It was Andy. He was knocking on the front door.

I groaned and got out of bed.

I went downstairs and opened the door. Andy was on the step swaying. He was pissed, looked like he had pissed himself as well. His trousers were soaking. He raised his head and looked at me with bloodshot eyes.

"I forgot my key."

"You'd better come in," I said.

"I'm drunk."

Andy took one step forward and I thought he was going to fall. He put a hand on my shoulder to steady himself. He grinned and burped. He stank of beer and curry. He stumbled through into the lounge and I followed him. I watched as he slumped on the sofa and considered saying something about his wet jeans but I didn't. I'd been young once. What was I saying, I was still young. I was only twenty-nine.

"Want a coffee?" I said.

There was no answer. Andy was leaning forward with his head in hands, his elbows on his knees.

"Andy," I said more loudly, "do you want a coffee or some water?"

He lifted his head and looked around the room. He spied me in the kitchen. Perhaps he spied several mes.

"I forgot my key," he said. "Sorry."

"That's OK," I said.

"I'm drunk," he said.

"You want a drink?"

"Honza?"

"Yes?"

"I'm going to be sick," he said. "I'm pissed. Sorry." He'd gone white.

I grabbed the bowl out of the sink and got to him just in time. I sat down on the sofa, placing the bowl at his feet and put my arm around him. I noticed again what I noticed earlier when he had come downstairs in his towel. He was very skinny. It was all those beans. I decided that I would teach him to cook. He threw up.

I suppose I was lucky. Not one drop of the vile green and yellow coloured albumen-like mixture went on my chequered rug, not one speck of it dripped onto the settee. Andy and I were a perfect shot, hitting the bowl spot on every time. After five or six flowing heaves Andy was retching, his stomach was cramping and he had nothing left to expectorate, regurgitate. I felt his pain with him and held him till he stopped.

I leant him back against the sofa. He looked like someone who had just given birth. There was a layer of sweat on his face, his cheeks were red and puffy and he had huge black rings under his eyes. He looked exactly like my sister had moments after they had placed Nicholas in her arms for the first time.

"Take him away!" she had screamed.

I went into the kitchen to get some roll to wipe his face with and when I went back into the lounge Andy was asleep. His mouth was open and he was snoring.

I had two choices. I could leave him there or I could take him upstairs to bed. If I left him there than it was likely that he would still be there in the morning when my sister brought Nicholas over. I had told her that my lodger was nice. I didn't want my sister to think my lodger was a piss-smelling drunk. I wanted my sister to think that I was holier than thou or at least holier than her.

That meant that I had to take Andy upstairs.

I grabbed his shoulder and shook. He half-opened his eyes. He grinned.

"Andy," I said, "you have to go to bed."

"Right," he said. He didn't move.

"Andy!" I said.

No answer.

I took his left hand and heaved and he came up easily. I put his left hand over my shoulder and my right hand around his waist. It wasn't as difficult as I expected. Even in his half-asleep, fully-drunk state Andy seemed to be bearing most of his weight and really it was just a question of taking it slowly and guiding him in the right direction.

I hadn't been in the spare room, Andy's room, since he had moved in. I pushed the door open with my foot, still holding Andy up. I don't know what I'd expected but I didn't expect what I saw. The room didn't look any different. I guess I expected to see some evidence of him in there, underpants on the floor, ashtrays, shirts on hangers. There wasn't anything. The room was tidier than when I had showed it to him. The bed was perfectly made, there was no sign of any clothes. I couldn't even see that bloody blue boiler suit.

I let Andy fall on the bed.

He had definitely wet himself.

I tried to remember if I had ever wet myself. I didn't think I had, not deliberately anyway. I once had this guy. He was absolutely beautiful. He wanted me to. He took me back to his house and gave me loads and loads of water. And then we waited. And waited. It's not easy. Try it. It's difficult to break the habit of a lifetime, years of doing it only in a toilet. Eventually with face scrunched tight with concentration I managed it.

I looked down at Andy.

I knew I should take off his trousers. It wasn't fair to leave him like that. It wasn't fair for him to sleep in the wet. But I was loath to do it, loath to remove the jeans. As you know I'm a sucker for a big cock regardless of what it is attached to. I didn't fancy Andy and I didn't want to do anything to jeopardise that. I didn't want to contemplate what might lurk in his nether regions. I didn't want to complicate our so far perfect coexistence. I wasn't keen to know if he had a wanger to end all wangers, I wasn't interested to find out if he could swing his hips and poke himself in the eye.

Decision time.

To remove or not to remove.

Andy was fast asleep.

It was windy outside. The room wasn't warm.

"Look at him," I told myself. "Not your type. You can resist."

Without pause I went over to the bed. I was a doctor with a patient, a mother with a son, a window dresser with a mannequin. I started whistling. Wrong choice. I Should Be So Lucky wasn't appropriate.

I undid the buckle. I undid the top button. I pulled down the zip.

Thank God, no button fly.

I tugged down the jeans.

Hallelujah! Praise the Lord! Sing hosanna! Three cheers! Hip Hip Hooray!

Andy was wearing boxer shorts. They were the most voluminous thick materialed boxer shorts I'd ever come into contact with.

There was no sight of cock, no glimmer of an outline. The underwear could have contained a walnut or a walnut tree trunk. I didn't have a clue. I was saved. My life was sorted. The boxer shorts were wet, it was true, but they would dry out. I didn't want to take them off, I didn't want to push my luck.

I had just hung Andy's trousers over the back of a chair, was just rolling him under the duvet when he opened his eyes. We were staring at each other.

"Honza," he said, "I didn't mean to kill him."

Six

I woke up. Outside it was light. Too light. Too light for before nine. There was panic in my stomach. I looked at the clock.

Shit!

It was eleven o'clock. I had overslept. Julie was supposed to have been bringing Nicholas at nine. If Julie was reliable about one thing, it was the time she dropped off Nicholas. She had never been late. Ever.

I leapt out bed and pulled on some pants. I ran downstairs. I ran into the lounge. I heard noises from the television and shouting.

Andy was there, Nicholas was there. Andy was on his hands and knees and Nicholas was on his back. With one hand Nicholas was holding onto Andy's hair and with the other he was slapping Andy's boxer shorts bum. Nicholas was shouting, "faster! faster!" at the top of his voice. As the pair of them rounded the corner of the sofa and negotiated the sharp sides of the Kaffatorp coffee table Nicholas spied me.

"Uncle!" he screamed. "Uncle!"

He jumped off Andy's back and ran to me, arms out like a quarter-size quarterback. He wrapped himself around my legs and I picked him up under the armpits. He giggled and wriggled against my body until he was comfortable. He patted my chest and turned to Andy.

"This is my uncle," he said.

Andy had stood up. He was breathing heavily. He was wearing boxer shorts and a T-shirt. The T-shirt was blue and had Adidas written on it in white letters. The boxer shorts were different to the soaked ones he had had on the night before.

"That's Andy," said Nicholas. He pointed at Andy. "He's a lodger. He's a horsey."

"I can see," I said.

In fact, Andy looked more sheepish than horseyish. His face was red and he was gazing at his bare feet, bouncing his big toe on the beech-wood floor. He had wrapped his arms around himself.

I wondered if his embarrassment was due to the state he'd been in the previous night, his drunkenness, his urinary slip or if it was due to something more profound. His confession. I'd lain awake for ages thinking about what he'd said. But from whichever angle I'd looked at it I hadn't been able to envisage Andy as a murderer. Not at all. So eventually I'd decided it was just one of those things you say when you're drunk. For example, "You're my best friend in the world", "I'm going to become a better person", "I love you".

"Uncle?" said Nicholas.

"Yes Nicholas?"

"Why aren't you wearing any clothes?"

I looked down. It wasn't entirely true. I was wearing a pair of Calvin Klein briefs but he had a point, these were less than modest. They were briefs that were sartorially designed for the imaginatively challenged. I lowered my nephew back onto the floor.

"I'll go and get dressed," I said. "And then I'll make you some breakfast."

"I had breakfast," said Nicholas. "With the lodger."

"Oh," I said. I glanced at Andy. He was scratching himself through the material of his boxer shorts. "What did you have?"

Nicholas screwed his face up like he did when he was really concentrating. He put his head on one side and put his left index fingers to the corner of his mouth.

"Croak Measure," he said.

"Croque monsieur," said Andy.

"Great," I said. "How was it?"

"Nice," said Andy. "Very French. The cheese was runny. Just how I like it."

"Like beans on toast," said Nicholas and looked at Andy. He grinned and then Andy grinned and then Nicholas started running around and around the coffee table, hands out in front of him as if he was driving a car. He was making loud noises through his pressed together lips. I half expected Andy to join him. He didn't.

"Thanks for looking after him," I said.

"I was awake," said Andy. "I heard the door. You were asleep. I woke you up last night. Sorry. Sorry."

"That's OK," I said.

Andy looked at Nicholas and then back at me.

"That woman," he said, "his mother?"

"Yes?"

"She your sister?"

"Yes," I said.

"She's very…" Andy looked around as if searching for the right words in the fixtures and fittings. We didn't have a slag pile, we didn't have shag carpet.

"Yes," I said. "She is. Very."

"He's a good kid," said Andy as Nicholas did a three-point turn around the corner of an armchair.

"Thank you," I said. "He is."

I looked at Nicholas. Andy looked at Nicholas.

Nicholas was now obviously growing bored of driving a car. Andy and I both watched as he shuffled backwards and parked. He leant one-handed on the coffee table and starting kicking his heels/wheels.

"Uncle?" he said. He was grinning cheekily, he wasn't looking me in the eye but at some point over my shoulder.

"Yes Nicholas?" I said.

"This lodger," he said, "he's a good horse but is he a good dinosaur?"

I didn't have to answer. Andy raised his hands in the air and was roaring and chasing Nicholas across the room and Nicholas was screeching and squawking and laughing. They went around the sofa and then when Nicholas found himself in a corner, under the spotlight of a downlight he turned to face his foe. He did his trademark Power Ranger kick and locked his arms in an X in front of him.

"I'm a Power Ranger!" he shouted contorting his face and added, "the red one" more quietly, and now he was after Andy and Andy was running.

I watched them for a while, watched them as they rolled onto the sofa together and watched as Andy, laid on his back, held Nicholas up at arm's length and Nicholas was a plane, flying through the sky with arms outstretched, swooping and diving.

I went over to them.

"Uncle, look at me," said Nicholas.

"I am," I said. "Very nice. Andy?"

"Yes?" said Andy, his face red again.

"Can you look after him while I have a shower?" I said. "I'll be ten minutes."

"Sure," said Andy. "No problem."

"No problem," said Nicholas and laughed.

I went upstairs to the bathroom and as I felt the first spurts of water on me I thought how much simpler this was with Andy in the house. Normally any action involving one adult and one child requires strategic planning, careful consideration. Usually when I had a shower I brought Nicholas upstairs with me. I checked my room for any sharp objects, any hazards and I let him play on my bed, shouting to him regularly from behind the shower curtain. Today, I didn't have to worry. Andy looked like he knew what he was doing. He looked like he was used to kids.

When I went downstairs, dressed and aromatic, Andy was on his hands and knees with Nicholas on his back once more, apparently being a horse again. I would certainly give him A for effort.

"Nicholas?" I said.

"Yes uncle?"

Andy stopped half on and half off the beech flooring, between lounge and kitchen, and Nicholas twizzled around to look at me. I walked up to them.

"What's the horsey's name?" I said.

"Horsey?" said Nicholas. "What horsey?" He looked puzzled.

I patted Andy's head. "This one," I said.

"Oh uncle," said Nicholas. "It's not a horsey, it's a donkey."

"Right," I said. "Of course."

"I'm not a donkey," said Andy.

I didn't answer. I still didn't know, still didn't want to know but I smiled to myself.

"Want some juice?" I said.

"Yes," Nicholas and Andy said together and the three of us laughed.

"Actually," said Andy standing and gathering Nicholas under his left arm, "a cup of tea would be nice. If you're making one."

"Of course," I said. "Go and sit down. I'll bring it over."

I flicked on the kettle. I opened the fridge. I took out the orange juice. I put tea bags in two cups.

When I took the drinks over Nicholas and Andy were sitting on the sofa. Andy was in his usual seat, Nicholas was in mine. They were huddled together and talking about something in whispers. Seeing me they both stopped.

"Uncle?" said Nicholas.

"Yes?" I said. I passed him the juice in his plastic Teletubbies cup. He took it in two hands.

"The lodger said," said Nicholas, "that I could go to the cinema."

"Heh," said Andy. He pinched Nicholas in the side. Nicholas

giggled and slipped off the settee. "I didn't," said Andy. "I said you had to ask your uncle. And my name's Andy. An-dy."

"An-dy said that at the cinema is *Toy Story. Two*," said Nicholas. "We saw Number One on video uncle. Remember? With Woody and Buzz and they fight." And Nicholas acted out the fight, jumping from one spot to another being first Buzz and then Woody, Woody and then Buzz. Then he stopped and looked at me. "Can we uncle? Can we go? Paulie went and Lucy went and Jane and Peter went and John and Simon and Susie and Mickey Mouse and the Teletubbies. They ALL went. Can we?" He looked at me, waiting.

I was thinking of our previous visit to the cinema.

"Remember when we saw *Antz*?" I said.

Last time, the first time we had ever gone to the cinema, Nicholas had talked constantly through the film. He had been going through his "why" period. He had asked why ants could talk, why ants didn't talk to him, why some ants were bigger than other ants. He asked which ants were good and which ants were bad and if he ever met an ant how would he know. And if he couldn't talk to strangers could he talk to ants? And when they had started fighting he had screamed and was scared and I had had to take him home.

"I remember," said Nicholas, looking at me with all the sagacity of a High Court judge, "and I made a deal with Andy and I promise not to talk. Not one word."

"A deal?" I said. I glanced at Andy. Andy was busy with the smooth knuckle on his left hand, kneading it between the fingers of the right.

"Can we go?" said Nicholas.

I sighed.

"Please."

I never could resist those big brown eyes.

"OK," I said.

"Hooray!" Nicholas clapped his hands. Nicholas was the only child I had ever heard say hooray. Nicholas ran around the room. Nicholas stopped and looked at me.

"Can Andy come?" he said.

I looked at Andy.

"I'm sure Andy has other things he wants to do..." I said.

"No," said Andy. "I haven't. I'd like to come. If that's OK?" He looked at me like Nicholas looks at me when he wants both cake and ice cream.

"Of course," I said. "That'll be nice. The three of us."

And I was surprised with myself because I meant it, it would be nice to go together. It wasn't that I was desperate to spend my time with Andy, to bask in his company. I meant it because it would be easy. I could buy the tickets and Andy could take care of Nicholas. I wouldn't have to worry how I was going to carry a cup of Coke, a box of popcorn and hold Nicholas's hand. Having Andy along would make my life more simple. And that's what I wanted, a simple life.

As I strapped Nicholas into the car seat that always sat in the back of my car he put his hand in the air. I'd been at school once too. I knew the meaning.

"Yes Nicholas?" I said.

He shook his head, his lips tightly pressed together. He pointed at Andy. Andy was already ensconced in the front passenger seat. I tapped Andy on the shoulder and he turned around.

"Andy," whispered Nicholas very quietly, "can I talk now or not?"

"Yes," said Andy. "Now, but not in the cinema."

"Good," said Nicholas and then he added. "When I'm watching the film can I laugh?"

"Yes," said Andy.

"Clap?"

"Yes," said Andy. "Quietly."

"Can I SHOUT!?" Nicholas giggled.

"No," said Andy. "No shouting. No screaming. No squeaking like a mouse. Deal?"

"Deal," said Nicholas. And Andy reached over the back of his seat and they shook hands, a big one in a little one.

"What is this deal?" I asked as I climbed in the front. "What are you getting me in to?"

"I'll tell you later," said Andy. He put on his seat-belt and looked out of the window, looked at the facade of my house. It didn't work, I could see his grin reflected in the glass.

My car was a Ford Ka. I had paid the deposit for it with the money from an article on gay men and jeeps for an American fashion magazine. Nicholas liked it, or at least he liked its name. On the way to the cinema he chanted his usual refrain. "It's not a car it's a Ka. It's not a CAR it's a Ka." Over and over.

I don't know who enjoyed the film more, Nicholas or Andy. They sat there like two kids. Nicholas had an excuse, he was a kid. They slurped Coke, they stuffed themselves with sugary popcorn. They laughed, they giggled, they put their hands over their eyes, they put their hands over each others eyes and they clapped when Woody the cowboy was rescued by Buzz the space ranger. Nicholas leapt from his seat and punched the air. But he didn't say one single word, not one syllable.

As the lights went up and the hubbub increased around us, as chocolate-coated kids were wiped clean with Kleenexes, Nicholas put his hand in the air.

"Yes Nicholas?" I said.

He shook his head and pointed at Andy. Andy was busy. He was pulling bits of stuck popcorn off his jeans and popping them in his mouth. I tapped him on the shoulder. I pointed at Nicholas.

"Andy," whispered Nicholas again, very quietly again, "can I talk now?"

"Yes," said Andy.

"Hooray!" said Nicholas. He clapped his hands. "So I won?"

"Yes," said Andy.

"You'll speak to uncle?"

"Yes," said Andy.

"Now?"

"Later," said Andy. "Tonight. I promise."

"Hooray!" said Nicholas and he went charging off up the aisle, shouting. "And then Woody went pow and Buzz went sock, bang, bam, kapow, kapow!" His little arms were flying.

I turned to Andy.

"So what's he won?" I said.

"Um..." said Andy.

"Andy?"

"Watch him!" said Andy. "Don't lose him," and he set off after my little, loveable, beautiful nephew.

In the car on the way back I put on a tape. Nicholas and I liked the same music. Indigo, Abbacadabra, Jackie O, Sarah Washington. As I pulled up at the house we were singing along at the tops of our voices to 'Lay All Your Love On Me'. Nicholas was clapping his hands and Andy was slapping the dashboard, stamping his feet on the floor. I put on the handbrake and turned off the cassette.

"We're home," said Andy.

I looked at him. He looked at me. He grinned.

He got out of the car and pulled up the lever to pull forward his seat. He reached in and undid Nicholas's straps while I fumbled for my keys and unlocked the door. Easy. We were in the house.

In the hall Andy scratched his stomach.

"I'm going for a piss," he said.

He bounded up the stairs three at a time. He left the door open. His aim was perfect, right in the centre of bowl. Splash, splash, splash.

"Andy's going for a piss," said Nicholas.

"Yes," I said.

Nicholas started laughing and then I was laughing. We were still laughing and still standing in the hall when Andy crashed back down the stairs.

"What's funny?" he said.

"Nothing," I said.

"Nothing," said Nicholas. He had put his hand over his mouth.

"Good," said Andy. "Anyone hungry? I'm going to cook. My speciality."

"Oh," I said.

Although Andy might tell us his speciality was gazpacho, couscous, Bohemian rabbit, Spanish rabbit or even Savoy cheese fondue, I knew what in fact his speciality would be. I could picture the single tin of spaghetti alphabet letters on the bottom shelf of his cupboard. On medium sliced white bread.

"Actually," I said, "I was going to order Chinese."

"That's my speciality," said Andy, "ordering Chinese. I know the girl. We can get a discount."

"Do it," I said.

"Uncle?" said Nicholas. He still had his hand over his mouth.

"Yes?" I said.

"I've done a pooh. Sorry."

I looked at Andy.

"I'll order that Chinese," he said. "Busy. Sorry."

"Come on my boy," I said. "Let's get you upstairs."

Later, dinner eaten, boy bathed, it was time for his bed. Supposedly Nicholas's room had always been the room Andy was in now, but only supposedly. Nicholas always wanted to sleep with me, always asked if he could and almost always did. I'd been trying to discourage him, telling him that he was becoming a big boy, but I figured now his supposed room was taken there was less chance then ever of getting him to sleep on his own. I did have a futon in my workroom but I didn't want Nicholas in there.

I could well imagine what damage little fingers could do to discs, manuscripts and A4 pages.

So Nicholas was in my room, in my bed, only a little head visible above the duvet.

"Goodnight Nicholas," I said.

"Night uncle."

"Sleep tight," I said.

"OK," he said.

I smiled at his answer. OK. Like he was in control. I liked that.

"Uncle?"

"Yes," I said.

"Can Andy read me a story?"

"Um…" I said.

"Please."

You know how it is, when Nicholas says please then I say yes. Usually.

Andy was in front of the tv watching a programme with big men standing in doorways, shouting. The ashtray was balanced on one sofa arm, his legs were open in a V and he was smoking a fag. Andy didn't smoke cigarettes, only fags. I realised that he hadn't had one all day, not in front of Nicholas.

I wasn't jealous that Nicholas wanted a story from Andy, not at all. I hadn't been jealous that they'd seemed to have taken to each other so much, had laughed together in the cinema, had had a competition to see who could get the most Chinese food in their mouth. I hadn't even been jealous when Nicholas had asked me quietly when he was in the bath if Andy might be his daddy. I wasn't jealous because I wasn't insecure about my love for Nicholas or his for me. It was the most secure thing in my life. If Nicholas was happy then I was too. So I was quite happy to ask Andy if he would be storyteller for the night.

"Sure," he said. He immediately stood and stubbed out his cigarette. "No problem. But one condition?"

"What?" I said. I was imagining rent concessions, piles of dirty laundry, cups of tea in the morning.

"Ten thirty, *Match of the Day*."

"Of course," I said. "Never miss it."

"You?" said Andy.

"Me," I said. "I'll go to the shop, get us some beers."

"Right," said Andy, "I'll give you some money."

"Don't worry," I said. "Just go and read that story."

I listened as he bounded up the stairs three at a time and then I went out of the door.

When I got back it was ten twenty-five. There was no sign of Andy in the living-room, in the kitchen. I knew that if I went upstairs and Nicholas was still awake and he saw me then it would be even longer before he went to sleep. So I put the beer in the fridge, kept one can and sat down on the sofa. On my side.

It was ten twenty-eight.

Ten twenty-nine.

At ten thirty exactly and just as the famous music started, ta ta ta ta tatata TA TA, music that made my heart beat as fast as any hi-NRG hit Andy appeared. There had been no footsteps on the stairs, no crash in the hallway.

"Beer's in the fridge," I said. "He asleep?"

"Thanks," said Andy. He took out a can. "Yes. Just. I was reading Ant and Bee."

"He likes that," I said.

"Yes," said Andy. He opened the can and beer fizzed over his hand. "All children like insects."

"You're good with kids."

"Thanks," said Andy. He sat down, took a swig from the can and placed it in the V of his crotch. His knee was touching mine. "I had a little brother once. He died. Six years old. Who's playing?"

"Sorry," I said. I was looking at Andy and he was looking at the screen. He took another drink of his beer, a long one.

"I said who's playing?" said Andy. He lit a cigarette. His hand was shaking.

"I don't know," I said. "Who do you support?"

"Liverpool," said Andy. "Since I was a little boy."

"Liverpool?"

"Yes," said Andy. "How about you?"

"Manchester United."

"Wankers," said Andy. He turned to me and grinned.

Gary Lineker had finished his commiserations for the death of Stanley Baxter and was now introducing the first game. Manchester United versus Liverpool. Andy nudged me in the side. The teams came out of the tunnel.

"Look at Beckham," said Andy. "He's such a poof."

I took a drink.

"A poof?" I said.

Andy was looking at the screen. The referee blew his whistle and the match started.

"Not a poof like you," said Andy. "Not a real poof but a poncey poof. Dyes his hair. Wears a skirt. Know what I mean?"

"Yeah," I said. "Suppose so."

"I don't like that wife of his either. Posh Spice. Thinks she's so beautiful. I hate her."

"Me too," I said. "But I am envious."

"Envious?" said Andy.

"Yeah," I said. "She gets to suck Beckham's cock whenever she wants."

Andy didn't answer. He leapt in the air, grabbing his can in the same movement, hoisting it to the ceiling and he started hopping from foot to foot.

"One nil. One nil."

Liverpool had scored. Patrick Berger had curled a free kick over the wall from more than thirty yards. It was a good goal, a great goal, one that would no doubt feature at a later date in the goal of the month competition. But I wasn't happy, not at all.

"Sit down Andy," I said. "I can't see the screen."

"One-nil," said Andy and sat down. He dug his elbow in my side again and I ignored him. Football always reduced me to a little boy. I put my elbows on my knees and leant closer to the tv.

I liked everything about football. I liked the game, I liked the facts, figures, statistics, tables and I liked the men. If I had a type then it was footballer. With notable exceptions I fancied them all. For example, I didn't fancy Gazza or the Hunchback himself, Peter Beardsley, but the rest, they did something to me. And it wasn't fantasy. I would never consider doing a David Mellor and getting one of my lays to put on a strip and then strip it off them. I loved the reality of it. I loved real footballers with real football legs, wearing real football boots, scoring real goals and after the match having real footballer showers and footballer Jacuzzis.

"I play football," said Andy. "On a Sunday. Non-league. Just a laugh."

I would have answered but just then Ryan Giggs made a blistering run down the left wing, fizzed the ball over to the centre and a waiting Solskjaer. Solskjaer, with his off-blond curls and baby-blue eyes, ghosted past one defender, squeezed past another and slid the ball under Westerveld into the back of the net.

I was over the moon.

I didn't leap into the air, that wasn't my style, but I did leap on the inside. I turned to Andy.

"One all," I said.

"Fuck off," he said and got up to go to the fridge.

He came back and thrust a beer into my hand without a word. I cracked open the can, still focused on the screen. Man United had turned up the pace. Solskjaer had a shot saved off the line and then so did Sheringham. I could feel Andy squirming next to me. Then suddenly he was up again. Owen, the wonder boy, was one-on-one with Van der Gouw, the United keeper. He had to score. Andy had his mouth half-open, ready to scream. The ball left Owen's boot, Van der Gouw lunged to his right. He missed it. The keeper had missed it. The ball was heading towards the goal. At the top of the picture the indefatigable Keane was running back. There was no way he would make it. I closed my eyes.

Nothing.

I felt Andy sit down.

I opened my eyes.

"What happened?" I said.

There was no answer from Andy but on the screen they were showing a replay. I watched as the ball bobbled and swerved at the last moment and went harmlessly past the right post. Owen had missed.

"Never mind," I said. "Not an easy chance."

"Fuck off," said Andy.

The match finished. It remained one each. Not a brilliant result but it kept the peace. Our teams done we watched the other games with less passion but equal interest. We didn't talk much. We both willed Southampton to lose and we discovered a mutual hatred for Glen Hoddle, their manager. We both said we didn't like Ginola's hair. And we both thought that Gary Lineker was doing a good job since the departure of Des Lynam.

As the final credits rolled Andy stood and stretched. He scratched his stomach.

"I'm going to bed. I'm knackered. Football tomorrow."

"OK," I said. And then I remembered, *Match of the Day* had put it out of my mind. I remembered about Nicholas. "But haven't you forgotten something?"

"Sorry," said Andy. "Thanks for beer and goodnight."

"No," I said. "Not that. You were going to tell me about your deal with Nicholas."

"Oh," said Andy. He yawned again and started to head towards the door.

"Andy?"

He stopped.

"Now, don't be angry," he said.

"What have you told him?" I said.

"It's just that..." He stopped.

"Come on," I said.

"Well I said, and you'll thank me in the end. I worry about you here all day by yourself..."

"What are you talking about?" I said.

"Um...you see on television there was this dog..."

"Dog?" I said. And then it clicked. "Andy, you haven't."

"... and Nicholas was so excited... and I said..."

"Andy, please, no!"

"I told Nicholas," said Andy, "that if he was quiet in the cinema then you would buy him a puppy."

"Oh my God!"

Seven

Julie was coming to pick up Nicholas at six o'clock. In this she was reliable. My sister was many things but she wasn't tardy. It was something I couldn't get my head around. How could someone inject poison into their blood, sell their body to disgusting lascivious old men and yet still have the punctiliousness of a most scrupulous railway signalman? I didn't know.

So when at five fifty-five there was a knock at the door I assumed it was her. I told Nicholas to put his things in his Power Rangers bag and I went into the hall. I fixed a smile on my face and opened the door.

"Hi," said Andy.

It wasn't Julie. It was Andy.

As usual, he was leaning against the jamb, smoking a cigarette. It was, however, a very unusual looking Andy. A very different Andy to the one that had gone out earlier.

"Andy!" screamed Nicholas. He had appeared behind me dragging his bag behind him.

"Hello Nicholas," said Andy and then added to me. "Sorry, forgot me key."

"Don't worry," I said. I wanted to say something else. I was wondering how to put it into words.

"Andy," said Nicholas placing his arms around my knees, "you're dirty."

Well done Nicholas. But he hadn't quite got it. To call Andy dirty would have been like calling a pig porcine, a cow bovine, a claret a bottle of wine. Andy was filthy. He was covered from head to toe in a thick black viscous mud. His once blond hair now wouldn't have looked out of place on the proudest of Negro's head. He was Mohammed Andy.

"I need a shower," said Andy. "Football got a bit mad."

"Yes," I said. "I can see. Were you the ball?"

"Ha ha," said Andy. A piece of mud slipped off his head and onto the pavement.

"Did you win?" I said.

"No," said Andy. "Don't ask. Eight nil. They said it was my fault. They dropped me. They sacked me. They said I was useless." He looked at Nicholas. "They said I was very useless, really very useless. They told me not to come back again."

"Oh," I said.

Andy threw down his cigarette and stubbed it out under a trainer that once, in a former life, might have been white.

"Better take those off outside," I said. I nodded to his shoes.

"Yes mum," said Andy.

"Mummy!" said Nicholas.

Julie had appeared behind Andy. She was almost wearing a miniskirt and a mini-top. Almost. Julie had a body that could make a prelate wolf-whistle and tent his cassock. It was a body that women would kill for, men would die for. And she knew it, liked everyone to know it. She put her hands on her hips and watched Andy as he pulled off his left shoe and then his holey sock.

"Getting them to undress in the street now, Honza?" she said. "Saves time I guess."

"He's the lodger," I said.

"And I'm the Queen of Sheba," said Julie.

As a retort that was quite good for my sister, not that she would have known the Queen of Sheba even if she had pulled up right there and then on a motorised burnished throne and invited her to the palace for tea and crumpets.

"Am I OK now?" said Andy. He ignored both my sibling's tartness and her tartiness. He was holding his shoes and socks in his hands. His feet and ankles were white in contrast to his caked skin.

"Fine," I said. "Come in."

He tentatively moved past me and bounded up the stairs three at a time to the bathroom. He left the door open and we all heard that distinctive sound.

"Andy's having a piss," said Nicholas and giggled.

"Nicholas!" said Julie. "Manners."

"Sorry," said Nicholas. He heaved his Power Rangers bag onto his shoulders. "Please, Andy's having a piss. Thank you."

"Well," I said. I patted Nicholas on the head. "He's ready."

"Say bye uncle," said Julie, pulling a face and glancing up the stairs as the sounds came to a splashing stop.

"Bye uncle," said Nicholas. "Thank you for having me." He held out his hand.

I looked at Julie. She shrugged.

"He gets it from school," she said.

I took Nicholas's hand and solemnly we shook.

"So," said Julie, "we'll be off."

"OK," I said.

"Can he come on Friday next week? Five o'clock?"

"Fine," I said.

"And the week after on the Friday again?"

"Of course," I said.

"I'll have a lot to sort out. Packing and stuff."

"Packing?" I said. I knew what was coming. I dreaded it, but I knew.

"For our move."

"You mean...?"

"Honza," said Julie, cutting me short, "I told you. I'm moving to London, I'm going to be a dancer. It's my big chance. I told you."

"Julie..."

"I don't want any lectures," said Julie. She scraped a glop of mascara from her left eyelid with a painted nail. "I'm going. I've decided. It's two and a half hours in the car, not the other side of the world. You can visit. You can come every week. I don't mind. But just don't give me that big brother hard time. Nicholas. Come on."

And Julie was already off, down the street. Nicholas stood watching for a moment and then set after her at a run.

"Bye uncle!" he shouted. "Thanks uncle! See you uncle! Be good uncle!"

"What you watching?" said Andy.

"Sorry?"

"I said," said Andy, "what you watching?"

"I dunno," I said. I'd put the tv on but I hadn't been watching it. I'd been thinking. Thinking and drinking. There was a half-empty bottle of whisky at my feet.

"I'm cooking," said Andy.

I resisted the temptation to ask what, I wasn't in the mood.

"I'm making baked beans," said Andy, "on toast. Want some?"

"No thanks," I said. Instead I poured myself another two fingers from the bottle.

I couldn't believe that Julie was really going. I couldn't believe that Nicholas wouldn't be here any more. I was trying to think of ways of stopping her, of making her not go. I would beg her if I had to. I would move to London. I couldn't let Nicholas just disappear out of my life. He needed me.

I needed him.

I took a slug of whiskey and stared at the screen and then Andy appeared next to me on the sofa. He placed the plate with beans on his knees. As usual he had used the whole can and the bread was invisible beneath a mountain of haricots and tomato sauce. My nostrils were filled with their distinctive aroma.

"Can I turn it over?" said Andy. *"London's Burning."*

"I wish it was," I said.

"It is," said Andy. "Nine pm Sunday nights, *London's Burning.*"

"No," I said. "I wish London would burn."

"Your sister?" said Andy, mouth full of beans, not looking at me.

"Yeah," I said.

"Nicholas told me," said Andy. "When I was reading him a story. Told me not to tell you. He's a good kid."

"Yeah," I said.

There was a pause. On Channel Four a bag of bones was talking about her battle with anorexia.

"Can I then?" said Andy.

"What?"

"Turn it over? She's putting me off my liver and bacon kebabs."

"Sure," I said.

Andy pressed a button and the woman was gone. Andy was right, London was burning. I took another swig of whisky and Andy sat shovelling beans into his mouth, shovelling until the plate was clean and we sat side by side watching hunky fire-fighters. They were a distraction. The adverts came on and Andy put the now clean plate on the floor. He scratched his stomach.

"Honza?" said Andy.

"Yes?" I said.

"I've got something to show you. Something to cheer you up."

"I'm OK," I said, raising the glass to my lips.

"No, you're not," said Andy. "You're not OK. I need to stand for this. Hang on."

He stood and turned to face me blocking my view to the television. There was a look of extreme concentration on his face. I'd once seen a documentary on Charlie Parker. The look was a bit like that, a bit like a trumpet genius only without the pursed puckered lips. Andy bent his knees slightly, leant forward slightly. And then he went for it.

The sound wasn't beautiful. It wasn't Enya performing 'Orinoco

Flow' with a gospel choir in a perfect acoustic environment but it was distinctive, tuneful almost. Not bad, although I didn't have much to compare it with. I'd never known anyone break wind with the cadence of a wind instrument before.

"*Match of the Day*?" I said.

"Exactly," said Andy.

"Very impressive," I said. "That's quite a talent."

"Thank you," said Andy. "I have perfect control of my arsehole. The boys at school loved it. Had them in stitches. Shhh now. *London's Burning.*"

And we didn't speak anymore but at least I wasn't thinking of Nicholas. I was thinking of the boys at my school and my own arsehole. I was smiling. At about half past nine and just as the next set of adverts came on I got up.

"You want the bathroom?" I said. "I'm having a shower. I'm going out."

Andy didn't speak, only shook his head and I went upstairs before he decided to entertain me with any more rectal displays. I wasn't sure how proud Andy was of his ability. But credit where it was due, it was the most I'd ever been interested in an arse without having an erection.

I pulled off my clothes and stood under the shower.

On Sunday nights I go out. Derby is not San Francisco, it is not Sydney, Paris or London. It is not even Mansfield. But it does have a gay scene. It does have a couple of bars and a club, L'Amour, which it just so happened was on the same street as my house. It was only a hundred metres from my door. After a weekend with my nephew usually I needed a few drinks, a few pints to relax. I needed music and dancing.

However much I loved Nicholas, he was tiring, draining. And anyway, Sunday night was the best night to go out. On a Sunday night there was a drag show and a stripper. On a Sunday night there were lots of men. On a Sunday night it was easy to get a shag.

This Sunday night I needed music, oblivion, sex, more than ever.

I came out of the shower, remembering to wrap a towel around my waist and went into my room which was still showing post-Nicholas devastation. There were crushed juice cartons on the bedside cabinet and toys on the floor. For now, I ignored them. I kicked aside a plastic Black Beauty and opened the doors of my white lacquer wardrobe.

I pulled out a Tommy Hilfiger white T-shirt, a Paul Smith canvas gilet and a pair of Full Circle stone utility pants and pulled them on. I was ready to go out, except for my hair. Hair is important, it can make the difference between looking like Arthur Scargill and Leonardo DiCaprio. Well, kind of.

In front of the mirror I teased the fringe into slender spikes with a dollop of ultra-fix gel. Generally, I hoped that these spikes would be teased out later by the rough hand of a handsome man. Generally I say, but tonight my feelings were far from general. As I looked in the mirror there was only one thought in my head, only one purpose in my groin.

The combination of the whiskey coursing through my veins and the anger at my sister had been sublimated into a raging desire.

Hair done, I went downstairs.

"Bye Andy!" I called from the hallway. I could hear the title music to the Royle Family coming from the television.

"You got your key?" Andy shouted back.

I smiled. I didn't answer. I pulled the door to with a bang and set off to L'Amour.

I wasn't wearing a coat, I never wore one, the walk was too short. Sometimes, if I hadn't pulled, then at the end of the night I would stand in the cloakroom queue, faking. Queues are good places to meet people. Even the corniest of lines in a queue smacks of the naturalism of a sentence in a novel by Emile Zola. I'd had some notable successes in queues. The technique was in the timing, you had to judge it just right so that you were either behind or in front of someone sexy.

That is what I was thinking as I arrived at the distinctive black door of L'Amour. I was hoping that tonight I wouldn't have to wait until the end to pull. I was hoping that I would be lucky. I needed cute, I needed handsome, I needed a man. No, more simply, I needed a cock. Not my own.

I paid my two pounds fifty and I was in the club. I walked through the red foyer and into the darkened dance room. The beat from the mega-powerful speakers was in my brain, my body. I could feel it in my nerve endings. I felt at home.

I don't know if this feeling is genetic, if the genes of a gay man respond to the disco beat in the same way that a robin responds to a nest, the way a pig responds to a pen, but I guess they probably do. In the dark interior lit by flashing lights and filled with pumping sounds I felt at home, the way I had felt at home the very first time I had gone to a small club on the outskirts of London. I felt I was in the right place at the right time and everything was going to be all right. Forever. Not necessarily here, not necessarily in L'Amour in Derby tonight, but for all time there would be places like this all over the world where I could go, where I could stand in a dingy space and ogle taut bodies to the backing of a banging track, where I could kiss, caress, stroke and fondle and still be part of the shadows.

I was early and there were few people there. I went to the bar, ordered a pint of Carling from the youthful barboy and then took it and stood facing the empty dance floor, staring into dark space lit intermittently by piercing colourful beams.

I would work something out. My instincts would prove to be right. My lodger wouldn't turn out to be a murderer, Julie wouldn't become an exotic dancer, Nicholas wouldn't leave. I wouldn't lose my nephew. Everything would be OK. As the beat bounced off my body I thought everything would be OK.

Someone pinched my bum. I spun around.

It was Mother Hen.

"Hello gorgeous," she said and placed a taloned hand on my chest.

"Hi," I said.

Mother Hen was the resident drag act. She answered to the name of Mother or Goose and on a Friday night when she appeared in mufti and worked as a somnambulant glass collector would even have answered to the name of Glen, although in my years of coming to the club I had never heard anyone call her this. She just wasn't a Glen.

Mother Hen had a bit of a thing for me. I had a bit of a thing for her, only it wasn't the same thing. We split the difference and somehow got along.

"You're looking good," I said.

"You too," said Mother Hen, "I could eat you all up."

"You look like you already have." I gently squeezed Mother's ample belly that in turn had been squeezed into a preposterous Lycra number.

"Thank you," she said. She put her tongue in her cheek so that it bulged like she was giving a Japanese man a blowjob. She was displeased.

"I'm sorry. You look beautiful. Nice wig."

"I didn't think it showed," she said and pulled down the hem of her miniskirt.

Mother Hen was the Jo Brand of drag queens. She was a cross between an electrified Cher and a blanched Barbar the Elephant. She had a mane of wild black hair and white pasty skin. She even had breasts. They were plastic. She had once told me she had stolen them from a double mastectomy patient while swimming at the Queen's Leisure Centre.

I always thought Mother Hen should have been a star and not stuck here in this second-rate club. I imagined her as one of the dancing girls who shimmy in and out of the breaks on *TFI Friday*.

"You look drunk," she said, "and you stink of whisky."

"I've got problems," I said.

"Well if you drink too much and think you might go home with someone you regret then please let it be me. And if it is going to be me," she added, "then let me know in advance, I've left me lippy in the changing room."

I smiled.

"Please let it be me," she said.

I still smiled.

"If I slept with you Mother," I said, "it would ruin a beautiful friendship."

"But I'd die happy."

And with that she was off. I watched as she pinched the bum of a young blond and fanned herself dramatically. She laughed at something he said, throwing back her head, her hair following in a hairsprayed solid and then the blond laughed and said something and Mother Hen did that thing with her tongue again. Then I lost them as people moved in front of them and I realised the place had started to fill up. I was surprised to see that my drink was nearly finished. I headed through the throng to get a refill.

I was served quickly. I returned to the edge of the dance floor and I drank, quickly. I needed to be drunk, drunker than I already was.

I went back to the bar.

This time, I had to wait. Ordering drinks were a group of deaf people. I knew straight away they were deaf because they were signing vigorously to each other and moving lips in an exaggerated way. This would have been pretty standard behaviour for a party of drag queens but as this group didn't have even a single spangle or a hint of blusher between them I worked out they were just hard of hearing.

I felt that feeling in my stomach. It had long been one of my fantasies to have a deaf boyfriend. I figured someone deaf wouldn't shout a lot. Joshua had always shouted and I hated it. I liked peace and quiet, a tranquil life.

I'd once told my friend Lisa about this, about my fetish for the aurally challenged, and she had been outraged. I couldn't understand it. She had argued that deaf people were normal people only with a disability and it was wrong of me to want someone just because they couldn't hear. She said it was patronising, insulting. I had said that I didn't agree. I said I was sure that deaf people suffered so much discrimination, so many people who couldn't be bothered with them just because of their inner silence. I was offering discrimination but of a positive kind. What was wrong with that? She had said a lot of things and we had agreed to differ.

The deaf people all had their drinks now and were moving away from the bar. Their conversation had died, it was difficult to sign and hold a pint of lager at the same time and as they shuffled along they resembled a New Orleans funeral march without the jazz. It was then, as I turned back to the counter and was ordering my third pint of Carling, that I spied him. Him. The One. The One that would do for that night only. When I saw his blond head I felt something stir, something stiffen.

I don't usually fancy blonds but this one had something else going for him. He was the spitting image of Solskjaer, the Manchester United forward. You could have put him on the centre circle at Old Trafford and not one of the sixty-one thousand fans would have known them apart. He had the same blue eyes, the same curls, the same hint of a cock and cheeky face. Whether he had Solskjaer's skill with the ball, Solskjaer's ability to twist and turn and score from any angle I didn't know. Yet.

And then came the *pièce de résistance*. As I was looking at him, contemplating what I'd like to do with him, he raised his hands and moved them for all the world like he was an assistant on Central's local news for the hearing-impaired. He was one of the deafies.

It was fate. I knew he was mine.

As my pint was placed on the bar in front of me, Solskjaer glanced over in my direction. I lifted my hand and did the only sign

I knew. I pointed my thumb and little finger. I clenched the other fingers down. It meant, I love you. I smiled. People had told me I had a nice smile. Solskjaer blushed and looked away and I took my pint and moved back to the dance-floor and out of his sight. If he liked what he saw then anticipation would be a great aphrodisiac.

I didn't want to make the mistake a lot of men made. I didn't want to become a stalker. It had happened to me so many times. You see someone and you think they're quite nice and they see you and then the next thing you know this person is marching up and down in front of you like a duck on a fairground shooting range. It wouldn't be so bad if they talked. But no, backwards and forwards they go and every time you look anywhere they are there. It takes between forty-five minutes and an hour and a half before they say anything and when they finally do you are so sick of the sight of them you can't be bothered to be nice. You just wish you had that air rifle.

So I left deafie and went and had a dance.

They were playing one of my favourite songs. Who can't dance to 'Better the Devil You Know'? For me it was up there with 'I Will Survive', 'Vogue', anything by Steps.

I was still dancing half an hour later, surrounded by a sea of bodies, sweat sticking my T-shirt to my body when Mother Hen took to the stage and told me to stop. Not only me, everyone. It was time for the stripper.

"Will you put your hands together," she said, "for the devilishly gorgeous Dark Angel."

I don't usually watch strippers. They don't do anything for me. I like muscles but not huge gym muscles and I don't find it particularly erotic to watch someone taking their clothes off while surrounded by other bodies. The whole thing was too much of a performance, too fake and it failed to stimulate me. It didn't even titillate. I had fantasies about the reality of sex, the taste of sweat and the stink of a man. If I took someone home and he put on music and started gyrating in a rehearsed way, ripping off his clothes in a prearranged sequence, building to the climax of the revelation of cock, then I wouldn't have been impressed. Not at all. It would seem to me too arrogant and arrogance wasn't attractive.

I used to have a straight female friend called Dom who had once told me a story about a guy she had taken home. The date had gone well and they were back at Dom's house. Dom had gone into the bathroom to clean her teeth, they had eaten garlic bread and having smelly breath was the sort of thing that bothered her. When she went back into the bedroom the guy, let's call him Dave, had taken off all his clothes. Dave was lying naked on the bed, legs apart and he had his hands behind his head. Dom told me she will never forget what he said. His exact words were, "Prepare to have the time of your life, baby." Dom told him to put on his clothes and get lost.

That's what strippers seemed to be saying to me, "Prepare to have the time of your life," and I just wasn't interested. So I was going to head upstairs to have a quiet snoop around, to see what was on offer when I spied the simulacrum of Solskjaer. He was at the front of the oval of audience clutching a half-full pint. He noticed me too and for a moment our gaze was locked and then he looked away, blushing. I decided to stay for the show, to stay to be near him.

As a stripper Dark Angel wasn't bad. He had the body of a gladiator, the moves of a ballerina suffering from steroid abuse. It was Schwarzenegger doing *Swan Lake* for the Swedish soft porn industry. But for erotic tension he had nothing on me and Solskjaer. Even the National Grid was like a six amp circuit next to us. Sparks were flying, fireworks were bursting. As the act started to the sounds of Divine's 'Walk Like a Man' me and the object of my affection were two metres apart. But almost imperceptibly throughout the performance, as items of clothing were shed, we moved closer to each other doing our own slower, more sexy dance of desire. The revelation of flesh on stage was mirroring the nakedness of our attraction.

As 'Walk Like a Man' segued into 'Rawhide' and Dark Angel cracked his whip there was one metre between us and then minutes later as a leather waistcoat was removed you couldn't have parked a bicycle in the space, there was only one slender man separating Solskjaer and me.

The crowd around us were getting into the spirit of the strip, whooping and cheering as chaps were ripped off and a PVC pouch was revealed. There were any number of volunteers to rub baby oil into Dark Angel's hirsute chest but it was fate, the hand of God was a kind one. The man chosen to do the honours was the last barrier between me and my football fantasy.

We were next to each other. Our thighs were touching, material of jean nestled against material of jean.

First contact.

I leant closer increasing the pressure and the pressure was returned.

The volunteer was kneeling on stage in front of Dark Angel. He was simulating oral sex, grinning like an idiot. I wasn't interested. I knew I was onto the real thing. I turned to look at my soon-to-be suitor and this time the look was held steady and there were no blushes. I smiled and Solskjaer smiled back.

We watched the rest of the show together, side by side, sexual tension mounting and mounting. We applauded together as finally the PVC pouch was whipped off and a nice thick dark dangling cock was revealed. That didn't turn me on; I was turned on already.

Dark Angel disappeared to cheers and someone came on stage with a broom to sweep up spilt oil and around us people were beginning to dance as the disco proper started up once more. And me and Solskjaer stood in the middle of this gay activity, looking at each other, smiling.

What do you say to someone who's deaf? How do you start a conversation? That had never been in my fantasy.

In the end, we didn't talk at all. Not a single word passed between us.

And my fantasy came true. More than true.

There was not even a preliminary kiss, no foreplay touch, no tender caress. Solskjaer took my hand and led me from the dance floor. L'Amour wasn't Hampton Court maze, it wasn't Daedalus's labyrinth home to the monstrous Minotaur. I knew where he was taking me. We were heading for the toilets.

There wasn't a single person at the aluminium urinal trough and the partitioned wooden cubicle was empty. Solskjaer dragged me inside here and pushed shut the door, sliding across the bolt, informing the outside world that we were engaged. And then we were on each other. I pressed him back against the white brick wall and my hands were in his hair, my tongue in his mouth. We were kissing, biting lips, fighting tongues, sharing saliva and his hands were on my belt, sliding out the leather tongue from the buckle. I pulled back my face and he looked at me and I looked at him and then he was leaning forward and he was kissing me, pushing me back now against the wooden side of the cubicle wall and he was pulling apart the fly of my jeans, popping buttons, freeing my cock, fondling my balls.

Solskjaer ran his thumb over my stickiness and then he raised his hand to his lips. I watched as he licked the glistening digit and smiled and then he was down on his knees in front of me.

I had done it, I had won. My shallowness had proved depthless. If anyone had asked me then if I had a nephew I wouldn't have said no but I wouldn't have understood the question. The question would have had no relevance in that moment. Desire had killed emotion, feeling, empathy. Right then I cared for no one, had no concept of deeper feelings. All I knew was that blond head going up and down. All I knew was that I was going to come. All I was worried about was whether he would spit or swallow. My hopes, dreams, ambitions had been reduced to this. I wanted to climax in the warm recesses of the orifice of his mouth.

I put my hands in hair and controlled the pace. Up and down.

And I felt no guilt in my desire, no sense that I should be at home being responsible. So many couples I knew avoided their problems through sex. I believed I was more honest than them. Their problem was with each other, sex was an escape and a momentary one at that. After sex they would still have their conflict, still have each other. This sex was other, distant, divorced from me and would be perfect in its imminent termination. I could walk away from it and it wouldn't blur my situation for it wasn't part of that situation. It existed only in itself, for itself.

Still sucking but with hands free, Solskjaer was busy with my left shoe. He had undone the laces, was levering it off, now managed to get it off. I knew what he was up to, I'd been here before. I raised my leg and he pulled the trousers and my half-mast underpants off of it so my left limb was liberated, emancipated from its bindings and my trousers and pants were heaped around my right leg.

Taking hold of my left ankle Solskjaer twisted me around using my right leg as a pivot. He placed my shoeless foot on the toilet seat. Now I had my back to him, one foot on the floor, one foot raised and I was balancing myself with my hands on the cistern. Solskjaer was still on his knees behind me. And then I felt his tongue between my cheeks.

Deafie liked rimming. I liked being rimmed. We were well suited.

Looking down through my parted legs I could see Solskjaer had one hand on his own cock and one hand on mine. I bent my right leg slightly, lowering myself, increasing the pressure on his face and reaching behind with my left hand I pulled apart my cheeks.

I couldn't stand it for long. I couldn't stand the probing sensation, the erogenic lapping of tongue on sphincter, the incredible intimacy in this most public of places.

"I'm going to come," I said.

Deafie couldn't have heard but he must have sensed something, felt the pressure mounting in the shaft of my cock, the extra surge of blood. He spun me around and his mouth was on me and I got what I wanted. I came in his mouth and I watched as he came too, shooting improbably high.

Nice.

Mission Impossible. Mission accomplished.

My problems hadn't gone, but they had been forgotten.

Or so I thought.

I hadn't expected Andy to be up. I knew that he had work in the morning and I thought he would have been in bed long before I came home. I had noticed from outside that there was light shining through the blinds but I thought Andy must have left it on for me. I thought he was being considerate. Even when I had put my key in the lock and discovered the door was open I didn't think he would be awake.

So when I heard the voice shouting from the lounge I was surprised.

"That you Honza?" he called.

"Who the fuck do you think it is?" I called back. I laughed.

I was drunk and still on a post-coital high.

"We've got a visitor," came the voice again.

"What?" I said. A visitor. It was one thirty in the morning.

I walked into the lounge. The tv wasn't on. Andy was sitting very straight in his usual seat. Opposite him, in the chair in front of the window, was our visitor.

"What time do you call this?" she said. "I've been waiting for hours."

Eight

"Hi mum," I said. It was my mother who was sitting in the chair.

"I spoke to Julie," said my mother. "She's going to London. Eleven thirty on a Sunday night she tells me she's going to London."

"I know," I said. I was swaying.

My mother leant forward, glared at me. "You know and you're gallivanting around town, getting drunk, carousing. Honza, I despair of you."

"Mum," I said. I sat down. "It's late."

"Yes," said Andy. He stood and stretched and yawned. "I'm tired. I'm going to bed. Work tomorrow. Night Mrs Drobloski."

"Drobrolowski," said my mother instantly and she watched Andy out the door. She followed the sounds with her head as he bounded up the stairs.

"And what sort of example is that?" she said.

"What?" I said. My head was spinning. I could still taste the final vodka and tonic in my mouth. It wasn't getting on with the whisky in my stomach.

"All these lodgers everywhere. What must Nicholas think?"

"Nicholas likes Andy," I said. "And he's just one lodger. He really is a lodger. He's got his own room."

"How middle-class," my mother said. "You always did have ideas above your station."

"Mum!" I said. I stood up and went to the kitchen. I filled a glass with water and drank it straight down. I filled it again and went back into the lounge. My mother had her head in her hands and she was quietly crying.

"Mum," I said again. I went over to her and put an arm around her shoulders.

"Where did I go wrong?" she said. She lifted her head and opened her handbag. She fished out a tissue. She started to dab her eyes. "Julie told me she's going to be a dancer. In London. I may be old but I'm not stupid. I know what these dancers get up to, sleeping around. I blame you, giving her fancy ideas, Bohemian ideals. It's not the sixties anymore Honza. There's no such thing as free love. Everything has a price."

I wanted to say that Julie more than anyone knew that everything had a price. But I didn't.

"Mum," I said. "I don't want her to go. I won't let her go. You know how much I love Nicholas."

"Oh," said my mother. She scrunched the Kleenex into a ball and held it tightly in her hand. She didn't say anything.

"You thought I was keen on the idea?" I said. "You thought I wanted her to go?"

"Well," said my mother. She paused. "It did cross my mind. You're always going off places. I can never keep track of you."

I sighed and sat down on the sofa. I rubbed my forehead with my hand. Where to start? Where would it end? I was tired of explaining.

"Mum," I said. "Look at me."

There must have been something in my voice. She did as she was told.

"I'm a gay man..." I saw my mother's mouth begin to open. I raised my hand. "I'm a gay man. Once I lived in Japan. Once I lived in Australia. Now I live here. I'm buying a house. This house. I'm settled, I like it here. I work as a writer and I make money but not enough money so I have a lodger. A lodger. He's not my lover. If I have a lover then I'll be on the phone to let you know. And finally I love my nephew. I adore my nephew. Those are the facts of my life. I won't have my own family but I love what I've got. I love you but give me some credit and give me a chance. I don't want Julie to go to London. Not one bit. Let's work together not against each other. OK?"

My mother sniffed.

"OK?" I said.

"OK," she said. "But settled? Honestly Honza. You haven't got a carpet. You haven't even got curtains. You live in a shell. You're like a snail."

It was too late in the day, too early in the morning to explain to my mother that floorboards were fashionable, that blinds were de rigueur in between the covers of *Vogue*. Instead I just smiled.

"We'll think of something," I said. "But now it really is late, and you were right, I am drunk. Let's talk about this in the morning. You can have my bed and I'll sleep in the office."

"In your bed?" said my mother. She stood with a click of joints. "Whatever will that lodger think? He seems like a nice boy to me, normal. You could do worse. Before you came he was entertaining me with his party piece."

"Sorry?" I said.

I had vision of my mother seated in a chair and Andy in front of her, knees bent, that look of concentration on his face, farting a medley of Cole Porter tunes.

"Yes," she said. "He really does have quick hands. Call me a taxi love and I'll be off home. You're right, it is late."

I wanted to ask what she meant by quick hands. I didn't dare. Instead I did as she said and called a cab. They said it would be minutes and they weren't wrong. Just as my mother was informing me of Aunty Irene's new bedroom suite (in pink!), we both heard the car pull up outside.

I showed my mother to the door. She hesitated on the step and then turned to me.

"I do love you Honza," she said. "I just need time. This gay thing is all new to me. I shouldn't blame you for your sister's faults. Bye son. We'll talk soon. I know you love Nicholas. Bye. I'm going. Bye."

I shut the door. Time. She needed time. It was nearly twelve years since I had told her I was gay.

I woke up sitting bolt upright in bed. My body was soaked in sweat. I had been having a bad dream and I still had the final image in my head. Andy was telling me that he hadn't meant to kill anyone. He was grinning maniacally and in his left hand he was gripping a wooden stake. On top of this stake was skewered the head of the deaf boy from L'Amour.

I looked at the clock. It was ten thirty. Andy would have long gone to work. Andy, the boy with the controllable sphincter and the drunken admission of murder. Murder. Over the weekend, with Nicholas there, I hadn't given the confession any thought. I'd put it to the back of my mind. The dream had reminded me. I didn't want to be reminded.

I groaned. My head was thumping.

I pulled aside the duvet and went into the bathroom naked. I looked at myself in the mirror. Red eyed but not too bad. Old age was still a distant dilemma. I emptied my bladder and then went downstairs naked for my first cup of tea of the day.

Routine.

I had another cup of tea and then the post came. There was nothing special, no incident with Simon and no return of the proposal for my novel. There was still hope, hope that neither would ever happen again.

By the third cup of tea I had both given Andy some thought and forgotten about him. The nightmare was just a nightmare. Without any facts and going only by what I knew of him I still couldn't imagine Andy murdering anyone. He would never be Colonel Mustard in the library with a lead pipe. I clung on to my earlier thought. It must have been the drink talking. Some people on acid believe they can fly, some people in movies believe they are king of the world. Maybe drink made Andy think he was Al Capone, Scarface, Bugsy Malone. Or something like that.

I went upstairs to have a shower.

By the time I was in my office it was nearly twelve. It was time to do some work. My notes from the previous week were still on my desk, untouched. The deadline for the article on the attraction of straights for gays was a week on Friday. I knew that all I needed was a hook, a single line or idea on which to hang the piece and then the rest would come easily. I sat down and picked up the couple of scruffily written-on pages. I read them over and then started working my way down them, expanding my ideas, weighing up my options. After an hour I had six possibilities, six different ways I could approach the article, six reasons why maybe gays were attracted to straights.

I went downstairs, had another cup of tea, and then set to work once more.

Virginity/Innocence: No. I didn't think that gay men cared about that. I didn't think gay men fancied straights because they wanted to be the first, the first to part and penetrate. Our culture was one of surface and image. Adam Rickett, Nathan from *Queer as Folk*, Leonardo DiCaprio were all huge icons, icons because they were young, boyish, fresh faced. They appeared virginal. I couldn't believe that I Can't Believe It's Not Butter would melt in their mouths. But never had sex? Probably not and it wasn't important. They could have seen more dicks than a clap clinic doctor and they still would have got a lay. The appearance of innocence was more important then the innocence itself. Those gorgeous boys were fanciable because they were gorgeous. No more, no less.

Historical Necessity: Once maybe but not now. Before the sixties there hadn't been an open culture, it hadn't been so easy to find people of the same inclination. Gaydar was more primitive, more hit and miss and mistakes were more dangerous. I'd read stories of aristocrats, the nineteenth-century meritocracy, the upper middle-classes paying silver shillings for the services of privates in the army, gardeners, barrow boys, all of whom saw the opportunity of a quick buck for a quick fuck regardless of sexual orientation. This was EM Forster territory. But he was dead now and I believed that if he were alive today then on a Saturday night he would have been in Heaven grooving with the best of them, making a living writing steamy romances for Harlequin publishers.

Straight-acting, Straight-looking: This was a possibility but after careful thought I rejected it as a no too. The common cry of straight-acting from endless personal advertisements was certainly true enough. But the desire was for straight-acting and not for straight. There was an important difference. Straight-acting as an adage existed only in its opposite, that which it was not. Straight-acting was not camp. We ask for straight-acting because we do not want camp.

Gay men's fear of camp and our use of the terms camp and straight-acting, I believed, was a kind of internalised homophobia. And a misplaced one at that. I am not camp. I do not have a limp wrist. I do not mince. But does that mean I am straight-acting? I act the way that I act. As Gloria Gaynor sang, 'I Am What I Am'. I am never anything but a gay man. I have sex with men, I listen to pop, I care what I wear. The terms we use to describe ourselves are reductive. Just because I am not camp it doesn't mean I am straight-acting and just because I don't fancy camp doesn't mean I want to have sex with straights.

And finally and importantly which gay man hasn't camped it up every now and again. I can bitch with the best of them. I can mince, I can pout. Camp is not something concrete, it is an overcoat we sometimes choose to wear. Camp is an act, a defence. It can be taken or it can be left.

Prestige: This was a possibility. If you managed to sleep with someone straight, someone who didn't normally sleep with men, then it was a boost to your own ego, it must mean that you were particularly good-looking, especially gorgeous, impossibly irresistible. Or so the fantasy goes. In reality a straight man who sleeps with gays is saying more about his own sexuality than yours. It is more to do with his own inability to face up to himself than your perfect pecs, your tight cheeks. Get over it.

The fantasy of masculinity/ A Real Man: Before my time, the Marlboro man had been the acme of masculinity, the face that launched a thousand wet dreams. But that was then. The seventies had been a time of experiment, a time blushing with the adolescence of new found freedoms. Gay men unsure of their own new identity, had played with others. They had posed, postured, faked their image. Think lumberjack shirt, think leather jacket, think handlebar moustaches, think Village People. We had exaggerated our own red-bloodedness. Even straighter than the real thing was our common battle-cry.

With growing confidence in our own community, however, these clichés were soon dropped. And besides a checked shirt just didn't go with Calvin Klein briefs, a leather jacket hung sadly on a Vesace top.

Bastards: Bastards. I looked at the word and smiled. Bastards. That was it. That was my hook. Gay men didn't fancy straight men because they were straight, we fancied them because they were unobtainable, not available. In our culture of easy sex, of saunas, cottages, cruising grounds and discos we were in a constant battle with our psyche, our indoctrinated ideology.

All our lives we had watched movies, listened to pop songs, sat in front of dramas that told us love is painful, sex is difficult, problematic, fraught with hurdles. And yet our life was different. If we had a hard-on it wasn't too difficult to find a use for it, a place to put it, and so our brain was telling us something was wrong. Subconsciously our lifestyle didn't fit with that which had been hammered into us, that which we saw in the media every day; love and pain are perfect bedfellows. And so if we fancied straights and suffered constant rejection then we could experience all those intense emotions. We could be Heathcliffe, Romeo, Inspector Morse. Our life could be that Kylie song, 'Tears on My Pillow', 'What Do I Have To Do?', 'I Should Be So Lucky'.

That would be the basis for my article, the hook I had been looking for.

And did I believe it? Not a word, but I could write two thousand words about it and that was all that mattered.

The reality of why gay men fancy straights is far more prosaic, far more mundane. On this planet there are millions of men, billions. There are men with blond hair, black hair, brown hair. There are short men, tall men, fat men, thin men and out of all these men only a tiny percentage are gay. Why should we fancy only this minority? The fact is we don't. Gay men like straight men because we like men. That's all.

I heard the sound of a key in the door downstairs.

I looked at my watch. Strange, it was only three o'clock and too early for Andy.

"Honza!" came the voice up the stairs. "It's me, Andy. I'm home."

I don't know why but I smiled. I put down my pen on top of my notes and went to see my lodger.

Andy was leaning against the breakfast bar. He was wearing his blue boiler suit with Ryder in white letters stitched on the pocket. He was chewing the knuckle of his left hand where his finger must once have been.

"You're early," I said.

"Yes," said Andy. "Half day. Holiday."

"That's nice."

"Yeah," he said. He wasn't looking at me. He was looking at a point on the wooden floorboards somewhere between us. "Honza?"

"Yes?" I said.

"I have to go out."

"OK," I said.

"Are you busy?"

"I'm writing," I said.

"Oh." Andy put his knuckle in his mouth again, pinched a fold of skin between his teeth and chewed it for a few seconds before pulling it out. He scratched his thigh and then pushed both hands in his pockets. "Your car Honza, it's very nice. I read that they're very economical. Kas."

"Yes," I said, "it is."

"I bet you get miles to the gallon?"

"Yes," I said.

"And it's convenient. Being able to go where you want. I hate public transport. And if you have to carry something, something big, heavy, it's difficult." Andy raised his eyes to look at

When I was young we had a dog. Every morning it would push open my door with its nose and then come and rest its head on my bed. It had a way of looking at me. A way which said, take me for a walk. Andy had the same look in his eyes now.

"Do you want a lift?" I said.

Andy grinned. "Yeah, if you don't mind. And you can give me a hand. It's a bit delicate."

"Delicate?"

"Yeah," said Andy. He shrugged. "You'll see."

"Right," I said. "Go and get ready and we'll be off."

"Ready?" said Andy. "I am ready."

I put my head on one side and looked at him and Andy looked back at me and then looked down at himself, at his blue boiler suit and scuffed heavy boots.

"I'm ready," he said and smiled. "But just let me have a piss."

You know the score. Bounds. Sounds. Crash in the hallway.

We were ready to go.

On the journey Andy directed me with all the skill of a pedestrian. He pointed down one-way streets, told me to turn left, right at the last moment so I had to swerve suddenly and at one point he even indicated a beaten-down grass path through a muddy field.

"Sorry," he said. "My family never had a car."

"Right," I said and then remembered. "But you're a delivery man, aren't you?"

"I'm not very good," said Andy. "They don't let me look at the maps anymore. They say I'm only good for carrying. They call me donkey. Especially Jim. I told you he's a bastard."

"Yes," I said.

But we were getting closer to wherever it was we were going. I could tell because Andy began chewing his knuckle more vigorously and he went very quiet. He wouldn't look me in the eye and he was gazing out of the window.

And in my mind were those words again, that midnight admission. "I didn't mean to kill him." Did where we were going now have something to do with that? Had Andy really killed someone? Had it been a moment of madness, an argument over a girlfriend, a crime of passion? Was it a childish prank gone wrong, a dare backfired? Or was it something more sinister? Was Andy involved in some kind of gang? Did it have something to do with a robbery? Or was it drugs?

My own tension was mounting. Andy had said it was delicate. I wondered what he expected me to do and if I was going to be in danger.

"Stop," said Andy. "We're here. This is it."

We were in front of a grey tower block. It stood alone and aloof on a concrete circle at the end of an otherwise normal row of terraced houses. The block should have been incongruous but somehow it wasn't. It was so huge, square, solid that it transcended its position. It could have been placed anywhere and it would have fitted in. It was typical of tower blocks all over England.

I pulled to a stop on a yellow-lined parking area. There were few other cars and the ones that were there were rusty old heaps, Austin Allegros, Morris Minors. Some were missing wheels and had been propped up on bricks. Others had smashed windscreens, broken lights.

Andy undid his seat-belt.

"You coming then?" he said.

I looked through the windscreen and up the concrete side looming before me. I could smell old chip fat, I could imagine latchkey kids with gap-toothed smiles pulling on found butts of fags in cat-piss alleyways.

"You don't want me to wait?" I said.

"I need you." Andy reached over and squeezed my bicep. "We have to put those muscles to use."

And he was opening the door and climbing out. Reluctantly I followed, wondering what I had let myself in for.

The glass doors that were supposed only to be opened by buzzer were swinging open, banging in the wind. Andy walked through and into a dingy foyer. The walls were covered in graffiti. Manchester United were going to do it, Sally loved Ben, Ben loved Kylie and Kylie was available twenty-four hours a day to supply oral pleasure in sixty-nine different ways.

"Come on," said Andy. He was propping open a fire door through which I could see concrete stairs.

"What about the lift?" I said. I nodded to the slight recess in the far wall where the lift was.

"It won't work," said Andy.

"But you haven't even tried."

"Trust me," said Andy.

I looked longingly at the rigidised stainless steel exterior and then set off after Andy up the echoing stairwell.

"Don't tell me," I said. "Top floor."

"No," said Andy looking back. "Fifteenth. One below."

"Right," I said.

We started up. First floor. Second. And so on.

Give me a gym and give me a step machine any day. On a step machine your nostrils are not assailed by the smell of urine. On a step machine you do not slip on slippery used condoms, you do not have to avoid standing on plastic disposable syringes. On a step machine there is a friendly LCD display informing you how many steps you have to go and you are aware that once you achieve that target you can go and stand under the relaxing spurt of a shower. And most importantly, on a step machine, while it may perfectly emulate the bio-mechanics of climbing, the action of ascension, you know that when you have reached the computerised summit you do not have to come all the way down again.

"Come on," said Andy. He stopped on what must have been the twelfth or thirteenth floor. "Don't lag. We'll be late."

"Late?" I said but Andy was already off again. I should have known that he would be an expert stair climber. He had bounded up and down mine enough times.

Eventually, just when I thought I couldn't lift my legs anymore, that I wouldn't be able to mount another step, Andy stopped and placed his hand on the handle of one of the identical fire doors, so many of which we had already passed. He pushed it open and turned to me.

"This is it," he said. "Let me do the talking."

Let him do the talking. I was dying. I couldn't breath, I was gasping for breath and my lungs were exploding. I went after him through the door and onto the balcony. We were very high up.

"The red door," said Andy. "You ready?"

Ready? I was having trouble standing, my heart was pounding. If Andy wanted me to be Starsky to his Hutch, Lewis to his Morse, Cagney to his Lacey then he was going to have to wait a minute. He didn't.

He knocked three times.

Nine

"There's no one in," I said. We had been waiting a few minutes, I could nearly breathe and the red door in front of us remained firmly closed.

"There is," said Andy. "Wait."

He knocked again. Three times. Loudly.

I looked out over the concrete wall of the balcony. Far below I could see my car. It seemed tiny. Over to the right, some kids were playing football on a piece of scrubland. They were chasing after the ball in a pack, no discipline, only the goalkeepers in position. Even from high up here I could hear their shouts, "Dickhead! Dickhead!" They were like a group of little Andies, all skinny limbs and rapid movement. I turned back to the real one.

"No one in," I said and I was going to say that we should go but I stopped.

The red door, the one on which Andy had knocked, was opening. I felt my heart beat faster.

It was show-time.

In the space where the door had been was standing a man. He was small, round, had no hair and was balanced on hospital crutches. He was wearing a grey shirt the front of which was heavily stained red. It might have been blood.

"Hi dad," said Andy.

Dad. Andy's dad.

It wasn't blood on the shirt. It was tomato sauce, the kind of tomato sauce that comes with baked beans in a tin.

The old man didn't say anything but he performed a rather difficult turn on his crutches and disappeared into the hallway and into a door on the left.

"Come in," said Andy.

"Your dad?" I said.

"Yeah," said Andy. "My dad. Who were you expecting?"

I shrugged and followed as Andy went inside.

The old man was now sitting in an armchair in the poky lounge of the flat. He still had his hands on the handles of the crutches and the poles were sticking out in front of him like thin metal legs. He was gazing at the television. Carol Vorderman was doing a difficult sum.

"So how are you dad?" said Andy. He was staring at the television with his arms folded.

"Not bad," said the old man. He didn't take his eyes off the screen. "Been better. Been worse."

"Right," said Andy. He scratched an armpit. "That nurse, she still coming?"

"She is. Yes."

"She helping you," said Andy, "bath and that?"

"She tries." Carol Vorderman had just made six hundred and fifty-four with the numbers one, ten, one, six, five and seventy-five. Andy's dad seemed fascinated. "But I don't like her round me bits."

"No," said Andy. He scratched his thigh and glanced over his shoulder at me. I was still standing in the doorway. The room smelt of old beans and unwashed old man. Andy looked back at his dad.

"You could do with a change of shirt dad," he said.

"It's OK."

"You've spilt sauce down it. It looks like a stab wound. I'll get you a clean one."

"Don't fuss," said the old man, eyes forward.

But Andy had already squeezed past me out of the room and now the old man twisted his head to look at me. He had deep blue eyes.

"I miss Andy," he said. "He makes a beautiful venison Saint-Hubert."

"Oh," I said, "yes. Yes he does."

He leant forward on the arm of the chair and spoke in a whisper. "Are you leading him astray too?"

"Um... no," I said and I didn't know what else to answer so I didn't say anything and we both turned to look at the screen and watched a contestant pick the letters, E, I, N, P, W, T, S, H, G.

Andy came back with an identical grey shirt, only clean, and I watched as he expertly pulled off the old one and replaced it. My mother was right, he did have quick hands. He had the job done before the *Countdown* clock had ticked away to zero.

"That better?" said Andy.

"Penis," said his dad.

"What?" said Andy.

"P.E.N.I.S. Penis. Five letters."

"Very good," said Andy and he looked at me and winked.

"Very good," I said. "Nice."

"Dad," said Andy. "I've just come to collect a few things. I can't stop now. Honza's," and he nodded at me, "a writer and he's busy. Will you be OK?"

"Fine," said his dad. "It's *Montel* next, then *Pet Rescue*, then *Friends*. I like *Friends*. You go. I'll be fine. Scrotum."

"Sorry?" said Andy.

"S.C.R.O.T.U.M. Scrotum. Seven letters."

"Excellent," said Andy and he shrugged and grinned at me. "We'll be off then."

There was no answer. It was Carol Vorderman and the numbers game again. Andy tugged my sleeve and guided me from the room, down the short corridor and into another smaller room at the end.

"This is… was my bedroom," he said.

The room was white, small and square. It had the insignificant transience of a room in a cheap hotel. A campsite caravan would have had more character. There was a wardrobe, a cupboard and on the far wall, opposite the door, was a narrow single bed, perfectly made. It had a red duvet and red pillows. Above the bed and the only hint of individuality in the room was a poster. I stood looking at it.

"Asterix," said Andy.

"I know."

"He was a Gaul."

"I know."

"It was my brother's," said Andy. "Before he died. Come on. You have to get back to your Work."

Andy said work like that, with a capital W. I liked the way he said it, it made me feel important. He said it the same way as M said Work in the Bond films. He said it as if he thought my work were indescribable and of national importance.

"So what are we doing here then?" I said.

"In here," said Andy. He opened the white badly-hinged melamine doors of the flat-pack wardrobe. "You take the speakers and I'll take the main unit."

Standing up in the wardrobe I could see a stereo. It wasn't just any stereo, it was the crown jewels of stereos. It was the kind of stereo stereo-freaks dream about one day owning. It was a Bang and Olufsen Beosound 9000. I recognised it from an article I had done for Wallpaper. Gay men and Gadgets.

"Nice equipment," I said.

"Thanks," said Andy. He looked down at his groin.

"The hi-fi," I said.

"I know," said Andy. "Will you help me carry it then?"

My legs were still sore from the journey up and they twinged in protest at the idea of not only making the journey down again but at the thought of doing it laden like a packhorse.

"Down all those steps?" I said.

Andy narrowed his eyes.

"Why don't you stand at the bottom and I'll drop it down to you from the balcony?"

Andy scratched his head.

"I'm joking," I said.

"Oh," said Andy. He paused. "Are you going to help me?"

I shrugged. "Yes," I said.

Andy pulled first one and then another speaker out of their resting place and placed them in my arms. They weren't light.

"And do you think you can manage a box of CDs as well?" he said.

"No," I said. "Definitely not."

"Thanks," said Andy. He put the box on top of the speakers. He smiled. "You're a very kind landlord."

"I'm a mug," I said.

"No," said Andy. "You're not. Let's go."

At the door to the lounge Andy stopped and popped his head in. He said goodbye.

"So you're off then?" said the old man.

"Yeah," said Andy.

"New place OK is it?"

"Yeah," said Andy.

"Andy...?"

"Yeah?"

"About Kevin."

"Yeah?"

There was a pause. My arms were already beginning to ache. This didn't bode well for my forthcoming ordeal.

"Dad," said Andy, "what is it?"

There was another pause.

"Dad?"

"Nothing son. Bye."

"Bye dad."

The first two floors weren't too bad but then my muscles started to burn, to beg for rest. The speakers were not only heavy but their bulk and their position in my arms meant that I couldn't see where I was putting my feet. Each step was an effort of muscular strain, of mental agility.

The next two floors were hard work. The two after that, agony.

In the gym I had once met a guy whose body had been like an alabaster statue of a Greek soldier. Every muscle was perfectly delineated, sharply defined. I was in awe, stupefied. I asked him how he had achieved such a pinnacle of fitness, such an apex of shapeliness. I didn't really want to know, didn't really care for his answer, I was only chatting him up, already imagining him in bed but I have never forgotten what he said.

He told me that muscles are formed in that moment when you are lifting a weight and you feel the most pain, the acutest anguish. It is at this point of purgatory that most people give up, drop the barbell and take to the showers. But, said the man, this is the very point when you do the most good. The trick is, he said, is to concentrate on an image, kind of like a Buddhist concentrates on nothingness, emptiness. You should fill your mind with this image, focusing on every detail, crowding out any pain, and you should continue pumping. The picture he said could be anything at all, it didn't matter what as long you could visualise it clearly.

I never did get him into bed but I had tried out his theory and it worked, it really worked.

I half closed my eyes.

I saw Andy's poster, the one that had been above his bed.

The tiny yellow-moustached Asterix is standing nose to nose with the bending Obelix. Their eyes are scrunched up and their mouths are open. Obelix has his fat arms crossed over his fat belly

and Asterix has clenched fists. At Obelix's feet is a very forlorn looking Dogmatix, his faithful and loving canine, and behind him in
the background, smiling slyly, is a little man dressed in the toga of
a Roman. This man is obviously very pleased that Asterix and
Obelix are so angry with each other. Asterix and Obelix I remembered are a pain in the side of the Romans.

The pain in my own arms is disappearing. I am descending.

The poster is evidently quite old. The top left corner is tatty and
dog-eared and in the bottom right corner you can clearly see where
an old piece of sellotape has been ripped off taking some of the
colour with it. I remembered. Andy said the poster had belonged to
his brother. Before he died. It must have been moved from one
room to the other. It was obvious that Andy loved his brother. Andy
wasn't a poster kind of guy, there were no others in the room, no
footballers, naked ladies, motor cars. Only that one reminder of the
dead boy.

I remembered how good Andy was with Nicholas, playing with
him without complaint.

Yes certainly he had been an excellent older brother.

Then I remembered Andy's confession. "I didn't mean to kill
him."

He didn't mean to kill him.

It suddenly struck me. One dead brother. One confession of
manslaughter.

Andy had killed his brother. Andy had killed his little brother.

"You OK?" said Andy. "You're white as a sheet."

We had reached the bottom.

"Fine," I said, my thoughts disappearing, the agony returning. I
put the speakers down on the floor of the foyer. "But I need a rest."

"OK," said Andy. "You mind if I have a fag?"

I shook my head, my lungs aching. I crouched down on my
haunches and watched as Andy pulled out first a packet and then a
lighter. We didn't speak and gradually as the cigarette disappeared,

Andy taking long drags, I felt more and more confident that I would be able to make the short distance to the car.

Andy dropped the butt and squashed it beneath the sole of his shoe.

"You ready then?" he said.

"Ready," I said.

He had just loaded the speakers into my arms again when there was a ping behind me. I turned in time to see the doors of the lift sliding open. Two kids ran out and passed us screaming. I looked at Andy. He shrugged.

"Exercise," he said. "It's good for you."

The journey home took ages. We got caught in rush hour traffic. I put the radio on and Andy fell asleep, his head snapping backwards and forwards, a line of saliva dribbling down his chin. Occasionally I glanced across at his nodding head and thought what an unlikely couple we made. And yet we got along. I was comfortable with him, with his boiler suit, his constant smoking, scruffy blond hair and staccato conversation. I was looking forward to getting home and collapsing in front of the television and having a nice cup of tea. Andy would make me tea. And then he would sit down and he wouldn't say much, only smoke and drink cans of beer and tell me when he was going to the toilet. He was easy. Simple. He was the human equivalent of one of those seventies lamps with the wax inside. I didn't have a clue how he worked but he gave the room a nice ambience.

The fact that he might have killed someone, might have killed his brother didn't seem important. The fact that I had just wasted half a day transporting a stereo across Derby didn't seem important. They weren't important. A nightmare lodger for me would be one who would barrage me with conversation, would knock on my door and require attention. This nightmare lodger would talk about the camp aesthetic of *Coronation Street*, would be able to recognise by the style alone which particular director it was who was doing that day's episode of *EastEnders*. Andy was none of those things. He was just there. He didn't invade my space, cramp my style. I could have written the most personal of love poetry with my pad balanced on his knee and his presence wouldn't have affected my train of thought.

As I saw the white sign saying Curzon Street I felt the same thrill as I always did when I had been away, even if only for a short time. It was my home, my sanctuary, my humble dwelling. Andy woke up as we stopped.

"We here?" he said.

"Home," I said.

"Home," said Andy. He stretched and pressed his hands against the ceiling of the car.

"Take the keys and open up," I said. "I'll wait here."

"What for?" said Andy.

"The stereo," I said. "Remember?"

"Oh yes," he said. He smiled. "Good idea."

"I'll pass you the stuff," I said, "and you take it in."

"Donkeywork," he said, "I'm good at that."

He got out of the car and unlocked the front door of the house and I got out my side and opened the boot. Andy came back and I handed him the first of the speakers. He was in and back for the next piece almost as soon as I had pulled it out of the boot.

Andy worked like a Trojan – hell, he was like a horse full of soldiers. The car was unloaded in almost no time at all. As I handed Andy the last box of CDs, slammed down the boot, locked it, I was thinking of my cup of tea, I was thinking of television, I was thinking of a peaceful evening. I was just heading inside when there was a tap on my shoulder. I turned and Brenda was there. Brenda was the single mother of Martin. Brenda and Martin were my next door neighbours.

"Bought a stereo, duck?" she said.

"It's Andy's," I said.

"Andy?" she said. She raised her eyebrows.

"He's the lodger," I said. I nodded at Andy's retreating back.

Brenda smiled. "A lodger lodger or a lodger?"

"He's just a lodger," I said.

"But," said Brenda, leaning closer, "the question is, do you want him to be a lodger lodger and not just a lodger?"

Brenda, although she was successfully bringing up Martin on her own and paled at the idea of having another man in her own life, was of the firm belief that I needed one in mine. I pretended to go along with her on this.

"He's not the one," I said.

"It's about time," said Brenda, "that you did find someone. About time you forget about Joshua."

"Yes," I said.

Brenda put a hand on my forearm. "Actually," she said, "it's me that's looking. I need a man."

"Oh," I said.

"In fact," said Brenda, "I need you."

"Me?"

"Do me a favour Honza," she said, "speak to Martin."

Martin the fifteen-year-old schoolboy, friend of Steve. Martin who had seen me standing naked on the step a week earlier.

"No problem," I said. I meant it. In the past Brenda had been there with tissues and shoulders, advice and comfort. "He's in trouble?" I said.

"No," said Brenda. "But it's delicate."

"Delicate?" Someone else not so far away had said that to me earlier and I had ended up carrying stereos down endless flights of stairs.

"Yes, delicate," she said. "Will you talk to him? I've been meaning to ask you for days. Will you?"

"Sure," I said. I liked Martin. "What's it about?"

"He'll tell you. I'll send him over. Five minutes. OK?"

Five minutes!

"OK," I said. "Five minutes."

"Thanks duck," said Brenda. "I owe you."

I watched Brenda go into her house and then I went into mine.

Andy was in the kitchen. I was pleased to see that the kettle was on and there were two cups ready by the side of it.

"Everything all right?" said Andy.

"We're having a visitor," I said. "Fifteen-year-old boy."

"Bit young," said Andy.

"He's coming for advice."

"Oh," said Andy. "Advice." He said the word slowly. He grinned.

I was just about to tell Andy not to be so cheeky and that he wasn't too old to have his bottom smacked, when there was a knock at the door. Martin.

"Come in!" I shouted.

There was another knock and I shouted again, louder and this time I heard the door open and then Martin appeared.

"Cup of tea?" said Andy.

Martin looked at me and then at Andy. He smiled.

"Cheers," he said. "Two sugars."

"Sit down," I said. I ignored Andy winking over Martin's shoulder. I ignored Martin winking with his back to Andy.

Martin came over and sat next to me, in the seat that had recently become Andy's. He was still wearing his school clothes, black trousers, green, jumper, striped tie. My house was becoming a fetishist's paradise, a uniform club.

"Well," I said after a few moments silence, "what's the problem?"

Martin, by the way, didn't look like he had a problem. He was leaning back on the sofa, his legs were apart and he was half-smiling. He was relaxation personified. No change there. Martin was the most relaxed at ease person I'd ever seen. He always seemed so comfortable

within himself. I remember what he had said that day he saw me
naked on the doorstep. "Cold day Honza?" And that wasn't the first
time he had seen me naked. A year earlier I had taught him to swim.
The very first day, before out first lesson and while we were getting
changed into our trunks he had looked at me in that couple of seconds I was naked. "Will I get as bushy as that?" he had said. "As dark
and big?"

So I shouldn't have been surprised by what he said then. I
should have been expecting it. I should have realised that embarrassment and Martin were two different species.

"It's sex," Martin said.

In the kitchen Andy dropped a cup.

"Sex?" I said. Well obviously there was going to be no beating
about the bush, no going around the houses. He'd gone straight for
the kill, straight for the jugular, the urethra.

"I know the basics," said Martin, "the biology but..." He
shrugged. "I want information."

Sex. There was a fifteen-year-old boy on my sofa who wanted to
know about sex and me, a fully qualified gay man. I felt out of my
depth.

Sex, what did I know about sex?

"Wait here," I said. "I'll speak to your mum. Andy, keep him
entertained."

"Sure," said Andy.

As I left the room I wondered what Andy would do to be entertaining. Farting and fifteen-year-old boys were a potent combination.

Brenda answered the door almost immediately. I got the feeling
that she had been standing there waiting for me.

"He wants to know about sex," I said.

"I know," she said.

"Brenda, I'm gay."

"And there was me thinking that the succession of young men

through your door were only auditioning for a boy band," she said. "I know you're gay. So what?"

"Um..." I said. I was still standing on the doorstep. She had a point. And she didn't look like she was going to invite me in. She wanted me in my house, speaking to her son.

"Honza," she said, "Please. He's driving me mad."

"So you've sent him to me?"

Brenda sighed and looked at me with those eyes of hers.

The list was growing. Nicholas's "Please uncle", Andy's grins, Brenda's eyes.

"Martin's not like other boys," she said. "Where they do things in the quiet, behind closed doors, he's all in the open. He asks me questions and I don't know the answers. The other morning over a bowl of cornflakes he wanted to know if it was normal to have wet dreams more than once a week. I didn't know. He looks up to you. Just speak to him. Please."

"Brenda..."

"It would mean a lot to him."

I could see that it meant a lot to her too. And I realised I should have been flattered. How many women would send an adolescent boy to a gay man for sex education? She trusted me and it was a trust I should repay. Only I was the one who felt awkward.

"Please."

"Right," I said, giving in. "I'll try."

"Thanks, Honza."

"But if he comes home whistling 'I Am What I Am', smelling of CK1 and tells you that he wants to take Home Economics and not Metalwork as an option next year then don't blame me."

Brenda didn't answer, she just closed the door.

I walked the couple of metres to my house. I braced myself. I could do it. I could be Doctor Ruth, I could be both up-front and informative. And besides, it was practice. One day I would have to do this with Nicholas. I opened the door and went into the lounge.

Martin was in the same place. Andy was now sitting in my seat. He had taken my place. In one hand Andy was holding a carrot upright by the base and over this vertical vegetable, with his other hand, he was rolling a condom. Martin was watching avidly.

"You have to hold the teat," Andy was saying, "to make sure air doesn't get in. It's easy. Look you even get instructions." He held up the slip of paper. "Try it a few times on your own at home."

Over Martin's shoulder I caught Andy's eye. He smiled and made to get up and I mouthed, "Continue." He seemed to be doing fine.

"OK," said Martin. "I will, I'll try it at home. But mum only buys tinned. Can I borrow the carrot? To practise."

"I didn't mean on the carrot," said Andy.

"Oh," said Martin. "Yes. I see."

He began to giggle and then they were both laughing, laughing more and more until they were helpless and holding on to each other. And when they had nearly recovered, were wiping tears from their eyes Andy held up the carrot and they were off again.

I went into the kitchen. I looked at the pair of them on the sofa, side by side. I suddenly felt a strange feeling coursing through my body, it was a feeling I usually only got on a good day with Nicholas or when my writing was going particularly well. It was happiness. I was happy.

"Excuse me," I called. "You want pasta. I'm making pasta."

They both turned to look at me and nodded.

As I was chopping onions, boiling water, heating oil I caught snippets of the conversation, words drifted over. Andy talked about different positions, about blowjobs, even masturbation techniques. I was amazed. I had neither never heard him talk so much nor talk about anything so personal. I realised that I didn't know Andy at all. I hadn't imagined him the touchy-feely type. I hadn't imagined him and his mates out on a Friday night discussing the beauty of sex with a loved one. I had been wrong. Or maybe I wasn't. We all had many sides to our character, clothes for different occasions. It was just that I had only seen Andy in his boiler suit.

"So," I heard Andy say as I lined up three plates on the breakfast bar, "any more questions?"

There was a pause. Martin scratched his head.

"Just one," he said.

"Yes?" said Andy.

"What if I'm gay?"

Andy looked at me. I shrugged. My shrug meant go ahead, you're doing fine.

"Are you gay?" Andy said.

"I don't think so," said Martin.

"Then don't worry."

"But I did once get an erection," said Martin, "when Ryan Giggs scored a goal against Arsenal. He ran with the ball all the way from the halfway line, dodged past three or four defenders and shot, bang! in the back of the net."

"I don't think that makes you gay," said Andy.

"Then what does it make me?" said Martin.

"A real fan," said Andy.

"Sure?"

"Sure," said Andy. "And even if you are gay, just think of the benefits."

"Benefits?" said Martin.

"Yeah," said Andy, "you'd never have to deal with PMT, you'd never have to worry if your partner was faking their orgasms and you'd have more in common with Stephen Gately than Stephen Hendry."

I couldn't have put it better myself. I was amazed that those words had come from Andy.

"Thanks Andy," said Martin.

"No problem," said Andy.

"Dinner's ready," I said.

We decided we would eat in front of the television. It was time for *EastEnders*. Andy turned up the sound. Peggy was ill in bed and

Frank and Dan were arguing. Ian Beale had sacked his nanny and was looking for a baby-sitter for his three kids while he planned the financial domination of the East End, and Phil still didn't want anything to do with Lisa and their unborn baby. Life, hey?

After *EastEnders* Martin said he had to go and he thanked us both, Andy for the advice, me for the food. We said no problem and Andy got up and sat where Martin had been sitting and I sat where Andy had been sitting so we were in our usual places. *This is Your Life* was just about to start. It was the turn of John Craven, of *Newsround* fame, to get the red book treatment, and he looked duly moved and teary eyed and we watched silently, only groaning when Noel Edmonds appeared. When it finished Andy stood and said he would get us some beers.

I did the washing up and I was just sitting down again when Andy came back. He had bought Czech beer in bottles and it tasted very nice. It was called Staropramen. It was only on the second one that I noticed that when I wasn't drinking I kept the bottle in the crotch of my legs like Andy did.

At ten o'clock Andy asked if it was all right if he put the tv on Channel Four. He wanted to watch *The Crucible*. This shouldn't have surprised me on a day of surprises, but it did. I didn't think Andy would like Arthur Miller. However, we both enjoyed the film very much. We both thought Daniel Day-Lewis was a fine actor and Winona Ryder didn't look out of place next to him. I told Andy the story was really about Communism and McCarthyism in fifties America and he said was it and he seemed quite interested but he said he liked the film because his grandmother had been a witch.

And then it was bedtime. I was quite drunk.

Andy did his usual routine, standing and scratching.

"Honza?" he said.

"Yeah," I said. "Just go to bed."

"No," said Andy. "Can I ask you to do a little favour for me?"

"It's late," I said. I was feeling all favoured out.

"It'll take five minutes," said Andy. He grinned.

That bloody grin.

"OK," I said. "What is it?" It was getting to the point where I couldn't say no to one of those grins. Nicholas must have been giving him lessons in how to get round me.

"Will you help me carry the stereo upstairs?" he said. "I like a bit of music when I wake up."

I looked at the stereo where it was currently resting on the floor next to the breakfast bar. It couldn't stay there.

"Come on then," I said.

Taking the speakers up twelve stairs was a doddle, was easy-peasy after what I had done earlier. It was a walk in the park, a stroll in the woods. A walk across hot coals in asbestos shoes.

"Where do you want it?" I said.

"On the table," said Andy. "Next to the bed."

Andy's room, I noticed, still looked the same as the last time I had seen it. It still looked as if no one lived there. There were no clothes on the floor, no personal objects. Even the bed was perfectly made.

While he was busy connecting wires I picked up one of the CD boxes. I flicked through it.

I blinked my eyes. I was amazed.

The Vengaboys, The Spice Girls, 5ive, Boyzone, Steps, Kylie Minogue.

"You like this stuff?" I said holding up an ABBA CD.

"Sure," said Andy. "I love ABBA. Everyone loves ABBA." And he snatched the CD off of me and started to sing, swinging his arms from side to side, gyrating his hips.

"You can dance, you can jive, having the time of your life. See that girl, watch that scene, digging the dancing queen."

What could I do? What could I say. Nothing.

I just joined in.

Ten

We all have a past. We all have secrets, something we are ashamed of, don't want to talk about. Believe me, I know.

I wasn't sure if I'd put two and two together and made five, six or even seven. But I came to believe that somewhere in Andy's past he had killed his brother, or at least he believed he had. I imagined that it had been some horrible accident, some tragic incident, a fall in the water, a running across a busy road, and that whatever had happened Andy hadn't been to blame. I didn't believe that he could harm anyone.

I didn't know then how wrong I was. How completely wrong.

After that Monday, for the rest of the week my life returned to normal. On Tuesday, Wednesday, Thursday and Friday mornings I woke up and Andy wasn't there. I walked around the house naked, I drank tea, coffee and I got on with my novel. I was averaging six or seven pages a day. That was good going.

In the evenings Andy came home at his usual time, he ate baked beans, he didn't take off his boiler suit and he told me every time he was going to the toilet, every single time. Sometimes we had beer he bought, sometimes we had beer I bought and every night we watched tv. I had never watched so much television and I was beginning to know the scheduling almost as well as Andy. I knew the days *Coronation Street* was on, what time I could tune into

Emmerdale, when *The Bill* would be doing their beat. And I even knew that you could rely on Channel Five to be showing a crap American telemovie at nine o'clock most nights. Andy loved these crap movies. He would sit there goggle-eyed, mesmerised as clichéd lawyers helped tarts with hearts out of sticky situations and he always seemed surprised when they ended up in the sack together.

Originally I had told myself that I was sitting there just to keep Andy company, because he was new and I didn't want to seem rude by going into my room to write every night. But after nearly two weeks that excuse was wearing a little thin. In fact, had worn out. In truth I liked it. I liked sitting there without having to say anything, without having to be entertaining, witty, convivial and yes, without sex ever getting in the way. Andy and I were like a married couple approaching our diamond anniversary. We were like a comfy jacket, a pair of old socks. We went together like chalk and chalk, cheese and cheese.

The only incident of note that week were the conversations with my mother. For once we seemed to be getting along. For once we had a common interest, keeping Nicholas in Derby. She wanted to report Julie to the Social Services, tell them that she was an unfit mother, but I convinced her that that wasn't a good idea. There was every chance it would backfire. It might turn Julie against us for good and then we would never see Nicholas again. And anyway I had a plan. It was a long shot but it might just work. It might.

So the week passed and Friday came as it always did, sneaking up behind Thursday.

And on Friday I was in my workroom and it was four o'clock when I heard a key in the door. I had forgotten that Andy had told me he was finishing early and more importantly I had forgotten that on Friday nights Andy went out. With his mates. That wouldn't have been a problem normally, shouldn't be a problem that day except I wanted Andy to do me a favour. I wasn't very good at asking for favours. I liked to do everything myself.

I went downstairs. Andy was in the kitchen standing by the kettle.

"Finished early," he said. "You want a cup of tea?"

"Thanks," I said. I sat on one of the bar stools.

"Bugger of a day," said Andy. He had his back to me, he was watching the kettle. "That Jim's a bastard. We got lost in Hucknall. He said it was my fault. I didn't even have the map. I'm not allowed the map. And then when I dropped a Servis Millennium Ecosave washer on his left foot he went mental. Said I did it on purpose. Said I was fucking useless. Useless. I need a drink. I need beer."

"You going out tonight then?" I said.

"Course," said Andy. "With me mates."

"Right," I said. Andy's mates. At that time I didn't think it odd that these mates had never been to the house, had never even called. I had other things on my mind. "What time you meeting them?" I said.

"Usual," said Andy. The kettle had boiled and he was pouring the steaming liquid into the cups.

"About seven?" I said.

"Yeah," said Andy. He mashed the tea bags, dropped the squashed sacks in the bin and then added the milk. We didn't have sugar.

He passed me a cup.

"So you're going about seven," I said as I took the first sip. "Can I ask you a favour? About tonight?"

Andy on the other side of the breakfast bar suddenly looked worried. He looked like my sister had looked when I was fifteen and she was seventeen and I wanted to go with her to see Duran Duran at Wembley Arena. She was thinking that I would cramp her style, not be cool. She was thinking how she could let me down gently. That was the look on Andy's face now. He was wondering how he could say no without hurting my feelings. He thought I wanted to go out with him. He had got the wrong end of the stick, the wrong stick even.

He was standing with his cup frozen between his mouth and the breakfast bar.

"You see," I said, "tonight..."

"I wouldn't mind," said Andy quickly, redness rising to his cheeks, "but I don't think you'd get on with the others. I don't think they're your type. I'm sorry Honza but..."

"Andy," I said, cutting short the incipient ignominy of my rejection, "I don't want to come with you."

"Oh," said Andy.

"Nicholas is coming shortly," I said, "and I just wondered if you would look after him for an hour. I want to speak to Julie. I'll be back before seven."

"Right," said Andy. His cheeks were redder than ever. "Look after Nicholas. Of course. I'll get ready now. I'll have my shower now. OK?"

"OK," I said to a retreating back.

If Andy hadn't always taken the stairs three at a time, hadn't always gone up them like he was being chased by wolves then I would have sworn that he was running away. He hadn't even touched his tea. His cup was there on the breakfast bar full and steaming. I looked at it and smiled to myself. Was the thought of going out with me so frightening, so nerve shattering? So embarrassing?

There wasn't much time to contemplate this, to dwell on my rejection because just then there was a crash in the hall. I didn't think a baby grand piano had fallen down the stairs. I recognised the sound. I turned to the lounge door as Andy reappeared. He was naked except for a towel wrapped around his waist. It was the second time I had seen him like this. He didn't look any more healthy. He still looked like a starved Bosnian refugee on his way to be deloused.

Let me explain.

Andy's skin was very pale, his body very skinny. The paleness was the whiteness of an Englishman who has never been abroad, who would go red at the hint of the sun and not the considered paleness of Madonna whose dermatological advisor had no doubt told her ultraviolet rays were damaging, ageing to the skin. Andy's skinniness was the skinniness of poverty, not the heroin-chic of a catwalk model, not the litheness of an Ethiopian middle-distance runner. And I felt guilty because I had promised myself that I would teach him to cook.

"Honza," he said, "the shower, it's not working. I think it's broken."

"Oh," I said.

"It's knackered," said Andy. "No flow. Haven't got time for a bath. Never mind. Just thought I'd let you know."

"Thanks," I said.

"Right," said Andy. He turned to go.

"Andy?" I said.

"Yes?" He twisted in the doorway, holding onto his towel.

"Did you turn it on? The shower." I made a flicking movement with my finger. "In the cupboard."

Andy didn't answer but he was back up the stairs again, the wolves still in hot pursuit and moments later I heard the spurts of water. I looked at my watch, it was twenty past four. Julie said she would be here around five o'clock. So I sat at the breakfast bar and went over in my head what I was going to say her, mouthing the words but making no sound. I finished my own tea and then started unconsciously on Andy's.

I had just reached the bottom of his cup when there was that smell again, the one that was reminiscent of Tendre Poison and Pledge floor polish. I turned and Andy was there.

"I didn't hear you come down," I said.

Andy lifted up his left knee and wiggled his blue and white trainer.

"I'm like a panther in these. Silent and deadly. Did I leave my tea in here?"

"Sorry," I said. I glanced at the cup. "I drank it."

"Charming," said Andy.

"I'll make you another one."

I got up and Andy sat where I had been sitting. I noticed that he was dressed much the same as he had been the week before. He had the same sports shoes, the same denim jeans, the same blue Ralph Lauren shirt with button-down collar. Only I hoped the clothes weren't the same. I hoped they were clean. I still remembered his accident the previous Friday, the dark patch on his jeans, the sodden material of his boxer shorts. And beneath that. I didn't know, didn't want to know. Donkey or not donkey, that wasn't the question.

As the kettle boiled there was a knock at the door.

I looked at my watch, instinctively. But I knew what the time would be. Five o'clock. Julie was here.

It was time to put my plan into action, time to put some action into my plan.

I walked into the hallway and saw that the flap through which the post dropped was up and that in this tiny oblong of space was a pair of eyes.

"Uncle!" came the cry.

"Sorry," I shouted, "not today thank you."

"It's me uncle! Nicholas!"

"Nicholas?"

"Yes, Me! Nicholas! The Power Ranger," said Nicholas. "The red one!"

I opened the door and Nicholas went charging past me, shouting, "Andy, lodger, Andy!"

"Someone's taken a shine to someone," said Julie.

Julie as usual wasn't wearing very much and what she was wearing was stuck to her like glue, like a colourful second skin. She was all legs, curves and breasts. But I had to admit she was sexy. In fact, she was stunning. Just for a moment I felt what I used to feel for my older sister, admiration, envy, pride. And then I heard Nicholas shout, "Donkey, donkey" and I remembered my plan.

"Here's his bag," Julie said, handing me a holdall. "I've put in extra underwear. He's been having little accidents. Big accidents. Don't ask me what happened in Sainsbury's. But if you do go out then make sure you take a change for him. And plenty of tissues. I'll be back on Sunday usual time."

"Julie," I said, "can we talk? In private."

"I'm busy," she said.

"One hour," I said, "that's all I'm asking."

She crossed her arms.

I tried Andy's grin, I tried Brenda's eyes, Nicholas's, "please". All the big guns.

They must have worked, Julie uncrossed her arms.

"OK," she said. "But at seven I have an appointment."

"Thanks," I said.

At that time of night I thought The Vine would be almost empty. I was right, it was. I nodded to Ian the barman and ordered myself a pint and Julie a vodka and tonic. We took our drinks and sat down at a table on a quiet corner of the raised platform that overlooked the bar.

"I know what this is about," said Julie.

I took a sip of my beer. I didn't say anything. I didn't want to fight, I just wanted to have a conversation, rational. I wanted Julie to see what she was doing and to talk herself out of it. This approach had worked when I was eight and she was ten and she had wanted to run away from home. I had only had to mention *The Wizard of Oz*, the Wicked Witch of the West and Julie had said herself that there was no place like home.

"It's London, isn't it?" Julie said. She fished the slice of lemon out of her drink, no mean feat with half-inch talons, and ripped off the alcohol-soaked flesh with her teeth, perfectly pulling apart her lips so as not to blemish her lipstick.

I nodded.

"Honza," she said, "I'm going to London. I'm going to be a dancer. I've been practising. Sandra says I'm good. Very good. She says I have fluid hips."

I took another sip of my pint and wiped froth from my top lip.

"I can make money," said Julie. "There's girls that make hundreds. In one night. Just think, in one night. I'll be able to buy Nicholas all the things that now I can't. I'll be able to make him happy."

"He's happy as he is," I said. Music was beginning to drift through from the disco in the back bar as the DJ geared up for the night. Geri Halliwell was singing 'Lift Me Up'.

"But I'm not," said Julie. "I'm not happy. I'm tired of Derby, I'm sick of this concrete city, the same faces, the same shops. Did I try and stop you when you went to Japan, to Australia?"

I didn't answer, but I took another sip of my beer.

"Did I?" said Julie insistently.

"No," I said, "but that was different. I didn't have a kid."

Julie laughed.

"That's not what this is about," she said. "Not really. What you want to say is that it's different because while you were a teacher I'm a common whore."

Julie said the last two words loudly. Ian, the barman, looked over briefly and then looked away again.

"I'm not ashamed of what I do," said Julie. "My body's my own and I don't take anything from anybody. Anybody. Sometimes when I'm lying there under a pumping ball of flabby flesh I think, that's a new pair of shoes for Nicholas, or that perhaps I'll be able to afford that Power Rangers costume he wants, that computer game he's seen, that holiday we deserve." Julie drank down about half of her vodka all in one go and then turned to look me in the eye. "And I pay for what I buy with my own money, with money I earned, money I worked for. All those women who live on handouts from the state and go out on a Friday night after any man make me sick. I'm not a slapper like them. At least I don't give it away. I charge."

Once more I was quiet. I took a long swig from my drink.

"Honza," said Julie, "why do you hate me so much?"

She looked at me and beneath the heavy make up, the mascara, foundation and lipstick was the sister I had once idolised, once thought was the bee's knees.

"I don't hate you," I said. "But Nicholas is four years old."

"I know," said Julie. "Four years, three months, twenty-one days. About as long as you've hated me."

"I don't," I said. "I don't hate you." From the other bar was now coming Robbie Williams. 'She's The One.'

"Remember when you told mum you were gay?" said Julie.

"What?" I said, surprised by her change of tack.

"You told her and she went mad. She said you were disgusting, abnormal, perverted."

"I remember," I said.

"Well, that's how you make me feel," said Julie. "Every time I come to drop off Nicholas or pick him up and you look at me the way you do, that's how I feel. That you think I am all of those things."

"I love Nicholas," I said.

"And so do I," said Julie.

"But I think of his little face," I said, "so sweet and innocent and then I think of what you do. How you make your money."

Julie laughed again.

"And you never have sex?" she said.

Unbidden into my mind came the scene from the previous Sunday night in the toilets at L'Amour. Solskjaer is on his knees before me and I have my hands in his hair, moving his head up and down.

I hated Julie, but she had a point. I took a sip of my drink.

"Don't go to London," I said.

Julie shrugged.

"Honza, I'm going. I'm going to London."

"Then leave Nicholas," I said. "Leave him with me until you're settled, until you make a go of it and you're really making the money that you thought you would. Who knows, it might not work out."

Julie picked up her glass and drained the remainder of her drink. She put the glass down carefully.

"I'm not going to get angry," she said slowly. "I don't want to be angry. But leave Nicholas? He's not a piece of luggage. Don't you get it? I love him. I love him to distraction. He's the last thing I think of before I go to sleep, the first thought when I wake up. He's my little boy, my love bug, my most precious thing. I am a prostitute, yes I am. I do take drugs, yes I do, but I am not, I repeat, I am not a bad mother. And now, it's ten to seven and in ten minutes I have a client. Will you take me home?"

I stood, leaving about half of my beer, and followed Julie out to the car. She crossed her arms again and waited for me to unlock her door. On the short journey to her house we didn't speak much but as I pulled up she turned to look at me.

"Honza," she said, "can we be friends? Please."

"Sure," I said, "sure."

And as she slammed the door shut I said to the empty car that I was sorry, that I had never meant to make her feel disgusting, perverted, ashamed of herself. I said that I had been wrong.

"I'm back!" I called.

There was no answer. I went into the lounge and there was nobody there. No Nicholas. No Andy.

My heart was in my mouth. My blood ran cold.

I felt panic, pure and simple, panic.

That's what four-year-old children do to you. Ask any mother, any father. Lose sight of a child for even a second and the most crazy thoughts enter your head, exploding like the bombs during the Allied attacks on Dresden. He's lost, he's run into the street, I'll never find him again ever. Never. Or he's been kidnapped, mugged. He's fallen down a big hole. His arm's broken, his leg's broken. He's dead. Dead.

I ran up the stairs. I was like Andy being chased by his wolves, only my wolves were real, more real. At the top of the stairs I heard noises. There was the sound of Nicholas's voice and water splashing. And then I saw the light in the bathroom through the half-open door.

Thank God. Thank God.

Nicholas was OK. He was just having a bath.

Relief flooded through me and I stopped outside the door, waiting for my equilibrium to be restored, for my respiration to become normal.

Inside Nicholas and Andy were talking. Nicholas was asking what was the difference between a donkey and a horse and Andy, obviously, was trying to wash his hair. And then Nicholas asked the question.

"Andy," he said, "are you my daddy?"

This question was both as sad as it sounded and not sad at all. I had heard Nicholas ask the same question many times before. He had asked the butcher, the baker and the only reason he hadn't asked the candlestick maker was because we hadn't come across one. But if ever we did then I'm sure he would be asked.

"No," said Andy. "I'm not."

"Oh," said Nicholas. "Is uncle my daddy?"

"No," said Andy, "Uncle's your uncle."

"Oh," said Nicholas.

"Do you want a daddy?" said Andy.

"Yes," said Nicholas and he must have thrown something in the air because I heard a loud splashing sound and then a delighted laugh.

"Why?" said Andy.

"Um," said Nicholas, "don't know."

"When you know then tell me," said Andy. "OK?"

"OK," said Nicholas and there was the sound of something landing in the bath again with an extra big splash and it was followed by an even louder laugh.

"Andy?" said Nicholas.

"Yes?" said Andy.

"Did you ask uncle about my doggie?" said Nicholas. "I want a big one with floppy ears and a waggy tail."

This I took as my cue. So far I had yet to be questioned about dogs. It was something I wanted to avoid. I pushed open the door.

"Uncle!" screamed Nicholas. "I'm having a bath."

"Hello Nicholas," I said.

"He's having a bath," said Andy, standing. He was shifting uncomfortably from foot to foot, looking like someone does when they are discovered doing something with your child and they are not sure whether you approve or not.

I did approve, I approved whole-heartedly.

"Who's having a bath?" I said. I glanced at Andy and smiled. "You're drenched." The front of his jeans were soaking wet, dark stains were running all the way down both thighs. "You'd better get changed," I said. "It's time for you to go out, isn't it?"

"I can't," said Andy pulling the sodden material away from his legs.

"You can't go out?" I said.

"Get changed. My other jeans are dirty. Kind of." He smiled.

"Andy's wet, uncle," said Nicholas joining in. "But he's not having a bath. I'm having a bath."

"Yes," I said to Nicholas. "Wait here," I said to Andy.

I went into my bedroom, pulled open a drawer and took out some jeans. With a belt they would be OK. I guessed that our legs were about the same length. I went back into the bathroom and handed Andy the pair of Calvin Klein pants.

"Put these on."

"You sure?" he asked.

"Sure."

"Thanks Honza," said Andy. He grinned. "Bye Nicholas. Bye Honza. Thanks Honza."

"Bye!" we said together and then he was gone, first into his room then out again and crashing down the stairs. The door was pulled to with a bang.

Andy had gone to meet his mates, gone to mill around Derby city centre drinking pint after pint in pub after pub, getting drunker and drunker until he was in no fit state to talk, walk, control his bladder. Or so I thought, so I believed. I had no reason to doubt it, to question. Why would I?

"The lodger's gone!" screamed Nicholas, smacking the water in front of him with the flats of his palms.

"Right young man," I said, rolling up my sleeves, "time to get you out of there and into your pyjamas."

Nicholas looked at me. He put his head on one side, he put it on the other and then he opened his mouth wide.

"No," he said.

Getting Nicholas out of the bath was never easy. It wasn't like taking candy from a kid. It wasn't money for old rope.

Sometimes I used brute force. I would lift Nicholas bodily out of the water while he would squeeze his elbows into his sides, scrunch up his face and kick with his feet. Sometimes I used cunning. Surreptitiously I would pull out the plug so that he would gradually find himself sitting in an empty bath. This didn't make him happy. And sometimes I just bribed him.

Bribery was the quietest of options, although it was a cop-out with implications. Bribery taught that if you inveigle enough you get what you want, if you are manipulative you can obtain what you desire. But tonight I opted for it anyway. The conversation with Julie had drained me, I just wanted a peaceful night.

I started out by saying that if he got out of the bath he could play with his farmyard set – open the bucket, tip on floor, play, put away. Nicholas said no, he wanted the Scalectrix – clear a floor space, piece together the track (one and a half hours), plug in, play with him, dismantle track, rearrange furniture. I said no, what about colouring – find some paper, later find marks on floor, walls, cupboards, body but easy and low maintenance. Nicholas said boring. What about computer games – sticky fingers on my keyboard, refusal to stop playing way past bedtime, nightmares, bed wetting. I said maybe not, but what about his train set. Nicholas opened his eyes wide, he opened his mouth in an O and put both hands over it.

We were in agreement.

The train set was, in fact, our favourite toy.

It was Swedish, wooden, well-made and very expensive. I had bought one yellow and red engine and just enough track to make a single oval two years before and I had been adding to it ever since. Like the Scalectrix it took ages to put together but unlike the Scalectrix Nicholas could piece the track together by himself. In fact, he loved doing it. He would spend ages making different patterns, figures of eight, complex circuits, looping loops incorporating flyovers, bridges and tunnels, and would only call me if he got stuck. Then, once he was happy with the layout, he was quite content to sit there by himself pushing the little wooden trains around and around, coupling and uncoupling carriages, dropping square painted passengers off at stations, picking up others.

While he played Nicholas would mouth whole histories quietly to himself. These stories were more complicated and involved than anything Thomas the Tank Engine could manage. And more than anything Nicholas liked orchestrating crashes, pile-ups, huge disasters. He would screech like a fire truck, wail like an ambulance.

So once the train was on the cards, Nicholas was out of the bath and into his pyjamas like a shot.

"Come on uncle," he said, tugging my fingers.

Downstairs, I moved one of the armchairs, moved one of the rugs, tipped out all the wooden pieces onto my floorboards and then I sat on one of the breakfast bar stools to watch him play. I tried not to think that the next weekend would be his last weekend here. I tried and tried not to think it but it was difficult. As Nicholas stopped every now and again and turned to look at me and said, "Watch uncle," I could only feel my heart breaking.

Right then life didn't seem very fair at all.

At about eight thirty I asked Nicholas if he was hungry and he said he was, a little bit, so I made us both cheese and ham sandwiches and I sat with him on the floor in the middle of his railway. We were surrounded by trains, wooden people, trees and houses and we ate side by side, Nicholas munching and telling me the story of every passenger of one particular green train. There was an astronaut, a fireman and a little old lady who was going to visit her pet elephant at the zoo. And then I lost track, and just nodded my head up and down and said, yes Nicholas, no Nicholas whenever there was a pause.

At last when Nicholas was quiet and was involved in creating a huge train disaster I escaped from the confines of the track, did the washing up and returned to my bar stool. I watched my nephew at play again and wondered what the future would bring, what would happen to our relationship when Julie had gone to London.

And the night crept on.

Usually it is me who has to cajole Nicholas into bed, usually it involves a fight, a battle of wills. But that evening Nicholas suddenly sat down in the centre of the network he had created and looked at me.

"Uncle?" he said.

"Yes Nicholas?"

"I'm tired. Can I go to sleep?" And he yawned a big, wide little boy yawn.

"To bed then," I said.

Nicholas didn't even want to walk up the stairs and I had to carry him. He was almost asleep in my arms by the time we reached the top. Without a murmur he slid under the covers I held up and slipped a thumb in his mouth. There was no "night uncle", no request for just one toy. The boy was tired out.

I did think about going downstairs to the lounge to clear up the mess, to pick up the pieces of the train but I was tired too. It could wait until the morning. I went into the bathroom, brushed my teeth, got undressed and went back into the bedroom. I got into bed.

And within minutes I was asleep. Nicholas and me, we were both asleep.

Fast asleep.

"Uncle," said Nicholas, "can I wake up Andy? Can I wake up Andy?"

"What?" I said. I opened my eyes.

Nicholas was sitting on my chest holding one of my cheeks in each of his hands.

"Can I wake up the donkey, the lodger?"

I turned my head and looked at the clock. It was nine o'clock. Nine o'clock. A miracle had taken place. I was usually lucky if Nicholas slept until eight. The unheard of had happened.

"After breakfast," I said.

I had no idea what time Andy had got in but I was sure it would-n't have been early and I was sure he wouldn't appreciate being woken at nine. Although, for one moment, I was almost tempted to send Nicholas in. I had never seen Andy upset, angry, in a bad mood. I wondered what he would be like.

But I couldn't be that cruel so instead I went downstairs with Nicholas on my shoulders and we had breakfast together watching tv. I had toast and Nicholas had Cheerios. To me Cheerios were bland, disgusting, tasteless, but he loved them. It happened that I had pretty much the same opinion of the tv programme we were watching, *SM:tv*.

At ten o'clock when I couldn't stand the blandishments of Ant and Dec anymore I said that Nicholas could go and wake Andy up, could jump on his head, pull his ears, and Nicholas went charging up the stairs. I went into the kitchen and put the kettle on. I was sure Andy would like a nice cup of tea.

Moments later Nicholas was back.

"Is he awake?" I said.

"He's not there," said Nicholas.

"What?" I said.

"He's not there," said Nicholas. "He's gone."

I don't know why but I rushed up the stairs and into the room.

The bed was empty. It hadn't been slept in.

Andy hadn't come home.

Eleven

I shouldn't have been surprised, Andy was a good-looking guy.
Well, maybe not good-looking, but he was cute in a wasted
Northern lad kind of way. And he had a nice manner. Quiet.
Unassuming. Some women would go for that, would probably
think he was quite a catch. Or a plaything. I'd recently seen
Afterglow, Julie Christie seducing the younger maintenance man,
trying to get back at her husband.

I suddenly had a vision of Andy in a plush hotel suite, his naked
white arm contrasting sharply with the burgundy crushed-velvet
bedspread. He wakes and caresses the perfectly coiffeured dyed
blonde hair of the *femme fatale* who has prised him away from the
cluster of his friends. His movement wakes her and she opens her
eyes and sees Andy, sees Andy's young fresh smooth cheeks so different from the wrinkled sagging lines of her husband's. She reach-
es under the cover and feels the youthful tumescence of a boy
newly woken. She feels desire, passion, exuberance.

"Make love to me," she says. "Make mad, crazy love to me and
then love me again."

Andy's face breaks into a grin.

"I'm just going for a piss," he says. He leaps from the bed,
bounds across the room, leaves the bathroom door wide open and
urinates copiously and noisily into a white marble bidet.

"Uncle," said Nicholas. He had appeared at my side, slipping his hand into mine. "Where's Andy? Where's the lodger?"

"Out," I said.

"Oh," said Nicholas. "Is he coming back?"

"Course."

"Uncle?" Nicholas tugged on my hand and I looked down at him. We smiled.

"Yes?" I said.

"Will you be the donkey then," he said, "until he does?"

"Sure," I said. "Now let's get you dressed." I picked Nicholas up under the armpits. "We're going out."

I carried Nicholas into my bedroom.

The wind was buffeting against the window and there was a hint of rain in the grey skies, but I felt the need to get out of the house. Suddenly I was in the mood for a beach, a sea. I wanted to think. I did my best thinking next to water. In Australia sometimes I had walked for hours, scrambling over sharp rocks, removing my shoes when I hit soft sand, following the coastline. And while I walked I would stare continually out over the placid waters, hidden depths, imagining Atlantis, Poseidon, Neptune, my life.

It was my dream to live next to the sea, to live in a flat with wide windows, broad vistas, to be able to wake up and see the ocean. But I didn't, I was here in Derby and the best Derby had to offer was a river and a collection of scrabbly ducks.

At least Nicholas liked ducks. He had never seen sand. Perhaps he would have liked that too.

I pulled Nicholas into a blue Gap fleece I had recently bought him and a pair of bright yellow combat trousers with more pockets than he would ever have sweets, tiny toys. Sitting on the side of the bed, twisting a small plastic horse around and around in his hands while I did up his boots Nicholas looked like a miniature extra for an advert starring the Oxo family. Somehow he had bluffed his way on set. He had kept quiet about his prostitute mother, his absent father, his gay uncle. It was all about appearance. With his black hair, his pale skin, blue eyes and cheeky grin he fitted the part, none of the rest was important.

"Where we going uncle?" he said, chewing one of the horse's plastic legs.

"To the park," I said. "To feed the ducks."

"Hooray!" he said. His shoes done up, he leapt from the bed and ran around the bedroom, flapping his arms, making quacking noises and then followed me down the stairs.

I wondered how much longer he would be like this, how much longer something so simple could make him so happy. And I wondered if I would be there to see the change.

In the lounge I dodged colourful engines, stepped over loops of tracks, carefully avoided standing on passengers standing on train-deserted stations and I retrieved my keys from the breakfast bar, picked up the bag I had packed earlier. I had remembered Julie's words of warning. I had spare underpants, spare trousers and enough tissue to satisfy the most diarrhoeic of Andrex puppies.

"Ready Nicholas?" I said.

"Ready."

I was just about to open the front door when I had an idea. I told Nicholas to wait a minute and I went back into the lounge. On the breakfast bar was a pad of Post-it notes and a Pentel pen. I pulled off the cap and wrote quickly, "Andy, we're at the park on London Road. See you at the duck pond?" I returned to an impatient Nicholas who was standing with his arms crossed and a scowl on his face. For the first time I realised how much he looked like his mother.

The scowl remained while I clipped him into his car-seat, started the engine and only disappeared when I put on Steps singing 'Tragedy'. Then his face broke into a broad grin. 'Tragedy' was currently Nicholas's favourite song. He liked it more than Madonna's 'American Pie', Aqua's 'Cartoon Heroes', the All Saints' 'Pure

Shores'. He knew all the words and all the dance movements and as I turned right at the bottom of Curzon Street I spied him in the rear-view mirror rotating his palms parallel to his dimpled cheeks. "Tragedy," he sang, smiling. Tragedy, he was too young to know what tragedy was, to know what suffering and pain were. But in my mind's eye I could see Steps miming in the video for the song and they were smiling too, smiling for all the world like they'd won the National Lottery, been told the Spice Girls weren't releasing a single that week and were guaranteed a number one spot.

Perhaps that's what the song was saying, what all pop was saying, nothing's a tragedy as long as you've got music, as long as you've got beats. Sing your troubles away. Smile and the world smiles with you.

So I joined in. I wound down the windows, I turned up the volume, and sang along at the top of my voice as we whizzed along the almost deserted lanes of London Road.

"Tragedy! When the feeling's gone and you can't go on, it's tragedy."

Some pedestrians turned to look and some didn't.

"Uncle?" said Nicholas.

"Yes?" I said.

"There aren't many ducks today."

I was sitting on a slatted wooden bench dedicated to the memory of Elsie Stokes. Elsie had, according to the already verdigris-coated plaque, come here to feed the ducks for fifty-five of her seventy years. I thought it a shame that the council had only decided to install a bench after her death. I'm sure she would have appreciated it more when she was alive. Fifty-five years seemed an awful long time to be standing.

Nicholas, it has to be said, was doing Elsie's memory proud, although I wasn't quite sure if he was feeding the birds or trying to bludgeon them to death with flying pieces of stale Sainsbury's medium-sliced white bread. With legs apart he would reach into the plastic bag and grab a handful of the food in his fist and then pulling this fist back behind his head he would launch the doughy missile with all his might directly at the ducks, screaming, "Power Rangers to the rescue!"

Quite who or what he was rescuing I didn't have a clue but he was right, there weren't many ducks. If they'd been geese they wouldn't have made a gaggle, if they'd been cows they wouldn't have managed a herd. Even if they'd been a strange breed of water-borne kangaroos they wouldn't have equalled a troop. Not quite. But as they were ducks, it has to be said they didn't make a team. They were missing at least a fly-half and a couple of wingers.

"Perhaps they've flown south for the summer," I said.

"Probably," said Nicholas.

In truth I had little idea about the migratory patterns of our web-footed friends and I thought it more likely that the majority of the birds had been tipped off by the greater-crested grebe I had seen loitering with intent beside the car as I'd parked. "Watch out," it would have said, "toddler about." I guessed all the park's wildfowl were currently hiding on the shores of the man-made island in the middle of the pond feasting on delicacies they had collected earlier, sniggering at us with beaks behind wings.

"Is that what I'm doing?" said Nicholas. Nicholas had grown suddenly bored of bread throwing and had come to sit next to me on the bench.

"What?" I said, putting an arm around his shoulder, pulling him closer.

"Going south?" he said. "Mummy says we're going to Condom."

"London."

"Yes London," said Nicholas. "Will the ducks be in London?"

"They could be," I said.

"I hope so." Nicholas scratched his nose and then looked up at me. "Uncle?"

"Yes?"

"Is London far?"

"It's quite far," I said.

"Oh," said Nicholas. "Further than the cinema?"

I nodded.

"Further than Robin Hood?"

By Robin Hood Nicholas meant Nottingham and the museum I had taken him to where you can learn all about Robin Hood's life. We had sat side by side in a cable car and Nicholas had been frightened by the smells, the noises, the wax figures that represented life in the old city.

I nodded again.

"That is far," he said. "Will you be there uncle?"

"Not always," I said. "But sometimes and you can speak to me on the telephone."

"I don't like telephones," said Nicholas just as there was a particularly freezing blast of air. We both shivered and cuddled for warmth and then Nicholas leapt up and away with a giggle.

"Mummy's been teaching me to dance," he said. "Like an Egyptian. Watch."

I watched.

I sat on the bench with my arms wrapped around myself as Nicholas showed me what he could do. If he'd have been caught up in an extra strong gust of wind and been carried on the eddies and thermals across continents to the African capital city of Cairo then I don't think he would have made his fortune as a tabletop belly dancer. Amidst the supple girls in diaphanous robes with fluid hips who'd had the ancient art beaten into them from birth he wouldn't have stood a chance. But if the same winds had dropped him in an insalubrious suburb of Manchester, Liverpool or Milton Keynes then he probably could have made a few bob. He was a natural. The boy could dance.

A nonagenarian couple with matching walking canes and a

scruffy terrier more frisky then I could imagine either of them had ever been were rounding the side of the pond and upon arriving adjacent to us they either stopped to see the show or stopped to catch their breath. Anyway, they started watching Nicholas.

And Nicholas was moving, sliding from side to side, one hand parallel to the ground at waist height, one hand level with his shoulders, his hips jigging left and·right and on his face was a huge grin. Even the ducks seemed entranced and I don't know if it was just my imagination but there seemed to be more of them than before.

"Come on uncle," said Nicholas, executing a twist and turn. "Dance."

I looked at the old couple and they looked at me and I saw laughter in their rheumy eyes, I saw a youthful tango beneath their layers of clothing.

"I will if you will," I said.

They didn't look at each other, not even a glance, but faster than I thought possible they were next to Nicholas. One hand clutching their sticks for support with their free hands they became half an Egyptian each, first one with palm high then the other, turning their white-topped heads perfectly in time as they shimmied in a mirror of my nephew.

What could I do but join in?

And so there we were, three generations performing arabesques, Dervish twirls to the orchestration of the wind, to an audience of one small dog and a collection of nervous ducks. And I was happy again. For a time.

Nicholas fell asleep in the car on the way home. It was a ten-minute journey, but he fell asleep, head bouncing on his left shoulder, snoring slightly, hands twitching. It was because I was so focused on parking gently, on making sure that I didn't wake my nephew that at first I didn't notice the man outside my house. It was only when I had undone the buckle strapping Nicholas into his car-seat and had carefully lifted his limp body into my arms that I saw him. He was banging loudly on my door.

I was sure that I hadn't seen him before. I was sure that he wasn't a trick I had forgotten about, someone I had used, abused or been used and abused by. He wasn't my type. On the quiet, from time to time, I am partial to a bit of rough, a squeeze from the wrong side of town, but this man was industrial strength sandpaper, toilet paper from a public toilet. He had a face that a heavyweight boxer would have killed for. Basically, he was big, bald and blocking my door.

"Hello," I whispered. The sleeping Nicholas was cradled in my arms.

"You live here?" said the man more quietly than even I had spoken. His accent was Home Counties, not East End crim.

"Yes," I said.

"I see," he said. He ran a hand over his bald pate. "I'm looking for Andy."

"He's out," I said. I didn't know that he was, but I was assuming that if Andy was in, then this wouldn't be a visitor he would want. The man looked like trouble. Hell, he was trouble. There was a chance he was going to wake Nicholas.

The man folded his arms and moved his feet apart slightly.

"Can I take a message?" I said. Nicholas mumbled something in his sleep. I wanted to get him inside and into bed and out of the cold.

"Just tell him I came," said the man, quietly, politely. But exuding menace like some people exude charm.

"And you are?" I asked.

"He'll know," said the man. "And tell him well done. Very well done."

And he walked off. I didn't know what he meant. I didn't want to know. I was only grateful that he hadn't raised his voice, not at all. The whole conversation could have taken place in a library without an eyebrow being raised, without a single tut. I watched briefly as he crossed the road and got into an old black BMW and then I opened the door and went straight upstairs. I removed Nicholas's shoes, slipped him into bed as he was and then I crept out of the room and down to the lounge.

I made myself a cup of tea and tried not to think too much about where Andy was or about his visitor. The man could have been any-one, could have been someone from work, an old school friend, a friend of the family. But probably wasn't. He probably was exactly what he looked, bad news.

Images of Andy and his *femme fatale* disappeared. Images of Andy in trouble took their place.

I finished my tea and put the cup in the sink.

I looked at the living-room, the tv switched off, the sofa empty, the absence of smoke. The lack of Andy.

The mess. I hadn't cleared up from the night before. Normally this wouldn't have bothered me. On days when I didn't have any-thing to think about I would have made a space and flicked on the tv.

Earlier that morning I had craved water, contemplation. Now I desired the opposite. I wanted not to think. I needed to be busy.

I picked up all the bits of Nicholas's train from off of the floor. I collected cups, ashtrays and old plates from the lounge and then I set to work on the kitchen. I cleaned all the surfaces, wiped down the cupboards, bleached my cups and even pulled on a pair of Marigolds and scrubbed the oven.

At five o'clock I went back upstairs to wake Nicholas. He sat up in bed, scratched his head and said, hello uncle. I said hello back and Nicholas asked if Andy was home and I said he wasn't and Nicholas said, oh. I asked Nicholas if he was hungry and he said yes he was hungry so I took us both downstairs and cooked. Nicholas helped/hindered me. He passed me some things from drawers I needed and some things I didn't. To make him happy I pricked the sausages with a corkscrew but refused to mash the potatoes with an egg slice.

We ate our tea with plates on our knees watching *Friends Like These* on the tv and then I did the washing up while Nicholas pretended to be a motorcar whizzing in and out from behind the chairs and the table. When I had finished, the pots drip-drying on the draining-board, I asked Nicholas if he wanted to watch a video and he clapped his hands. We put on shoes and walked hand in hand to the video shop and after careful consideration came back with *Mulan*, a bottle of Coke and a giant bag of Maltesers. We enjoyed the film. We laughed at the antics of the little lizard who thought he was a dragon, we marvelled at the battle scenes in the snow-capped mountains with a million horses and we screamed with delight at the fat and thin cartoon characters dressing up in drag for the grand finale assault on the palace.

And then it was time for bed. I read Nicholas a story and another and another until eventually he fell asleep.

My life was back to normal. Except it wasn't. Andy was missing and the next weekend Nicholas would be going to London.

I wanted to go to the off-licence to get some beer but I couldn't, I couldn't leave Nicholas by himself. I had to watch *Match of the Day* completely sober. And alone. The sofa seemed huge without Andy in the seat next to me dressed in his boiler suit, scratching and announcing his urinary intentions. I cheered Manchester United when they scored against Bradford and I was pleased that Dwight Yorke got a hat-trick, really I was, but it was a Pyrrhic celebration. I didn't have anyone to celebrate it with.

I didn't have anyone to nudge in the side, to rib, to tease. I didn't have anyone to say, more simply, "Good goal that."

Nice shot. Great pass. Beautiful cross.

What was I saying? Until a few weeks ago I had gloried in my privacy, in my life without complication. Every tiny thing I had done was a victory in itself in its very simplicity. For everything I did I didn't have Joshua telling me that I was wrong, or that I shouldn't have done it like that, I should have done it this way, his way. After the split I had been sad, tormented, demented but concurrent with that had been another feeling. I had been drunk with freedom. I could do what I liked, when I liked. And yet here I was missing Andy and he wasn't even a boyfriend, nor was ever likely to be. He was just a low-maintenance lodger who had an extraordinary ability with his arsehole and who was missing an important finger.

I didn't understand.

So I did what I always did in times of stress when I wanted to empty my mind of all worries. After the football had finished I flicked off the screen and I pulled down my trousers. I thought of Solskjaer in the showers being jockeyed by his team-mates. I thought of the deaf Solskjaer look-alike I had met in L'Amour the week before. I thought of many wondrous things, trawling a history of fantasies and *faits accomplis* until I reached that stabbing climax.

And then I cleaned up and went to bed, sneaking in beside my snoring darling nephew.

On Sunday I took Nicholas to see my mother. She had promised us Sunday lunch. Actually it was more of a threat than a promise. I warned Nicholas that he was to be on his best behaviour.

Nicholas was at an age now where he could distinguish between what was good and what was bad. For example he knew that refusing a kiss and asking to put the tv on as soon as he got in the door was bad. He knew that holding out his hand and saying thank you when offered an almost inedible Werther's Original was good.

And he was good. He was almost better than me. He didn't turn his nose up at the frazzled chicken and even seemed to enjoy its crunchy texture. He managed to eat not only one but two of the roast potatoes that could only have been roasted in the fiery furnaces of hell and must surely have been dumb-waitered up to my mother's kitchen. He even wolfed down a whole bowl of the pudding put in front of him. I didn't know what it was meant to be, I really had never seen its kind before. Its colour alone could have won a competition for kitsch shades of the seventies and it tasted like a collection of the more deadly E-numbers with a hint of cream. It was just the sort of thing the EC was trying to legislate against and my mother would say England should be proud of. "It was our biggest mistake joining with those foreigners. God didn't put a stretch of water between us for nothing."

It wasn't only the food that Nicholas was good about but other things too. He remembered to say that he was going to the toilet and not that he needed a piss. He listened patiently while my mother told him stories of her youth in Buxton and he even had questions to ask about the accompanying photographs. Most importantly, when he was asked if he had learnt anything new he did not roll up his T-shirt and do an impromptu belly dance on the dining-room floor but instead said that he now knew the names of eight planets and he named them all, bending down a finger as he said each one. Mercury, Venus, The Moon, Mars, Jupiter, Saturn, Uranus, Pluto. He wasn't sure, he said, which planet he would like to go to most, Mars because he liked chocolate or Pluto because he believed the Disney animals lived there when they weren't working. My mother laughed and said how adorable he was. I agreed with her.

When he yawned and my mother said it was time for his afternoon nap I became tense. I knew that once he was asleep it would be time for my third degree, time for an update on operation Julie. I didn't know how to break it to my mother that my opinion of Julie had changed since I'd had that conversation with her in The

Vine. I didn't know how to tell my mother that although I still believed that Julie was making a big mistake, it was her right to make mistakes and whatever she did and how she lived her life were her choices. I didn't know how to say that I had to admit what I had always begrudgingly told myself, Julie was a good mother.

So when my mother came down the stairs and said, "well" and looked at me with those eyes of hers I had no choice. I lied. I told her that I hadn't had chance to speak to Julie but I would do when she came to pick up Nicholas that evening. My mother, good for her, took this in her stride and then went on to ask about the Lodger. I lied. I said he was fine. She then asked about my writing and was I still only writing for Gays and if I was I should try and branch out because Gays weren't the only people who could read, you know. I lied again and said that I had my fingers in other pies too and my mother told me not to become greedy, not to run before I could walk, not to count my chickens before they were hatched. And so on.

I did well, I did very well. I didn't lose my temper at all, I didn't even get a little bit angry. When I became the slightest bit upset I went into the kitchen to make a cup of tea, or upstairs to the bathroom. After one particularly painful set of questions on how my novel was going I sat on the toilet for ten minutes with my underpants around my ankles counting to ten over and over.

At last five o'clock came and I said we had better go because Julie was coming at six and I wanted to give Nicholas a bath before I sent him home. I woke Nicholas and he hugged my mother and kissed her on the cheek and we said our goodbyes and then in the car he asked if all old women smelt like that.

"Like what?" I said.

"Funny," said Nicholas. "Like a church pew."

"Like what?" I said laughing. "When did you go to church?"

"Mummy took me?" said Nicholas.

"To a church?"

"Yes," he said. "The vicar left his bible at our house."

"Oh," I said.

I had expected to see the lights on in our house, to see some sign that Andy was back. There was none. The house was in darkness. I unlocked the door and went into the emptiness. I told Nicholas to go upstairs and start his bath while I 1471ed the phone for missed calls and then moments later Nicholas was shouting to me, saying that he couldn't reach the bathroom light cord. Of course. So I went up after him and then stayed to help. I had just got him undressed, we were just testing the water with our elbows and making exaggerated Ows! when I heard the key in the lock.

Andy.

"Andy!" screamed Nicholas and before I could stop him he was rushing dangerously down the stairs. I wanted to shout at him to be careful, not to go so quickly but I knew how he felt. I wanted to be rushing down the stairs too. I wanted to ask where Andy'd been, what he'd been doing and why hadn't he called. But I knew I had no right. He was just the lodger and I was a bastard who didn't want involvement on any level with anyone except my nephew so I stayed where I was adding cold to the too hot bath water.

"Nicholas!" said Andy and there were sounds of a hug and a smacking of lips. "How's my favourite boy?"

"Andy," said Nicholas, serious, "what happened to your face?"

I turned off the water and checked it again with my elbow. Perfect.

His face?

"It's nothing," said Andy. "Just a little accident. And where are your clothes?"

An accident? Perhaps he'd been in hospital.

"I'm having a bath," said Nicholas. "You can help."

"Okey-dokey," said Andy.

I could hear them both coming up the stairs. Nicholas was telling Andy about his weekend, about feeding the ducks, about going to my mother's, everything all at once in an incomprehensible jumble.

And then Andy appeared in the bathroom door.

Oh my God!

Twelve

Andy looked like a contestant on *Battered Housewife of the Year*, both facial injury and overall champion categories. I could imagine the compère in his flashy white suit and toothy smile.

"Andy, as you can see," he would say, placing a hand on Andy's elbow, "is sporting a pair of matching shiners, the blueness of the left a perfect counterbalance to the swolleness of the right. Those lips, ladies and gentlemen, owe nothing to the magic of collagen, they are perfectly hand crafted, a glorious example of what fist can do to flesh, of how flesh can be moulded. Show them a profile Andy." Andy does a twirl for the audience and a little curtsey. There is a round of applause. "And the nose," the compère continues, "Roman? Grecian? No, beaten to smithereens, smashed to a pulp. It's a work of art that couldn't be passed off as a meeting with a cupboard door, a trip on the stairs. It has real thing written all over it. And finally," the compère says grinning broadly for the camera, "the whole ensemble is nicely set off by the weeping cut above the eye, notice the seeping blood, the delicate crust forming. Andy's hobbies are grovelling and whimpering. He would like to work with children and animals but his husband won't let him."

"Oh my God!" I said.

"Oh my God," said Nicholas, giggling and copying me.

"It's nothing," said Andy. "An accident."

Andy picked Nicholas up and blew a raspberry on his stomach. Under the circumstances, with a mouth like tenderised beef, this seemed like a very brave thing to do.

"Can I bath him?" said Andy. He looked at me. "Please."

It was not an everyday please. It was not a please can I have a cup of tea, please can I watch *EastEnders*, it was a please loaded with meaning. It was a please that summed up a weekend that was beyond my comprehension, a please that begged for a return to normality.

"Please uncle," said Nicholas, laughing as Andy did another raspberry under his left armpit.

"Sure," I said and added, "Andy, I'll talk to you later."

I left the room quickly, not giving Andy chance to refuse my offer of conversation and as I went into the bedroom I heard Nicholas splashing into the bath, Nicholas laughing, young, carefree.

It was a quarter to six. Julie would be arriving shortly to reclaim her child.

I rushed around gathering Nicholas's discarded clothes, picking up every last flung T-shirt, every single dropped sock. I folded them neatly into the Power Rangers bag, remembering to leave out a pair of trousers and an Adidas sweatshirt for the journey home. Then I took the bag downstairs and filled it with the things I had put in the tumble-drier earlier that day. They were dry and I folded them too.

I was operating on autopilot. I was thinking who had caused such damage to my lodger. And why.

I went back upstairs and back into the bathroom. There was nobody there but the bath was half-full and half-dirty water was still draining away. I heard noises from my bedroom. I went in.

"It's a miracle," I said.

"Newcastle won away from home?" said Andy.

"Nicholas," I said, "you're dressed."

"I am," said Nicholas.

Andy was wielding a hairbrush and Nicholas was standing perfectly still as his sticking-up wet hair was brushed down.

"Good boy," said Andy and he lifted Nicholas and put him into my arms. "All yours and ready for delivery."

I think Andy grinned but it was difficult to tell because his lips were so twisted, so misshapen. It might have been a leer but as Andy didn't have much to leer about the grin got the benefit of the doubt.

There was a knock at the front door. It was six o'clock. It would be Julie.

"Mummy!" said Nicholas.

"Say bye Andy," I said.

"Bye Andy! Bye Andy!" shouted Nicholas over and over as I carried him down the stairs.

"Bye Nicholas," said Andy. He leant over the banister. "See you next week."

"Bye Andy," said Nicholas again and then as we opened the door he shouted, "Hello mummy," one smile segueing into another.

"Hello Nicholas," said Julie from the step. "You been a good boy?"

"Yes," said Nicholas and he patted me on the chest, "haven't I uncle?"

"Yes," I said.

"Any accidents?" said Julie. She held out her arms for her son.

"Andy had an accident," said Nicholas. "He looks like Tom."

"Tom?"

"Yeah," said Nicholas. "In Tom and Jerry. Bang! Smash! Bang!"

Julie looked at me and I shrugged.

"Don't ask," I said. Don't ask because I didn't know.

"Same time next week?" said Julie not asking. "Friday night again if that's OK with you?"

"Sure," I said and we exchanged goodbyes. Briefly. Like a nanny and a mother, not like a brother and a sister.

I had planned to speak to Julie, to say the things that I hadn't said to my mother, about how I thought she was a good mother, how it was her right to make her own mistakes but Andy had thrown me. I wanted to know what had happened to him, to find out if he was really OK. And more honestly, I was copping out. Saying sorry wasn't an easy thing to do, not for me, not at all.

So I didn't say anything, only watched Julie walk up the street, bum wiggling, Nicholas in tow lugging his Power Rangers bag behind him. I closed the door.

Time for Andy.

I went upstairs.

The bathroom door was shut but I could hear the sound of the shower going, the rush of water. And beneath this noise was something else, another noise. I pressed my ear close to the door. The noise was crying. Not wild breathless sobbing, but crying nevertheless, gentle and monotonous. I pulled back and went back down the stairs. It was almost time for *Star Trek Voyager*.

I flicked on the tv, filling the room with comforting noises, Andy's music of the womb, and I slipped out to the off-licence where I bought eight cans of Grolsch. Grolsch is strong lager.

When I got back Andy was there on the sofa, his blond hair gleaming, skinny arms sticking out of a white T-shirt, legs comfortable in bobbled jogging pants. But his face was where I was looking. Clean it didn't look any better. If anything, it seemed more red and raw.

"*Voyager,*" said Andy. "It starts in five minutes. Captain Janeway. She's such a bitch."

"Andy," I said, "do you want to talk about it?"

"There's nothing to talk about," he said. He was looking at the screen. "She is a bitch. But I like her."

"About the weekend?" I said, "About your face?"

"She boldly goes," he said, "seeking out new life, facing every danger but really she just wants to get home, to get back to where she started from."

"Andy?" I said.

"Shhh," he said, "*Voyager*'s starting."

I knew when I was being brushed off. I could take the hint. And I understood.

Once when I was fifteen some older boys had lain in wait for me outside the school gates. It wasn't a gay thing, a homophobic attack, they just didn't like me. They said I was too clever for my own good, whatever that meant. They beat me up pretty badly, blackened my eye, cut my lip and more than anything hurt my pride because I cried and begged them to stop.

When I got home my mum had demanded to know what had happened, who had done this damage to me, but I had refused to tell her, told her to leave me be and she must have heard something in my voice because for once she did.

Sometimes, not always, you have to deal with things on your own. I got those boys back, one by one, by myself. And after that I was never touched again. That wasn't always the best approach, doing things by yourself, but sometimes it was. I trusted Andy's judgement. I had seen him with Nicholas, I had listened to him advise Martin. He seemed to have his head screwed on. I felt sure that if he thought I could help then he would ask me for help. So I didn't press.

Later, I thought I should have done. It would have saved time.

"At least let me look at those cuts," was all I said.

Andy shrugged.

"They might get infected," I said.

"Can I watch *Voyager* at the same time?"

"Of course," I said and I went to get the first-aid kit.

I was glad that *Casualty* or *ER* weren't on. The nurses and doctors in those programmes would either have shown me up with their professionalism, the ease with which they dispensed with patients, applied bandages, offered caring words, or I would have got caught up in one of the plots and thrown Andy back on the sofa and attempted to shock his heart using an ashtray and the tv remote control as an impromptu defibrillator.

So while Andy was mesmerised by intergalactic travel, the moral problems of alien species, I treated his earthly wounds. I put antiseptic cream where I thought necessary, massaging it in with the tips of my fingers. I dabbed iodine on swollen lips and watched as it was instantly washed off with sips of beer. I fixed a piece of gauze over the cut above his eye, gently pressing down the ends of sticky tape on his forehead and cheek. That was as far as my professionalism extended.

When I had finished Andy said thank you and I said no problem and we slipped cosily back into our old routine. Andy told me there was a drama on ITV starring Sarah Lancashire. He said it was a true story about a seventies actress who had opened a children's home. Did I want to watch it? I said that I did so he flicked it over.

You know the story. We both sat there with cans of lager in our crotches. Andy told me whenever he was going to the toilet and I said OK and we didn't talk about our problems. There was no mention of the fact that Andy hadn't been home for two nights and no mention that the next weekend would be Nicholas's last before he went to London. We worked our way through the eight cans of Grolsch and they did their work on my head, relaxed my body. By the end of the television drama I had forgotten my own real-life drama.

Life is as easy as you make it. Apparently.

After a tribute to Larry Grayson – no comment – Andy stood and stretched and yawned. He didn't scratch his stomach and I almost felt as if I should reach out and do it for him.

"I'm tired," he said.

"Why don't you go to bed?"

"OK," he said. "And Honza?"

"Yes?" I said.

"Thank you."

Before I had time to ask thank you for what, Andy was out the door and up the stairs. Wolves still chasing. Did he want to thank me for the beer, the ointment to his face or just thank me for being there?

I didn't know but there was a strange feeling in my jeans. Well, actually not so strange, I'd had it many times before. I was horny.

I had almost forgotten, it was Sunday night. L'Amour night. Time to see Mother Hen and friends. Time to be gorgeous, to knock them dead with my killer repartee, my dazzling dancing. Time to find a partner.

I was changed and out of the door within ten minutes.

Oh my God.
  Oh my God.
  My head hurt.

I turned it slightly, as much as I could bear, and looked at the clock. It was ten thirty. I had slept until ten thirty. I couldn't remember what time had I got back. I couldn't remember much about the night before at all. Vaguely I recalled Mother Hen telling me to go easy on the vodka. Mother Hen telling someone to go easy on the drink was like Mick Jagger telling Jack Nicholson not to play around. Pop star calling the kettle black. And then I had a picture of myself in an alleyway and someone on their knees in front of me. I saw short blond hair and teeth.

I must have been drunk, I don't go for blonds. Not usually.

At this point my video show of memories was rudely interrupted by a spasm in my stomach. I was going to be sick. I was going to vomit. This couldn't be, I'm never sick. Never. There was another spasm and before I proved myself wrong in glorious technicolour all over the bedroom carpet I leapt out of bed and ran into the bathroom. I got to the toilet just in time.

Now I remembered why I was never sick. It wasn't very nice. Clutching onto the sides of toilet bowl spewing out a thick mixture of bile, mucus and pieces of semi-digested food I wished that I was anywhere else doing anything else. I wished that I was in the elephant enclosure at London zoo cleaning up after a dinner party the Indian elephants had thrown for their African counterparts. I wished that I was being offered a lightly sautéed sheep's eye by some Arab emirate.

"Morning Honza," said a voice behind me.

I wished that I hadn't just heard that voice behind me. I had thought things couldn't have got any worse.

In between a spasm I turned to look and there was Andy. Andy not in a blue boiler suit and not at work. And then my stomach was clenching again.

"You all right?" said Andy.

Even in the state I was in I was aware of what a state I looked. My position itself was a dead give-away. Crouching naked in front of a toilet was not how I usually spent my Monday mornings. So I didn't answer the question. I only felt embarrassed.

"Can I get you anything?" said Andy.

A new stomach I wanted to say, a new head. But I didn't. I said I needed water and Andy was gone, charging down the stairs. Thankfully, it seemed that the spasms had relented so I took the opportunity to wipe my mouth on a piece of toilet tissue and head back into my room. I had just slipped under the covers when there was a knock at my door and Andy reappeared, glass of water in one hand and box of paracetamol in the other. He sat down on the edge of the bed.

I popped two of the tablets in my mouth and drank down half of the water.

"You're not at work," I said.

"No," said Andy. "I'm on holiday. Week off. Derek'll have to manage by himself."

"And Jim?" I said.

"Jim's a bastard."

"I know," I said. I shifted down the bed and lay back down on the pillow. I felt rough. I felt worse than rough.

Andy scratched his thigh and let his eyes wander around the room. I was looking at him, concentrating on something other than my own ill feeling. The bruises on his face had deepened to a darker more lived-in colour, but the cuts looked less raw. The gauze over his eye had gone crooked in the night where it had been slept on and I thought it needed changing.

"You were drunk last night," Andy said. He stood.

"Was I?" I said.

"Yes," he said. "You forgot your key."

Did I?

"Did I?" I said.

Andy smiled. "You woke me up at three in the morning singing 'Things Can Only Get Better'. Should think you woke the whole street up."

"Oh My God!" I put my hand to my head. My hurting head. "Sorry."

"No worries," said Andy. "Glad to return the favour. I put you to bed and you were out like a light. No more singing."

Andy had put me to bed. My brain was foggy, but I still remembered. I had woken up naked. Completely naked. Somehow it bothered me. I felt like I used to when I was a teacher and I got drunk with my adult students. Somehow it didn't seem like the right thing to do, the right thing to have happened.

And besides it wasn't fair. Andy was now *au fait* with my donkey-status, I was ignorant of his. Not that I wanted to know, not really, but some things in this life are reciprocal. Ask any kid in the playground.

You show me yours and I'll show you mine.

"Thanks," I mumbled.

"Don't worry," said Andy. "Any time. And if you want anything today just give me a shout. I'm not going out. OK?"

"OK," I said.

And Andy left.

When I was younger, still living at home, and I had a hangover my mother showed no sympathy at all. She said it was my fault. She was right. But fault is a slippery slope. Do we blame people who smoke and get cancer? Should we treat someone who was driving too fast and has an accident? Should hospitals in Scotland, where people eat fried Mars Bars and bags and bags of chips, have cardiology departments?

Andy would have said yes to all of the above. He was an angel all morning and looked after me as though my illness was something that had happened out of the blue, was a family tragedy, a shock to everyone. He was up and down the stairs with cups of tea, kind words, a collection of magazines from the local newsagents. I couldn't have wished for a better carer.

By lunch-time I had given up all hope of doing any work that day. The coming Friday was the deadline for my article on gay/straight attraction but I had my hook and I only needed a couple of long stints at the keyboard to write it. So I decided to extend my weekend and have another day off. I decided to make use of my nurse.

"Andy!"

There were footsteps on the stairs. Andy poked his head around the door.

"I'm hungry," I said. Even though I was still feeling queasy I thought I should eat something. Something that Andy could cook. Something out of a tin. Not beans on toast.

"Tomato soup?" said Andy.

"Perfect," I said.

"No problem," said Andy and the head disappeared.

Tomato soup. I thought I would be fairly safe with tomato soup. I put my hands behind my head and waited. It was nice having someone run around after me. Joshua had never been a very sympathetic person. Everything he had done for me on the occasions I had been sick had had to be congratulated so many times it had been more effort than it was worth. But Andy required no reward. He was like a very faithful dog. A faithful dog who could open a tin. Look after my nephew. Educate my neighbour. Spend quiet evenings with me. Make me laugh.

The soup arrived. With four slices of bread and a cup of tea.

It wasn't bad, tasty even.

After eating I drifted off to sleep. I dreamt of ducks and ponds, dancing and flashing lights. I dreamt of ducks at L'Amour paddling in the urinals and laughing behind their wings. I dreamt of Nicholas throwing pieces of bread to a football eleven of Solskjaer look-alikes. I woke up.

My head wasn't hurting. I didn't feel too bad.

"Andy!" I called.

I expected to hear him bounding up the stairs. I didn't, but he appeared in the room.

"Yes?" he said. "How do you feel?"

"Awful," I said, pulling a face. "You wouldn't run me a bath, would you?"

"Sure," he said.

"Hot and to the top," I said.

"No problem."

When Andy was gone I rubbed my hands together and allowed myself a smile. Tomorrow I would go back to work. Today, I would milk the situation for all it was worth. I heard water starting in the next room. I heard singing. 'Lay All Your Love On Me'. I smiled.

Ten minutes later, ten minutes of lying there relaxing and thinking that London wasn't so far away, was just a hop in the car and a drive down the motorway on a Friday night, Saturday morning. Andy's head appeared around the door again.

"Ready," he said. "Radox has been added."

"Lovely," I said and I got out of bed and went into the bathroom.

I was wearing boxer shorts, I wasn't naked. You can get too much of a good thing. Andy had already had his eyeful. "Thanks," I said looking at the frothy water.

"No problem," said Andy and he crashed down the stairs.

Normally I didn't like baths, I was more of a shower man. Showers are the casual sex of washing. No foreplay is required, no expensive offerings. You just dive in there, get what you want and then leave with barely a thank you. Baths however require commitment. It takes patience even to get them ready, at the right temperature, in the mood. And once started it is difficult to stop. You can't just get in and out. Others get involved. The boiler gives you hard stares. "I spent hours on that water," he says, "and you treated him like shit."

But today I was in the mood for a bath, for a long soak. I wanted to breath in the scented steam, to feel it inside me in my lungs, to feel the water pressing on my body, wrinkling my skin. I wanted to feel my muscles loosening, unknotting, until on standing I would find myself in a weakened infant-like state, red and raw, newly born and baptised. And after, I would snuggle into a big woollen jumper and curl up in front of the telly. With a video. With a bottle of wine. Heaven.

I had been in the bath two minutes when there was a knock on the door.

"It's me," said Andy. "Andy."

"Yes?" I said.

"I need the bathroom."

I didn't answer. There was another knock.

"Honza, please. I'm desperate."

I sighed. "Can't you go in the garden? Against a tree."

"It's not that kind of needing the bathroom."

"Sorry?" I said.

"I need a dump," said Andy.

Relaxing baths and someone sitting on the toilet did not seem to belong together.

"Why didn't you go before?" I said.

"I forgot," said Andy. "Please."

What could I do? When a man's gotta go, a man's gotta go.

"OK," I said. "I'm getting out. Hang on."

The door started to open. There wasn't a lock on my door. There hadn't been one when I'd moved in and I hadn't ever bothered adding one.

"I said, hang on," I said, not angrily, but not happy, not Laa-Laa in Teletubby land.

Andy's head was there, peering in. He was grinning again or leering. It was still difficult to tell.

"You don't have to get out," he said. "I don't mind if you don't."

It seemed that I didn't have much choice, Andy was already crossing the room.

It seemed that one of my fantasies was about to come true. Well, not fantasy exactly.

Let me explain. There are two parts.

Part one. A few years earlier I had seen a BBC2 programme about a group of young straight lads on holiday. I forget where they were, but it was somewhere cheap and cheerful with beaches and beer, sun and nightclubs. It was kind of an *Ibiza Uncovered* before producers realised they could get away with so much sex and swearing. Anyway, there were four of these lads and they were sharing one apartment in a hotel. It must have been the first time they had been away from their parents, the first time away from parental authority because they were all giddy with joy, had the exuberance of liberty, were revelling in making decisions for themselves.

Apart from the filmed segments in and around the resort, days on the beach, hiring of motorcycles, throwing up in tacky discos, the lads had been given a camcorder to film themselves in the apartment. And the one sequence that sticks in my mind took place one evening while the lads were getting ready to go out. It is a sequence more powerful for me than Orson Welles's dropping of the glass ball in *Citizen Kane*, more dramatic than the eponymous English Patient carrying his dead lover across the desert, more poignant than the piece of dust in the eye in *Brief Encounter*. In this sequence John is sitting on the toilet and Kevin is filming him, holding the camera, having a conversation.

John's trousers and underpants are around his ankles, his arms are on his knees and he is looking up at the camera with his newly suntanned face. He is talking how he hopes to find a girl that evening and Kevin is asking him what kinds of girls he likes. There is nothing smutty or seedy about the scene, nothing scatological. It is only natural and innocent. It said something to me about friendship, about the closeness possible between two straight guys. For we are at our most vulnerable, animal, when on the toilet, and to show that naturally to another is a greater gift than an expensive watch, a new car. And Kevin and John make no mention of where he is or what he is doing. John could have been suited and next to Parkinson for all the honesty with which he was answering Kevin's questions.

I was touched. And jealous as hell.

Part two. A few years earlier, right after I had finished university, I went to Prague. It's a long story to explain how it happened but somehow I ended up sharing an apartment with five straight guys. We had only one room, one bed and one toilet. And one topic of conversation. The conversation centred around the arsehole. Those lads talked about nothing but things going in the arsehole and things coming out of it. Quite simply, buggery and shitting. And yet somehow I was never included. Somehow, although they talked about buggering each other quite gaily, and leapt on each other's backs more regularly than a group of five-year-olds playing endless games of leapfrog, my butt was never the butt of their jokes.

I knew why. It was because in their perception of me as a gay man they thought I probably enjoyed buggery. They could not joke about anal penetration with me because it would have been too close to the bone, too close to the boner, as an American would say. Their fun was in the fantasy and I was too much of a reality in their midst. So I felt left out, was left out. Nick would nip into the bathroom and joke what a hairy bum Mike had, or Johnnie would complain what a smell Andy had made in the toilet. My bum, however, went unnoticed. My sojourns in the karsey were odourless. Apparently.

And once again I was jealous as hell.

But now my time had come. My day was dawning.

Andy had reached the toilet. He was undoing his belt.

Was it polite to turn my head or was it rude to look away? He was directly in my line of vision, framed between the taps.

He was pulling apart the buttons on his jeans.

Was I about to find out whether Nicholas was right, whether Derek and Jim were right. They called Andy donkey. By the end of this evening, as we settled in front of *EastEnders*, would I be calling Andy donkey too?

In one swift motion Andy descended his trousers and pants and he was sitting on the black plastic seat.

I hadn't seen a thing. Not even a glimpse of a thing. But Andy had been right, he was desperate. There were four successive explosions of noise. There was no problem. Shit wasn't hitting the fan, it was merely hitting water.

"Honza?" Andy said, saying my name with unconscious stress on the second syllable as he pushed waste down and out of himself.

"Yes?" I said. I inched myself down in the water. I felt suds nestling against my chin, water lapping at my clavicle.

"I've been thinking," said Andy.

"Yes?" I said.

Andy turned to look at me, my lodger with the beaten up face, my lodger on the toilet, my lodger who could evacuate in front of me but who couldn't tell me the shit he was in. "You won't take this the wrong way, will you?" he said.

"I think we know each other well enough by now," I said. The irony of my statement wasn't lost on me. Only on Andy.

"Well," said Andy, he had torn of a section of paper and was beginning to wipe, "I've been thinking that this room could do with painting." He dropped the soiled paper into the pan and tore off another piece. "It's looking a bit dull," he said.

I looked around the room.

"And as I've got a week off," said Andy. "I thought I might do it. I've got some paint at my dad's house. We never used it. Dad went off the idea of purple. What do you think?"

"Purple?" I said.

"Yes," said Andy, tearing another piece of tissue. "Purple."

Purple. Might be nice.

"OK," I said. "Go ahead."

"Right," said Andy.

He had finished wiping and now stood, somehow managing to pull up his trousers so again I didn't see anything. Not that I was desperate for a look. It was just one of those things. Instinctive. Like a cat with a fish, a dog with a bone, a vampire with blood. I still didn't fancy Andy. This whole bathroom episode had taken place without even the hint of an underwater erection, without a subtle arrangement of bubbles being necessary. I was happy with Andy as he was. Very happy.

"I'll start tomorrow," said Andy.

He was standing at the sink, washing his hands, looking at himself in the mirror, at his damaged face.

"I'll go to my dad's first thing," he said. "I'll clear out the room and I'll get to work. You won't know I'm here. You can get on with your writing."

He was now leaning against the sink.

"Andy," I said, "I'm having a bath."

"Yes," he said, "I can see. Do you want me to wash your back?"

"Andy," I said, "fuck off."

He did that thing again with his face. I would be happy when his lips were normal. I missed that grin.

"See you then Honza," he said. "Oh and Honza?"

"Yes?" I said.

"Nice dick."

I threw a sponge at the closing door.

Thirteen

Tuesday morning I woke up feeling much better, much better indeed. My headache was gone, my limbs weren't aching, my eyes weren't throbbing. Everything was OK, in order. I looked at the clock. It was twelve o'clock.

Twelve o'clock!

I couldn't believe it. Andy and I had gone to bed at midnight after watching a dull football show on ITV. Martin O'Neill, the Leicester City manager, had bored us both into cocked hats and we had felt done in. Andy had tried livening up proceedings by farting 'Here We Go, Here We Go, Here We Go' over O'Neill's droning voice but even that hadn't done the trick. O'Neill talked like he had a bad smell under his nose at the best of times.

So after the programme had finished, Andy had yawned and stretched, I had yawned and stretched and we had gone to bed together. Separately.

I looked again at the clock. I had slept for twelve hours. Oh my God. I pulled aside the duvet and remembering my vacationing lodger pulled on a pair of Active underpants and a Moto T-shirt. I went into the bathroom, looked in the mirror, thought not too bad and went downstairs.

Andy was sitting at the breakfast bar, having a cup of tea, munching a piece of toast.

"Morning Honza," he said, spraying motes of semi-masticated bread.

"Morning Andy."

"This came for you." He held up an oblong brown envelope in his left hand. I recognised the writing. I didn't need to recognise it.

My day had suddenly got worse. Much worse.

Shit!

"That postman," said Andy, "he's very..."

"Yes," I said. I flicked on the kettle. I wanted to throw it at the eggshell walls.

"He knocked on the door at seven thirty and said through the letterbox that he had something that was too big for my hole."

"That's Simon," I said. I poured boiling water onto the tea bag in my cup. Concentrating hard. Trying to breath easily. "If you kiss him he usually shuts up. If you're naked, he always does."

"Oh," said Andy. "Actually, he told me to kiss you for him."

"How are your lips?" I said. I mashed the tea bag. Viciously.

"Still a bit tender," said Andy. "We'll leave it, shall we?" He took another bite of his toast. "And anyway, you've got your letter to open. Go on." He pushed the envelope towards me.

It was an envelope I didn't want to be seeing. Not ever. I wanted a nice white oblong mysterious in its plainness, nestled between a phone bill and an unwanted offer of a bank loan. I wanted to rip open its gummed down label, not sure of its contents and then be surprised at the concise phrasing that said so much, meant so much. I would read it once, twice, three times, blinking like a Disney dog who has just been given two bowls of food. We would like, the letter would say, to read the whole of your manuscript on an exclusive basis.

"It's a rejection," I said to Andy. "From a publisher."

If Andy had said then that everybody gets rejections, or made a sympathetic pout, come out with some hackneyed aphorism, I would have screamed, shouted, gone mad. He didn't.

"Oh," he said. "Well, I've got something to cheer you up, something that will brighten up your day.

"You've joined the Royal Philharmonic Orchestra?" I said. "Wind section."

"No," said Andy. "Paint. Purple paint."

And then I noticed what Andy was wearing, what he had been wearing since I had come down. It was a boiler suit. But it wasn't blue, it was green and it didn't have Ryder stitched on the left pocket in white letters, it didn't have a left pocket. It also differed from Andy's usual attire in two other respects. Firstly, the suit was about six or eight sizes too large. The arms and the legs had been rolled up and loose material billowed around the groin as if the design allowed for the occurrence of a man becoming superglued to his Portaloo. And secondly, the suit was filthy. Not filthy dirty, but filthy covered with paint. It looked like someone had been wearing it while they had painted miniature rainbows all along the one thousand four hundred and ten metre span of the Humber Bridge. The suit was more colourful than anything Joseph could ever have professed to own and I wouldn't have been remotely surprised if Andy with his blond hair and boyish appearance had leapt off the stool right there and then and broken into 'Any Dream Will Do'. But he didn't. Andy was his usual quiet unassuming self, drinking his tea, eating his toast.

"You've been to your father's?" I said.

"Yes," said Andy. "I collected this stuff," he nodded to the cans, brushes, buckets I hadn't noticed on the lounge floor, "and also I cooked for him."

I had to ask, I just had to.

"What did you make?" I said.

"Breton scallops," said Andy totally deadpan. "They're one of his favourites."

"Nice," I said.

"Yes," said Andy. "With a hint of garlic. He enjoyed them. And now I'm going to get started.

"Fine," I said.

"Right," said Andy.

He popped the last piece of toast in his mouth, took a last gulp of tea, climbed down off of the stool and set to work, picking up pots, carrying them upstairs.

Andy, I knew, could sit for hours, could spend whole evenings in front of the television scarcely moving, a scratch of the leg, a journey to the toilet, the fridge. And yet what little I had seen of him at work made me think he could toil like a trooper. I remembered our day climbing stairs at his father's flat. I remembered they called him donkey at work. Watching him now, I thought that was unfair, he was much faster than a donkey. Within minutes the pile of equipment in the lounge was gone, diminishing with each bounding movement, each haring up the stairs. And when it was gone and there were no more appearances of the thoroughbred who was my lodger, the noises became louder from above, things been moved, picked up, dropped.

Andy was at work. Work. Which was what I should have been doing too. I had a piece to write. I had a deadline approaching. I drank down my tea and headed up to my workroom. I switched on my computer and pulled out my notes.

Time to finish my article.

I remembered clearly.

Bastards.

Gay men are attracted to straights because in a culture of easy sex by loving someone who has no chance of returning that love we open ourselves up to the whole gamut of emotions. We are not in love if we are not in pain. And pain is what we crave. It is the basis of every tragedy, every comedy.

I started with a pastiche, Romeo loves Romeo. Everything goes well. The family are happy, the two boys have good business ideas and a business partnership is much more preferable to the families than a matrimonial one. Also there isn't the expense of a wedding. But Romeo gets bored of Romeo, of uncomplicated fun, easy sex and meets Juliet. Shit happens. And a story is born. A story that has been told over and over again in many ways.

This latter kind of fiction, this archetypal R & J, I argue, is what we are bombarded with, faced with every time we turn on the tv, open a book, love and pain and we can't help but desire it, gays and straights alike. It is a powerful addiction. We thrive on our disasters, dwell on them, rake over them with friends. I had, we all had. "I was so in love with him. I'm so lonely." Well, boo hoo. Get a life. Get a man. And that's just it, getting a man is so easy. Go to a sauna, a cottage, a club. But we don't want someone easy. We want this rejection, we want these disasters, these feelings that we see on our television screens. We want pain.

And all the gay men are saying poo-poo. No way. What rubbish. You're just confusing sex and love.

But look inside yourself. Ask yourself if you have ever had a crush on someone straight. And remember how delightful that pain was. How initially you thought that he could be gay, you knew he was not. How you would look forward to seeing him, you would position yourself so he would brush by you, notice you casually as you had so carefully arranged. So much more rewarding than eye-contact in a gay club. Isn't it?

And remember that first kiss.

So painful.

Painful because he was kissing a woman and not you. But how you tossed and turned on your bed at night for all the world like a star crossed lover. Bastard, you said.

What a bastard!

I felt a presence behind me. I saw a dull reflection in the screen. It was Andy.

"Brought you some tea," he said. He put a cup down next to me.

"Thanks," I said.

"How's it going?" he said. "The writing."

"Fine," I said. "How's it going? The painting."

"Fine," he said. He had nudged over a pile of papers and was sitting on the edge of the desk, the material of his voluminous crotch draped over the corner like a muslin throw.

I took a sip of the tea.

"What you writing about?" he said.

I didn't like talking about my writing. It wasn't a superstitious thing. It was just I found it difficult to put into words what I had put into words.

"Gays fancying straights," I said.

"Oh," he said. "I just fancy who I fancy."

"Right," I said.

"If you see someone," he said, scratching his left armpit with his disfigured hand, "you don't think of their sexuality. You just think if you like them. Or not."

"I know," I said.

"Oh well," said Andy, "I better get on."

I watched Andy leave. The straight exits. If what I had said in my article was true then I should be in love with Andy. In Romantic Love with Andy. My heart should beat when he entered the room, I should glimpse sunlight in his hair on the darkest of nights. I should thrill at his closeness, die at his parting, dream of his skin, his eyes, his slender nose.

I should love Andy because he could never love me.

But I didn't. I didn't do any of those things. I didn't even want to fuck him.

Andy the straight and me the gay man would never be an item.

Because I'm a bastard. People told me. I tell myself.

I don't want commitment, I just want an easy life. Because of my past.

I worked for one more hour. I finished my rough draft and I saved it to disc. I would look at it again tomorrow and then I would e-mail it to my agent. No doubt she would have another assignment for me, another piece that required the hand of a pink specialist, something else I didn't believe in. But as far as today was concerned, the day was over.

I got up to go to the bathroom.

Andy was kneeling on the floor between the bath and the toilet, bum in the air, brush in hand. He was at work on a skirting board applying a deep purple gloss. As far as I could see he hadn't touched the walls. Not yet.

"I need to go to the toilet," I said.

"Go ahead," said Andy not even turning around, dipping his brush in the open pot of paint at his side.

Go ahead. Go ahead. I was that boy in the hotel room. My life was that good, that splendid. And seeing Andy's wriggling bum in the air I had suddenly had an idea. I had done some work and now I wanted to relax.

"Andy?" I said, urine hitting water.

"Yes?" he said, shuffling to the left to start a new section.

"You fancy getting a video this afternoon?" I said. "Now."

"I'm painting."

"You can paint tomorrow." I said. "Go on. Please."

I knew that he would. I knew that he would agree. I had been practising my please, studying Nicholas, watching his face as he said it. I had noticed how he started off gently and then emphasised the sibilant of the s turning it into a winning smile.

"OK," Andy said. He looked around over his shoulder, "But two conditions."

"What's that?" I said. I pulled up my zip.

"Firstly," said Andy, "next time you have a piss, you try not to splash me."

"Sorry," I said.

"And secondly," he said, "you help me tomorrow. Paint."

"Fine," I said. "You can admire my strokes."

"Right," said Andy. He put the brush down and stood. "It's a deal. Video it is."

"Get changed then," I said. "We'll go to the video shop."

"Changed," said Andy, holding out his baggy arms. "I am changed."

We watched our video, we ate, we watched another video, we drank beer and then we slept. Each in our room. Not together. You have to be careful with the first person plural, with we, people jump to the wrong conclusions. Like when you say you have a lodger.

The next day, in the end, we didn't paint. It took me longer than I expected to finish my article, to write a new covering letter for yet another publisher and then at lunch-time Andy got a phone call from his father. His help hadn't turned up and he didn't have any food. So Andy went shopping for him.

While Andy was out I called a friend. We had sex in the kitchen, on the stairs, in my room. Then I told him to leave. I told him I had an appointment with my psychiatrist. I wanted him out of the house before Andy was back.

I was behaving like a teenager deceiving his parents, a young Muslim appearing devout but in fact without a thought of a mosque in his head. Andy wouldn't care what I got up to and yet somehow subconsciously I was keeping my sex life secret, out from under his nose.

And perhaps he was doing the same with his. Perhaps.

Then it was Thursday. Time was flying by. As it so often does. Except when you want it to.

Right now I didn't want it do, I didn't want time to fly. Because each day that passed was another day closer to Nicholas and Julie's departure. They were on my mind a lot, so much so that I still hadn't questioned Andy about the previous weekend, about where he had been and what had happened to his face.

Maybe it was none of my business. And maybe I was scared. Scared that I cared.

On Thursday Andy and I promised ourselves we would get up early and do the whole job in one day, the decorator's equivalent of a purple patch. So when my alarm went at eight o'clock I wasn't surprised. I wasn't surprised but I wasn't happy. I pulled aside the duvet, pulled on underpants and a T-shirt and went down to make some tea. There was no sign of Andy, only two empty bottles on the draining-board from the red wine we had drunk the night before. We had spent the evening watching Jean-Claude Van Damme films. Andy liked the bullets, the explosions. I liked Van Damme's body, the fact that he could do the splits.

I poured hot water into two cups, mashed two tea bags and added two splashes of milk. I took a sip from one cup and carried the other one back upstairs.

I knocked on Andy's door. No answer.

I knocked again and went in.

Andy was lying on his right side with one bare arm sticking out of the duvet. And something was very strange. It wasn't that Andy wasn't snoring. It wasn't that his short blond hair was sticking up. It wasn't even that there was the open case of the Vengaboys' first album on his bedside table. Those things were all normal. What was strange was that Andy was sucking his thumb. He was sucking the thumb of his left hand, the hand with the missing index finger, so in fact he wasn't only sucking his thumb, he was sucking his knuckle too. He looked like a little boy.

"Andy!" I said.

He didn't stir.

I put down his tea and gently shook his shoulder.

The thumb flew out of his mouth and he sat bolt upright with his eyes wide open, his mouth wide open as if about to let out a scream. It was a look of terror if ever I've seen one.

"Andy," I said, "I brought you tea."

"Thanks," he said, breathing out and twisting to grab the cup.

"You were having a nightmare," I said.

"No," he said. "I'm OK. Fine. Thanks for the tea." He grinned. "Time to get started. Painting."

He took one sip from the cup and then he was climbing out of bed. He yawned, stretched, scratched and bent to pick up his boiler suit. It was neatly folded on the 1991 'vik-ter chair.

He put in his legs, put in his arms, buttoned up the front. He put on his shoes. One minute. He was ready.

This, no doubt, was his routine every day. One minute and ready. One minute and nightmare forgotten, buried at the back of the mind.

He looked at me.

"I've got something for you," he said.

"Oh yes," I said.

"Yes."

Andy opened a drawer and pulled out another one of the circus tent-like boiler suits. It looked exactly the same as the one he was wearing. It had the same paint marks, the same abundance of material at the crotch. And I had thought his was an original. I had thought such frippery was a one-off, such foliate, floriate patterns were uncopyable. I had been wrong.

"Thanks," I said. I held it at arm's length.

"I brought them from my father's," said Andy. "He used to wear them to work."

"Right," I said, slipping in a leg. "He was a painter and decorator?"

"No," said Andy. "He worked in the city."

Good one Andy. Not even a second's pause. You are on form this morning.

"Perfect," said Andy. "Fits like a treat."

Haha.

"Go and get your tea," said Andy, "and I'll meet you in the bathroom."

I could see there was going to be no messing around, no sitting at the breakfast bar for hours on end, gearing ourselves up, contemplating the work ahead over cups of coffee.

"Hurry up," said Andy.

"Yes boss," I said.

"Not boss," said Andy, "sir will do."

I didn't say anything, I just left the room. I went down the stairs and got my tea and when I got back Andy was waiting in the bathroom with a brush.

"You can do the walls," he said. "I'll work on the skirting-boards. You can follow me round."

"Right," I said. I was going to say sir but I didn't.

We started to work.

You would think that being stuck in a room together all day would give us chance to speak to each other. You would think it would allow me space and time to ask Andy naturally, in the course of conversation, where he had gone for two days, what had happened to his face and who he had killed. You would think that away from the distraction of the television that all of the above would have been possible.

It would have been possible but it didn't happen. For two reasons.

The first reason was that part of me didn't want to know. Although I had worried about Andy, had wondered what had happened to him, Andy's beauty was in his low-maintenance. In spite of all that had gone on this was still what I thought of him. Andy was easy and was becoming more and more easy even as his problems grew. Our growing closeness was indirectly proportional to the obvious amount I didn't know about him. He could sit on the toilet and talk to me about decorating, I could go to the toilet and ask him about videos and always, always in the evening we could sit side by side and devour television, hour after hour of family entertainment. But I still had no clue what went on in his head, what was going on in his life.

And look at today. We were painting a bathroom, from top to bottom. Decorating, I had read in an article on stress, was one of the most stressful things a couple could do together. It followed closely behind losing a loved one, divorce and going on holiday. And we were as happy as two pigs on cheap day-returns to Trufflesville. Our conversation never became more contentious than "Do you want a cup of tea?", "Could you pass me that mug, pot, brush, etc?" or, "You're doing a good job, nice work," and so on.

So I didn't feel it appropriate to ask Andy about murder, GBH or mysterious disappearances.

The second reason we didn't delve into each other's inner secrets was music. After we had been at work for ten minutes Andy said why didn't he put on some music. I said this was a great idea so Andy had gone back into his bedroom to find an album. I had heard him rattling in one of his plastic boxes and then the sound of the CD tray sliding out.

The music started.

Geri Halliwell. He had chosen the Geri Halliwell album.

Now I like Geri Halliwell, I love her. But her music is not conducive to serious debate. I could not slip easily from the chorus of 'Lift Me Up' to a question concerning severe bruising. 'Mi Chica Latina' and manslaughter were of a different key completely.

So while Andy and I had a great morning, while we managed to paint a good half of the interior, I got no nearer to Andy's problems.

I should have done.

At one o'clock we stopped for lunch. I made us sandwiches, tuna, mayonnaise, sweetcorn in wedges of yesterday-fresh bread. Andy ate his standing up. He said that he didn't want us to get lazy, to drop off in front of daytime telly and as soon as he had finished eating, he made two more cups of tea and was on my back. Not literally.

"Come on," he said a cup in each hand. "Upstairs."

Give him a piccolo and he'd have been the Pied Piper of

Hamelin. I was no rat, but I followed. It wasn't that I was putty in Andy's hands. It was just that it was nice to be busy, to be doing real work. It was nice to see an immediate result to my industry. I felt like I did when I had done my garden. My hands had been sore, my back had ached but the garden had looked great. And I had done it. So I went back upstairs but not into the bathroom.

First I had a more important task. The CD needed changing and it was my turn to choose. I looked along the rows of Andy's collection. Barbra Streisand. Too torchy. Bette Midler. Too brassy. The Rolling Stones. Too rock-'n'-roll. And then I saw it. The distinctive blue cover. It couldn't be. Eagerly I pulled out the case. It was. I opened it up, flipped over the inner plastic leaf and took out disc two. I slipped it in the CD player.

Queer as Folk. Series one. In the mix.

It started with 'I Am What I Am'. That was always a good place to start anything.

I went back into the bathroom and back to work.

Although Andy was only doing the skirting-boards, the gloss work, I was catching him up. I had a bigger brush and I moved it in long parabolic sweeps, coating acres of wall. My job was easy whereas Andy's was fiddly, mostly on the floor, in awkward corners. He had been stalled for ages by the pipes of the radiator, the radiator itself. Then, that completed, there had only been half a metre of board before he got to the airing cupboard. I was only inches behind him and getting ever nearer.

Just as Andy reached the bathroom door I caught him up, was working directly above his crouched form. His bum was still wiggling in the air, to the left and the right and I couldn't resist such an easy target, such an opportunity. I nudged his bottom with my big toe, knocking Andy to one side.

"Hey!" he said. "Watch out."

"Come on then slowcoach," I said. "You're holding up a professional at work."

"A professional?" he said. He looked up at me over his shoulder. "You could stick that brush up a horse's arse, take it for a walk around the room and it would do just as good a job."

"Charming," I said.

And then I started it. I have to admit, everything that followed was my fault.

It was childish, it was immature but I did it. I did it to the sound of Hannah Jones singing 'Young Hearts Run Free'. I blame the music, it put me in the mood, it made me giddy. As I was dipping my brush in the lighter purple pot that now stood next to Andy's darker shade, deliberately I didn't wipe off the viscous excess that clung to the hairs. And then as I was reaching up to stroke paint onto the wall, equally deliberately, I let a few drops fall. With a spatter they landed on Andy's head. Four purple dots.

"Hey!" he said. He patted his head with his hand and looked at the resultant imprint.

"Sorry," I said. "Accident."

Andy didn't say anything. Not one word. He stood, bent over the sink and spurted water over his head. He shook himself dry and then returned to work.

That morning I hadn't put on shoes. I had got dressed in Andy's room, pulling on the boiler suit over my underpants and T-shirt and I hadn't added anything else. So I should have expected what happened next, should have been aware of my Achilles heel. I should have known what was on the cards. But I didn't.

As I was reaching up to a high spot, rubricating with purple, I felt a tickling on my foot. I imagined a hairy spider, the brush of a lover's long hair. I looked down.

Thank you Andy.

Adidas has three stripes, Nike has a single white tick, DCshoeCoUSA an interlocking D and C. I had none of these. I had a single purple line running along the base of my toes.

"Nice," I said.

"That's OK," said Andy. "Suits you."

"Thank you," I said.

We went back to work, Bianca singing 'Crush' in the background, Andy still on his knees, me waiting for an opportunity for revenge.

I had never thought Andy was stupid. I had never believed he was dumb, thick or dense. But he didn't see what was coming, he didn't even take precautions. He wasn't on guard. At all.

"I need a piss," he said. He stood up.

I imagined it was part of the game, that he was going to do something terrible to me, mark me for life, but no, he was walking over to the toilet.

The fly on Andy's boiler suit at some point in its long history had broken, so relieving himself was a more protracted affair than a simple parting of metal teeth, a pulling out of flesh. The only way Andy could gain access to his nether regions was through an unbuttoning of the whole top half of the garment.

Andy accomplished this without a glance back at me, without caution and was now pulling out his arms, pulling down the mountains of material to waist height, stretching the elastic at the top of his underpants.

I heard the distinctive sound of him going to the toilet.

He didn't suspect a thing. There was not a thought in his head of the senatorial stripe on my foot.

In the bedroom Cinnamon was singing 'Showin' Out'.

I picked up the paint brush, I dipped it in the can. I would have to be quick. We had drunk a lot of tea but not that much.

In comedy films, war movies, *EastEnders*, when somebody sneaks up on someone to deliver the killer blow, the *coup de grâce*, they do it in sublime slow motion, taking delicate little pecks at steps. That's not how it works at all, not in reality. I had once had sex with an SAS soldier. He had told me that the important element of surprise was that you had to do it quickly, with celerity. Don't give your enemy time to know you are there. I believed him and for the rest of the evening every time he moved one of his powerful arms, twisted a foot I expected a deadly chop. When he had walked into the room brushing his teeth I had nearly had a heart attack. So many rapid movements.

But he had been right. If you want to surprise someone, do it fast.

Paintbrush in hand I took two long strides and I was behind Andy. He jiggled his hips as he began to shake off. It didn't seem as if he had noticed me.

I transferred the paintbrush to my left hand and in one movement with my right I gripped all the material of Andy's boiler suit and underpants and pulled down, yanking with all my might.

Andy gave a shout of surprise and started to twirl around.

Whiter than white flesh of bum was revealed, skin snowier than any catamite's cheeks and Andy began to struggle. Speed was of the essence, now was no time to be admiring globate orbs, curvaceous buttocks. So while still clutching the material in my right hand, twisting it around my fist to fix Andy in prime position, with my left hand I performed one deft stroke of the wide brush.

Picasso could not have been more pleased with his work, Van Gogh would not have turned a deaf ear. I had produced a perfect purple line right down the centre of Andy's arse.

A most beautiful of skid marks.

We both stopped dead and for a second just looked at each other.

"Nice bum," I said. "Suits you."

Andy didn't answer. He didn't say anything, he only grinned.

It wasn't his usual childish grin, his grin of pleasure expected, a special reward received. It was the grin of a Hollywood bad guy, the kind of bad guy that is always played by a British actor. Think Alan Rickman in *Die Hard*, think Jeremy Irons in *Die Hard with a Vengeance*, think Terence Stamp in *Superman*. It was a grin that was insidious, leery, a grin that said I am going to get you. And then rule the world.

With a pounce Andy was on me and it was my turn to be caught by surprise. I wouldn't ever have said that Andy was strong. I would never have asked him to pick up the Yellow Pages and the phone book, not at the same time. Oh no. But strong he was. What I had seen as the skinniness of poverty was in fact the muscularity of poverty. Andy was like one of those stick-limbed Indian men who perform tricks in the street, perform feats of amazing strength. They lift old fat ladies and balance them on their thumbs, they break piles of red bricks with a single flick of the wrist, they bend forks with their eyebrows.

Andy's grip was as strong as that, almost superhuman, almost superIndian showman. He had me round the biceps and with a twist of his foot behind my ankle I was toppling over, falling on my back. I landed with a thump with Andy on top of me, on my chest, his knees pinning down my arms, immobilising me.

"Andy! No!" I shouted. And I was laughing, laughing like a child engaged in a pillow fight, gleefully, freely. "I'm sorry, I'm sorry."

"It's payback time," said Andy. "No one paints my bum and gets away with it."

It was a line Mel Gibson, Bruce Willis would die for.

"Andy," I said. "Please."

Andy didn't answer, but reached over for his brush. And while he did this, expertly he maintained the pressure on my arms. I really couldn't move.

"Now," he said carefully, "if you struggle then I will paint your whole face. Understand?"

I nodded. I understood.

"You painted me, so I paint you. Fair?"

I nodded again. The brush was hovering over my face.

In the bedroom Shirley Lewis was singing 'Armed and Extremely Dangerous'. She wasn't wrong.

"Right," said Andy.

I kept my head still, kept my eyes closed.

I felt Andy do two little strokes, felt a tickling under my nose and then nothing more. Nothing more. I opened my eyes.

"What have you done?" I said.

Andy got off of me, stood up and stood back to admire his work. At first his lips just twitched up at the sides, then I saw teeth and then he put his hand over his mouth and he was laughing, laughing.

"What?" I said.

Andy had dropped the paintbrush and had doubled up, clutching himself. I realised I had never heard Andy laugh, not really, not completely like this. Beneath his bruising his face had gone red and he was gasping for breath. He was pointing at me.

"What?" I said.

"Look at you," he managed.

And now I did turn and look in the mirror.

Oh my God!

Sometimes it is the little gesture that can outdo the grand one, the pithy comment that is more effective than the diatribe. Whereas the stripe on Andy's bum was pure Carry On, what Andy had done to me was Monty Python. It was his genius compared to my slapstick.

On my face Andy had drawn a very small pencil moustache, curled up at the ends.

I looked like Dick van Dyke in any number of Disney movies, I looked like a suitor to one of the sisters in *The House of Eliott*. I looked like an idiot.

Downstairs, there was a knock at the front door.

I looked at Andy, he looked at me. We went quiet, guiltily quiet. We were like two school kids caught with a deck of naughty playing cards.

"It's your house," he said wiping his eyes.

It was, it was my house. I glanced at myself in the mirror.

There was another knock, louder more insistent.

"Answer it," said Andy. "You look nice. Lovely. You suit facial hair."

Like missed phone calls I hated missed callers. It was the kind of thing I would dwell on, wonder who it was, might have been. With another look at Andy I headed down the stairs and answered the door.

I recognised the man immediately. I had seen him once before. He was big, bald and blocking my door. He was the man who had come looking for Andy the previous weekend, the man I had completely forgotten to tell Andy about.

"Is Andy in?" he said.

I should have lied, I would have lied if only at that moment Andy hadn't shouted down the stairs, "Who is it Honza?"

The bald face in front of me broke into a grin. It was the same grin I had so recently seen on Andy's face. The man that wants to take over the world. Only this guy looked like he meant it.

Andy crashed in the hallway. I turned at the sound and saw Andy as Andy saw the man. I saw him go pale. I had never seen anyone go pale. I thought it was just an expression.

"Hello Andy," said the man. "You did well on Friday. Very well. It's time to go again."

"Right," said Andy. "OK."

He came walking towards the door, zombie-like. He was still wearing his boiler suit, he still had smudges of purple paint in his hair. It was the most colourful thing about him, his face was deathly. As he passed me he squeezed my arm.

"I don't think I'll be back tonight Honza," he said. "Or Friday."

Andy's voice was lifeless, flat and as the big man put an arm around his shoulders I wanted to grab Andy and pull him back, say that he wasn't allowed to go, say he had to stay with me. I wanted to say I would protect him from the trouble whatever it was. I wanted to say that I would try.

But I didn't, I only watched as he crossed the road and opened the passenger door of the old black BMW. He didn't look back, he didn't turn to wave goodbye and then he was gone, the car roaring up the street.

I closed the door.

It was happening again.

Fourteen

"Where's Andy?" shouted Nicholas pushing past me.

"He's not here," I said, but to unlistening ears. Nicholas had already gone into the lounge.

"Your lodger's definitely a hit with him," said Julie. "You sure he's not a lodger lodger?"

"Yes," I said.

It was Friday evening, six o'clock and Julie was on my doorstep. She was as on time as ever, as dressed to kill as ever. She had on even fewer clothes than usual. If she'd had a bright light behind her, put her arms in the air and wiggled her hips she would have looked like one of the curvy silhouettes that appear at the start of every Bond film. If I'd have had the Broccoli family's phone number I would have been on to them directly. "I've got just the girl for you," I would have said and then, perhaps, perhaps Julie wouldn't go to London and become an erotic dancer. I was clutching at straws.

Nicholas's head now reappeared around the lounge door.

"Uncle," he said, "where's Andy?"

Where's Andy? Good question.

It was a question I had been trying both to answer and not to answer ever since Andy had left with the goon in black, the hulk in a suit. After he had been whisked away I had gone back upstairs to scrub off my purple moustache, and just seeing the paint equipment and the scene of our recent fun had made me sad. I had gone to the off licence and spent the evening getting drunk, downing glass after glass of red wine. I wished I had remembered to tell Andy about his visitor and then maybe he would have confessed all, told me the trouble he was in. But I hadn't. So there was no use crying over spilt milk, splashed paint.

During the day on Friday I had finished off the bathroom by myself. I had put music on loud in Andy's room, pop beats, and worked off my hangover. I had wanted to keep myself busy, to surround myself with sound so I didn't have to think. It wasn't that I missed Andy, or was pining for him, I just felt that somehow I had let him down. I didn't like letting people down.

"Uncle?" said Nicholas again. He was now standing next to me and had wrapped his arms around my knees. "Where's Andy?"

"Um..." I said. "He's gone to see his daddy."

"Oh," said Nicholas.

I could see him thinking, I knew that he was going to ask a question about daddies, about where his own daddy was, but then Julie interrupted.

"Honza," she said, "can I come in, for a chat?"

"Course," I said. I moved aside and picked Nicholas up under the armpits. I followed Julie into the lounge.

Julie wanted a chat. It was time to make her feel not disgusting, perverted, ashamed of herself. It was time to be the brother I hadn't been.

I tipped the pieces of Nicholas's train set onto the floor to keep him quiet and then I made me and Julie a cup of tea. We sat side by side at the breakfast bar. Julie was sitting on the stool where Andy usually sat, where he drank his tea, ate his toast.

"So..." said Julie.

"So..." I said.

Julie wasn't looking at me, she was looking at Nicholas on the floor. Nicholas was deep in concentration building a track, muttering under his breath.

"He likes it here," she said.

I shrugged. Of course he did. I liked him here. He could be a permanent fixture any day. Julie knew that.

"I just wanted to tell you my plans," said Julie. "About London."

"He thinks he's going to Condom."

Julie put her hand over her mouth and giggled. It was nice to see her giggle.

"Oh my God," she said, "he said that to you too. I once blew up a whole box of condoms into balloons and now he thinks he's going to some fantasy land full of balloons."

"And ducks."

"What?"

"Long story," I said.

"Anyway," said Julie, "I wanted to let you know, we're leaving on Sunday. So I'll come and pick him up on Sunday morning around eleven. OK?"

"Fine," I said.

Fine. What was I saying?

When I was younger I had travelled around the USA on the Greyhound buses. Somehow, one day, I had ended up in Milwaukee, Wisconsin, home of beer, cheese and obese Americans. While I was ambling around the modern city centre, killing time, it had started raining, pouring down, and with nothing better to do, nowhere better to go I had slipped into an art museum.

I soon discovered that it wasn't an art museum with paintings, with a fine collection of works of the Renaissance, Art Deco styling, Picasso's blue period. No, it was a museum with installations. I was intrigued, I had never seen anything like it. There were whole rooms filled with angle-mounted television screens, metal pipes, videos showing microscopically different footage slightly out of synch. I read the idiot cards and learned that the artists wanted to say something about war, about society, about the relation of man to the media.

And then I went downstairs to the basement. Down here the lighting was more subdued, more intimate, the installations smaller, less elaborate. And there wasn't a single other person around. I was all alone. Passing one exhibit, another, I found myself in a darkened room and I paused to allow my eyes to adjust. I wasn't sure if I had wandered into an out-of-use storeroom or if this was part of the collection. Then, as my pupils widened I saw that there was something in the room. Dead in the centre was a solitary wooden chair, high-backed and with thick wooden arms. And resting on one of these arms, incongruous, was a set of headphones. They were big chunky headphones with foam ear-pieces that covered the whole of your ears.

I had no choice, I had to sit down.

As soon as my bum touched the planking of the seat a screen flicked on in front of me. I could see now that there was a television positioned exactly in the centre of the wall, exactly opposite the chair. It wasn't a flashy flat-screened, super-duper tv like upstairs. This television was old, from the fifties, housed in a wooden cabinet. And the image on the screen was strange. It was an image of the room I was in. The same blank walls, the same chair dead in the centre, the same set of headphones.

I picked them up and put them on.

My ears were filled with the sound of someone breathing. In and out. In and out.

And my eyes were fixed firmly on the tv in front of me.

I don't know how long I sat like that, watching the static image of the place where I was, but wasn't. The chair on the screen remained empty. But the breathing continued and my breathing adapted and we were breathing together like two twins in a womb.

And then it happened.

Oh my God.

On the tv screen in the doorway behind the chair, the doorway behind me, appeared a man. It all happened so fast. It was that surprise thing again. Speed, celerity. The man was dressed in black, was wearing a black balaclava I think and I would have turned around to see if he was really behind me, was really in the doorway and not just part of the programme but I didn't have time.

The man rushed into the room. Stopped behind the chair and in a single movement raised what I could now see he was holding in his hands.

It was a huge mallet.

He brought the mallet down with a crash on the chair, smashing it to smithereens.

The breathing stopped, the picture went dead.

And I had nearly had a heart attack.

I left that place and caught the first bus to sunny California.

So when I answered fine to Julie, what I wanted to say was that I felt like I had that day, that someone had just hit me over the head with a large hammer. I felt like I needed a long holiday in San Francisco.

"I'll write down the address for you," said Julie. "So you can get in touch."

"Fine," I said again. I passed her a piece of paper.

I watched as she wrote and past her I watched Nicholas on the floor. He had completed a simple oval and was sitting in the centre of it pushing a train around and around, saying choo choo and making the noises of wheels on tracks.

"There," said Julie, pushing the paper towards me.

"Thanks," I said. I picked up the paper and looked at it. "I can come and visit?"

"Sure," said Julie. "We're friends, right? Just give me time to get settled."

"OK," I said. "Friends."

It was all so civilised. There was no begging, no pleading. I didn't ask Julie to stay, tell her she was making a mistake. I'd done that already. But seeing the address, the house number, the street name it hit me that she was really going. She was really going to London.

In my family I had always been the one to do the going, the one saying goodbye and leaving on a jet plane. I'd always somehow assumed that my mum and my sister would be there when I got back. They had been my stability. And now that the boot was on the other foot I wondered if they had felt this sense of loss when I had gone. This jealousy.

"Right then," said Julie. "I'd better be off. I've got an appointment."

"OK," I said.

"Bye Nicholas."

"Bye mummy."

"Be good."

"Yes mummy."

"Love you."

"Love you too mummy."

And she was gone. Gone to do what she did, what she would do with or without my approbation.

"Uncle," said Nicholas, looking up from the centre of the track barely seconds after the door had closed, "can we get a video?"

He didn't say please. Perhaps he sensed that he didn't need to, that right then I would have given him anything he wished for, anything in the world if I could.

"Sure," I said. "Let's go."

And we went, a short walk of fifty metres. Me walking in a straight line, directly. Nicholas spinning around in my orbit, arms out, one moment behind, one moment in front, looping my path in the dizziness of his youth.

"Hello!" screamed Nicholas running past the counter, going straight, as he always did, to the children's section.

"Hello Nicholas," said John, the store manager, to Nicholas's back and he smiled at me, indulgent, sincere.

When you have a kid people are friendly to you. They are

patient and understanding while you try to extricate money and hold a tiny hand at the same time. They help you off buses, let you in front of them in queues, don't bang trolleys into your ankles in supermarkets.

That wasn't something I would miss about not having Nicholas however, other people's reactions. I would miss Nicholas himself, his smile, the smell of his breath, him tugging my hair in the morning, wrapping himself around me, looking at me from under his eyebrows and grinning when he knew he had done something wrong. Him saying "Uncle". Him saying "Please".

"Uncle!" said Nicholas, appearing in an aisle, dragging a video case behind him. "Can we have this one?"

I didn't think *Pulp Fiction* was suitable, not for a four-year-old, so I took his hand and we went back to shelves and then went home.

That evening I began to understand why I liked Andy so much, why he had fitted so easily into my life. Andy was just a bigger version of Nicholas. It hit me while we were watching the video, watching *101 Dalmatians*. Nicholas was sitting where Andy usually sat, his legs were apart and his glass of Coke was balanced in the V of his crotch. There was a big bag of Maltesers between us.

"I don't like Cruella de Vil," said Nicholas.

"No," I said.

"She's cruel."

"Yes," I said.

"Nice doggie," said Nicholas and he popped a Malteser in his mouth. "Uncle, I'm going to the toilet."

"Right," I said, "I'll pause it for you."

I could have had the same conversation with Andy, the same easy phrasing, the same saying nothing but saying everything. I often felt that most speech was a waste of words, people trying to fill awkward moments, perceived pauses. But Andy and I had never had an awkward moment, I had never felt that I should say something just to fill a gap. And that was amazing for a man who dreamt of living with someone deaf, who guarded his privacy.

But that was it, Andy never invaded my privacy, encroached on my space. Somehow we got along without getting along. I couldn't pinpoint a single conversation we'd had when either of us had strung more than ten words together. Maybe that just made us shallow. But I didn't think

"Uncle?" said Nicholas.

His eyes were on the screen. Perdita was giving birth to puppies. Mr Darling was pacing the room. Pongo, Perdita's dog boyfriend was pacing the room and tiny spotted newly-borns kept coming. One, two, three...

I knew what Nicholas was going to say. This was the boy who could remember everything, the boy who one night had had me searching for a horsey, a small blue plastic horsey he swore he had and was at my house. And he was right. I had found it in a cupboard inside an old shoe where Nicholas had said it would be. It was a toy he had got in a Christmas cracker more than a year earlier.

Nicholas was the boy with the memory of an elephant. And on the screen the puppies kept coming.

"Uncle," said Nicholas, "when am I getting my doggie?"

He hadn't forgotten Andy's promise.

I didn't want to let him down.

"Next time you come here," I said, "then you shall have a doggie? OK?"

"OK," said Nicholas, matter of fact. "Shhh now uncle, I'm watching the film."

Waking on Saturday morning I felt my potential to be like one of those fathers, the estranged partners of divorce or separation, who only get to see their offspring once a month, longer in the holidays if they're lucky. It is so rare that these fathers get to spend time with their progeny that they overdo it. They want the day to be so indelibly marked in the young one's mind that they go over the top. They organise ice-skating dressed as a favourite Disney character, they arrange firework displays lighting up the midnight sky, they plan trips to zoos with special passes to feed dangerous wildlife.

What these fathers never learn is that something so co-ordinated always go wrong, something so anticipated is always a let down. They discover that their much-loved distant-living child no longer loves Mickey Mouse but would rather glide across the ice dressed as a Pokémon. They curse themselves for not checking the forecast as the firework show turns out to be damp squib due to an unseasonal sub-tropical storm on the commuter belt of London. And finally their eyes are opened to the fact that a lion and a five-year-old boy are always a heady mixture. And bloody.

Felicity, as any good Buddhist will tell you, is found through the abandonment of worldly pleasures. Reaching a state of nirvana is achieved by meditating on nothingness, clearing out your mind. Peace and happiness are on the inside.

So with Nicholas, that day, I resolved to do nothing. As little as possible.

Our last day together we would spend just being.

We would reach a state of pure essence. Togetherness on a higher plane.

And the day started with Nicholas wetting the bed.

"Sorry uncle," he said, shaking me awake, holding the damp patch of his pyjamas away from himself.

"Never mind," I said.

I climbed out from under the duvet and picked Nicholas up, tossing him on his back further down the bed, away from the soaking sheet. I pulled off his sodden trousers and flung them dramatically over my shoulder. I tickled his sides and he giggled and leapt up and ran half-naked around the room shouting over and over that I couldn't catch him.

I pretended I couldn't until eventually I gave in. Nicholas was the winner, the champion, the best boy in the whole world. I found him some fresh underpants and trousers and we went down to breakfast.

I didn't check Andy's room on the way down. I knew he wouldn't be back.

"What are we doing today?" Nicholas asked. He was sitting at the breakfast bar.

"Nothing," I said.

"Oh," he said, "What's nothing?"

"It's something and everything," I said. "Not this and not that. Nothing is just what you want it to be. And not."

"Right," said Nicholas. He put the index finger of his left hand to the corner of his lips and put his head on one side. He was thinking. "So," he said, slowly, "I can have ice cream for breakfast then?"

"Sure," I said.

And he did. We did. He had chocolate and I had vanilla, big bowls full which we didn't wash up afterwards, we just licked them clean with our tongues.

Doing nothing meant a lot of things. A lot of not things. It meant that I didn't have to change out of the underpants and T-shirt I had slept in. It meant that I didn't have to brush my hair, my teeth, have a shower. It meant that Nicholas and I could sneak out to the shop in horrendous old jogging pants and flip-flops and buy two big bags of Maltesers and come home and close the shutters, close out the world outside. It meant that we could pull the cushions off of the sofa and the chairs and line them up on the floor and that we could lie there, arms and legs tangled and watch *101 Dalmatians* again even though we had only seen it the night before. It meant that we didn't care about anything, anybody but ourselves.

So when *101 Dalmatians* finished and Nicholas said could we get another video I said of course we could. We could even go out in our flip-flops again.

"Hooray!" he said.

This time we chose *The Rescuers* and a bottle of Coke. We were both tired of Maltesers, chocolate altogether, and Nicholas said he wanted some food, real food. I asked if pizza was real food and Nicholas said it was, it was the most real food he could think of right then so I ordered it by telephone and we put on the video.

We fast forwarded through the trailers because on this day of nothing we didn't care for future releases, what we might see next time. We cared only for now, today. Or rather we didn't care. We just were. We were just being in a Disney Buddhist sense.

And I was all too aware, somewhere deep down that this was my last day of Elysium, Eden, Asgard, Heaven.

The film started.

Two mice, a very ladylike one and a fat clumsy one, are called on to rescue a girl, Penny, who has a large diamond hidden in her teddy and has been kidnapped by the evil Madam Medusa. Nicholas asked me, not taking his eyes off the screen, that when he went to Condom if he got into trouble, if a diamond happened to slip into one of his toys and he was kidnapped then would two mice come and rescue him. I said that he wouldn't get into trouble and if he did then I would be there, I would come and he had looked disappointed and said not even one mouse, the one with the funny accent, the plump one who made him laugh every time he bumped into something, fell over something and I said, I said...

I was saved from saying anything by a knock at the door. I paused the video and got up to answer it.

It was the pizza.

And Andy.

"Andy!" I said.

"Is that pizza?" he said, gazing at the square box. "I'm starving."

He looked starving, he looked done in, as if he hadn't slept for days. He had huge bags under his eyes, stubble on his chin, his jaw. But the swelling on his face had subsided and there was no evidence of a new attack, less evidence of the old one. His bruises had evened out and spread now so that his whole face had a pale purple gleam. If he'd have stood next to the newly-painted bathroom wall dressed in a plum suit I wouldn't have been able to see him.

I paid the pizza man and we went inside.

"Andy!" screamed Nicholas. "Pizza!" And he ran around and around the makeshift bed we had made on the floor until Andy grabbed him and blew a raspberry on his forehead.

"Don't I get a kiss?" said Andy. He looked at Nicholas and Nicholas looked at him and at the same time they both pulled a face, said, "yuck" and both started running around the room, first Nicholas chasing Andy and then Andy chasing Nicholas.

I said enough and calm down and it was time to eat.

"Can we eat on the floor?" said Nicholas. "Watching *The Rescuers*?"

"Of course," I said and went in the kitchen to get some plates and tissues.

Andy followed me.

"Honza?" he said.

"Yes?"

"I have to warn you."

My heart started beating. Fast.

"What?" I said, thinking danger, thinking trouble.

"Pizza doesn't agree with me," he said. "I like it, but it gives me wind."

"Wind?" I said. This was a boy whose sphincter had a greater range than Mariah Carey's vocal cords.

"Pizza," said Andy, "makes me smell. A lot."

"Right," I said. "Thanks for telling me. And Andy?"

"Yeah?"

"I want to talk to you," I said. "I want to know what's going on. If you want to stay here."

"Oh," said Andy.

The last bit, the threat, I didn't mean. But I wanted to help. Andy was twenty-one, twenty-two next birthday as he had said. He was young and seemed younger, as if he had never lived. So I threatened him, just a bit. Threats usually work with little boys and problems are usually better shared.

I'd given Andy chance to sort out things by himself. He hadn't. Now it was my turn, my turn to be Sir Lancelot, Odysseus, Inspector Morse. It was time I got involved, time I admitted that I was already involved, that Greta Garbo and me didn't have as much in common as I liked to believe.

"Uncle!" shouted Nicholas from the living-room. "Andy! I'm hungry!"

"Later," I said to Andy.

"OK," he said. "But I warned you."

Warned me of what? Of the effect pizza had on him or what I was going to find out? I wasn't sure, but it was time to eat.

Andy and I joined Nicholas in the front room and we all sat cross-legged on the chair and sofa cushions, plates balanced on our knees and thighs, stuffing ourselves with doughy pizza, drinking gallons of fizzy Coke. While Nicholas was eating, picking out the bits of pineapple he didn't like and feeding them to an imaginary dog called Bonza who was apparently resting on the opened lid of the pizza box, he tried to explain the story of *The Rescuers* to Andy. Andy was nodding his head but he didn't seem to get it.

"So who are they rescuing?" he said. He wiped tomato sauce from his bottom lip.

Nicholas slapped his forehead in mock horror.

"Andy," he said, "for someone so old, you're not very clever."

"But who is it?" said Andy.

"They're rescuing the little girl with the diamond in her teddy."

"Oh," said Andy. "Why?"

Nicholas fell backwards pretending to choke and then I had the idea of starting the video again from the beginning, after the trailers. This was greeted by the sound of four hands clapping and two big grins.

So we watched the whole thing together lying on our cushions, surrounded by the dirty cutlery, empty glasses, clothed in our clothes from the day before, the days before and nobody spoke, nobody moved except for a gradual gravitation towards the centre of the mound. By the end of the film we were a tangle of bodies, arms, legs, our heads leaning on shoulders not our own. And if any of us could have chosen one moment, if God had said that was what heaven was, a choice of a single moment to be replayed over and over again for all eternity, then I believe we all would have chosen that one, a perpetual muddled huddle stuck in front of a rodent Disney movie, mousey antics flickering before our eyes, our brains free and somewhere in the region that a Buddhist would call bliss.

Bath time.

Andy was nominated by Nicholas to be the chief washer and I watched them bound up the stairs together, Nicholas first, Andy chasing. After I heard the water start and Nicholas say, "not too hot, no" as he always did, I slipped out to buy some wine. Wine, I believed was needed if Andy and I were going to have that talk, that chat about what was going on. And then when I was back from the off licence I listened for the splashes, the giggling and water noises, just checking everything was all right before I started to tidy the lounge.

I tried not to think that next week there would be no more mess, no more pizzas on the floor. I tried not to think that the very next day Nicholas would be going to London. I tried but I did think it and I felt sad. I told myself to snap out of it. It wasn't over until the fat lady sang. And at that moment from upstairs, as if on cue, came the sound of Andy and Nicholas singing 'Bag it Up' at the tops of their voices. I wasn't worried. Andy, Nicholas, and Geri Halliwell all together didn't even make one plump proletarian, let alone an obese woman of the nobility, one fat lady. Putting the last of the cushions back in place I noticed the time, it was just after ten and way past Nicholas's bedtime.

I rushed up the stairs.

I wasn't one of these people who believe in dragging out the moment. I wasn't going to make Nicholas sit up all night just so we could spend the last few hours together. I wanted everything to be as normal as possible. I was the same at airports. Get off, I would say, don't hang around. Hanging around only made things worse. Hanging around, searching for the right words to say goodbye, was the emotional equivalent of a funeral, designed to make you cry, upset, think about what you had lost, were losing. And anyway, pregnant pauses usually only gave birth to tired clichés.

I stormed into the bathroom.

There was nobody there, only the emptying bath, the final wreaths of steam. I heard voices from the bedroom, my room.

I put my ear to the ajar door.

Andy was reading Nicholas a story. Reading properly. It was a story from *The House at Pooh Corner*, the one in which Pooh invents Pooh-Sticks and Eeyore gets knocked into the river. I had never heard Andy read before. He was good, very good. He did the voices of all the characters, Pooh's surprised aspirations, Piglet's squeak, Roo's childish keenness. And best of all, Eeyore's lugubrious drawl. He got them all perfectly.

I stood listening.

Eeyore has been bounced into the river by a bouncing Tigger and Rabbit asks Eeyore what he is doing as Eeyore floats by on his back, carried by the current. Andy as Eeyore says, "I'll give you three guesses, Rabbit. Digging holes in the ground? Wrong. Leaping from branch to branch of a young oak-tree? Wrong. Waiting for somebody to help me out of the river? Right. Give Rabbit time, and he'll always get the answer."

Lovely.

And so true. In the end we always get the right answer, see the obvious that has been under our nose.

I felt something stir in my stomach.

I had eaten too much pizza. I went into the toilet and closed the door.

*

"I didn't think you'd make it," I said. "Is he asleep?"

"Fast," said Andy.

Match of the Day was just starting. There was Gary Lineker's torso, the teak bookends of Alan Hansen and Trevor Brooking.

"There's your wine," I said, indicating the glass I had put by the side of the sofa.

"Cheers," said Andy. He scratched a thigh. "I'm dying for a fag." He pulled a packet out of a pocket on the side of his trousers.

Andy, I only now realised, wasn't wearing the paint-splattered boiler suit he had left the house in. He had on a pair of khaki combat pants and a long-sleeved Hilfiger fleece over a white T-shirt. It wasn't the kind of garb I had seen him in before. It seemed as if he was developing a fashion sense.

"So..." I said. I was ready, willing and able. To talk.

"So," said Andy, "do you think Manchester United will beat Bradford?"

Did I? There wasn't much doubt but that wasn't what my so meant.

"Andy?" I said.

He turned to look at me. His hair was ruffled, but not spiky. It looked like it had been brushed down to hide the gash above the eye that was still in a semi-healed state. And the rest of the face was in that same state of flux. It was the face of a champion prize-fighter a week after a particularly gruesome set of bouts. Except Andy's face wasn't mean like a boxer's was supposed to be, ideally was. Andy's face was vulnerable, hurt. Andy's expression was like Bambi's when he is learning to walk and slips on the ice.

"Can we just watch the football?" he said. He took a drag on his cigarette and a drink of his wine. "Tonight."

I was glad he had added that final noun. It suggested another time. Soon.

"Sure," I said. "Tonight."

"I'm just going for a piss," said Andy, standing. "Before they start. It's Liverpool and Newcastle."

He went upstairs quieter than a mouse, much quieter certainly than the clumsy mouse, Bernard, from *The Rescuers* and there was no crash in the hall on the way down. Not even a minor incident.

"Any score?" said Andy. He sat down.

"Not yet," I said. "No goals."

And we settled down to watch, side by side, Andy in his seat, me in mine, drinks between our legs.

In all fairness Andy had warned me about the pizza. He had told me what it did to him but I hadn't given it a second thought. For the first game he was OK. And then it started.

"Excuse me," said Andy. "Sorry."

When I was very young and my parents were still together, for a few years in a row we had holidayed on the Norfolk Broads. We hired a cruiser and spent a leisurely two weeks meandering up and down the peaceful waterways. One year, on a particularly blustery day, our one and only map and guide had been blown over the side. For several hours we had drifted listlessly not sure of where we were, where we were going.

And then we had noticed a small village beginning to rise on the left bank and in the distance the ominous looking shape of a huge factory building. Unbeknownst to us we had washed up in the region of a large turkey factory. There had been no warning signs. Not one. There should have been.

It was me who noticed the smell first. My nose was the youngest and most sensitive.

"Yuck," I said. "What's that?"

"What?" my mother said and then just as she had said it, she turned pale green and vomited projectilely over the side, scoring a direct hit on my father's martini glass which had been balanced precariously there.

The smell was appalling, disgusting. You could feel it in your lungs, behind your eyes. It was the kind of smell a stink bomb man-ufacturer would have given his left nostril to own. If Willy Wonka from *Charlie and the Chocolate Factory* had opened a bad odour fac-tory as mythical and magical as his chocolate one then surely, even with the help of a nation of Oompa Loompas, he could not have eclipsed that stink. It was as if the sweat from a million Chinese rail workers' armpits had been distilled and added to vat containing a farmyard of bad eggs, a dozen skunks' tails, a polecat's skin and the bottom, most fetid layer of a hussar's month-old latrine. It wasn't nice.

And now I was faced with that smell again.

I felt like Luke Skywalker must have done when he found out the evil Darth Vadar was, in fact, his father.

It couldn't be happening.

"Excuse me," said Andy.

I tried to ignore it, I tried to concentrate on the game. I tried to think football, goals, nice men in shorts. But it was useless. It was the fight against the Zulus without a Hollywood ending. It was the Vietnam war without Rambo. It was the Conservative party without Margaret Thatcher.

On the television Owen scored.

Next to me Andy celebrated.

"Christ Andy," I said. "Put a cork in it."

"Do you think that would work?"

"What?" I said.

"Good idea," said Andy. He was standing and walking to the kitchen.

And then it hit me.

He wouldn't would he? Surely not.

I could only watch as he moved behind the breakfast bar. Only his top half was visible. I saw him pick up the discarded cork from the wine bottle I had opened earlier. I saw him take the lid off the butter jar and smear the cork. I saw his hands disappear beneath the surface of the breakfast bar and then I heard a belt being undone, a zip being lowered. His left hand appeared again and took the cork.

Of all the stupid ideas in all the world he had to take me up on mine.

Watching his face I detected a small twitch of discomfort and then the zip was done up, the buckle was buckled and Andy came back to sit down.

I had nothing to say.

Liverpool–Newcastle finished, then it was Everton–Sunderland, Watford–Tottenham.

There was not a peep out of Andy. Not a toot.

He turned to me and grinned.

"Seems to have done the trick."

"Yes," I said. "Want some more wine? We should finish the bottle. I don't fancy re-corking it."

For the second time Andy laughed, laughed like he had done a pact with the devil, laughed like all his eternity in heaven had been swapped for this one joyous moment. And he couldn't stop laughing, was clutching his sides.

I took the glasses and went to the kitchen. I wanted to get out of the way. It wasn't that I thought the laughter infectious, I was only worried Andy was going to have a heart attack, pop his clogs, pop his cork. Now, that could have done us both an injury.

I filled our glasses. To the brim.

After *Match of the Day* Andy stood, scratched his stomach and said he was tired.

"Go to bed," I said.

"Right," he said. "Goodnight."

"Goodnight," I said.

Andy went upstairs and I picked up the empty wine glasses, took them into the kitchen, washed them up. Then, job done, I went up myself. The toilet door was closed, there was a chink of light under it.

I needed to go before I got into bed so I waited on the landing.

I waited and I waited.

"Andy?" I whispered finally, tapping gently on the door. I didn't want to wake Nicholas.

There was no answer.

"Andy?" I said again, slightly louder.

The door opened.

Andy was standing there in just his fleece and underpants. I could see his combat trousers on the floor behind him. He looked worried.

"Honza," he said. "The cork, I've lost it. It won't come out. I can feel it inside. It hurts."

"Right," I said.

Fifteen

I woke up. Someone was shaking me.

"What is it?" I said. I opened my eyes.

Nicholas was standing by my left shoulder. It was he who was shaking me.

"It's Andy," said Nicholas.

"Andy?" I said.

Then I saw Andy. He was hovering at the end of the bed. He had on the same T-shirt as the night before, the same boxer shorts. He had large circles under his eyes. His eyes were red and jumpy. He looked like he might not have slept all night.

"Honza," said Andy, "I couldn't sleep all night."

"It didn't come out?" I said. I rolled over and sat up.

"Sorry?" said Andy.

I put my finger in my mouth, in the corner of my lips and made a popping sound. Nicholas giggled and did the same thing, copying me.

"No," said Andy, "but I didn't mean that. Not only that. You said you wanted to talk to me. I've been thinking about it. For hours." He rubbed his hands down the front of his thighs and then crossed his arms. "But one condition."

"Which is?" I said. I grabbed both of Nicholas's hands in mine. He had just made his forth and fifth popping noises.

"No police."

No police. Looking at Andy again I thought he wasn't the sort of person who would even have passed the audition to be an extra on *The Bill*. He seemed too young, too innocent. I didn't think, as Humphrey Bogart once said, that his problems would amount to a hill of beans. The whole thing was probably a storm in a coffee cup. So no police was an easy promise.

"Sure," I said. "No police. But one condition."

"What's that?" said Andy.

"If there's no sign of that cork by lunch-time I take you to the hospital."

"Hospital," said Nicholas, his ears pricking up, "can I come?"

He jumped off the bed and started to run around the bedroom making noises like an ambulance. He loved hospitals. Hospitals. Police stations. Fire stations. Rubbish dumps.

"You my boy," I said, picking him up, holding him wriggling in my arms, "have to get ready. You're going to London today."

"London," said Andy. He looked at Nicholas and then looked at me. "Oh my God. I'm so sorry. I forgot. Forget about me."

"Andy," I said, manoeuvring Nicholas up onto my shoulders, "let's get this boy fed, let's hand him over to his mother and then let's sort you out. Here." I kicked Andy's bum. "And here." I tapped him on the head.

"Uncle," said Nicholas from above me, "why are you hitting the donkey?"

"Because he is a donkey," I said. "A big stupid, silly donkey."

And I ran out of the room and down the stairs with Nicholas bouncing on my back screaming for joy and clinging onto my hair and with an image of Andy's face still in my mind. The face had on it an expression that was somewhere between indignation and pleasure, anger and amusement.

In the kitchen Nicholas said that he didn't want ice cream for breakfast, not today, but could he have Weetabix. I said of course he could and I sat him on a stool. I reached up to get a bowl, to get the cereal packet.

When I turned back Andy was there. He had Nicholas on his knee and he had his arms around him. He was looking at me.

"Honza," he said, "can I have Weetabix too?"

"Sure," I said.

"And Honza?"

"Yes?"

"Do I really have to go to hospital?"

"Yes."

"But what do I tell them?"

I smiled. "We'll think of something. We'll tell them we were playing a very rough game of pin the tail on the donkey."

"Using the cork as a tail? Thanks Honza."

I shrugged and tried to look gracious. Then I noticed the time. It was ten o'clock. This meant that there was only one hour to go. One hour before Julie arrived. One hour before Nicholas left. Sometimes one hour can seem like a lifetime, when you are waiting to see a dentist, when you are waiting for a hunk who is late for a date. And sometimes the minutes go so quickly. So painfully.

London wasn't the ends of the Earth but it wasn't around the corner either, it wasn't a couple of streets away. Nicholas had been a part of my life for all of his life. He had always spent his weekends with me. Always. Our days together were sacred, special, the metre by which I ruled my life. And, more than anything, I dreaded that what had happened to Joshua would happen to me. Because Joshua had been very fond of Nicholas once, he still sent birthday cards, Christmas presents but inevitably, since I had thrown him out of the house, my house, he was no longer the fixture for Nicholas he had once been.

For the first few weeks after the departure Nicholas had asked where Joshua was, when he was coming back and then as the weeks had passed he had asked less and less until finally one day he had stopped asking all together. I didn't want to become that, the person Nicholas stopped asking about. I didn't want to become that ever. Never.

But what could I do?

I didn't know.

And in that final hour I found no answer. Weetabix was eaten, dishes were washed and then we went upstairs to collect his things, to pack them in his bag. I asked him what he wanted to take with him. To London. Nicholas hummed and hahed, put his head on one side and sweetly said me and I said no and so he said could he take one of his wooden trains. He knew that he couldn't take the whole set, no uncle, the track wouldn't fit in his bag but could he take just one engine and a carriage. He could push it across the floor. And think of here. Me.

So he said.

Nicholas didn't have any concept of space and time outside his own physical world. Things were here now or they didn't exist, not really. A person speaking on the phone was here, he or she existed. Nicholas often asked me when I called him to look at this, that. Voice and body were one, the telephone line the work of magic merging place and place. And next year, for example, had no meaning. See you next week was only something he said, copying me. Concurrently London was just a name, something his mummy had told him about. London was one location, exciting, new. My house was another location, safe, comforting. And Nicholas didn't understand that going to one was at the cost of the other.

Therefore he had no unhappiness. No sadness.

It was only me who was cracking up, breaking up. On the inside.

On the surface I was the same old uncle.

"It's mummy!" I said.

A big truck had pulled up outside, its red body blocking the light through the window. I knew as soon as I had heard the noise down the street, the descending notes of a musical klaxon, the roar of an engine that it would be Julie. It was just like her to leave in style, with drama and a tarantara.

There was a knock at the door and Nicholas flew out of my arms. I ignored my heart. My heart was telling me close the shutters, batten down the hatches, pull up the drawbridge. I went into the hall.

"Come on uncle!" shouted Nicholas.

And I was coming on, fighting my instincts.

"Hello Julie," I said, the door open.

"Hi Honza," she said to me. "You been a good boy?" she said to Nicholas.

"He has," I said.

"I have," said Nicholas.

"Very good," I said.

Julie looked at me and pulled up her mouth in a smile that wasn't a smile. She knew that today for me wasn't a day for sharing teeth, beaming joy.

"Well," she said. "We'll be off. The truck's waiting." Unnecessarily she nodded behind her over her shoulder to the waiting monster.

"Yes," I said.

"You have my address," she said. "And my phone number."

"Yes," I said.

Julie took Nicholas's bag from me and then picked up her son in her arms. Her property. Her flesh and blood.

Not mine.

"Say bye uncle."

"Bye uncle! Bye uncle!"

And then I remembered.

"Wait here," I said. I dashed up the stairs and into my room. What I had forgotten was in a small ring box in my sock drawer. I quickly retrieved it and then was crashing back into the hall, landing like Andy did.

"I got you a present," I said. "Both of you."

I opened the box and took out two matching silver chains with triangular grooved pendants dangling from them. First I fastened one around Nicholas's neck and then one around Julie's.

"They're St. Christophers," I said. "They'll protect you on your travels."

"Thanks Honza," said Julie.

"Thanks Honza," said Nicholas and giggled.

"Bye Honza," said Julie."

"Bye Honza," said Nicholas.

"Bye," I said.

I closed the door. I didn't watch them walk to the truck. I didn't watch them get in. I didn't watch the truck pull away.

And I tried not to think.

"You OK?" said Andy.

He was loitering by the breakfast bar, nursing a cup of tea, looking nervous.

OK. OK. Was I OK?

The answer to that was simple. No.

"Yes," I said. "Come on, go and get changed. We'll get that arse of yours sorted out."

"Now?" said Andy.

"Yes now," I said. "I need to see other people suffering. I need to see the terminally ill sucking for one last drag on the tube of a cigarette that has already almost killed them. I need to see fountains of blood seeping from knife-wielding haemophiliacs. I need to see the mangled remains of road traffic accidents."

"Honza," said Andy. "that's not nice."

Nice, I didn't feel nice.

"I'll be in the car in ten minutes," I said.

Andy looked at me as if he was going to say something and then he didn't and he was haring up the stairs. I listened to the shower going, I concentrated on the noise. In my head I followed the water on its journey, dripping off Andy's skinny pale body, down the plug hole, past the skeins of hair in the pipes and on and on to the sea. I filled my mind with anything, any detail in counterpoise to yesterday's nothingness.

You know what I mean.

The water stopped and then there were the sounds of footsteps across the landing. Quick. I envisaged Andy rubbing off the excess water, his naked flesh, him choosing and pulling on clothes from neatly folded piles in drawers. I saw his hand hovering by the on switch to his stereo and then move away. I saw him sit on the bed, put on socks, shoes, tie his laces, stand. I heard him cross the floor, crash down the stairs. He came into the lounge.

Andy was wearing the same clothes as the day before. His new get-up. The Hilfiger fleece and khaki combat trousers.

"Well done," I said. I stood and rattled the car keys. "Nine minutes."

"Eight and a half," said Andy and then he looked at me, hard. "Honza?" he said.

I knew what he was going to say. I could see it on his face.

"Yes, we have to," I said.

In the car Andy clicked on his seat-belt and then sat fidgeting. As I drove he tapped the dashboard, looked out of the window, showed an extraordinary interest in old women crossing the street, a group of kids kicking a squashed Coke can. And I concentrated on him concentrating on other things.

The hospital wasn't far, the Sunday lunch-time traffic sparse and soon we were pulling into the visitors' car park.

"Honza," said Andy gazing at a teenager manipulating crutches, his leg in plaster, "what do you think they'll do? You know. To get it out."

I shrugged. I was an expert only on anal insertion. I had little idea about retraction. It wouldn't have been my specialist subject on *Mastermind*. If I'd been asked a question concerning proctology on *Who Wants To Be a Millionaire?* I probably would have phoned a friend, asked the audience.

"I don't know," I said. And then added, "Perhaps they'll have a giant corkscrew. Or a doctor with small hands."

"Honza," said Andy as we came to a stop in one of the many empty spaces, "thanks."

"Don't worry," I said. I put on the handbrake. "It'll be fine."

Once inside, Andy didn't want to go up to the reception desk.

"What do I say?" he said.

"The truth," I said and pushed him forward.

So Andy started talking. The receptionist was a young nurse. She had her hair in pigtails. It was probably her first day, Andy her first client, and to be fair to her I didn't know what Andy was talking about either. He hadn't even mentioned corks yet. He was talking about pizza, fast food in general and somehow he had managed to mention the score in the Liverpool–Newcastle game. Two–one. Redknapp headed in a great goal. The nurse had begun to chew the end of her pencil and she had one hand under the desk. Maybe she was toying with the idea of pressing the security button.

"He has a cork," I said, "up his bum."

"Oh," she said. She didn't bat an eyelid. She didn't even take the pencil out of her mouth. She looked bored.

"Right up," Andy said following my lead. "I can feel it, it hurts. It won't come out."

"How long?" said the nurse.

Andy held up his thumb and middle finger indicating a distance. "About an inch and a half," he said. "A big one. From a litre bottle."

"No," said the nurse. Deadpan. "How long ago did it happen?"

"Oh," said Andy. He had gone red. "Last night. During *Match of the Day*."

"Football," said the nurse and tutted.

She took down some details and then told us to go and wait.

We sat down in a cavernous waiting area on uncomfortable orange plastic seats.

There was a tv in one corner of the room. It was too far away to see the picture clearly and the sound was too low to hear distinctly. It was just an annoying buzz in the background, distracting and persistent. I bought us both coffee and we sat sipping it, resting the scalding plastic cups between our legs. Every now and then a nurse would appear with a clipboard and somebody would be called and then somebody else would appear through the automatic sliding doors.

It was boring. So boring. But it wasn't conducive to thought. Or speech. We only sat there side by side like we did at home, companionably, Andy scratching and getting up to go to the toilet often. "Any luck?" I would say each time he came back and he would shake his head and sit down.

It was exactly the kind of thing I need to be doing on the day my nephew left. I would recommend it to anyone in a similar position.

And finally Andy was called. A small very white nurse with a clipboard bigger than her torso appeared and shouted out Andy's name. We stood up.

"And you are?" she said to me.

"He's my landlord," said Andy. "I'm his lodger. Can he come?"

The nurse nodded her head and smiled. Kind of. Then I smiled and Andy smiled.

"This way," said the nurse and spun around on a heel and we all set off together.

It was funny because even though Andy hadn't said anything I'd assumed he would want me with him. To mentally hold his hand. It was funny because it wasn't the sort of thing you would usually ask a friend to do for you. It was the sort of problem most people would sort out by themselves. And then keep quiet. Very quiet. Classified. Hush hush.

I felt flattered that Andy wanted to involve me in his rectum.

We followed her to a line of green curtained cubicles. She indicated one that was empty, handed Andy a hospital gown to put on and told us a doctor would be with us shortly.

She drew across the curtain.

"Well..." I said.

"Well..." said Andy.

"You better put that on." I nodded to the gown.

"Yes," said Andy. "Right."

There was nowhere to look in the six metre square space, so I looked at Andy. He untied his laces, took off his shoes and put his socks inside them. He pulled off his fleece. He folded it neatly and placed it on the end of the examination bed. He turned his back to me. A buckle was undone, a zip was lowered. Andy removed his underpants and jeans at the same time, hopping from one foot to the other as he pulled his feet out from the legs.

I saw his bum.

I put my hand over my mouth.

Oh my God.

Andy pulled on the gown. The flaps didn't meet at the back. I could still see his bum.

I put my other hand over the one at my mouth. Tears were leaking out the corners of my eyes.

Andy turned around so he was facing me again.

"Honza," he said, "what's wrong?"

I wanted to say that nothing was wrong but as I took my hands away from my mouth, the laughter exploded out of me.

"Honza," said Andy, "what is it?"

I couldn't stop. I collapsed onto the single chair in the room, bent forward with my elbows on my knees, trying to take deep breaths.

Andy sat down opposite me, pulling himself up onto the bed. He folded his arms. He waited patiently. He didn't say anything, only stared at me.

Finally, I was able to talk. I wiped the wetness from under my eyes.

"Well," said Andy, "what is it?"

"Andy," I said. "Your bum. It's purple."

Andy's bum still retained a perfect purple stripe from where I had painted him the Thursday before. It hadn't faded, not at all. You could have put a frame around it and sold it to a food magazine as a prime example of a photo of a ripe aubergine cut in half and ready to eat.

"Come on," said Andy. He got off the bed. "That's it. I'm going." He was reaching for his jeans.

"Andy," I said, grabbing his hands, still smiling, my sides still aching with laughter, "you can't leave. Not now."

"But what will the doctor think?" said Andy.

We were face to face in the middle of the cubicle, me holding onto Andy, preventing him from escaping. He looked so vulnerable, his slender white limbs poking out of the green hospital gown, his still damaged face. I felt sorry for him, wanted to put my arms around him. I was supposed to be offering support. Helping.

"He'll have seen it all before," I said. "You'd be surprised. They see all sorts these doctors."

"What?" said Andy. "A twenty-one-year-old male with a purple stripe on his behind and a cork up it?"

"When you put it like that..." I said. I was still holding onto Andy's hands but he wasn't resisting anymore. I guided him back over to the examination bed and I manoeuvred us both onto it. We were sitting side by side.

"It's embarrassing," said Andy.

"I'll explain everything to him," I said. "About the decorating. About the pizza. About the cork."

"Would you?" said Andy.

"Yes," I said. "I will."

"Thanks Honza."

"That's OK," I said. "You'll stay?"

"I can't have a cork inside me forever, can I?"

"No," I said.

"Thanks Honza."

And then we both went quiet sitting next to each other on that doctor's bed. Our silence was punctuated only by the noises of the bustle outside. People walking up and down. Rattling equipment trolleys. The gentle noise of someone else's tears. And yet in our cubicle we were separate from it all. We could have been on our own private island, miles from anywhere, just the two if us.

"Honza," said Andy, "can we talk?"

"Sure," I said.

"It's difficult," he said.

I didn't say anything.

"I remember you know," said Andy. "What I told you that night. When I was drunk. That I killed someone."

"Oh," I said. "Your brother?"

"What?" said Andy. "No, not at all. Kevin Miller. I killed Kevin Miller. I killed him."

"Oh," I said. I had got it wrong. "Tell me," I said.

From outside there was the sound of an old man coughing.

"I went to school with him," said Andy, shifting in his place and starting. "He was cool. One of the lads. All the girls fancied him and all the boys wanted to be his mate. You know?"

"Yes," I said. I did.

"He wasn't my friend," said Andy, "not really. But I never forgot him. He was something I never was. I hadn't seen him for years and then one day last March I delivered a Bosch Maxx washing machine to his house. That's top of the range. Six hundred quid. Beautiful house too. It was him that recognised me. Andy, he said, Andy Johnson and he held out his hand. He gave me his phone number and said we would have to meet up, go for a drink. And that was the start of it."

Andy was looking ahead, folding an edge of the gown in his hands. I was looking at Andy. I didn't say anything.

"I was flattered," said Andy. "Me and Jim and Derek don't get on. They think I'm thick, don't let me read the maps, call me donkey. Only good for lifting. Kevin was glamorous. So I called him. And my life changed. Completely."

Andy said the word completely. But from his expression I knew he meant irrevocably, irretrievably. He said it like it represented a loss of something, a fall from somewhere. And I knew what. Innocence.

"Kevin had loads of money," said Andy. "He always paid for everything, beer, fancy food in restaurants, clothes. I didn't argue. Nobody had ever spoilt me before, nobody had been that interested. Kevin seemed to like me. I liked him." Andy took a deep breath and ran a hand through his hair. "We used to go back to his house after the pub shut. We'd watch videos and drink loads. Kevin always had lots to drink. In the morning I'd get a taxi home. Kevin would pay. He always paid for everything. He insisted and I let him. We were mates. Then one night it all came out."

"What did?" I said.

Andy ran a hand through his hair. "As usual," he said, "we were drunk. We'd gone from one pub to another. I wanted to go home but Kevin insisted. He said he would pay for me to get a taxi home later. He always paid. He said he had something to tell me."

"What?" I said.

"He started as soon as we got in," Andy said. "I remember. He said poverty was for beggars. He said I wasn't a beggar. He said he liked me and he wanted me to have all that he had. The nice house, money, a car. He said that I could take care of my dad properly. I asked him what he was going on about and then he told me."

Andy stopped talking and stood up. He folded his arms.

"It's OK," I said.

"Drugs," said Andy. "Kevin was selling drugs." He sat down again.

"Oh," I said.

Where did I stand on drugs? I was a gay man, I'd taken them of course. LSD, ecstasy, speed. But not anymore. I liked my brain to be clear nowadays. But I didn't know that I was anti-them as such. And when Andy said drugs I wasn't shocked, I didn't fall off the bed.

"It wasn't like the movies," said Andy. "It was over so quick. I was drunk, we were both drunk, and when Kevin said drugs I went mad. My mother took drugs. My brother died. And I liked Kevin so much. He liked me. I was drunk. I started shouting and Kevin got angry and stood up. I only pushed him once. He fell and hit his head on the corner of a coffee table. He was dead."

"Oh," I said.

"I need a fag," said Andy.

"You can't," I said. "Not in here."

"I know," said Andy.

"Why didn't you go to the police?" I said. "It was an accident."

"I was going to," said Andy. "But Nigel turned up."

"Nigel?"

"You've seen him," said Andy. "Big. Bald head."

"Yes," I said.

"Kevin's dead, I said. I was crying. Nigel pushed me out of the way. He checked the pulse and told me to go."

"He told you to go?"

"Yes," said Andy. "And I did. I got home, threw up in the stairwell and got into bed. I couldn't sleep but then I woke up and the bed was wet." Andy scratched his left arm. The nails left a white scar there. "I changed the sheets and then cooked my dad's breakfast. I got on with things. I went to work and in the evenings I watched telly sitting side by side on the sofa with my dad."

"I don't understand," I said.

Andy held up his hand. "One day Nigel called. He said he needed my help. He said I needed his help. I understood. At first I was just making deliveries. I was a courier. But gradually the jobs got bigger. I was working in clubs. I was making money. What Kevin had told me that night was right."

"What?" I said.

"I had money," said Andy, "and I was popular. Everyone wanted to be my friend. I'd watch the people dancing, seeing what a great time they were having. I wished that Kevin was there. Kevin liked dancing. And that's it."

"Oh," I said.

"That's all," said Andy.

"You should go to the police," I said.

Andy shrugged. "Drug-pusher kills dealer."

"Oh," I said.

"It'll never stop," said Andy. "The week after I moved into yours, the week that I got drunk, Nigel said I had done so well that he was going to give me a bigger patch. He drove me down to London. To Brixton. Now I work in The Cube."

"The gay club?"

"The gay club," said Andy. "There are thousands in there. I don't have to move. There's a queue for the bar and a queue for me. And that's the ironic thing."

"What is?"

"That I've changed my mind about drugs. They're OK. What I do is OK but I want out. I don't want to be doing this. I don't want this life. Not ever. What I do is not me."

I understood that, I understood perfectly.

"I don't touch the money I earn," said Andy. "I keep it in a box. I look at it sometimes and think I could buy anything. I could go to a shop and buy CDs, clothes, electrical equipment. But I don't."

I looked at Andy and this time he looked at me. He smiled. His lips were nearly back to normal. Not bruised.

"But the bruises," I said, "last weekend?"

"I was beaten up," said Andy. "It's what happens to people like me. I'm going for a piss."

Andy slipped off the bed and holding the two edges of the robe to hide his purple bum he disappeared out of the side of the cubicle.

Andy the murderer and drug-dealer. Andy who scratched furiously and nestled a can in his crotch. Andy who knew the tv programming schedule. Andy who got on so well with my nephew, who liked the same music as me.

Andy who had kept my mother entertained for two hours and never asked for payment.

Andy the sex educator with an intimate knowledge of carrots.

Andy my lodger.

Andy appeared again through the curtains. He was smiling. It was like *Stars In Their Eyes*. He had gone out a murderer, had come back a comedian. But that's how he lived his life. How he coped.

"Honza," he said, "it came out."

"What?" I said. I knew what.

"The cork," said Andy.

"Are you sure?"

"Sure," said Andy. "It popped like a bottle of expensive champagne. The drunk in the next cubicle shouted hip hip hooray and started singing 'For He's a Jolly Good Fellow'. Come on, let's go. We don't need to be here anymore."

Andy began to put on his clothes, turning his back to me once again. Shy, modest. Not a killer. Not a dealer. He pulled on his underpants, his jeans. Just as he had the fleece over his head the curtain was pulled aside and a man in a white coat was standing there. The doctor.

"Mr Johnson?" he said.

"It came out," I said. "The cork."

"Yeah," said Andy his blond head appearing from the fleece. "All gone."

The doctor looked first at Andy and then at me. He was old. He had a grey beard, thinning

"Now," he said with gravitas, holding his hands in front of him,

"I don't care what you people get up to in private but next time be a little more careful. It's a waste of hospital time."

My mouth was open. I wanted to say something, wanted to be angry, make some vituperative retort but nothing came out.

"And quite frankly," said the doctor, "lodger, landlord. Come off it boys."

"I'll go and get some wine," said Andy. "Screw top."

"Fine," I said. I put the car keys on the breakfast bar. "I'm making a curry for tonight. Want some?"

Andy nodded.

"We'll eat about six."

"Fine," said Andy, "six."

He went out. I chopped vegetables. The knife slipped on a carrot and I cut my finger. I ran it under the tap. Andy came back.

"I'll put the wine in the fridge," he said. He did it and then stretched and yawned. "I'm tired," he said.

I stopped chopping. "Why don't you have a sleep?"

He said he would and he went upstairs.

Normal. We were back to normal. Back to our staccato speech, our easy ambience. The conversation in the hospital might not have happened. But it had and I had the beginnings of a plan. I took a pad and pen out of a drawer in the kitchen and I sat at the breakfast bar. I turned Andy's story into a list of points, a logical progression of events. When Andy had been speaking I had thought something didn't ring true, something wasn't quite right and now in front of me in black and white I spotted it. Tomorrow I would check out my theory and then perhaps I could help Andy.

And all the time I was working, constantly while I was sitting at the breakfast bar, in the back of my mind was an image. It was the image of a big red truck heading south, getting closer and closer to London, and in the front of this truck was one small black-haired boy with a cute smile singing along to 'Tragedy'.

I looked at the clock. It was five thirty.

I made two cups of tea and took one upstairs. Andy wasn't asleep. He was lying under the covers with his hands behind his head, staring up at the ceiling.

"Curry in half an hour," I said. I put the cup down on the bedside table.

"Fine," said Andy.

I turned to go.

"Honza?"

"Yes?"

"Thanks."

"That's OK," I said. I paused and then I sat down on the bed next to the mound of Andy. "I think I have a plan. To sort things out or you."

Andy sat up. He didn't ask what the plan was, how I was going to help him. He only grinned. It was that boy-who's-got-more-than-he-expected grin again. It was a grin that surrendered authority, gave trust. It was a grin that believed in me. "Thanks Honza," he said. "You're a hero."

A hero. That was a problem, because I wasn't. For a long time with Joshua I'd tried to be, tried to solve his problems. But I couldn't. Everything I did only seemed to have made him worse.

So I was better on my own.

"Don't thank me yet," I said. "Just come and get your dinner."

"Right Honza," said Andy. "Thanks Honza."

We ate the curry sitting side by side. We drank Andy's wine. We didn't talk much. We watched the Brazilian Grand Prix, we watched *Coronation Street*, we watched *Who Wants To Be a Millionaire?* Andy didn't know many of the answers. I knew a lot. He said that I should call the number, try and get on the show. I said yes but I knew I wouldn't. I tried not to put myself in any position where I could be disappointed.

After *Millionaire* I went upstairs to have a shower. It was Sunday night, L'Amour night. I wasn't in the mood but music might do me good, cleanse my soul. And I needed a shag, the escape of sex. So I pulled on a pair of green cotton and nylon Diesel pants, a C17 white tight T-shirt and gelled my hair.

Downstairs Andy was watching a romantic drama. He had spread out on the sofa, was half in my space, was engrossed. He was smoking a cigarette, drinking wine. He looked like he didn't have a care in the world. I knew better. Now.

"Bye," I said.

"Bye Honza," he said. "Have you got your key?"

I patted my pocket.

"Yes."

"See you later," he said. He hadn't turned around. He hadn't taken his eyes off of the television screen.

"See you," I said and went out.

I made the short walk down the road and I was in the club.

Sometimes you can hear that music and suddenly you are in the mood, you want to dance, you want to move to the beat, to lose yourself in it. You want to spy a gorgeous hunk across the floor and you want to score, to take him somewhere, anywhere and do all those things you dream of on lazy mornings alone.

And sometimes the music just gives you a headache.

"You OK?" said Mother Hen. She had spotted me at the bar and had sashayed over, swinging those full hips, licking those lipstick lips.

"My lodger's a murderer," I said, "and I'm never going to see my nephew again."

"And apart from that?" said Mother, adjusting one of her plastic breasts.

"Everything's great."

"We have a fantastic show tonight," said Mother. "I'm doing 'Tragedy'."

"Oh," I said. I took a long swig of my beer. A very long swig. I put my glass down and Mother had gone.

I knew the evening wasn't going to get any better when I saw Solskjaer. He raised his hand and did that one deaf sign I knew and nodded his head towards the toilet and smiled. I felt nothing. There wasn't even the glimmer of a girding in my loins.

I decided to go home. I decided to go home and have an early night. I would get up tomorrow and I would be organised. I would do something for Andy and I would phone my nephew to check that he had settled in all right.

I left the club and walked back up the street. It was deserted. Quiet. Except for my house.

A wall of sound hit me as I opened my front door. It was Moloko doing 'The Time is Now'. At full volume.

"Andy?" I called.

Of course there was no answer. You couldn't have heard a bomb drop. A pin? Get out of here.

I looked in the lounge. There was no sign of Andy there. The tv was off and I noticed the washing up had been done. The dishes were drying on the draining-board. I went upstairs. Moloko had given way to Madonna singing 'American Pie', William Orbit's trademark beeps in the background.

Oh my God.

The door to Andy's room was open but that wasn't what surprised me. The door to my workroom was also open and light was poring out of it. I knew that I hadn't been in there that evening. I knew that it must be Andy.

I walked in.

Andy was sitting in the swivel chair where I usually worked. He had spun it around away from the desk and had his naked feet crossed and up on a short cabinet I used for filing. He was smoking a cigarette. He didn't see me, he was deep in concentration. Resting on his thighs was a thick wad of A4 pages. I knew what it was. I recognised the vellum tint. I had spent hours and hours looking at that surface myself. Andy was reading the manuscript of my novel.

"Andy?" I said, loudly but not angrily. I just wanted to be heard.

Andy leapt. The cigarette flew out of his mouth and he stood and bent to retrieve it all in one motion. He put the stub in an ashtray on my desk. Then he looked at me and didn't say anything. He looked very guilty. He looked like someone about to face a firing squad.

I had once read a survey about trust. The worst thing, I read, that someone could do to you was to read your papers, your letters. It was the ultimate breach of confidence, the thing which could not be forgiven.

When I had been living in Japan the guy who had had the flat upstairs from me had given me his spare key in case he locked himself out. I was in love with him. He kept a diary. Those are the facts, you can guess the rest. Every morning once I had heard his footsteps going down the stairs I would sneak up the stairs and would read what he had recently written. And it was boring so boring. But I was addicted. I couldn't help myself. Until one day Marc, the guy upstairs, caught me helping myself. He asked for his key back and never spoke to me again. End of story and I didn't blame him.

I went into Andy's bedroom and turned down the music. Andy followed me in.

"Honza," he said, "I'm sorry."

He was looking at the floor.

"I'm really sorry," he said. "I'll move out."

I shrugged. "Andy," I said, "it doesn't matter."

"It does," he said. He was looking at the deep green of the carpet as if it was water and he wanted to drown himself in it. "It does matter."

"I don't care," I said. And I didn't. Somehow it wasn't important. If I'd have been angry, I'd have been a hypocrite, the anger would have been fake. I'd seen Andy sitting on the toilet, I'd painted his bum purple, he'd bathed my nephew, he'd told me he'd killed someone. All he'd done was read my novel and that, after all, was what I had written it for.

"But..." said Andy. He sat down on the bed and put his head in his hands.

"Andy," I said, "really. It's not important."

"Oh," said Andy. He looked at me. "Sure?"

"Sure," I said.

"You still want to help me?"

"Of course."

Andy grinned. He stood up, walked over to me, put his arms around me and held me tight. "It's excellent," he said in my ear.

"Oh," I said. "Thanks."

He let me go and sat back down on the bed.

"I've read it twice. The whole thing. It's excellent."

Excellent.

"You're not going to go all Betty Blue on me, are you?" I said.

And now Andy did raise his head. For the first time since I had been back he looked me in the eyes.

"Who's Betty Blue?" he said.

"What?" I said.

"I said, who's Betty Blue?"

Andy didn't know who Betty Blue was. He didn't know that *Betty Blue* was a French eighties art house film by Jean-Jacques Beineix. He didn't know that Béatrice Dalle played the eponymous hero, a destructive passionate woman who falls in love with a quiet man living in a shack by the sea. He didn't know that Betty discovers this man's secret manuscripts and believes him to be a literary genius and will stop at nothing to get him published. Sacrificing everything to do so. Andy didn't know that *Betty Blue* was a love story. Andy didn't know any of this.

Sixteen

I opened my eyes. I had been awake for ages. I had listened to Andy descending the stairs, the metallic spring of the toaster, the bang of the door closing as he went to work. And then I had listened to the silence until I couldn't stand it anymore.

I got out of bed and walked naked into the bathroom. I looked at myself in the mirror, went to the toilet and then went downstairs. The post was lying on the mat. I collected it on my way into the kitchen.

On the breakfast bar was a pile of money and a single Post-It note. I unpeeled the yellow oblong from the laminated surface and read the message that was written in Andy's almost illegible scrawl. "This is just to say I have drunk all the milk that was in the fridge. I'm sorry but I couldn't go to work without tea. Thirty-seven pounds fifty for rent. Back about six. I'll cook. See you, Andy. PS It was April last year. I'm sure."

I smiled, crumpled the note in my hand and tossed it into the bin. I made myself a cup of tea, sat down on a stool to drink it, black, and sorted through my letters.

There was a statement from the bank telling me I was teetering on the edge of red. There was a letter from Marks and Spencers offering me the loan of a lifetime. A lifetime to pay it back I assumed. And then there was a brown envelope with a printed sticker with my name on the front. It looked like a bill.

I ripped open the flap and pulled out the single white page. I unfolded it. I read the few short lines. I looked away from the page, blinked and then looked back and read the letter again.

No way.

I jumped from the stool and did a jig around the living room. I danced a quarter of a quadrille with a lamp stand. I shouted for joy.

"Fucking yes!"

The publisher had liked my proposal. They wanted to read the rest of my manuscript.

I wasn't going to be published, not for sure, not yet, it was only a step up the ladder. But I had a feeling. It was fate.

Fate.

My sister had once said to me that what goes around comes around. She had told me this while we were lying on our backs on opposite sides of a spinning wooden roundabout, looking up at the clouds. It had made sense to me then as cumuli came back and back into view, and it made sense to me now. It suggested both that everything we do has a consequence and a consequence we deserve. We are masters of our own destiny.

A few weeks earlier I had put an advertisement in the paper for a lodger. I had got a lodger. My lodger had problems and I was helping him. A few years ago my sister had had a baby and I had supported her, loved him. The balance in my fatalistic scales had been tipped and now something good was happening to me.

It wasn't a case of you scratch my back and I'll scratch yours. It wasn't about giving to be given something back, about negotiation, the checking and balancing of behaviour in an eternal metaphysical account book. It was much simpler than that. In this life you must do what you believe to be right for the right reasons, without regard to laws or religion. You must do what is in your heart. And if you have a good heart.

What goes around comes around.

Karma.

I went upstairs to have a shower. I was excited, ecstatic about my letter but I hadn't forgotten my plan, my course of action for the day, what I had promised Andy I would do. I hadn't forgotten what we had talked about sitting in his room side by side on his bed, my bed, our heads gradually wreathed in smoke as he lit one after another cigarette. I hadn't forgotten at all.

The only difference was that now I would do it with a lighter heart, a spring in my step. Now, I felt like I was king of the world. I felt as if I could wave a magic wand and solve all of Andy's problems. I felt as if today was the day. My day. The beginning of something new.

I felt everything would go right.

And I was right.

Everything was going right.

I managed to get the water temperature of the shower perfect first time, not too hot, not too cold, the runner on my sock drawer didn't stick, my underpants were without holes, gel and my hair went together in perfect harmony. A lark wasn't singing on my window ledge but I didn't go in for that stuff much anyhow.

Within fifteen minutes I was ready to go out.

I only needed one thing. I went into the workroom and it was there in its box where Andy had left it. The copy of my manuscript, the result of so much work, so many hours alone, sitting at the keyboard, punching keys.

I picked it up and went first to the post office.

Then I had a couple of places to go.

Karma time.

Chameleon time.

Time to pull on my old bullshit suit.

"Graham," I said, "fantastic to see you."

"Honza!" said Graham. "Simply lovely to see you too my boy."

I was in the lobby of the offices of the *Derby Evening Telegraph*. Graham was a staff writer on the paper. He had appeared striding from the lift, hand out, seconds after I had summoned him from the front desk. He must have sniffed a good story. Or something else.

"How are things?" I said.

"Looking up," said Graham. "If you get my meaning."

I did. Perfectly. The way he was looking at me left nothing to the imagination.

"I have a little problem," I said.

"Oh yes," said Graham.

"I need your help."

"My help?" said Graham. He looked surprised. He'd probably thought I'd popped over for a quick one. He'd be disappointed. But not yet.

"Yes," I said. "Help."

There was a pause, just enough time for Graham's brain to receive a message from his crotch.

"I'll do what I can," he said, "if you do what you can."

Sir Lancelot du Lac he wasn't. Mind you, damsel in distress I wasn't. Graham hadn't changed in the two years since I had last seen him. He was still gagging for it. I could see it in his eyes.

It was something I could use to my advantage.

"If you scratch mine," I said, "then I'll scratch yours."

Clichéd I know, but then Graham worked for a local newspaper. Clichés were his bread and butter. To Graham mornings still broke, people still got on like houses on fire and gays were still self-confessed.

"Where is it, this itch?" said Graham, glancing around the lobby. "Below the belt I hope?"

"Might be," I said. I shoved my hands in my pockets, I thrust out my hips. "Could be. How about you take me upstairs? And then we'll see if we can sort this scratch out. Big time." I moved a little closer. "I just need to exercise my fingers across your computer first. I need to access your database."

Mentally I crossed my fingers.

"Database?" Graham said, eyes dropping to my crotch. "Is that what you're calling it nowadays? I must get out more. I must keep up with the lingo."

If he was the same Graham I remembered then I was sure he was getting out plenty. I was sure he still hung around in park toilets, still spent his Saturday afternoons on train station platforms, still frequented seedy saunas.

"Please," I said, "I'm serious."

"Well," said Graham, running a finger around his collar, "it's strictly against the rules."

"Go on," I said, "for old times' sake."

Old times were a couple of Tuesday afternoons in a Midlands steam room. I had been bored, Graham over the moon. He was a good twenty years older than me and at least thirty pounds heavier.

"Well," said Graham, "I suppose it couldn't hurt."

"Thanks," I said, brushing my thigh against Graham's and winking. "I'll owe you."

Graham returned the wink. The lascivious smile was all his own.

"If anyone asks," said Graham, "just tell them you're my nephew. You're still looking young enough."

"Yes aunty," I said and I grinned.

The grin I had borrowed off Andy. It did the trick. Graham told me to follow and turned on his heels. I did as I was told, watching the undulating buttocks lead the way back to the lift he had recently emerged from. I wondered how I had ever done it, what I had been thinking of, who I had been thinking of. But at least it was making my life easier today.

Our former meeting had not only been kissing. It was kismet.

Up we went. Thank God we weren't alone in that metal box. Thank God for brown-coated janitors.

The lift doors pinged open.

The office was open plan and contained a dozen or so desks separated by wooden partitions with Perspex windows. It wasn't a hubbub of activity, not exactly, but there was a background noise of phones ringing, voices mumbling. A few harassed looking people clutching sheets of paper were milling around the aisles and other harassed looking people were seated at desks. Graham indicated for me to follow again and I did.

At one work station we passed, a blonde woman was furiously tapping at keys. Her hair was wild, her make-up skew-whiff, the area in front of her a cluttered jumble of office stationery, furry gonks and family photographs.

"She's doing an article on Feng Shui," whispered Graham conspiratorially.

I laughed conspiratorially. It was all part of the plan.

Graham's desk was in a corner, out of the way. If I had been an expert on Feng Shui then I would have put Graham in just such a place. Or at the bottom of a garden in a shed.

"Sit down," said Graham.

"Thanks," I said. I sat down.

Apart from the computer the desk was almost completely empty. There was only one small sign. The proof is in the pudding, it said.

"So what can I do you for?" said Graham. He had perched himself on the corner of the desk. His knee was very near my arm.

"I just need to see back copies of the paper," I said. "April last year."

"Oh," he said.

He seemed disappointed. He'd obviously thought I was up to no good, although what delicate information he could possibly have on his computer was beyond me. Did he think I was involved in some kind of industrial espionage? Did he think I was planning to steal next week's gardening tips and syndicate them nationwide? I didn't know.

"I'll be very grateful," I said.

"I'll hold you to that," said Graham.

"You'll do it?" I said. I smiled my best smile.

"No problem," said Graham and then added more quietly, "I'll do it and then you'll do it."

"Yes," I said. Or so he thought.

Positioning himself far closer to me than was necessary Graham showed me how to locate the correct files, scroll the pages. It was easy. I soon got the hang of it, soon got tired of Graham's halitotic breath on my cheek.

"This might take ages," I said. "Why don't you go and get us a coffee?"

"And what do I get?" said Graham, winking.

I returned the wink. I smiled again. I was dazzling. Cute.

"Just you wait and see," I said.

Graham bounced off the desk, his face alight and he scuttled off to get us that dose of caffeine.

Andy had said April so I started at the first. If he had killed Kevin Miller then I figured it would have been in the papers. I'd asked Andy if he'd seen it, heard anything about it but he said that he didn't get the papers, watch the news. I should have known that already.

"But didn't you check?" I'd asked.

He had just shrugged and said that he had tried to forget, hadn't wanted to know.

By the time Graham got back I was already up to April tenth. It was quick work. I only had to scan the first few pages of each paper. That's where all the news was. After that it was all adverts, jobs, opinion columns with no opinion.

"Any luck?" said Graham. He put down a plastic cup of coffee.

"Not yet," I said.

I told Graham that he didn't have to stay, that it would be boring just watching me but he said he didn't mind. Obviously. As the days flicked by before my eyes, I remained under Graham's gaze. He never took his eyes off of me. I could imagine what he was thinking. He didn't have to imagine. He had seen me naked.

I got to the end of April. I had skipped past articles on missing children, burnt houses, council taxes, governmental budgets but no murders. Not even one.

"You finished?" said Graham.

Had I?

"Just a minute," I said.

I went back to before April, to the end of March, just in case Andy had been a few days out. But there was nothing. Not a sausage. Not a dead drugs-dealer.

And then I had an idea.

I tapped a few keys, scrolled a few pages and I found it. I found what I was looking for.

I was right. I had been right.

I exited from the file.

"All done," I said to Graham.

"You find what you were looking for?" he said. He had slid off the desk and was standing with his hands in his pockets.

"I suppose I did." I didn't smile, I didn't need to.

"Now," said Graham, "how about I take you to dinner? Tonight. And then I know a little place."

"How about you take your wife?" I said loudly and I pinched his stomach.

His face dropped. The penny dropped.

"Honza," he said, "you're still a bastard."

I grabbed his tie and I pulled him towards me. I kissed his nose. No one had called me a bastard for a few weeks. I was beginning to forget what it felt like.

"Thanks Graham," I said.

And I walked out of there swinging my hips. I could feel Graham's eyes on my bum all the way to the door.

*

"Can I speak to Sergeant Harris?" I said.

I had walked to the police station in Chaddesden to make my enquiries in person. I hadn't phoned because I knew that Sergeant Harris, Paul, wouldn't have been too pleased to hear from me. I knew that Sergeant Harris would have hung up. Sergeant Harris was happily married. Supposedly.

The policeman on the desk looked me up and down with his government-issue X-ray eyes, scanning me for weapons, stolen goods and then asked my name.

"Honza Drobrolowski," I said. I doubted whether he got many sons of Polacks in there so I added, "just tell him Honza. He'll know who I am."

The desk officer picked up the phone, said exactly what I'd told him and obviously I was given the all clear because I was ushered through a door, down a corridor and into a whitewashed room. I was looking around at perfect whitewashed walls when the door behind me opened and then closed again with a bang.

"What the fuck are you doing here?"

I turned around. Sergeant Harris was there. Paul. He was leaning against the closed door like he didn't want me to escape, or for anyone to get in. He didn't look happy. He looked like the Kray twins had just been released into community care in Derby.

"Nice to see you too," I said. I was tempted to blow a kiss. I didn't.

"I told you not to come to my work," said Paul. "What the hell are you doing here?"

He'd got from fuck to hell. He was evidently getting used to the idea of me. Or he was just practising his expletives.

"Cut the bad cop bad cop routine," I said, "I need your help."

I grinned. I was getting good at it, bloody good. Paul nearly grinned too. Nearly.

I knew Paul's outburst was more a demonstration of his

masculinity than anything else. I knew he was a pussy cat in bed. A pussy cat with the body of a god.

"But shit Honza," he said, folding his arms, "turning up at work."

"I had no choice," I said. "You never answer my calls."

"Don't lie," he said. "You never called. You're not the type. You made that clear."

"You never wanted me to," I said. "You made that clear."

He unfolded his arms. He moved away from the door. One point to me.

"I've got a reputation," he said. "I've got a wife."

That's not what he'd said twelve months ago. Not at first. I had met him in L'Amour shortly after the split with Joshua, when I was still working him out of my system. I had been leaning against the wall adjacent to the dance floor, drinking a pint of lager, when a gorgeous man had come up to me, told me he was a policeman and would I like to see his truncheon. Just that.

The little wife thing at home had come later.

Sergeant Paul Harris wasn't my favourite person but he had got what he wanted from me. Now I wanted something from him.

"Relax," I said. "I'm not here for sex."

"Oh," he said.

"I'm not here for a shag."

"Oh," he said.

"I wasn't about to leap on the reception desk and sing 'I Am What I Am'," I said. "Please Paul, it's important. I just need your help."

He looked around the room resignedly. There was nobody there to help him. Only me, and I wasn't going anywhere.

"OK," he said. "What do you want?"

"A name," I said. "I just want you to check a name for me."

Bang on six there was the sound of a key in the lock. I was in my workroom. I was sitting at the keyboard and I was writing.

My novel, maybe, just maybe, was about to be accepted by a publisher. My nephew had gone to London. My sister was probably getting ready for her first night as an erotic dancer. I had spent the day visiting old flames trying to sort out the life of my lodger who was both a drug-dealer and a murderer. And I was writing.

The words were pouring out of me, spilling onto the page. I was writing like a man on speed talks, quickly, lost to anything but his own speech, his own ideas.

When life gets too much, head for the hills. That's where the muses live.

"Honza!" came the voice up the stairs. "I'm home."

"Hi," I shouted back. "I'll be down in a minute."

I saved the file to disc and then I saved it to a backup disc and then I went downstairs.

Andy was in the kitchen. He was wearing his blue boiler suit, the one with Ryder stitched on the pocket. There were two bulging plastic carrier bags on the breakfast bar.

"Been shopping?" I said.

"Yes," said Andy. "I'm cooking tonight. For us. And I bought some wine."

"Oh," I said. "Nice. What are you making?"

"Basque chicken and rice," said Andy. "It's my speciality."

I was waiting for the punch line. I was looking for the tin, waiting for Andy to raise the can opener and grin. None of these things happened. Instead, I watched as Andy pulled a net of onions and a pack of coloured peppers out of one of the bags. He was serious.

"Lovely," I said. "Andy," I said, "I have some news. Good news about your problem."

My good news could wait until later. It had paled in significance.

"Right," said Andy. He had taken a knife out of a drawer and was beginning to chop one of the onions. He had his back to me. "Can you tell me while I cook? I'm starving."

"Sure," I said.

I had never been the harbinger of good news before and I didn't know how to do it. I wasn't sure if I should have hired a herald, whether I should shout it from the roof tops or do it intimately over a candlelit meal. I didn't know whether to throw my arms around Andy or give him a stiff drink and tell him to sit down.

In the end I just told him, like that, while he was chopping an onion.

"Andy," I said, "Kevin Miller's not dead."

Momentarily I saw the knife pause, the shoulders tighten, and then Andy was chopping again.

"But I killed him," he said. "I saw the body. He was dead."

"He's not," I said.

Andy was still chopping. His back was still turned.

"I pushed him," he said. "He banged his head."

"Andy," I said, "look at me."

He turned around. He was still clutching the knife in his left hand, the one with the missing finger. There were tears running down his face, dripping from his chin.

"These onions," he said, "they're strong."

"Andy," I said. "Kevin Miller's in prison. In Brixton. He got caught for possession last May. Two thousand Es. He got four years. He had a record. That guy Nigel set you up. He needs people he can use. You gave him the perfect opportunity."

Andy wiped the tears from his eyes, his face, using the dirty cuff of his blue Ryder boiler suit.

"So," he said, "Kevin's not dead."

"No," I said. "Not at all."

"Why didn't he tell me?" Andy said. "I thought he was my friend."

I didn't know the answer to that, or rather I didn't know how to answer that. Not really. So I didn't.

"I'm just going for a piss," said Andy.

He put knife down carefully on the side and walked out of the room. I didn't hear footsteps on the stairs as he bounded up. I didn't hear footsteps on the Gerlor sand-tile flooring in the bathroom. I didn't hear a steady stream hitting the water in the toilet bowl. I didn't hear anything. I just sat at the breakfast bar and waited.

And waited.

After five minutes I got up to go and see if Andy was OK. I went up the stairs.

The bathroom was empty. The door to Andy's bedroom was half open.

"Andy?" I said. I knocked gently on the door.

"Yes," he said. "Come in."

I did. Andy was sitting on the end of his bed.

"Why didn't he tell me?"

I shrugged.

"They used you."

"But Kevin..." Andy stopped speaking and brought his knuckle up to his mouth and started chewing.

"Yes?"

Andy wiped his face again with the sleeve of his boiler suit.

"We used to watch tv together. We were friends."

"I'm sorry."

"We..."

"Yes?" I said.

"It's all right," said Andy. "Sorry. I thought he was dead."

"I know."

"I thought I killed him," said Andy. "I kept seeing his face."

"I know."

And then Andy was quiet. He sat looking down at his hands, crossing and uncrossing the fingers. I went over to the bed and sat next to him.

"I have a plan," I said.

"A plan?"

"A plan so you don't have to sell drugs anymore."

"Honza," said Andy, "it's not your problem."

"It is. We're friends right?"

Andy looked at me. He almost smiled. "Friends, yeah. Neat."

"So you want to hear it?"

"Yeah," said Andy. "But Nigel won't let me stop. Not now."

"He won't let you," I said, "but we can make him. Fight fire with fire."

"Oh," said Andy.

"You want to hear my plan?"

"Sure," said Andy. He wiped his nose on his sleeve. "But I promised to cook for you." He made a chopping motion with his left hand onto his right palm.

"You don't have to," I said.

"I want to," said Andy.

"You sure?"

"Sure," said Andy. "Unless you want to order a pizza?"

"Let's get you downstairs," I said laughing. "You're cooking."

Andy followed me down. I sat on the stool at the breakfast bar and Andy picked up his knife and I explained my plan while he was cooking. I explained that as far as Kevin was concerned he had done nothing wrong. I explained that although this was good news, great news it didn't mean necessarily that he could just tell Nigel and Nigel would let him stop. Andy said he knew that, knew that he was in deep and it wasn't so easy to go back. I explained to Andy what my idea was, what we could do, and all the while he was cooking. I sat on a stool at the breakfast bar and Andy cooked.

I got to the end of my plan just as Andy was chopping fresh parsley for a garnish and sprinkling it on the stir-fried chicken.

"*Voilà*," he said.

"Looks nice," I said. It did. It looked very nice.

"Thanks," said Andy. "And Honza?"

"Yes?" I said.

"About the plan."

"Yes?" I said.

"I like it, but there's something I have to tell you about Kevin. Something important. Something I should have told you."

"Yes?" I said.

There was a knock at the door. Loud. Very loud.

"You better answer that," said Andy.

Seventeen

"Hide," I said.

"What?" said Andy. He was moving the spicy-smelling chicken dish onto the breakfast bar.

"It might be Nigel. I don't want you to see him. We're not ready for him. Yet."

I could see Andy's mouth opening. He was about to say something. Some objection. There was another knock at the door. Loud.

"Just hide," I said and I went to answer it.

It wasn't a question of being brave, not really. It wasn't a question of walking a tightrope blindfold across the span of the Niagara falls, not exactly, but I still felt nervous. And excited. Because something was happening.

I put my hand on the handle, pushed down and pulled.

"Honza! Oh Honza!"

It was my mother. She had a handkerchief held up to her face and she was crying. She looked like she had been crying for some time.

"Mum," I said. "What is it?"

She didn't answer. She just stood there crying.

I didn't know what to do. My mother was the master of saying the wrong thing at the wrong time, the unapt aphorism, the inappropriate adage. She was an expert at popping the balloon of your pride. Over the years she had made me scream, shout, punch inanimate objects. She had made me cry. But it was very rare that she had a tear in her own eye. Very rare.

I guided her into the lounge and into the chair in front of the window. There was no sign of Andy. I sat down on the sofa.

"Mum," I said again. "What is it?"

"It's Julie."

Julie. The name ricocheted through me, scoring points on my nerves. If there was a problem with Julie, then there was a problem with Nicholas.

"What about Julie?" I said.

"She's gone," said my mother. "She's gone to London." And then she started crying again.

My mother hadn't known. Julie hadn't told her, Julie hadn't told her that she was actually going, that it wasn't just another one of her schemes that fell through. Well done sis. What a way to go. I could imagine my mother turning up at Julie's house, expecting to see the smiling face of her grandson and just finding an empty shell. Or maybe new tenants. No wonder she was upset. My mother didn't like surprises, shocks. She had trouble coping with easy truths sitting in her favourite chair with a nice cup of tea.

"Tea," said Andy, springing upright like a rifle range target from where he had evidently been hiding, from behind my mother's chair. "I'll make tea."

My mother, surprised by the newly vertical Andy, bounced out of her seat, spun around and landed squarely in the centre of the room on the checkerboard russet rug.

"The lodger," she said looking at Andy.

In old Hollywood movies when women are panicking, sobbing hysterically, caterwauling uncontrollably they are slapped. This seems to calm them down, restore their equilibrium. Andy had just given my mother the equivalent of a good hard slap.

"The lodger was behind the chair," she said. She had stopped crying.

"I was looking for a contact lens," said Andy. He was crossing the room to the kitchen. "Tea? You need tea."

"Tea mum?" I said.

My mum looked from me to Andy and then back again. Her shoulders had stopped heaving.

"You'll be the death of me," she said. "You and Julie."

"Sit down mum," I said. "Andy'll make you a nice cup of tea."

My mother sat down.

"Julie's really gone," she said. She wiped her eyes with her handkerchief. "She gone to London. She's going to be a dancer. And she's taken Nicholas. She's taken my one and only grandson to London."

"I know," I said.

"You knew?" said my mother. Her head snapped up.

"Yes," I said.

"You knew and you let her go?" My mother folded the handkerchief into the sleeve of her cardigan. I recognised the sign. She was going into battle. She was putting away her white flag.

"I knew," I said. "But I didn't let her go. She went. I didn't know she hadn't told you."

"You knew?" said my mother again. She shook her head and sighed. "Thank goodness you don't have any children of your own Honza. You seem to let them slip through your fingers so easily."

I put my hand in my pocket and pinched myself. Hard. I needed pain. Something to concentrate on.

"I couldn't stop her," I said. "I thought she'd told you."

"Couldn't stop her," said my mother. "A real man would have stopped her."

A real man.

We were back to this. Twelve years down the track and we were back to this. I let it pass. I knew she was angry and for once I could understand why. So I didn't say anything, I only waited for my mother to finish. I knew there would be more, I knew from experience.

"A real man," continued my mother rising up in her chair, straightening her back, "a real brother wouldn't have let her go, would have put his foot down. But no, you're too busy playing silly buggers with your lodger. Lodger. You make me laugh. You want me to treat you as normal, but I come round and you have men hiding behind chairs. You think I don't know what's going on."

I'd preferred the crying mother. This mother I could do without. I was just about to say that there was nothing going on between me and Andy when the man himself came out of the kitchen with a big smile on his face holding a steaming mug in his hand.

"Tea," he said, glancing at me, looking at my mother. "This'll make you feel better. A nice cup of tea."

He put the mug down next to my mother and came and sat beside me on the sofa. His usual seat.

"Mrs Dobrowski?" he said.

"Mrs Drobrolowski," she said. She picked up the cup and took a sip, eyeing us both over the rim.

"Yes, that's right," Andy said. "Before you came Honza was just telling me his plans."

I looked at Andy. My mother looked at Andy.

"Plans?" said my mother.

"Yes," said Andy. "Honza was telling me that once a month he was intending on taking you down to London. To see Nicholas."

"Oh yes," said my mother. "He said that, did he?"

"Yes," said Andy. "And once a month, if your sister agrees, he'll bring Nicholas here. It's only two and a half hours in the car, he said."

"Oh yes," said my mother.

"It's not the end of the world," said Andy.

"No," said my mother.

"It's not Australia," said Andy.

"No," said my mother.

"And in the meantime," said Andy, "Honza said that he would

just have to hope that Julie misses her family, gives up her job, and comes home to Derby. Honza thinks she will."

"Is this right Honza?" said my mother.

I nodded.

"Mrs Drobrolowski?" said Andy.

"Well done," said my mother. She had almost smiled.

"I've just cooked," said Andy. "Basque chicken and rice. Would you like to stay to dinner?"

My mother looked at me and then at Andy.

"That would be very nice," she said. "Why don't you get changed and then we'll eat."

"Changed," said Andy peering down at himself, at his blue boiler suit with Ryder stitched in white on the left chest pocket. "I am changed."

Dinner was excellent, Andy was charming, effervescent. He didn't look like someone who had just found out that a person who they thought they had killed was in fact alive and well, not dead at all. Or perhaps he did. Perhaps it was just the kind of news that would make you charming, effervescent. And my mother was charmed, effervesced.

"And for dessert," said Andy. "Apple pie."

He pulled the steaming tray from the oven.

"Ooo!" said my mother. "My favourite. Did you make it yourself?"

I had seen the Iceland box. Apple pie just like your mother makes, it had said. I had hoped not.

"Yes," I said. "He did. All by himself."

"Your lodger," said my mother, loading the word lodger with so much meaning I feared it would collapse under the pressure and confess to being another word all together, "is very talented."

"No," said Andy, ladling a piece of pie into a waiting bowl, "your son is talented. I've read his book."

My mother raised her eyebrows, the left and the right. She raised them so high they could have been mistaken for a pair of very small wigs holidaying on her upper cranium. She didn't know how many times my book had been rejected, but she had a good idea. I could see her mouth beginning to open. I knew it would be to say something hurtful, upsetting, so I got in before her.

"I got a letter from a publisher," I said.

"What?" said Andy, the piece of apple pie hovering in mid-air.

"They want to read the whole of my manuscript."

"Really?" said Andy. He grinned.

"Really."

"Neat," he said.

He threw the ladle into the air, spraying pieces of pie across the tiles of the kitchen floor. He came around from behind the breakfast bar and put both his arms around me and pulled me to him.

"Well done," he said and then quietly, in my ear, "fucking amazing."

He held me out at arm's length, his hands around my biceps. "Why didn't you tell me?" he said.

"We had other things to talk about." I glanced at my mother. "About Julie."

"Oh yes," he said, "about Julie," and he pulled me to him again.

My mother coughed. Not politely.

"Well," she said, slipping off her stool, "I'll leave you boys to it. You've obviously got a lot to talk about."

"Mum," I said as Andy released me, "you don't have to go. Stay for a coffee."

"I don't drink coffee." She looked at me and then she looked at Andy. Pointedly. "It disagrees with me."

"Oh," said Andy.

"What about the apple pie?" I said.

"Next time," said my mother. "In the future. Thank you anyway." She was already heading out of the lounge.

"OK," I said. "Next time."

"It was nice to see you again," said Andy. "And don't worry about Julie. She'll be OK."

"A mother," said my mother, "always worries. It's what we do."

"Oh," said Andy.

"Thank you for the chicken," she said. "It was lovely. Bit crispy, but lovely."

"Oh," said Andy. "Bye."

I showed my mother to the door. I promised her that I would arrange something with Julie and I apologised for not letting her know Julie's plans. She said that she forgave me and she apologised because maybe she had been a little short with me.

"Will you be OK getting home?" I said.

"Fine," she said. "And Honza?"

"Yes?"

"That Andy, he's all right. You could do worse."

And then she turned and was walking down the street, head straight, eyes forward, ready to lambast any vagrants who made the mistake of asking her for alms. My mother.

In the kitchen Andy had his arms in water, doing the washing-up. The sleeves of his boiler suit were rolled up to the elbow, I could see the sinews in forearm flexing. He looked back over his shoulder.

"There's wine in the fridge," he said. "To celebrate. Your novel."

"Thanks."

"Pour me a glass and we'll watch *Millionaire*."

I went to the fridge and took out the bottle. I opened it with a pop and filled two glasses. I carried them into the lounge and sat down and switched on the television. It was the adverts. A snail race was selling Guinness, Heather Locklear was selling hair colour, a hamsters' tea-party was selling Iceland. Then it was time for Chris Tarrant and *Who Wants To Be a Millionaire?*

Andy plopped down next to me in his usual seat. He wiped his hands dry on the thighs of his boiler suit. He picked up his wine glass.

"Cheers," he said.

"Cheers," I said.

"To the author."

"To plans."

We clinked glasses. We took sips, rested our glasses in the V of our crotches and then we turned our attention to the television, to *Who Wants To Be a Millionaire?*

In the studio the lights had gone down, the audience were quiet and the first question was being asked. Andy knew the answer. He said it out loud, looked at me and grinned. He was OK on two hundred pounds, five hundred, a thousand. At two thousand he started to struggle. I knew the answer but I kept quiet. I wasn't even tempted. I also knew the four thousand, the eight thousand, the sixteen, thirty-two, sixty-four and the one hundred and twenty-five thousand pound questions. But I still didn't say anything and Andy was still silent. We drank our wine. The adverts came on and Andy took our glasses to the kitchen and refilled them.

When the adverts were over Chris Tarrant came back looking excited. He asked the audience to be quiet and the house lights went down, the spotlights up. He told the contestant he had no lifelines left, he had already gone fifty-fifty, phoned a friend, asked the audience. He told the contestant that the next question, thirteen of a possible fifteen was worth two hundred and fifty thousand pounds, a cool quarter of a million. The contestant nodded his head. He looked tense, expectant, keyed up.

The question appeared on the screen.

I had no idea, not a clue. Not the foggiest.

"C," said Andy. "The answer's C. Easy."

The contestant on the screen was looking nervous. He was wiping his forehead, closing his eyes, staring blind up at the ceiling.

"Any ideas?" said Chris on the box.

"C," said Andy. "Easy."

I didn't know.

"I don't know," said the contestant. He leant forward in his chair.

"What are you thinking?" said Chris.

There was a long pause. The camera zoomed in and the contestant's face filled the screen. He was sweating.

"Really, no idea," said the contestant finally. He wiped his palms on the thighs of his jeans. "Chris," he said, "I've had a great time. A hundred and twenty-five thousand is a lot of money. I don't want to risk it. I'll take the money. I'll give someone else a chance."

"Sure?" said Chris Tarrant.

"Sure," said the contestant.

"Is that your final answer?" said Chris Tarrant.

"Final answer," said the contestant.

"Idiot," said Andy. "It's C. Obvious."

There was a round of applause. Chris Tarrant handed over the cheque as the lights came up. There were smiles all round.

"I can tell you," said Chris Tarrant, "not that you give a monkey's, that the correct answer was in fact C."

"I told you," said Andy. "Easy."

Andy had been right.

That about summed Andy up. He didn't know the answer to the simple questions, he didn't know the two thousand, four thousand, eight thousand pound answers, but he knew the big one, the one that other people struggled on. He knew how to get around my mother, how to handle the sexual questions of an adolescent, how to get my nephew to do as he was told without complaint. They were all things I struggled with. Yet on the surface Andy seemed to lack these people skills. He worked as a manual labourer, a donkey, he said. His life was routine, his speech monosyllabic, he watched endless television. And yet again and again he surprised me.

"Can I put it on Channel Five?" said Andy. "There's a good film on. *Under Siege. Two.*"

"Sure," I said.

"I'm just going for a piss."

He bounded up the stairs, he left the door open, he crashed in the hall.

"More wine Honza?"

"Thanks," I said. "The film's starting."

"OK," said Andy. "Coming."

The film was generic Hollywood. A transcontinental train has been hijacked by a team of mercenaries as part of their plan to seize control of a satellite weapon orbiting the Earth. But they had not allowed for the presence of Steven Seagal's character, a former navy SEAL. There were many explosions, fight sequences, chases through carriages. Good guys beating bad guys. Heroes saving the day.

At the end Andy stood and stretched.

"Good film," he said.

"Yes," I said.

"I'm knackered."

"Why don't you go to bed?"

"I will," said Andy. He bent to pick up the two empty wine glasses and then hesitated. "Honza?"

"Yes?" I said.

"I just wanted to say well done, about your book. I'm pleased for you. And thank you."

"Thank you?"

"For what you've done. Are going to do this weekend. Thank you."

"It's OK," I said.

Andy went into the kitchen. He put the glasses in the sink. I remembered something.

"Andy?" I said.

"Yes Honza?"

"You said you had something to tell me about Kevin. You said it was important."

"Oh," said Andy, coming out of the kitchen, standing in the door to the hallway. "It was nothing. Forget it. It was nothing. Goodnight."

And he was up those stairs as if the wolves were chasing him again.

Eighteen

If I'd have had a convertible I would have put the top down, driven with the wind in my hair, like Thelma, like Louise. It was one of those perfect blue-skied early spring days. The sun was shining and it was crisply cold.

I beeped the horn.

I was waiting in the car for Andy. I had been waiting five minutes. He'd already been in the passenger seat once, showered and shaved, booted and suited but suddenly he'd leapt out telling me that he just had to go to the toilet before we left. I should have known, should have expected it.

I beeped the horn again and then I saw the front door reopening, Andy in the doorway. He had changed his clothes. He had changed from jeans and Ralph Lauren shirt to the Hilfiger fleece and combat trousers. He got in the car.

"You changed," I said.

"Yes," said Andy. "Sorry."

He slammed the door shut and pulled the seat-belt across his body. He looked at me. I looked at him. I noticed that he had also put gel on his hair. It was spiky at the front, like mine.

"So," I said, "why the change?"

"I splashed my jeans. When I was washing my hands. Looked like I'd wet myself."

"Andy," I said, "you never wash your hands."

Andy's face began to go red. He scratched his thigh, watching the nail.

"Doesn't matter," I said. "You don't have to tell me."

I put the key in the ignition, turned it and started the engine. I checked in the wing mirror, in the rear-view mirror.

"You seen that Hilfiger advert?" said Andy. "With all those androgynous Americans?"

"Androgynous?" I said. I put my hands on the steering wheel and looked over my shoulder. "Have you swallowed a dictionary?"

"They're on a beach," said Andy. "Perfect sand. Perfect water. They're walking and laughing with their arms round each other. Young, tanned and beautiful. And carefree. They look like nothing can hurt them." He shrugged. "I want that to be me. Can I put some music on?"

He didn't wait for an answer but pulled a tape out of the side pocket of his trousers and slipped it in the Sony cassette tuner. As I pressed my foot gently on the accelerator and pulled out into the road, All Saints singing 'Pure Shores' came over the hundred-and-forty-watt speakers. "Take me to your beach."

"London here we come," I said.

"Yes," said Andy. The knuckle of his left hand was in his mouth. "You nervous?"

"No." Andy glanced to look at me. "I trust you."

I trust you.

I turned left at the junction at the bottom of Curzon Street.

I trust you.

It was Friday lunch-time. I had phoned Andy's work, told them he was ill, was in bed and wouldn't be coming in. And Andy, on my instructions, had phoned Nigel. He had told him that this week he would be travelling down to London on his own. He had told him that he would meet him in the car park of the Tesco on Acre Lane in Brixton at five pm. Nigel hadn't been happy but there wasn't much he could do. So the first part of the plan had gone OK.

I trust you.

All Saints gave way to Shaft. 'Mambo Italiano'. Derby city centre gave way to the A6. The beat was faster, the traffic increased.

"You mind if I smoke?" said Andy.

I was concentrating on the road, watching out for maniacs, wary of road rage. I was steady, tapping the steering-wheel in time to the music.

"You always smoke," I said.

"So you mind?" said Andy. "In the car? Some people mind. Kevin minded."

I shrugged. "No."

"It's for my nerves," said Andy. He lifted his waist and dug in a pocket for the cardboard oblong box.

"I thought you weren't nervous."

Outside a black BMW overtook dangerously on the inside. The driver of a red Ford Escort beeped furiously and shook his fist. I didn't know people did that in reality. Shake fists.

"I'm not," said Andy. He pulled on the cigarette nestled between the middle and ring fingers of his left hand, he tapped his knee with his right. "But..." He stopped.

"But?" I said, looking ahead, watching the Ford Escort set off in pursuit of the BMW.

"But..." said Andy, "what if it goes wrong?"

"It won't."

"But if it does," said Andy, looking out of the side window, looking out of the front window. "If it does go wrong."

I shrugged. "We go to the police."

Andy flicked his head to look at me, smoking hand poised in mid-flight. In front the BMW swerved from behind one and in front of another car. The Ford Escort followed.

"I can't go to the police," he said. "I sell drugs. I'll go to prison."

"My plan won't go wrong. Don't worry." The plan could go wrong. I was worried.

"But if…" said Andy. "Tell me."

I trust you.

"You run away," I said smiling, moving into the fast lane. "You must have a lot of money. You can go to a Caribbean island. You can sip piña colada from a coconut shell on a sunset beach." I was joking. Half.

"I can't run away," said Andy. "Derby's my home. There's my dad, my dad needs me, there's my job and…"

He pulled out the ashtray and stubbed out his cigarette. He pushed in the dashboard cigarette lighter.

"And…?" I said.

"Nothing," he said and looked again out of his window.

We were going past the turning for Alvaston Castle. Tom Jones and the Stereophonics were singing 'Mama Told Me Not To Come'. The car had become a haze of exhaled smoke and so I wound down my window a little. I felt a rush of cold air against my neck. The cigarette lighter popped out and Andy took it and lit another cigarette.

"Andy," I said, going over in my mind the reasons why he said he didn't want to leave Derby, "why did you leave your father's?"

Andy shrugged. "I'm twenty-one. Twenty-two next birthday."

"So you wanted independence?"

"It's overrated," said Andy. "Independence. Supporting yourself. Being on your own. Can I turn the music up?"

"Sure."

Andy reached out a hand to the volume control and then his fingers on it, he hesitated.

"Honza?"

"Yes?"

"I just want it to be over. I just want tomorrow morning to be a free man and to go and visit your nephew. And right now I just want loud music, I don't want to think. You know what I mean?"

"Yes," I said. And I did. "Turn it up then."

And he did.

Tom Jones has a voice that is loud even when he's quiet and when he really is loud, he is really loud. You couldn't think and listen to Tom Jones. There wouldn't be space in your brain. I guess that's what Andy wanted. Wanted more than anything.

We were now on the M1, motoring south on our way to London, the big smoke. The traffic was sparse, much heavier on the other side with people leaving the capital for the weekend, escaping the rat race. And we were cocooned in our car trying to make a similar escape from our own different rat race.

Andy sat smoking, one cigarette after another and the music stayed loud. Gabrielle, 5ive, A1, Bewitched, Mel C, Geri Halliwell, NSync. An endless procession of frothy pop noises.

Time passed.

And we got closer and closer.

And we didn't talk. Hardly at all. I didn't turn down the sounds and fill the air with otiose conversation, hiding what was beneath it. I wasn't effusive, reassuring. After all, it's easy to tell someone everything's going to be all right because at the end of the day it's not you. It wasn't me who had to stand there week after week and sell drugs. It wasn't me who had been beaten up. It wasn't me who dreaded the sound of the phone ringing, a knock at the door. I only hoped I could change that.

And did I hope that at the end Andy would fall into my arms and call me a hero? No, because that's not why you do things. You have only to do what you believe is right.

Everything else has to fall into place by itself.

What goes around comes around.

As we pulled off the M1 and onto the A5 on the outskirts of London I reached over and turned down the music.

"Look in the glove compartment," I said.

Andy leant forward and pulled it open.

"A box of condoms," he said, "and a tube of KY Jelly."

I'd forgotten that.

"Not that," I said. "The *A-Z*."

I knew it was there. It had been for ages. In our time Joshua and I had come down to London often. We had drunk in bars, gone to theatres, danced in chic clubs, trying to convince ourselves we were having a good time. Trying to manufacture one.

"Got it," said Andy.

"Right. Find Brixton."

I had booked us into a bed and breakfast. For the weekend.

"I can't read maps," said Andy. "I'm hopeless."

"Try," I said. "You can do it."

"OK," said Andy putting out his cigarette. "But don't blame me if we end up in Buxton. Where are we now?"

"Edgware Road. Coming up to Marble Arch."

Andy flicked to the index, flicked to a page. He rested the book on his thighs and concentrated.

"Found it," he said.

"Right," I said, "which way?"

"Um..." said Andy. "Go straight."

"You been speaking to my mother?"

"What?" said Andy. "Oh yeah. Haha. Left. LEFT."

If I had been Robert Falcon Scott on an expedition to the South Pole then I don't think I would have taken Andy as an alternative to a compass but he wasn't bad, wasn't bad at all. He directed us past the Dorchester Hotel, over Westminster Bridge, over the grey flowing Thames to the long busy stretch of Kennington Road. He looked down at the book on his knees constantly, moving fingers along numbered rows, down alphabetised columns, looking up to check landmarks, street signs. He told me when to turn left, right, go over roundabouts, and I guided the car through the heavy London traffic, avoiding cars pulling out suddenly, motorcycle messengers, meandering pedestrians, and finally we were nearing Brixton. Our goal.

I'd never been to Brixton but I remembered Mother Hen telling me a story about it. I remembered it while we were stuck in traffic on Kennington Road, stuck behind a red double-decker, while Andy was engrossed, poring over his maps. Mother Hen had told me that when she was young Brixton hadn't been the cosmopolitan place it was now. "Then it wasn't all niggers and queers," she said, "it was just niggers." And the only gays who would go there, she said, were the drag queens to buy their high-heeled shoes. Why there? I had asked. "Well," said Mother, licking her lips, nudging her plastic breasts together. "What they say about a black man's cock could also be said of a Jamaican woman's feet." She held out her hands like a fisherman describing a large catch, a young boy who has just spent the night with Tom of Finland. "Large," she said. "It was the only place that sold women's shoes bigger than a size eight." And then she had cackled like a hyena giving birth.

"We're here," said Andy. He looked up from the pages of his book. "There's the bridges of Brixton. Where's this B and B?"

"Brixton Hill."

"I know it," said Andy. He grinned. "It's where The Cube is. Straight on. Brixton Hill is at the end of Brixton Road. This road."

This road was busy. The going was slow, the traffic dense. We crawled past the Spudulike on the left, the red-fronted Our Price on the right, inching forward, even the jam-packed shoppers on the pavements overtaking us. So many people, so much noise. Litter everywhere.

Outside the oblong hole of the entrance to Brixton tube was a tawny-skinned skinny-flanked peripatetic preacher with a battered amp and mike. He stood shouting to the unconverted, the never-to-be-converted stream of shoppers, single mothers, gays and their lovers. "Jesus was put on this Earth to save you. Confess your sins. Cleanse your soul. He WILL forgive you. He WILL love you."

And then he faded into the hubbub.

The glitzy Ritzy. A paean to inner-city regeneration.

The curved facade of McDonalds.

And up the hill, getting closer to where we were going.

"There," said Andy. "It's there."

There was a paint-flaking semi-detached house set slightly back from the road in the shade of a sycamore tree. Outside was a freshly painted sign. B and B it said. No name.

"You did it," I said. "You got us here."

"Yes," said Andy. "I did. I did it."

"And we're not in Buxton."

"No," said Andy.

I followed the whitewashed dripping arrow on the MDF board to the parking at the back. There were four demarcated spaces, no other cars. I parked as near to the house as possible, for safety. I put on the handbrake and got out. Andy joined me from the other side. We looked up at the building.

"Nice," he said.

It was many things but it wasn't nice. It was decaying bricks, rotten woodwork. It was four floors straddled by a rusty iron staircase. It was ramshackle, urban. It was to be our home for the next couple of days.

"Nice," said Andy. "Let's go."

I opened the boot and took out our luggage, Andy's plastic bag, my rucksack, and I followed Andy round to the front.

The green door was open and I went in without knocking, stepping over empty milk bottles. Andy was close behind me.

"Neat," he said.

We were in a dingy entrance hall. There were stairs going up, doors on the left and right. There was no reception desk, only a dog-eared sign sellotaped to a paint-flaking wall telling you to press the bell for service. I pressed the brass circle and there was a loud buzz above my head.

The door on my right was immediately whipped open, as if

someone had been waiting for us behind it. Standing there was a voluminous old black woman in a voluminous flower-patterned flowing cotton dress that did little to hide massive breasts, round stomach. She had glasses hanging around her neck on a chain.

"Honza Drobrolowski," I said. "Room for two."

She put on her glasses, perched them on the end of her nose and leant her head back to look at me through them.

"That's a funny name, innit?" She smiled revealing a mouth full of white teeth.

"His father's Polish," said Andy.

"Polish," she said, with a short 'o', "my father hated to polish."

"No..." started Andy.

"The room?" I said. I recognised her smile. I could see that she was just pulling our legs.

"Third floor," said the old woman. She removed the glasses, letting them drop. "First door. Key's on the bedside table."

Andy looked at me and grinned and then he was squeezing past the old woman and bounding up the stairs. The woman watched him as he disappeared around the landing.

"Nice boy, innit?" she said. "He yours?"

"Um..." I said.

"I was young once. Doesn't last forever. Catch it while you can." And she winked and turned to make her way back into her room.

"Excuse me?"

She stopped but didn't look back.

"What time's breakfast?" I said. "In the morning?"

She laughed, like Mother Hen laughed, like a hyena giving birth.

"Breakfast," she said, "there is no breakfast." And then she was closing her door again.

I went on up.

It was easy to find our room, Andy already had the door open. He was sitting on one of the twin beds.

"Neat," he said.

"Yes," I said, looking around.

If the walls had been further apart the room would have been bigger. As it was, it was tiny. It had orange curtains and a bare bulb and apart from the twin beds with their matching orange cotton covers there wasn't much else. There was another door, through which I could see a shower, smell a toilet. There was a single coffee-cup-stained bedside cabinet separating the two beds. Nothing more. Well, nothing except something very important. Balanced on an upturned milk crate at the bottom of the beds was a very small, very old black and white television.

"Look," said Andy, "they've got a telly."

"Yes," I said. "Great."

"Tomorrow, when everything's sorted we can bring Nicholas here and watch telly, can't we?"

"Andy, we're in London. We can find something better to do."

"Oh yes. Suppose."

"It's four o'clock," I said. I put down my Adidas bag. "We should go."

"Yes," said Andy. He looked at me like Nicholas looked at me when I told him he had to get out of the bath.

"It'll be OK," I said.

"Yes," he said.

"It will."

"Come on then," said Andy. "Let's do it. Let's get this show on the road."

He stood and crossed the threadbare carpet to the door.

Nineteen

"Park there," said Andy pointing, "where you can see the wall."

"OK," I said, manoeuvring the car over to a free space in a line of free spaces.

"I'll wait by the bins."

"All right," I said. "Just act normal."

Andy looked at me. "Yes. I know. Normal."

I tried the smile I used when Nicholas woke up from a nightmare. "Don't worry," I said. "When Nigel hands you the drugs I'll take the picture. After, I'll meet you in Tescos by the fruit. By the apples. Then we'll get the film developed."

There was a pause.

"You think it'll work?"

"Course," I said. "Fight fire with fire."

"Yes," said Andy. "Like Steven Seagal. Like Jean-Claude Van Damme." He pulled the cigarette box out of his side pocket. "What time is it?"

"Quarter to five. You better go."

"OK." Andy put the cigarette box back. He chewed his knuckle. "See you later."

"See you," I said.

"See you Honza. Bye Honza."

Andy unbuckled his seat-belt and got out of the car. I watched as he crossed and stood next to the bins. There were four of them, round, dully metallic, slightly taller than him and overflowing with rubbish. Andy folded his arms, unfolded them and scratched his thigh, shifted his feet. Breath was pluming out of his mouth. The sun was going down and it was getting colder now, freezing. I watched as he did up the zip on his Hilfiger fleece until it was right under his chin. He looked around him but not towards me, not at the car, and he reached down to the side pocket of his trousers and pulled out the packet of cigarettes again. I saw the brief flare of a match and then smoke rising from the white tube.

Andy was about ten metres away. It was easily near enough for a clear shot with my camera. It had a two hundred millimetre zoom lens. For a moment I considered climbing over the to the back seat, balancing the camera on the headrest like some ardent ornithologist waiting for that rare bird, a once in a lifetime shot. Then I discounted it. Sitting here in the front I was any husband, any boyfriend waiting for a loved one, their someone to come back laden with shopping, bags bulging. All I had to do was pick up the camera and click. Once. Twice.

I was John Wayne. Wyatt Earp. Doc Holliday. Billy the Kid. And so on.

It was *High Noon*. Rorke's Drift. Or something like it.

Andy dropped his cigarette and squashed the butt under the sole of his shoe. I remembered the first time I had seen him, the second, leaning against the jamb of my front door in his blue boiler suit smoking. That grin.

It was five to five.

Andy reached into his pocket and took out another cigarette. Lit it. For his nerves.

Then it started to go wrong.

I recognised Nigel straight away of course. The large rugby body and bald head were unmistakable even at a distance. He came walking around the corner of the wall that ran at ninety degrees to the road, his collar turned up. He was on foot. I'd expected him to be in his battered BMW, to park somewhere in the car park. I'd expected more time.

But that was OK.

I put my hands on the camera on my lap. Ready.

Andy noticed Nigel and turned to face him. He dropped his cigarette, half-finished. He stubbed it out with his toe. Deliberately. He put his hands in his pockets.

Nigel continued walking towards Andy, walked right up to him and they nodded a greeting to each other. Nigel said something and Andy shook his head. He didn't open his mouth. Nigel said something else, breath freezing in short sharp shocks and Andy shrugged and shook his head again and this time he said something. No.

I didn't know it was going wrong. Not yet.

Nigel reached out a massive hand and put it on the small of Andy's back. The meaning was evident. Come with me. It wasn't threatening, violent. But...

Andy looked around again. Not at me. Just around. Casual. And they were walking off together. Like two friends. Pally.

They were already twenty-five metres away. Thirty.

I trust you.

Shit!

I got out of the car and set off after them. I didn't know what I was going to do. Cry, "Oi you stop!" And then what. Fight fire with fire. I didn't have any fire.

Ahead of me Andy and Nigel were reaching the point where the crumbling brick boundary wall of the car park finished, gave way to Acre Lane. There was traffic going past.

I was twenty metres behind now and closing. Walking quickly. Thinking. I can bump into Andy. He's an old friend. What are you doing here? No, Nigel knows me. Then what. I was gaining ground

Nigel and Andy weren't talking and Nigel's hand had moved now from Andy's back to his elbow. With his other hand Nigel reached into his pocket, took out a mobile phone. He spoke into it, just a few words I couldn't catch. Too far. Andy didn't look back or around now. Just straight in front. I was getting nearer.

Think.

I don't know why but just then I looked right, down the road at the traffic coming towards us. And there was the black BMW. Approaching. Fast. Nigel shut his mobile as the car pulled up.

A door was opened. Andy was inside first, bending at the waist, a hand on the shoulder guiding him. Nigel was next. Then the car was off. Roaring up the road.

I broke into a run. Uselessly. Hopelessly.

Well done Honza. Good plan.

I trust you.

I stood staring up Acre Lane. The BMW was out of sight. Gone with Andy in it. I stood like that for five minutes, five seconds, I don't know and then I walked back to the car. My car. The one I had driven down from Derby in with Andy at my side. The door was open. I'd left it unlocked in my hurry. In my alarm I hadn't beeped on the alarm. I noticed someone had taken my camera. It wasn't on the seat. Never mind. It could be replaced. I got in and slammed the door shut. And I sat there.

I'd said after Joshua that I didn't want anyone else. I didn't want anyone else because I didn't want the pain of losing them. Of them not being there. Of not being in control. I'd chosen Andy as my lodger because I didn't think he would interfere in my privacy. I thought he wasn't interested in my work, wouldn't disturb my life.

Andy was supposed to be like writing for magazines, something easy, that paid the bills and I could put away at the end of the day.

I had been wrong.

I turned the key in the ignition and drove back up Brixton Hill to the bed and breakfast. I parked in the same spot and climbed the same stairs to our room. I didn't see the fat woman in the hall, I didn't see her on the stairs.

I sat down on the orange-covered bed. I could see the gloom gathering outside, lowering over the back yards of brick houses. It was the time of day when people were returning from work, oven-ready meals were in cookers, subdued greetings were given from in front of turned-on televisions. It was the time when I usually heard Andy's key in the lock, his shout up the stairs.

Not today. Next to me Andy's bed remained empty. The plastic Sainsbury's carrier containing whatever he had brought with him was still there. Unmoved. And Andy was with Nigel. No doubt Nigel would be planning his evening, sorting him out. Telling him he was the man. Or whatever. However it went.

Later I could go to The Cube and Andy would be there, with his queue and with his drugs. All right. If that's what you want. If that's what he wanted. But he didn't and I said I would stop it.

I flicked on the tv. Channel Four came up, a hazy picture. I could see Chris Evans behind the snow surrounded by a group of kids shouting yes at the tops of their voices. I kicked off my shoes and lay back on the bed with my hands behind my head, staring at the ceiling. I heard some pop protégé talking about her exhaustion, the grind of self promotion, a boy band being interviewed about their mums, someone singing a generic country-and-western ditty. But I wasn't listening, not really. It was just there. Noise.

I was thinking. I was thinking about Joshua.

Joshua hadn't been able to cope with life. No, not exactly that, he hadn't been able to cope with the little things. If any little thing went wrong he would go berserk, would worry about it for days, be in the depths of despair. He used to get so angry, mental. He could change in a second from being a lovely smiley gorgeous person to a demon. And that demon was usually reserved for me, in the privacy of our lives. He didn't have anyone else to blame because all his life was centred on me. I was his universe.

Anything could set him off. Once he bought a cantilever bridge for Nicholas's train set and the mechanism for raising and lowering it was too stiff, too difficult for a small boy to turn. He went mad. He bought a bag and the strap became frayed in a day. He was crazy. And CDs. He loved CDs, would spend hours in the shop listening to them, testing them before he bought them and then when he got home inevitably wouldn't like them. It was anything and everything.

And when it wasn't perfect he would be in turmoil. He would extrapolate this tiny imperfection to encompass his whole life. Because he wanted our love to be perfect too. He wanted my attention all the time, for me to say that I loved him all the time. He didn't want me to watch television, read a book, write. He wanted all those shows of love that I didn't think were love anyway. He wanted walks along moonlit beaches, violins and bouquets of flowers. He couldn't see that they weren't real.

The saddest thing was that I did love him, like I had never loved anyone. When he was asleep I used to stoke his black hair and kiss his cheek and just wish and wish that I could take away his pain, make everything right. But I never could. Whatever I did it was never enough. If I gave him attention he wanted more. More and more. Until I couldn't give anymore.

In the end with Joshua I had never been able to do anything for the worry that it would go wrong, the worry I would be a failure. That I would upset him. The worry that I couldn't love enough. The worry that I couldn't do enough. I. Me.

Because I had wanted to make him so happy. I had stayed with Joshua for two and a half years. He had fed on something in me and me on something in him. I had some latent instinct that wanted to protect, care for, look after. And the more the little things went wrong the greater was my desire to put them right. To sort everything out.

I wanted to sort everything out. I wanted to be a hero.

Chris Evans had stopped talking and the Channel Four news was about to start. I got off of the bed and went over to the television. I pushed a button, the third one down, figuring it to be ITV. Lines on the screen appeared, static, interference. No picture. I twisted the free-standing aerial, this way, around. I stood with it, moved to the window, set it on the ledge and *Catchphrase* came into view. Success.

I lay back down on the bed, resting my head on my outstretched arm, watching the tv now, giving it the full attention it didn't deserve, concentrating like the man in the gym had told me, pushing out all thoughts.

I mouthed the answers to the stupid *Catchphrase* questions in the empty room and when its jaunty jingles eventually gave way to the ersatz grime of *Coronation Street* I followed the antics of the soap's characters with the gaze of a fanatic. Then it was Michael Barrymore with *My Kind of Music*, Chris Tarrant with *Who Wants To Be a Millionaire?* As *Millionaire* finished I flicked over for the end of *Parkinson*, the start of a movie with gunslingers and horses in the American West.

I didn't move all evening, only in the adverts to go the toilet. Outside the sky turned from cornelian to a dark grey with pinpricks of light and in the room it grew colder. There was no heating, no double-glazing. The wind had picked up and drafts were audibly shooting around the edges of the window. At some point I pulled the orange bedspread over me, trying to keep warm. And I gazed at the screen.

At exactly eleven o'clock I stood and stretched. I bent and turned the tv off, cutting off Wyatt Earp in full swagger, tight hips swaying and I went into the bathroom and looked at myself in the mirror. It was the blanched Bart Simpson again staring at me. I went back into the main room, took out my toilet bag and returned once more to the bathroom. I ran water from the hot tap into the stained sink. I waited with my fingers under the flow but the water didn't get hot. I splashed some on my hair anyway, shivered as drops slipped down my back and then twisted the cap off my firm hold hair gel. It took a minute to brush flat the top, brush spiky the front.

The clothes I was wearing would do, a Full Circle crew neck, tight on me, and Virgin action pants. I was ready to go out. I took one last look around the room, pulled to the curtains and left closing the door behind me.

There was no one in the hallways, no sounds from other rooms and downstairs the door from behind which the large landlady had appeared was firmly closed, silent within.

I hadn't put on a coat and it was freezing out, the cold air goosebumping my bare arms instantly, but it was only a short walk down The Cube. I walked quickly with my hands thrust deep in my pockets, my left hand turning the key to the B & B over and over, over and over.

Eleven fifteen I was there. A queue had formed already outside the white facade, stretching fifty metres down the road. There were groups of young giggling gays and girls. There were men by themselves. There was short hair, gelled hair, tight T-shirts, plastic smiles. There was me on other nights, on another night. I joined the end of this slow-moving procession, turning my back on the single smiling person there and slowly we shuffled forward. Slowly, slowly, until it was my turn to enter.

At the door I was frisked by a bouncer. I was found not to have any concealed guns, deadly blades and I was let past the security. I paid a spangly woman who called me love and I went up stairs, was in the club proper. For a moment I stopped dead. It was a long time since I had been to a club in London and I had forgotten what it was like.

I had become used to L'Amour. L'Amour would only have a hundred, a hundred and fifty people in at one time. Sometimes on a Friday there would only be thirty or forty. The difference was enormous. The Cube had a capacity of more than a thousand. A thousand men looking for men. I was looking for one.

I went and stood by the metal railing overlooking the huge

dance floor, the roof cavernous above me. Few people were dancing yet. There were only lights flicking back and forth over the expanse of space in an antipathetical movement to the already pumped up noise. It was that gay beat, the one that can sometimes grab you and bounce your feet, sashay your groin. Not tonight, not this evening. I left the railing and started to make a circuit, going past the bar, around the dance floor, through a set of doors and upstairs to another bar. Here, people stood chatting, holding drinks, eyes shuttling from bums to biceps to eyes. Waiting for the one, for tonight or every night. But not me. I was on a very specific cruise.

I went down the stairs again, the noise increasing as I came back into the main dance area. It was busier already. More people were dancing, but lazily, indolently, not with the frenzy that would come later. It was the waltz compared to the samba. A daring few had taken shirts off, were showing off bodies created in back street gyms. I turned away from them and the pleasures they had to offer and went to the bar. I bought a can of lager from a slim-waisted bar-boy and when I turned back Andy was there. I saw him through the crowd, leaning against the black side of the DJs' shed.

I walked over.

"Andy," I said. Loud because of the music.

"Honza," he said, not surprised just flat and beaten. "What'll it be? An E? Some speed? Acid?" He was smoking a cigarette.

"Andy," I said again and put a hand on his arm.

He smiled grimly. "Sorry. Bad joke."

"You all right?"

"Yeah." He shrugged and took a drag on his fag.

"What happened?"

"You saw. The usual. I'm sorry."

"Sorry?"

"Yeah. I shouldn't have said anything. My problem. It's OK."

I was going to say that I wanted to help, that we were friends when someone appeared and leaning close to Andy whispered something in his ear. Andy nodded to me and walked off a few paces with this guy. I saw the hint of a note, the passing of something between hands and then Andy was coming back, leaning his back against the wooden side of the DJ box.

"It's what I do."

I didn't say anything. Andy stood smoking.

"I'll be busy soon," he said, not brightly, but trying. "Why don't you dance?"

It was my turn to shrug.

"We can still see Nicholas tomorrow?"

"Yeah. Of course."

"We can still drive back on Sunday. I'll go to work. Nothing's changed."

"Yeah," I said but I was lying. Things had changed.

"That's life," said Andy. He finished his cigarette and dropped the butt on the floor. He squashed it under his shoe. "I'll be finished around one. No one buys anything after that. I'll give the money to Nigel and we can go."

"What?" I said. It was difficult to catch every word. We were behind two huge speakers and I wasn't sure if I'd heard right. "What did you say?"

"I said I'll be finished around one," said Andy. "Are you OK?"

"Yes," I said admonishingly, eagerly. "Fine. But what did you say after that? About Nigel?"

"I said," said Andy, his voice louder, "that I have to give him what I don't sell. And then I'm free. Every week the same. What? What is it Honza?"

I was smiling. "You mean that Nigel's here?"

"Sure," said Andy. "Always."

He pulled the cigarette box out of his pocket and lit one. Then someone else appeared, tapped him on the shoulder and Andy was off again, a few paces.

I leant over the railings and looked out over the dance floor.

There were more and more dancers now, a mass of bare worked-out torsos, a sea of bodies moving in waves of movement. Andy came back, was next to me and we stood side by side, not talking. My mind was racing.

"Andy," I said, "where did Nigel take you?"

"Some house."

"But where?"

"It was in Brixton."

He was missing the point. "But what was the address," I said. "Exactly."

He told me, shouting almost into my ear.

"Again," I said.

"What?"

"Tell me again."

He did and I repeated it over and over in my head.

"Why?" said Andy after a few moments. There was a lull in the music, the haunting start of a new track.

"I've got a plan."

"Oh," said Andy. He took a drag on his cigarette. A cry went up from the dance floor as the beat proper began. "Honza?"

"Yes?"

"I've been thinking."

"Yes," I said.

"The important thing is about Kevin. He's not dead."

"I know," I said.

"But when you told me," Andy shrugged. "I don't know. I just realised. He's not dead. Fuck him. This." He spread his arms. "It's OK. I can manage. I'm not a killer."

I was quiet a minute.

"You want to do it?"

"No," said Andy. "Not at all." He rubbed a hand over his forehead. "You know what I want?"

"What?"

"Peace," he said. "An easy life. A few beers. Telly. A packet of fags."

"Then I'll sort it."

Andy looked at me and grinned. Grinned.

"Thanks Honza."

There was no question of how or what I was going to do. Nothing like that. And then there was another tap on Andy's shoulder. A guy with a shaved head and a tattoo on his bicep stood waiting.

"I'll see you later," I said to Andy. "I'm going to find Nigel."

"Right," said Andy. "Be careful."

"If I can't be good," I said.

"What?" said Andy.

"Nothing," I said. And was gone.

Sometimes in big clubs you can lose friends and spend hours looking for them, keep missing them in an endless search, an endless farce of one door opening another closing. And sometimes you find them straight away. Right in front of your nose. And The Cube, after all, wasn't a labyrinth. I wasn't in an Egyptian souk. I shouldn't have been surprised.

Turning away from Andy and edging around the side of the dance floor I saw Nigel through the crowd. He was heading to the door by the stairs. By himself.

Opportunity knocks. Fortune favours the brave.

I pushed my way past people, not fast, not desperate because I knew I had all night. I knew that I had time. Nigel wasn't going anywhere. I made it to the door, ignoring a pinched bum and a wink from a man propping up the jamb and I went through. Nigel was already at the top of the stairs, his massive body filling the gap between wall and wall, and then he disappeared through the door.

I didn't run. I took it calmly, slowly. I felt I had the upper hand. It was that karma thing again. I had the right on my side.

Reaching the top I went into the bar. It was quieter up here now.

As the night had gone on people had moved downstairs to the dance floor where the action was, where they had more chance of pulling. There were only a few people at the spread out tables, a few loners, old friends chatting, newly copped-off couples exchanging saliva.

I saw Nigel. He was at the bar ordering a drink, saying something to the barboy who was laughing. Too much. I went over and stood next to the huge body, leaning my elbows on the counter.

"Nigel?" I said.

He turned his big bald head to look at me. Up close with his black eyes and hard expressionless face he looked like the leader of some well-funded terrorist militia group. There was no hint of recognition there and from his breath it was obvious he had been drinking heavily.

"Nigel?" I said again.

He didn't answer. Just looked.

"I'm Andy's landlord. I'm Honza. Can I speak to you?"

If Nigel thought it strange, that I was there or that I wanted to speak to him he didn't show any sign of it. Not at all.

"The pleasure would be mine," he said. Evenly. His voice as blank as his face.

"Shall we sit down?" I said.

He slowly nodded his head. "Lead the way. But first. Let me buy you a drink."

I said no. I didn't want to turn our encounter into a social meeting but Nigel insisted. He was all politeness, kindness, wouldn't take my negative for an answer. So I said I would have a lager and Nigel ordered and paid and held the glass for me, proprietorially.

There were some round metallic tables by a glass wall that over-looked the dance floor. They were empty except for discarded crushed cans and overflowing ashtrays. I nodded to Nigel and went over and sat in one of the seats. Nigel followed. I could feel him behind me, a huge presence.

Glancing through the glass I noticed that the dance floor was heaving, packed with a mass of bodies, everyone having a good time, a great time. And over by the side of the dance floor just as he had said was Andy. A queue had formed in front of him. Long and thin. Orderly. Like in a post office. Andy's hands were flying between different pockets and he still had a cigarette in his left hand. I turned back to my new companion.

"Thanks for the drink," I said. I raised my glass.

"Cheers," said Nigel.

We were like two old friends. Distant cousins. Or maybe a matey David and Goliath.

Time, however, to cut short the comradeship. Time for my plan. My stupid idea.

"I'm a reporter," I said. I moved my glass to the centre of the table. "Freelance."

Nigel picked up his drink and took a sip. He raised his eyebrows. Some people walked past, stumbling drunk, propping each other up. Nigel didn't say anything.

"I sell stories. To newspapers."

Nigel lowered his glass.

I'd seen a film about drugs. Kind of about drugs. *Lock, Stock and Two Smoking Barrels.* I remembered the black dealer with an Afro, loquacious and dangerous. "If you hold back anything I'll kill yer. If you bend the truth or I think you're bending the truth I'll kill yer. If you forget anything, I'll kill yer. In fact, you're going to have to work very hard to stay alive."

"We took your picture today."

Nigel raised his eyebrows again.

"When you gave Andy the drugs," I said and then I repeated the address, the one Andy had told me.

It was obvious what my meaning was. I have your pictures. I'm a reporter. I'll sell my pictures. You're in trouble. It was blackmail. It was up to Nigel to ask me what I wanted. Money, whatever. And then I'd tell him that I just wanted Andy to be free, to not have to sell drugs any more. Nigel would tell me that he could break my legs, have me killed and I would say that the pictures were in a safe location, that if anything happened to me then they would go to the press.

"What do you see?" said Nigel. He nodded towards the window.

I looked through it following his gaze but I knew already what I would see. It was my turn not to say anything.

"They're having a good time. Nobody gets hurt."

I shrugged.

"And nobody cares. You think the police don't know? The press?" Nigel took another sip of his beer, slowly. "There are scenes like this in every club in the country. Every weekend. Everywhere. People taking drugs. People selling them. It happens. And the police and the press let it happen. You know why?"

I shook my head. It wasn't going according to plan. Nigel didn't look scared. He didn't look like he gave a shit. I had talked about karma. Nigel with his bald head and calmness reminded me of Buddha.

"The police don't care," continued Nigel, leaning back on his seat, fixing me with his gaze, "because here they can control it. It's not out in the streets. It's not a hundred little guys in back rooms concocting deadly pills. Here, it's not a problem. No trouble. Their job is just about maintaining the status quo. And the press don't care because they are only interested in the individual. If someone dies, if its someone famous. They don't care about all these people. Where's the story in that? Where's the human interest? Nobody'll touch your pictures Honza. You won't get any money for them. Not a penny."

Downstairs, momentarily the music went dead. There was a round of applause and then it started again.

"I don't want money."

"Then what?"

There was a pause. I was thinking. And Nigel was looking at me.

I could see something in his eyes now, something I hadn't expected, something I had seen before in other eyes, a thousand times. It
was desire.

"Andy," I said finally. "I want Andy."

And I meant it.

"Andy?" Nigel leant forward on the table. Leaning his massive
arms on it. He seemed genuinely puzzled.

"He knows Kevin's not dead."

Nigel almost smiled. Almost. "I never said he was."

"Andy thought he'd killed him," I said.

"It was convenient."

"Convenient?"

"These sellers," he said with a hint of amusement in his eyes,
"they tend to be, how can I put it? Untrustworthy. Flighty. It was
convenient. Andy didn't want to do anything wrong, would do as
he was told. It was easy."

"But he doesn't want to do it. He doesn't want to sell drugs. It's
his life."

Nigel ran a hand over his bald head and looked out of the window at where Andy and his queue was. Then he looked back at me.

"Fine," he said. He leant back on his chair.

"Fine?"

And now Nigel did smile. It wasn't the smile I had seen before.
The Hollywood baddie. This smile was genuinely amused.

"What did you expect?" he said. "An episode of *The Bill*? *Miami
Vice*? You watch too much television. Fine. If he doesn't want to do
it then fine. I don't need this every week. Meeting in car parks.
Secret pictures. I can find someone else. Someone who wants to
make money. Someone uncomplicated. Easy. I want an easy life. But
one condition."

"What's that?" I said. Nigel was still smiling.

"You come with me to the toilets."

"What?" I said. I knew what.

"It's a small price to pay, isn't it?"

Under the table I felt his leg press against mine. He was serious.

"It's just a game," I said, "all this."

"Not a game exactly," said Nigel. "I'm a man of my word. Andy for a little fun with you. Why not? You don't get something for nothing, not in this world. You scratch my back and I'll scratch yours."

It was *reductio ad absurdum*. A murder reduced to a knee trembler in an upstairs toilet. Little lives fucked over by a big man with a cock. That it should all come down to this. It didn't seem right, fair. It wasn't karma. Or maybe it was. What goes around comes around.

I'm a sucker for a big cock. I can have sex anywhere, anytime, on my front, on my back, once even standing on my head. My words. My own stupid words. It was time to eat them.

I stood up.

"Come on then," I said. "Andy for me, right?"

"Right," said Nigel. He smiled. "Andy for you."

I went after Nigel to the toilets.

There were five or six people at the urinals, some pissing, some just hanging around with flies open, waiting, looking over shoulders. A couple of the cubicles had doors open. I followed Nigel into one of them, pushed the door closed with my back and slid the bolt across. From the next cubicle came groaning.

"Do you kiss?" said Nigel.

Is this what people said to Julie?

"Fine," I said.

Nigel put one of his massive hands behind my head and pulled me to him. His tongue was in my mouth. I had to stand on tiptoe, support myself with my hands on his waist.

We kissed. A couple of minutes.

Nigel forced a hand into my jeans between my body and my belt, his wrist squashing my stomach. He played with my cock.

He pulled out his hand, licked his fingers and pushed my

shoulders down until my head was level with his crotch.

I knew the score. I'd been here before.

I undid the buckle on his belt. He had a button fly. I pulled apart the buttons. I pulled out his cock.

It was hard. Massive. Like I hadn't seen before.

I put it in my mouth and he put his hands on my head. Pushed it backwards and forwards.

It was huge inside me, squashing flat my tongue, rubbing against my palate. And as Nigel thrust deeper I was gagging. I wanted to throw up.

I wanted to get it out of my mouth.

Nigel came. Quickly. Holding my head stiff. My mouth was full of his hot bitter come.

I spat into the toilet bowl, the semen hitting the water and then slowly it sank, spreading out, swimming for the U-bend.

Nigel did up his trousers, buckled his belt.

"A deal. Andy's yours."

"Right. He's finishing early tonight."

Nigel looked at his watch. "Fine, whatever. The busiest time is over. Send him to me."

"Fine," I said.

I turned to unbolt the door.

"Honza?" said Nigel.

"Yes?" I said, pausing, leaving my hand on the door, wanting to get out of there.

"Kevin tells me Andy's got a great arse. But he's a bit clingy. Like a dog. Kevin was glad to get rid of him, jumped at the chance of being dead."

I didn't answer and I didn't look back. I knew Nigel would be smiling. I knew that he knew that I didn't know Andy was Kevin's boyfriend.

The upstairs bar was as quiet as before. I went past the seat where we had been sitting. There was a single man there, young, but with a moustache. He looked worse for wear, his head was lolling back, his arms were over the back of the chair, supporting himself. He caught my eye.

"How about it?" he said.

"Fuck off," I said and walked down the stairs.

The whole of the club seemed to have moved onto the dance floor now. The music was so loud it was almost distorted, just a bass pumping, banging in your head, filling your mind. Bare bodies were rubbing against other bare bodies, the contact lubricated by sweat and arms were in the air in abandonment to the god of the beat. I had to fight my way through to the downstairs bar. Someone grabbed my chest and squeezed and I turned to catch a smile that a different person would be pleased to return and glazed eyes that another person would meet with their own. I shimmied away and continued on my way. Finally I made it to the other side.

Andy was there, alone. He was leaning over the rail, one leg crossed in front of the other. I watched him looking and then he saw me. He smiled.

And I smiled too.

"Go and see Nigel," I said.

"Later," said Andy. "It's not time yet."

"It's time," I said. "Give him what you owe him and that's it."

"What?"

"It's over."

"Over?"

"No more drugs. No more coming to London."

"Right," said Andy and grinned. "I'll be back in a minute then."

And he was gone.

I don't know what I'd expected. Tears of joy. Arms thrown around me and a spinning dance. Euphoria. But I should have expected just that, a terse statement and a grin.

I stood where Andy had been standing and looked out over the people dancing. Like Nigel said, they were having a good time. They weren't hurting anyone, just chemically changing their brains from their routine boring lives. They were escaping for a few hours from the humdrum, the mundane, eschewing their daily identities to become one in this seething community of movement and music. I'd done it in the past. But not anymore. Not the drugs. It wasn't a moral stand. It was just a question of doing what you want to do. Doing what's in your heart. That's what's important.

Andy came back. Pulled a cigarette out of his pocket and lit it.

"You want to dance?"

"You?"

He shrugged. "I want to go home. To the B & B. It's been a long day."

"Come on then," I said.

"You don't mind?"

"No. I don't mind."

We didn't have coats either of us, so we didn't have to stand in a queue. We were straight out of the doors nodding a goodbye to the bouncers. The night was really freezing now. The sky clear, stars bright. We set off up the hill.

"It's cold," said Andy.

"Yes," I said.

"Bloody cold," said Andy. He slapped his arms around himself.

"Yes," I said.

"Honza?" said Andy.

"Yes," I said.

"Thanks."

"That's OK," I said. "That's OK. Anytime."

Then we didn't talk anymore. Just walked up the hill. Side by side, footsteps in synch. Together.

The B & B was in darkness. I fumbled for the keyhole and then having found it twisted the key gently. I pushed the door open. Silence. I couldn't find a switch for the landing lights so we had to ascend the stairs in the pitch black, carefully feeling our way until eventually we got to our room. I unlocked this door too, fumbling once more for the keyhole. I pushed open the door and flicked on the light.

It was as cold inside as it was out. Our breath froze as soon as it left our mouths.

"It's cold in here," said Andy.

"Yes."

Andy yawned and stretched. "I'm knackered."

"Why don't you go to bed?"

"I will," said Andy. "I'm just going for a piss."

"OK," I said.

There weren't any stairs to bound up but he did walk briskly. He left the door open and his aim was as accurate as ever. Right in the middle. I heard him shake off and then I followed him in. I wanted to brush my teeth. I could still taste Nigel.

When I had finished and rinsed vigorously I switched off the light and came out into the main room. Andy was sitting on the end of the bed nearest the door, still in his Hilfiger fleece and combat trousers and with his hands pressed between his legs.

"It's cold," he said.

"Yes," I said.

"Honza?" he said without looking up, looking at a spot on the floor.

"Yes?" I said.

"You going to bed?"

"Yes," I said.

There was a pause.

"Can I sleep with you?"

He still wasn't looking at me, still at the floor.

Could he sleep with me? What had I said, I didn't want a boyfriend, I didn't want commitment. I had already eaten my words once that evening. I was getting a taste for them.

"Yes," I said.

Andy looked up. He was grinning.

"I always sleep naked," he said.

"Me too," I said.

"That's all right then," said Andy.

Twenty

I woke up and opened my eyes. I was in the single bed in the bed and breakfast. I was alone. The other bed, the one under the window, was unslept in. I couldn't see Andy. I sat up.

"Morning," said a voice.

I looked towards the bathroom, towards the sound. There was a pair of bare feet on the tiled floor, the curve of a knee, the start of a thigh then hidden by door post. Andy was sitting on the toilet.

"Morning!" I called.

"It's freezing," said Andy.

"Yes," I said. It was.

I looked at my watch. It was nine thirty.

I lay back down on the bed, pulling the sheet and blanket up under my chin. Nine thirty. It was early. I wanted to get to Julie's about lunch-time, surprise her. And Nicholas. I was going to see Nicholas.

The toilet was flushed and then I heard Andy padding quickly across the floor. He pulled the covers slightly aside and got in next to me. His body was cold next to the warmth of mine.

"You're cold," I said.

"Sorry," said Andy. He smiled and put his hand flat on my stomach.

"Get off!" I laughed and squirmed out from under the hand,

ending up on my side, my back nearly against the icy plaster of the wall.

"Sorry," said Andy again. He was still smiling. "Accident."

The smile was cute, gleeful. Innocent. I felt myself hardening.

We hadn't had sex. I don't know why. The night before we had taken off our clothes and got into bed, jumped into bed, away from the frigid air. Andy had twisted around so that his back was against my front, had pressed his bum back against my groin and I had threaded my arm under his and across his stomach and we had held hands. We had held hands like Vince Virgin and Trudy Never Been Touched and Andy had fallen asleep almost straight away, snoring gently.

I had lain awake for ages, just thinking, thinking about how things had panned out. I thought about how I seemed to have kept passing over big cocks for this guy in my arms. First there had been Dave who had come to look at the room, and then Nigel last night in the toilet at The Cube. They both had cocks as thick as a builder's arms, as long as carpenter's spirit levels, and yet I had rejected them for the cute grin on a tv monster.

I won't tell anyone if you won't. I've got my reputation to think of.

I like casual sex in outdoor places. I don't like commitment.

I'm a bastard.

"Do you mind if I put the telly on?" said Andy, scratching an armpit.

"No problem," I said. "Anything you like."

Andy climbed out of the bed and crossed the floor, exaggeratedly hopping on tiptoe and flapping his arms because of the cold. I watched as he bent to turn on the television, tendons in the back of his thighs flexing, the cheeks of his bum slightly parting to reveal a slash of dark hair. What had Nigel said? That Kevin had said he had a great arse. Beautiful.

Kevin was right. Kevin the boyfriend. Kevin Andy's lover.

I should have worked it out.

"Andy?" I said as the television came on, filling the room with the noise of static.

"Yes?" he said. He had his back to me. He was fiddling with the aerial.

"Can I ask you something?"

"Sure."

I paused, not sure what question I was going to ask. If I was going to ask about Kevin.

"What?" said Andy.

"What channel you looking for?" I said. I lay back down on the bed with my hands behind my head.

"ITV. It's *SM:tv* with Ant and Dec."

"Oh," I said. "You need to put the aerial on the window-ledge. The reception's better there."

"Thanks," said Andy.

I heard the curtains being drawn.

"Fuck!" said Andy.

"What is it?" I said. I sat up, wondering what could have gone wrong now.

"Honza! Come here. Quick!"

I climbed out of the bed, naked. I walked across the room to the window, naked. I stood behind Andy.

"Fuck!" I said. I looked through the glass.

It was snowing. It was April and it was snowing. Big thick flakes were falling from the sky, filling the air, landing on the already white blanket below. Backyards and dividing walls, heaps of cars and rubbish bins had been transformed into a virginal vista of discordant shapes. In my head flashed kiddy memories of Christmas mornings, waking up with thoughts of wondrous presents and mad snowball fights.

"Beautiful, isn't it?" said Andy. "Romantic."

"Yes," I said. I didn't believe in romance. "Nice. Very nice."

I put my arms around Andy's waist and pulled him to me, rested my head on his shoulder. I let my hands drop to his groin. I noticed that Andy's cock was circumcised. I ran my fingers around the head, along the shaft, weighing it my hand like a fresh egg. The cock wasn't huge it was true, it wasn't massive, not like Nigel's, not like Dave's, but it was thick. What it lacked in length it made up for in girth. You would need an Olympic triple jump judge and his tape measure to know if its circumference would beat those two former champions. I guessed it wouldn't but it would be up there in the medals in any other competition. A bronze at least.

It was hard.

"I'm cold," said Andy. He dropped the aerial and reached around to put a hand on my erection.

"Me too," I said. I pulled him closer, running my hands up his body.

"I love the snow though."

"Me too," I said, moving my hands to Andy's balls. The scrotum was tight, the skin thick, the balls squeezed against his crotch.

"Honza?" said Andy.

"Yes?" I said.

"Do you like me?"

"Yes," I said.

"Fuck me then."

"OK," I said.

We were still standing in front of the window, almost shivering, looking at the snow. Locked together. I put a hand on Andy's face and turned his head from the window, towards me and we kissed. We kissed. I was kissing my lodger. Andy.

I was kissing my lodger. I stopped kissing.

"We have a problem," I said. "About the fuck."

"What?" said Andy. He twizzled around in my arms and put his hands on my bum.

"I don't have any condoms."

"Wait." Andy moved away from me, kissing me lightly on the lips.

The plastic carrier bag Andy had brought from Derby was still on the unslept in bed. Untouched. Andy bent and gripping the bottom, tipped the contents out onto the orange blanket. He started to rummage through the pile of socks, T-shirts, underwear. He was leaning over the bed, looking for something.

I moved behind Andy and placed a hand on his bum, palm flat. Andy looked back at me over his shoulder and smiled. I flexed the middle finger of my hand, moving it between Andy's cheeks, through black hair, and he leant forward more. He pushed back towards my hand and my finger at the same time, placing his elbows on the bed.

"You find what you were looking for?" I said.

"Condoms," said Andy, "KY jelly. I found them."

"Nice," I said.

The tv was still hissing static in the background, forgotten. The cold, forgotten.

I dropped to my knees so my face was level with Andy's bum. I caressed the gluteal fold, the line that forms between thigh and arse, and then I moved up, licking. I put one hand on each of the cheeks, holding them like you hold a basketball before you shoot and I pulled them apart, using my thumbs to divide, moving inwards with my tongue. Andy pushed back again towards my face and I was lapping at the sphincter. Rimming.

Rimming.

I had told some female friends about rimming and they had been disgusted. I had sat up one drunken vodka-fuelled night with Kelly and Jan and the conversation had come around, as it does, to sex. I had wanted to know what straight people got up to, if they did the same things as me. Kelly had said that she had tried anal sex once and that it was OK, not bad. The good feeling was in her mind, she said, the erotic charge in the sexual transgression, she said. Jan said she had never done it but that she would with the right man, if he wanted to and loved her. And then I had asked them about rimming. Rimming, Jan had said, what's that? Licking arse, I had said, and they had both pulled repulsed faces. I had guessed that meant a no. Kelly said that she would never go near her boyfriend Simon's bottom with her tongue in a million years. She said that she had to leave the room even when he farted. Jan just looked me in the eye with such sympathy and said, you know, doesn't it taste, you know, awful, disgusting. Like someone's taking a shit in your mouth, said Kelly. Well, she had had a few.

I said that no it didn't. (I didn't tell the story about the one time it did. That story was best forgotten, filed away and the drawer locked, the key thrown away.) I said that it didn't at all. I said the taste was like lips, only better, like cock, only fresher and the smell, I said, was reminiscent of elderflower water, of cleanliness, freshness, as if bath water had been trapped there. And I said that to me rimming was the best pleasure because it was the most intimate, the most personal, the closest you could get to someone.

In what sense? said Kelly taking a sip of her vodka.

When someone is being rimmed, I said, they are at their most vulnerable, passive. It is not purely sexual like the blow job, it does not lead to orgasm. It is not reciprocal like kissing, only one partner is active. It is not physical like fucking, it does not make you sweat. When you are being rimmed you are surrendering yourself to someone, totally. And there is also the anticipation factor.

Anticipation? said Kelly, leaning forward across the table we were sitting at. Jan had gone quiet, had crossed her legs.

Well, I said, if you are rimming someone it is a form of lubrication, it is more than likely going to lead to penetration. That's the expectation. And any philosopher will tell you heightened anticipation is noblest form of pleasure. The looking forward is better than the happening, the idea of Christmas better than Christmas, the best part of a holiday the plane taking off.

Right, said Kelly. Maybe.

And anyway, I said, the sphincter itself is a thing of beauty, amazing, indescribable. It's unexplainable in words, I said. It's like standing on the edge of the Grand Canyon and shouting, it's like seeing the sunset on the horizon, like Tom Cruise's bum, I said. Impossible to express with vocabulary of shape or form but you know you like it. The sphincter I said is the acme of the human body, the bulls-eye of desire.

Can we change the topic, Jan had said, I think I'm going to be sick.

Andy was now lying flat on the bed we hadn't slept in, lying on the contents of his upturned bag, one leg straight, the other at ninety degrees to it, bent at the knee. And I was rimming him.

"Honza," he said.

Andy was still holding the condoms he had recently found. He had squashed the packet in his hand. I reached for them and in the same movement slipped my hand under his stomach and pulled him back up onto his knees and his elbows. His head was resting on the pillow.

"Hang on," I said.

And Andy remained like he was, in that position, goose-bumps on his legs and arms, from desire or cold. Waiting, expectant.

The lodger was about to become a lodger lodger.

Who had I been trying to kid?

I ripped the blue foil square with my teeth and rolled on the condom.

"Honza?" said Andy.

"Yes?" I said.

"Thank you. For everything."

If it had been anyone else, I would have said that they hadn't had everything, not yet. But it wasn't anyone else, it was Andy, so I didn't say anything.

I positioned myself on my knees behind Andy and guided the

head of my penis into the sphincter, slowly. I paused momentarily as the rectal muscles relaxed around the intrusion and then pushed further in, and further in until the shaft was all the way in, in that realm where we all walk with everyone, where everyone is the exception and the same. And I fucked him. I fucked Andy my lodger. The one I had told everyone wasn't my type. The one I told myself wasn't my type. Me. Me the one who didn't want to get involved.

It wasn't the best fuck I'd ever had in my life and it certainly wasn't the longest. Andy came in a minute, shooting onto a pair of his socks on the bed and me soon after him, in him, in the latex teat of the condom. There was no groaning, no wailing, no noise to disturb the neighbours. There was no sweat and sweet nothings. We didn't change position, use techniques dreamt of on long winter nights, scale the heights of porno movie stars. But it was nice. Something I could get used to.

"Honza," said Andy.

Slowly, sensitive now, I pulled out and rolled us both over onto the bed, intertwining our legs. I hugged Andy to me.

"Honza?" said Andy.

"Yes?" I said.

"I need a fag."

Andy leant across to grab the packet and lighter. They were on the table between the two beds. He pulled out one of the white tubes, lit it, and started to smoke holding the cigarette between the middle finger and ring finger of his left hand.

"Thank you," said Andy. "It was nice. This is nice."

He reached down to grab my cock. I was still wearing the condom. I pulled it off of me and I threw it towards the bathroom. We watched it land on the lino floor with a gentle splat.

Condom.

"Andy?"

"Yes?"

"What did you bring the condoms for?" I said.

Andy shrugged, his face starting to go red. And then he smiled.

"You never know when you might have to educate adolescent boys."

I sat up. "Sorry?" I said.

"Martin," said Andy. "Remember? The carrot."

I remembered. I remembered Andy and Martin sitting side by side on the sofa, laughing.

"So that's the reason?" I said. I slid an arm around Andy's waist.

"Sure," said Andy and then added. "He's cute, isn't he? Martin."

"He's a bit young."

"For you maybe," said Andy. The smile turned into a grin. "For an older man. But I'm twenty-one."

"Heh," I said. I pulled Andy towards me, pushed him down on the bed and manoeuvred myself on top of him, my legs astride his body, pinning him to the sheets. "Watch yourself."

"Honza," he said, struggling, "I can't breathe. You're squashing me."

"It's all that smoking," I said, squeezing his sides, tickling him.

"Honza! Stop!" he said. "Get off!"

He tried to wriggle out from under me, but I gripped him tighter, tickled him again. And again, until he was helpless, red-faced, gasping for breath, tears running down the sides of his cheeks.

"I brought them for you," he said. "All right, I brought them for you."

"That's better," I said and I leant forward to kiss him.

There was a knock at the door behind us and as I looked around and Andy looked up, it swung open.

The large Jamaican landlady was standing in the doorway. She had the same voluminous dress, the same enormous breasts. She was out of breath and she was holding a tray.

"Yes?" I said. I moved off of Andy, trying to pull the orange blanket over us.

"Breakfast, innit," she said and walked into the room. "You wanted breakfast, right?"

We both nodded. It seemed like the right thing to do.

She put the tray down on the cabinet between the beds where Andy's cigarettes had previously been and then she turned and beamed revealing all her many and splendid teeth.

"You boys wanna watch yourselves," she said. "Cold." She pronounced the word cold with two syllables and mimed a shiver, rippling flesh and cotton all the way down to the toes, and she laughed, the noise deep and booming. It was a laugh that came all the way from Jamaica, a laugh that was full of sandy shores and blue lagoons. It was a laugh to frighten away the most frightening of obeah spirits.

"Thank you," said Andy. "For breakfast."

"Yeah," I said. "Thanks."

"Problema none," she said, throwing her hands into the air and then was gone as suddenly as she had come, turning and leaving closing the door behind her.

She was like a Dada fairy godmother bearing gifts.

And I believed in fairy godmothers about as much as I did romance.

"That's neat," said Andy. "I'm starving."

"Yes," I said.

Breakfast consisted of two cups of very sweet, very milky coffee, one in a chipped cup and one in a chipped mug, four pieces of toast, two white and two brown, a dollop of something on a saucer that might have been raspberry jam and one very large bowl with two spoons of what Andy said was definitely Weetabix. Whatever, it was perfect. I hadn't eaten since the previous lunch-time, not anything. We snuggled under the covers and ate sitting side by side, munching happily, watching the snow fall outside, surrounded by the debris of our clothes.

After breakfast Andy ducked down under the blanket and gave

me one of those blowjobs that is more toast crumbs under foreskin than fluid motion but in this case it was nice anyway and then I said we should get ready because we were going to see Nicholas. I said that Andy could go in the shower first and he pulled the covers tight under his chin and said that he didn't need a shower so I had one by myself, shocking myself with the freezing water, making myself gasp. I could only stand the flow for a couple of minutes before I leapt out and danced out of the bathroom, jumping up and down, trying to get warm.

I dried myself as quickly as possible and then pulled on clean underwear, clean socks, jeans, a T-shirt and a jumper, remembering the freezing weather outside. After I had put moisturiser on my face and gel on my hair, brushed it, spiked it at the front, I was ready. Andy was still in bed, smoking, watching me, smiling.

"Come on," I said. "Get ready."

"OK," he said. "Coming."

He put out the cigarette, crushing it in the ashtray and then got out of bed. He picked up the briefs he had been wearing the day before and put them on. They were white and had a yellow stain on the crotch. Then he sat on the bed and pulled on the socks he had been wearing the day before. They had a hole so his left big toe was sticking out. And then he put on his combat trousers and Hilfiger fleece.

"Ready," he said and smiled.

Ready. He was ready. What would Mother Hen say?

"Let's go then," I said. I walked to the door.

"Just a minute," said Andy, "I'm just going to..."

"... have a piss?"

"No," said Andy. "Brush my teeth."

"Fine," I said.

"And Honza?" Andy said and looked at me.

"Yes?"

Andy brought his knuckle up to his mouth and chewed it.

"Yes?" I said again.

"Nothing," he said and disappeared into the bathroom.

I sat on the bed and waited. I looked at my watch. It was quarter to eleven.

I was going to see Nicholas.

It was freezing outside. The snow had already settled about an inch and was still falling. I put my head down and made for the bus stop I had spied the night before on my way to The Cube. Half way there I looked back to check on Andy and saw him five metres behind me walking in my footsteps, trying to fit his shoes exactly in the depressions I had just made.

At the shelter there was no one else waiting.

Andy leant against the glass wall. "You not driving then?" he said.

"No," I said. I pushed my hands down into my pockets.

"Right," said Andy and pulled his box of cigarettes out the side pocket of his combat trousers. He looked around him. "Honza?"

"Yes?" I said.

"Thanks for the fuck."

"No problem," I said and smiled.

Andy smiled back.

We stood smiling at each other in a South London bus shelter on a freezing spring day and we didn't say anything else because we didn't need to.

The bus soon came and we paid and ran upstairs, banging snow from our shoes. We sat at the front side by side with our feet on the window ledge looking out at the tumbling snow. Andy farted the tune to 'Santa Claus is Coming to Town' and some people behind us laughed and gave a short round of applause and then it was time to get off. The bus stopped right outside Brixton tube station. It was only a case of crossing the road.

Everything was easy.

The preacher was there again with his speaker and amp. He was shouting more loudly today but to less of a crowd. People were hurrying by, ignoring him, trying to get to where they were going as quickly as possible. But the preacher didn't care. He was on a mission.

"Confess your SINS and Jesus will save you. HE saved me. HE can SAVE you. HE can SAVE you."

"Hear that," I said to Andy, "Jesus will save you."

"I'm already saved thank you," said Andy and we descended the stone steps into the station.

I bought two tickets and then we were through the barriers and on the escalator, Andy on the step in front of me.

"What you fancy doing?" said Andy. "With Nicholas?"

"I don't know."

"We could go to the British Museum or Madame Tussaud's, or the Planetarium, or London Zoo."

"Yes," I said.

But I didn't care. Just seeing Nicholas would be enough. I thought again of those weekend fathers and their grand plans. Plans that could go wrong. But I wasn't like that, didn't need to do that.

There was a tube waiting on the right hand platform with doors open. The digital indicator told us we had three minutes before it left so we wandered down to the front, got on the first carriage. There was only one ancient woman there, hunched forward and leaning on a stick, chewing something in her mouth.

Andy yawned, stretching his hands in the air, opening his mouth wide, sticking out his stomach and the old woman looked at him and nodded, tutted. Andy looked at her, looked at me and grabbed me and kissed me full on the lips and she nodded again, tutted again and said something under her breath.

The doors closed with a hiss and we were off, shooting and rattling into the darkness of the underground tunnels on our journey to see one small boy.

People got on at Stockwell, Vauxhall, Pimlico. There was standing room only.

People got off at Victoria and were replaced by more people. The same people but different.

Andy and I didn't talk. We just sat side by side. Together.

After Victoria Andy fell asleep on my shoulder and he slept through Green Park, Oxford Circus, Warren Street and Euston, waking only at King's Cross St Pancras when a backpacker dropped a backpack on his foot.

"We nearly there?" he said. He rubbed his eyes and stretched as the bag was lifted off. It was the sort of thing that would have made Joshua scream.

"Yes," I said, looking up at the blue line on the wall that represented our journey. "Next stop."

And I was quiet. There was a strange feeling in my stomach and as we got closer to our destination and this feeling grew I realised it was nerves. In this day of new beginnings I was scared that today would be the beginning of the end for me and Nicholas. The beginning of the end of the perfection we had now. Because the Nicholas that grew up in London would be a different one to the one that grew up in Derby. He would be streetwise. Tubewise. Unclefree. Those days of Disney would be gone too quickly. And I would miss them. I would become someone on the periphery, only seen with an effort.

The train shuddered to a stop and the doors hissed open.

"This it?" said Andy.

"Yes," I said.

"Come on then," said Andy.

And I stood up and we got off.

Julie had said that the house was near a park and I saw the park as soon as we emerged from the entrance. It was covered in snow.

"It's snowing everywhere," said Andy.

I pulled the slip of paper out of my pocket and read the address

I had written. There was no one around to ask so I went back into the station and asked the man in the ticket office. He scratched his head once, again and then said he thought it was the street that bordered the park. Look, he said, I think you can see the houses from here. I looked but could see only snow.

We followed the path around the park and there on a street sign I saw the words I was looking for. We were in the right place.

The houses were tall and elegant, four or five storeys. I thought it wasn't a bad place to live, a bad place for a boy to grow up, and it seemed safe, but I felt sad all the same.

As we went past doors I checked the numbers, counting up in twos.

And then we were there, outside.

"This is it," I said to Andy.

"Go on then," he said, "knock."

There was no gate and no front garden, only four steps leading to a bottle green door.

I went up the steps and knocked.

There was no answer.

I knocked again and this time I heard someone behind the door. Slowly it opened.

A thin beautiful woman in a white nightgown was standing there looking as if she had just woken up.

"I've come to see Julie," I said. "I'm her brother."

"Julie?" said the woman, rubbing her eyes.

"Yes, Julie," I said.

"Julie's gone," said the woman.

Twenty-one

"Gone?" I said. "Gone where?"

"Dunno," said the woman. "She was here and now she's gone."

Julie had just fallen off that knife edge I felt she'd been walking along for years. She'd fallen off it and someone had used the knife to stab me in the heart. And then they'd twisted it.

"She can't be gone," I said.

"She is," said the woman, "gone. Not here. *Comprenez?*"

On another day I wouldn't have stood someone talking to me in flippant French, on a day when I hadn't just found my sister had disappeared.

"What's happening?" said Andy. He had come up the steps behind me. He was smoking a cigarette.

"Julie's gone," I said.

"Yeah," said the woman. "Gone. Now if you don't mind I'd like to close the door. It's not warm and my nipples are about to cut through this nightie. It was expensive."

I watched the door start to close.

"Hang on," I said, quickly, having an idea. "Sandra? Is Sandra here?" I remembered Julie's friend, my acquaintance. Sandra was the one who had taught Julie to dance, the one who had told her about the job. Sandra should be here.

"Dunno," said the woman, just a head now in the gap.

"Well," I said calmly, trying to remain calm, "can you find out?"

The woman looked at me and then looked at the snow. She could see I wasn't going anywhere, not without an answer. She sighed.

"Come in," she said.

We went in.

The hallway was massive, more like a reception room. The floor was chequered black and white, and the walls were cream. There was a staircase leading up to infinity, two closed doors on the right and a passage leading through to a kitchen. Just inside the front door were three Mackintosh style high-backed chairs and an occasional table. If it hadn't been for the wank mags with insalubrious titles spread liberally on this table you might have thought you had happened into a high court judge's elegant pied-à-terre and not into a high-class brothel.

"Wait in the kitchen," said our hostess without the mostest, "I'll go and see if Sandra's about."

She spoke this last sentence like a seasoned hostage negotiator hours from retirement ordered to do one last job involving a breakaway unit of the IRA and several minor members of the royal family. She wasn't happy. She stomped barefooted up the stairs and Andy and I made our way to the kitchen.

"Very posh," said Andy, twirling around, taking in the gleaming appliances, the curvilinear marble work surfaces.

"It's Smeg," I said.

"No," said Andy. "I think it's nice."

"No," I said, "The make. It's Smeg. It's expensive."

"Right," said Andy. "Course. Looks like it's never been used."

He was right. It was a kitchen that was just for show. It looked like no one had ever cooked in it. It wasn't the sort of place that would ever be homely, welcoming. It wasn't the sort of place I would want my nephew to be even if he was here.

But then I didn't have a choice. That's what I had to remind myself. That's what I couldn't accept.

"Honza! Darling!"

I spun around. It was Sandra. My sister's soi-disant friend. Unlike Julie's more lithe figure, Sandra was voluptuous. She had more curves than Nicholas's Brio train set. But like Julie Sandra was perfectly turned out. Her make-up was precise, even, her hair coiffured, brushed. If she hadn't been wearing a kimono nightgown you might have thought she was going to the opera. If it hadn't been for the explicit shortness of the gown, you might have thought she was a lady not a ...

"Who's the bit of rough?" Sandra said, glancing at Andy.

Andy looked at me. I opened my mouth. Andy spoke first.

"I'm the lodger," he said, "I'm Andy, Honza's lodger. Nice to meet you."

"And very cute you are too," said Sandra with a growl Eartha Kitt would have scratched her eyes out for. "I could sell you tomorrow. I could buy you back the next day."

"Sandra," I said, "where's Julie? Where's Nicholas?"

"Ah," said Sandra.

"What?" I said.

"I couldn't do anything," said Sandra. "It wasn't my fault."

"What wasn't?" I said. The dread was beginning to grow like visible libido at a sexual health check-up.

"Sit down," said Sandra.

We sat down, pulling ourselves onto high bar stools at an oak-topped breakfast bar.

"I don't know where to start," said Sandra.

"Start at the beginning," I said, "and work forwards until you get to the end."

Sandra opened her mouth, once, twice, but didn't say anything.

"Please," I said.

"Julie got the sack," said Sandra finally. "She, how shall I say it, upset the club manager. The owner of this house. He threw her out."

"Oh my God," I said.

"I'm sorry, Honza," said Sandra, "She's gone."

This I knew. What I wanted was more information. Details. I was feeling like I had felt that day at the art gallery in America, like someone had just hit me over the head with a very large blunt instrument.

"Where?" I said. "Where has she gone?"

"I don't know," said Sandra. "Has either of you two got a fag?"

Andy pulled out his packet and held it towards Sandra. Sandra took a cigarette with nail-polished fingers and placed it delicately in her mouth. She leant closer to Andy, the end of the cigarette hovering inches from his own mouth. Sandra had the moves of an actress in a fifties Hollywood movie. Andy had seen enough of these, he knew what to do. He ignited his lighter.

"I was at work when it happened," said Sandra, taking a long drag on the cigarette. "It was all over by the time I got back. Julie and Nicholas had already gone. Susie, the girl who answered the door, told me about it."

"Tell me," I said.

Sandra leant her elbows on the oak surface, looked both left and right and started to speak in a low whisper. Andy and I leant closer to hear.

"It's a bit sensitive," said Sandra. "Gerald's been crabby ever since he got back from hospital."

"Who's Gerald?" said Andy.

I was glad he'd asked, it seemed important.

"Gerald's the owner of the house," said Sandra, "the owner of the club where we work. He's the one Julie had the run-in with. It was because she was new." Sandra took another drag on the cigarette. "You see, Gerald likes to try out all the new girls. Says he's giving us an MOT. More like GBH we say. He's got an action that makes a pneumatic drill seem gentle, an appendage the size of a rugby player's calf. I should have warned Julie about him, I should have told her. But she was so excited about this whole gig I didn't want to spoil it. And anyway it all comes with the job."

"What job?" said Andy.

Sandra looked at him, looked at me and then back at Andy. He didn't know. He only knew that Julie was a dancer.

"Let's just say," said Sandra, "that it's the oldest profession."

"What is?" said Andy. It hadn't clicked.

"Being a hooker," said Sandra, "a whore, a lady of the night, a bitch, a callgirl, a harlot."

"Oh," said Andy, starting to blush, lighting his own cigarette. It had clicked.

"Gerald left Julie alone for the first couple of days," said Sandra, "and she was doing well at the club, seemed to be doing well here. Moved her hips like a real pro. The punters loved her. And then on the third day it happened."

Sandra moved her head closer. We moved our heads closer. Her voice dropped.

"It was a Wednesday. I had to leave early to collect my snake. Nicholas was downstairs playing with Gloria and Julie was having a rest. Susie tells me she saw Gerald slip into Julie's room soon after I had gone." Sandra looked to the left and the right again. There was nobody here but us homosexuals. "Now," said Sandra, "Gerald always likes a bit of oral before he does the job. It's at times like those you wished you'd trained as a sword swallower, not as an erotic dancer. But everything would have been OK if it hadn't been for Gerald's strange proclivity."

Sandra paused and took a puff on her cigarette. She looked first Andy in the eye and then me. When she lost her looks no doubt she could get a job as a cabaret raconteur. She seemed to be enjoying herself. Or maybe she was just milking the situation. It couldn't have been often that she had two men interested in her for her conversational ability.

"So what is it?" said Andy. "What happened?"

"While you are sliding the greasy pole," said Sandra, hiatus over, "Gerald likes to shout out the name of Disney heroines, Cruella De Vil, Pocahontas, Snow White, Cinderella and so on. He had just uttered the words Bambi when it all went wrong. Nicholas, who had been playing downstairs with Gloria, hearing all these names he recognised, must have thought he was missing out on something because he ran into the room. Gerald, seeing him, shouted for him to fuck off, fuck off. And Julie gave one of those knee-jerk reactions any mother would have done in the same situation when her child is sworn at. And let me tell you a knee-jerk reaction with a cock in your mouth can lead to much unpleasantness."

"Oh my God!" said Andy quietly.

I didn't say anything. I just wondered how it was how everything came back to this.

A blowjob.

What goes around come around. If you live by the sword you die by the sword.

And I don't mean that in a moral sense. Morals seem Christian, implying a didactically ordained right and wrong. Karma just is.

"Of course Julie had to go," said Sandra. "Her bags were packed, her room cleared by the time I got back."

"And you've no idea where she went?" I said.

"Not a clue," said Sandra.

In the hallway the telephone started to ring.

Sandra stubbed out her cigarette and went to answer it.

Andy put an arm around my shoulder and pulled me to him, gave me a hug.

Sandra came back into the room.

"It's Julie," she said. "She wants to talk to you."

The address Julie had given us was on the other side of London, near Elephant and Castle tube. It didn't take me and Andy long to get there and we didn't talk much on the journey. I was thinking and

Andy just was, being Andy. I had another plan. I decided I was going to be more of a man, more assertive, make my mother proud of me. I decided I was going to do what I should have done in the first place.

Whereas the house in Highbury had been elegant, the one we found ourselves outside now was inelegant. In fact, it was decrepit, dirty, ramshackle. It exuded an aura of poverty and dissoluteness. Blankets were hung in the downstairs windows and there was a crate of empty wine bottles on the front step. Even Andy couldn't find a kind word to say. He said nothing but squeezed my arm.

Next to the battered brown door were six white buzzers. Julie had told us hers was the top flat and so I tried the top one.

I pressed it and waited.

There was a hiss and then through the broken wire mesh of the intercom came a voice. It was Julie. She told us to come up, the door was open, the latch was broken she said and it was never locked.

The hallway was dimly lit and stank of old vomit and hamburgers. There was the sound of shouts in a guttural foreign language coming from one of the ground floor flats. And then the shouts stopped and there was a different voice, a squeaky man's voice whimpering.

We went on up, me first, Andy behind. The stairs were uncarpeted, wooden, dusty, with nails that must once have held a carpet jutting out on the edges.

It wasn't nice. Not at all.

Julie's flat was on the third floor. She was standing in the doorway, waiting.

"Honza," she said before I had chance to see the whites of her eyes, "don't say anything. I know."

She looked like Michael Caine standing behind sandbags gazing out at the horizon in that *Zulu* film, putting on a brave face despite horrendous odds.

And then from behind Julie appeared Nicholas, a ball of lightning, faster.

"Uncle!" he screamed. "Andy! Donkey! Lodger!"

I bent to catch his hurtling form in my arms and I swung him up in the air, held him up at arm's length.

"Hello uncle," he said, grinning down at me.

"Hello Nicholas," I said.

"I live in London."

"I know," I said.

"It smells," said Nicholas. "London smells. Do you want to see my house? It's not very big."

I caught Julie's eye. She was warning me again. Her look said, not one word.

"Well," said Julie. "You'd better both come in."

Flat would have been too grand a word for the place where Julie lived. Bedsit would have been giving it the benefit of the doubt. It was tiny. If she'd had more floor space she could have called it a boxroom. But she didn't. As it was it was just four walls and some floorboards.

"Sit down," said Julie.

There was nowhere to sit, no tables and chairs, so we sat on the bed, Andy next to me, Nicholas on my knee.

"Where's all your stuff?" I said.

"There." Julie pointed to two suitcases by the side of the bed, one on top of the other.

"But," I said, "what about the other things? Furniture. I saw the truck."

I remembered the big red-sided lorry that had pulled up outside my house on the day Julie had picked up Nicholas for the last time.

"That was George," said Julie, "a client. He drives a truck. He offered to take me to London. I didn't bring much."

"Oh," I said.

"Want a cup of tea?"

"Yes please," said Andy.

"OK," I said.

"No thanks," said Nicholas. He was playing with a button on my T-shirt. He was very quiet.

Julie turned to where an electric kettle was on the floor in the corner. She picked it up and walked out of the room. Nicholas climbed from me to Andy and started telling him a story about Power Rangers. It wasn't a wham, bam usual Power Ranger story. It was a Power Rangers at home kind of story where they are having tea and talking about their favourite toys.

And I was thinking.

I was thinking that there was no way I could let Julie stay here, let Nicholas live here. I was also thinking about how stubborn Julie was. I remembered that she didn't like to be told what to do. When we were young she had always stood up to mum, done her own thing. Always. She had worn the make-up she wanted, the clothes she wanted, brought home who she wanted and at sixteen she had left home and supported herself. I admired her for that. So I expected a fight. I didn't expect to win. I expected her to say that she would find another dancing job in another bar. I expected her to say there were plenty more fish in the sea, plenty more tabletops to wiggle on. I expected her to say that this room was just a stepping stone to greater things, wonderful things, a happy life.

Julie came back into the room.

She knelt on the floor and put the cord into the kettle. She stood and turned to face me. She looked strong, determined.

I was ready for battle.

"Honza?" she said.

"Yes?" I said.

"Before I came to London you said that me and Nicholas could live with you. Does your offer still stand?"

Julie wanted to live with me. Nicholas would live with me.

"Yes," I said. "It does." It did.

"Good," said Julie. "Then I want to. I want to live with you."

"Right," I said. I wanted to say great, amazing, fantastic. I wanted to leap up off of the bed, grab Julie's cases and run all the way back to the my car. I didn't.

"If there's room," said Julie. She looked at Andy.

"You can have my room," said Andy, looking back at Julie. "I'll sleep with Honza."

Andy would sleep with me. Every night. Me, the one who didn't want a boyfriend, commitment, the one who liked his own company.

What had I said about privacy?

What had Scrooge said about Christmas?

Humbug.

We would all live together and it would be easy. Perfect.

I was happy.

"So you are a couple?" said Julie. She smiled.

"Don't label us with heterosexual terms," said Andy.

It was something I had written in an article.

"Idiot," I said. I hit Andy on the arm.

He grinned.

"But there are a few conditions," said Julie.

"Right," I said.

"One. I will carry on working. I'll get a studio flat in Derby."

"OK," I said.

"Two. I am Nicholas's mother. My decision is final."

"OK," I said.

"Three. I am not a failure. I do not require sympathy, care or condolence. I do need you or anybody else to feel sorry for me. I am not a damsel in distress and you have not rescued me."

"OK," I said.

"Four. You will buy Nicholas a dog. For the past week I have nothing but dog this and dog that."

I looked at Andy. Andy looked at the floor. I looked back at Julie. "A dog," I said. "Fine."

"Five. And this is the last one. And the most important. Are you listening?"

"Yes," I said.

"Yes," said Andy.

"Yes mummy," said Nicholas.

"No Steps," said Julie. "There will be no playing of Steps. Agreed?"

"Agreed," I said.

"Agreed," said Andy.

"A greed," said Nicholas and giggled and pulled me to him and whispered in my ear. "Uncle, what's a greed?"

"It means," I said hugging him to me, "that you come and live at uncle's house."

"Hurrah!" said Nicholas and started running around the room, which due to its smallness didn't take very much time at all. He was flapping his arms and shouting hurrah and hurrah at the top of his voice.

The kettle flicked off.

"We'll have a cup of tea," said Julie, "and then we'll be off."

"Home," said Andy.

"Home," I said. And we kissed.

"Mummy," I heard Nicholas say, "uncle's kissing the lodger."

"He's not the lodger," said Julie. "He's the lodger lodger."

"Oh," said Nicholas.

And he ran around and around the room again until he got tired and came and lay down on the bed.